THE PICTURE OF DORIAN GRAY

AND OTHER WRITINGS

THE PICTURE OF
DORIAN GRAY
AND OTHER WRITINGS

Oscar Wilde

Supplementary material written by Moira Muldoon
Series edited by Cynthia Brantley Johnson

POCKET BOOKS
NEW YORK LONDON TORONTO SYDNEY

POCKET BOOKS, a division of Simon & Schuster, Inc.
1230 Avenue of the Americas, New York, NY 10020

This book is a work of fiction. Names, characters, places and incidents are
products of the author's imagination or are used fictitiously. Any resemblance
to actual events or locales or persons, living or dead, is entirely coincidental.

Supplementary materials copyright © 2005
by Simon & Schuster, Inc.

ISBN 13: 978-1-4165-0027-8
ISBN 10: 1-4165-0027-8

First Pocket Books paperback edition May 2005

10 9 8 7 6 5 4 3 2

POCKET and colophon are registered trademarks of
Simon & Schuster, Inc.

Cover illustration by Mark Hess

Manufactured in the United States of America

For information regarding special discounts for bulk purchases,
please contact Simon & Schuster Special Sales at 1-800-456-6798
or business@simonandschuster.com

CONTENTS

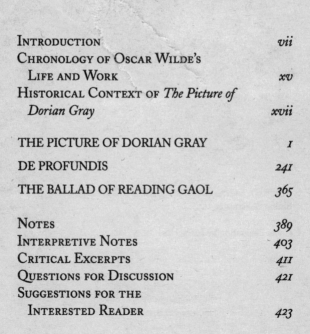

Contents

INTRODUCTION

The Picture of Dorian Gray:
THE DANGERS OF BEAUTY

———————— ⚜ ————————

The Picture of Dorian Gray arrived in prim Victorian England in 1891 like a naked man at a tea party, and was just about as well received. The novel tells the story of Dorian, a beautiful young man who remains eerily unmarked by age and excess, while, hidden away from view, his painted portrait registers every detail of his dissolute life. At once a Gothic tale of horror and a philosophical exploration of aestheticism, *Dorian Gray* probes the pleasures and dangers of life devoted to gratifying the senses.

When *Dorian Gray* was first published in *Lippincott's Monthly Magazine* as a short story, Victorian readers were shocked by the morals of its title character and the story's scandalous homoerotic subtext. When the story was published as a novel, Wilde added, along with another six chapters, an equally shocking preface that announced art had no moral responsibility. Art, he argued, should strive only to be a beautiful object entirely separate from its creator.

And yet it is almost impossible not to see a moral in *Dorian Gray*. Dorian, who lived his life as though it were a work of art unconnected to the question of ethics, dies by his own hand. Basil, who puts too much of himself into his art, is murdered. People cannot exist separately from morality, as works of art can. Wilde himself admitted that his novel contained a moral, calling it the book's "only flaw."

Flaws—personal flaws—were certainly the subject of the first half of *De Profundis*, the letter that Wilde wrote to his former lover Lord Alfred Douglas. Though it begins as a chronicle of his tempestuous relationship with Douglas (a relationship that ultimately led to Wilde's personal, professional, and financial ruin), it ends as a record of Wilde's own spiritual quest. *The Ballad of Reading Gaol*, Wilde's final work, is a fitting conclusion to the soul-searching of *De Profundis*. The provocative refrain "for each man kills the thing he loves" rings chillingly throughout the long ballad, and it rings true for Wilde, too. He had destroyed all that was beautiful in his life, and accepted the blame and the punishment fully.

As with many of Wilde's works, *The Ballad of Reading Gaol*, *De Profundis*, and *Dorian Gray* cannot be fully separated from the details of their author's life. In a letter defending *Dorian Gray*, Wilde wrote: "Basil Hallward is what I think I am: Lord Henry what the world thinks me: Dorian is what I would like to be—in other ages perhaps." In this sense, Wilde's works contradict the main tenets of aestheticism: they are both moral and entwined with their author. However, *The Picture of Dorian Gray*'s central questions remains aesthetic ones: What does it mean to live life as a work of art? And what happens to the person who tries?

Life and Work of Oscar Wilde

Oscar Fingal O'Flahertie Wills Wilde was born on October 16, 1854, to the Irish nationalist and writer "Speranza" Wilde and eye and ear doctor William Wilde. Young Oscar did exceptionally well at school, earning scholarships and taking high honors at both Trinity College, Dublin, and Oxford. While there, he met his teacher and mentor, Walter Pater, and became an enthusiastic follower of the Aesthetic Movement, which Pater championed.

After graduating from Oxford in 1878, Wilde moved to London. He quickly gained notoriety for his sharp wit and flamboyant style of dress—he was especially famous for wearing a dyed-green carnation in his lapel. In addition to writing plays and criticism, Wilde traveled in London's most brilliant social circles, becoming a kind of local celebrity. When he went to America to speak on aestheticism in 1882, he thrilled audiences from New York City socialites to Western miners. By the time he returned to London, he was a transatlantic sensation.

In the early 1880s, Wilde was regularly publishing plays and poems, but they were received badly. It wasn't until the late 1880s and early 1890s that he published some of his best-loved works, including *The Happy Prince and Other Tales* (1888) as well as a number of influential critical volumes, including *Intentions* (1891) and "The Soul of Man under Socialism" (1891).

Wilde married Constance Lloyd in 1884. They had two sons in quick succession—Cyril in 1885, and Vyvyan in 1886. Wilde had been married only two years, however, when he met Robert Ross, who claimed to have initiated him into homosexuality. Whether or not he did, Ross became a close and loyal friend to Wilde and later his literary executor.

In 1891, the thirty-seven-year-old Wilde was captivated by the handsome, spoiled twenty-year-old playboy Lord Alfred "Bosie" Douglas and began the major affair of his life, one whose volatility would soon endanger him. The same year, Wilde's greatly expanded version of the "Dorian Gray" story was published as a novel. Dorian's sensual life caused enormous controversy—almost as much as Wilde's life itself. Together, Dorian and Bosie spelled disaster for Wilde.

Wilde's relationship with Douglas infuriated Bosie's father, the Marquess of Queensberry. When Queensberry left a card for Wilde at his club, addressed to "Oscar Wilde, Somdomite" [sic], Wilde foolishly sued for libel. He lost, and Queensberry retaliated by instituting proceedings against Wilde for homosexuality. Waving aside opportunities to flee

England, Wilde stood two trials. The first ended without a verdict. At the end of the second trial, Wilde was convicted and sentenced to two years in prison. Because Queensberry forced him into bankruptcy, all his possessions were auctioned. Tragically, Wilde's downfall came at the height of his career. His plays, *An Ideal Husband* and *The Importance of Being Earnest,* had been playing to full houses in London.

Though he was allowed only one sheet of paper at a time while in prison, Wilde managed to compose *De Profundis,* a chronicle of Wilde's spiritual quest. During Wilde's years in prison, his mother died and Constance moved abroad and took the name "Holland" for herself and their sons. After her death in 1898, Wilde was denied access to his sons. Wilde, greatly weakened by the privations of prison life, moved to Paris and took the name Sebastian Melmoth, after the protaganist of *Melmoth the Wanderer,* a novel about a man who sells his soul to the devil. (The novel was written by his great-uncle Reverend Charles Maturin.) In the final years of his life, Wilde wrote little besides *The Ballad of Reading Gaol,* which he signed only as C.3.3, the number of his cell. Wilde died in a hotel room, either of syphilis or complications from an ear surgery, in Paris, on November 30, 1900.

Historical and Literary Context

The Victorian Era

Queen Victoria was crowned in 1837 and ruled until 1901. The "Victorian era" is used to describe the whole of her reign. "Victorianism" is synonymous in many people's minds with the elaborate, oppressive moral codes instituted under the genteel queen. Piety and family were exalted. Sex, and anything that brought sex to mind, was strictly taboo, and gender roles were equally strictly enforced. Not only were women forbidden to show so much as an ankle, even table legs—guilty by metaphorical association—were covered up. Didactic literature meant to train children and adults in the proper way to behave flourished. Underneath these codes seethed a populace deeply anxious about huge changes in science, technology, religion, politics, and social mores. Charles Darwin's *Origin of the Species* was published in 1859, but his theory of evolution was so radical, it took several decades for his ideas to have their full impact. The growing Industrial Revolution sent millions of country people to the cities to work, producing huge wealth and horrible slums and doubling London's size to two million people.

So much change occurred during the tumultuous Victorian era that the early, middle, and late Victorian periods each has its own particular characteristics. Wilde's life and work belong to the late Victorian era, a period marked by both genteel country house parties and growing political unrest. The complicated tangle of political matters known as the "Irish Question" were particularly urgent. Home Rule, the idea that the Irish could and should rule themselves, was one of the great controversies of the day. Karl Marx and Friedrich Engels had also published their famous works—*The Communist Manifesto* and *Capital*—and the question of the laborer and his role in society was fiercely debated, especially as some workers gained the vote and the labor movement became an important force in politics. In the face of such complex and difficult questions, a number of writers, including Wilde's teacher and friend Walter Pater, felt little could be accomplished in the way of resolution. Instead, they turned to the idea that people should seek out and enjoy each fleeting moment of beauty the world offered.

Aestheticism, Decadence, and The Yellow Book

Walter Pater, Wilde's teacher and mentor at Oxford, was among the founders of the Aesthetic Movement. In his *Studies in the History of the Renaissance*, Pater called for his readers to fan the "hard, gem-like flame" of self-fulfillment through a devotion to their senses. As *Dorian Gray*'s Lord Henry puts it, "Nothing can cure the soul but the senses, just as nothing can cure the senses but the soul." This was a radical idea in a culture devoted to suppressing sensuality. Aestheticists pushed harder against the Victorian tide by arguing that art's role was not to be moral or useful, or to teach "lessons," but to make art an object of beauty that transcended humans and human questions. They also believed that life should strive to emulate art and become as beautiful as possible and that, as Wilde puts it in *Dorian*, "the search for beauty is the real secret of life." Victorian aestheticists found an outlet in an influential literary journal called *The Yellow Book*, founded in 1894 by Aubrey Beardsley, an artist who illustrated some of Wilde's work.

Aestheticism is sometimes thought of as the English branch of the French decadence movement. One of the main tenets of French decadence was "art for art's sake," the idea that art didn't need to have a purpose or moral. In fact, the decadents embraced the gruesome, immoral, and perverse aspects of life and championed them in their art. The father of the decadence movement was Charles Baudelaire, whose 1857 collection of poems, *Les Fleurs du Mal* (*The Flowers of Evil*), was so scandalous that Baudelaire, his publisher, and even his printer were founded guilty of blasphemy and obscenity. Joris Karl Huysmans was another key figure in the movement. His 1884 novel, *À Rebours* (*Against the Grain*), referred to as "the little yellow book," was treated almost as a textbook for decadence. Wilde was profoundly influenced by *À Rebours*, and refers to the yellow book in *Dorian Gray*. Other poets associated with the decadence movement include Arthur Rimbaud, Paul Verlaine, and Stéphane Mallarmé.

The Gothic

An extension of Romanticism, the Gothic rebelled against the reasonable, controlled, sun-lit world of the Enlightenment. Gothic novels are full of mystery, terror, the supernatural, and monstrosities—all the dark things that lurk beneath the conscious, daylight world. These novels are often set in places once inhabited and now abandoned such as ruins, medieval castles, or old houses. The supernatural transformation of Dorian's portrait, Dorian's descent into the nightmarish worlds of vice, opium dens, murder, and the monstrous portrait itself, hanging in an abandoned schoolroom, clearly mark *The Picture of Dorian Gray* as a Gothic novel. Classic examples of gothic literature include Mary Shelley's *Frankenstein*, Bram Stoker's *Dracula,* and Robert Louis Stevenson's *The Strange Case of Dr. Jekyll and Mr. Hyde*.

Homosexuality and Victorian Morals

In Victorian society, men and women occupied distinctly separate spheres. Men had intense friendships and spent a great deal of time with one another in the absence of women. These basic facts of social life, combined with strict enforcement of traditional gender roles, made sexual policing and paranoia almost inevitable. In 1885, England made "gross indecency" (a code term for the unspeakable sin of male sodomy) punishable by up to two years in prison. Four years later, several male members of the nobility were accused of hiring young male prostitutes in the scandal known as "The Cleveland Street Affair." Rumor had it that even one of the Prince of Wales's sons was involved. The papers—and society tongues—went wild.

The homosexual subtext of *Dorian Gray* is unmistakable. As Wilde biographer Richard Ellmann explains, it's not "that all Wilde's principals are homosexuals, but they are scarcely anything else." Though Lord Henry has a wife (who divorces him), he spends all his time mentoring Dorian, and Basil's adoration of Dorian is clearly homoerotic. Dorian himself is said to have "ruined" several young men. Wilde's novel was even offered as evidence of his homosexuality in his trial for "gross indecency." The sensational trial was not simply about Wilde himself. It was an effort to suppress the idea of homosexuality, "immoral" books like *Dorian Gray,* and everything else outside the bounds of "decent" society.

CHRONOLOGY OF OSCAR WILDE'S LIFE AND WORK

1854: Oscar Fingal O'Flahertie Wills Wilde is born in Dublin on October 16.

1871: Studies Classics at Trinity College, Dublin, on scholarship.

1874: Wins scholarship to Magdalen College, Oxford. Studies Greek and Classics. Meets teachers John Ruskin and Walter Pater, whose ideas strongly influence him.

1877: Reviews the Grovesnor Gallery, his first published prose and criticism.

1878: Wins the Newdigate prize for poetry for "Ravenna"; graduates from Oxford.

1880: Publishes play *Vera*, which is badly received.

1881: Self-publishes *Poems*, which is badly received.

1881: Goes to America; wildly successful lecture tour.

1883: Writes *The Duchess of Padua*, which is not successful.

1884: Marries Constance Lloyd.

1885: Son Cyril born.

1886: Son Vyvyan born; meets close friend Robert Ross.

1887: Becomes editor of *The Lady's World* for two years.

1888: Publishes fairy tales, *The Happy Prince and Other Tales*.

1890: "The Picture of Dorian Gray" published as a story in *Lippincott's Monthly Magazine*; controversy ensues.

1891: The revised version of "Dorian Gray" story released as a book. Meets Lord Alfred "Bosie" Douglas. Publishes *Intentions, Lord Arthur's Savile Crime and Other Stories*, "The Soul of Man under Socialism," and *A House of Pomegranates*. In November and December, he writes *Salomé*.

1892: *Salomé* banned from the British stage and *Lady Windermere's Fan* produced to critical and general acclaim.

1893: *A Woman of No Importance* produced successfully.

1895: The hits *The Importance of Being Earnest* and *An Ideal Husband* produced. Wilde on trial for homosexuality. The first trial ends without a verdict. A second trial begins. On May 25, Wilde is convicted and sentenced to two years in prison.

1896: Wilde's mother dies.

1897: Wilde composes *De Profundis* in prison. In May, he is released, adopts the name Sebastian Melmoth, and moves to France.

1898: Publishes *The Ballad of Reading Gaol* under the name "C.3.3."—the number of his cell. Constance dies.

1900: Ill, penniless, and exiled, Wilde converts to Catholicism on his deathbed, and dies in Paris.

HISTORICAL CONTEXT OF
The Picture of Dorian Gray

1837: Queen Victoria is crowned.

1853: France outlaws cross-dressing.

1854: French poet Arthur Rimbaud born.

1855: Walt Whitman publishes the first edition of *Leaves of Grass*.

1859: Charles Darwin publishes *On the Origin of Species*.

1861: The death penalty as a punishment for sodomy in England is abolished.

1865: *The Fortnightly Review* founded by Anthony Trollope and others; W. B. Yeats born.

1868–69: The Spanish Revolution; Queen Isabella abdicates.

1869: André Gide born.

1870: The Second Industrial Revolution begins. Isaac Butt introduces "Home Rule" in Dublin, proposing the Irish rule themselves.

1872: Théophile Gautier dies.

1873: Walter Pater's *Studies in the History of the Renaissance* published.

1882: Henry James's *The Portrait of a Lady* published.

1883: The Orient Express makes its first run.

1885–98: Height of French symbolism and artistic "decadence" movement.

1885–1940: Irish Literary Renaissance.

1885: The Criminal Law Amendment Act, calling for two years' imprisonment for any male convicted of "gross indecency" passed in England.

1888: In the Whitechapel area of London, Jack the Ripper kills several prostitutes.

1894: *The Yellow Book*, a magazine of aesthetic arts and literature, is founded by Aubrey Beardsley, Henry Harland, and John Lane.

1895: The Aesthetic Movement widely considered to end with Wilde's trial.

1967: England decriminalizes sodomy.

THE PICTURE OF DORIAN GRAY

PREFACE

The artist is the creator of beautiful things.

To reveal art and conceal the artist is art's aim.

The critic is he who can translate into another manner or a new material his impression of beautiful things.

> *The highest as the lowest form of criticism is a mode of autobiography.*

Those who find ugly meanings in beautiful things are corrupt without being charming. This is a fault.

> *Those who find beautiful meanings in beautiful things are the cultivated. For these there is hope.*

They are the elect to whom beautiful things mean only beauty.

> *There is no such thing as a moral or an immoral book.*

> *Books are well written, or badly written. That is all.*

The nineteenth-century dislike of realism is the rage of Caliban seeing his own face in a glass.

> *The nineteenth-century dislike of romanticism is the rage of Caliban not seeing his own face in a glass.*

> *The moral life of man forms part of the subject matter*

3

of the artist, but the morality of art consists in the perfect use of an imperfect medium.

No artist desires to prove anything. Even things that are true can be proved.

No artist has ethical sympathies. An ethical sympathy in an artist is an unpardonable mannerism of style.

No artist is ever morbid. The artist can express everything.

Thought and language are to the artist instruments of an art.

Vice and virtue are to the artist materials for an art.

From the point of view of form, the type of all the arts is the art of the musician. From the point of view of feeling, the actor's craft is the type.

All art is at once surface and symbol.

Those who go beneath the surface do so at their peril.

Those who read the symbol do so at their peril.

It is the spectator, and not life, that art really mirrors.

Diversity of opinion about a work of art shows that the work is new, complex, and vital.

When critics disagree the artist is in accord with himself.

We can forgive a man for making a useful thing as long as he does not admire it. The only excuse for making a useless thing is that one admires it intensely.

All art is quite useless.

I

THE STUDIO was filled with the rich odour of roses, and when the light summer wind stirred amidst the trees of the garden there came through the open door the heavy scent of the lilac, or the more delicate perfume of the pink-flowering thorn.

From the corner of the divan of Persian saddle-bags on which he was lying, smoking, as was his custom, innumerable cigarettes, Lord Henry Wotton could just catch the gleam of the honey-sweet and honey-coloured blossoms of a laburnum,[1] whose tremulous branches seemed hardly able to bear the burden of a beauty so flame-like as theirs; and now and then the fantastic shadows of birds in flight flitted across the long tussore-silk[2] curtains that were stretched in front of the huge window, producing a kind of momentary Japanese effect, and making him think of those pallid jade-faced painters of Tokyo who, through the medium of an art that is necessarily immobile, seek to convey the sense of swiftness and motion. The sullen murmur of the bees shouldering their way through the long unmown grass, or circling with monotonous insistence round the dusty gilt horns of the straggling woodbine, seemed to make the stillness more oppressive. The dim roar of London was like the bourdon[3] note of a distant organ.

In the centre of the room, clamped to an upright easel, stood the full-length portrait of a young man of extraordinary personal beauty, and in front of it, some little distance away, was sitting the artist himself, Basil Hallward, whose sudden disappearance some years ago caused, at the time, such public excitement, and gave rise to so many strange conjectures.

As the painter looked at the gracious and comely form he had so skilfully mirrored in his art, a smile of pleasure passed across his face, and seemed about to linger there. But he suddenly started up, and, closing his eyes, placed his fingers upon the lids, as though he sought to imprison within his brain some curious dream from which he feared he might awake.

"It is your best work, Basil, the best thing you have ever done," said Lord Henry, languidly. "You must certainly send it next year to the Grosvenor.[4] The Academy[5] is too large and too vulgar. Whenever I have gone there, there have been either so many people that I have not been able to see the pictures, which was dreadful, or so many pictures that I have not been able to see the people, which was worse. The Grosvenor is really the only place."

"I don't think I shall send it anywhere," he answered, tossing his head back in that odd way that used to make his friends laugh at him at Oxford. "No, I won't send it anywhere."

Lord Henry elevated his eyebrows, and looked at him in amazement through the thin blue wreaths of smoke that curled up in such fanciful whorls from his heavy opium-tainted cigarette.

"Not send it anywhere? My dear fellow, why? Have you any reason? What odd chaps you painters are! You do anything in the world to gain a reputation. As soon as you have one, you seem to want to throw it away. It is silly of you, for there is only one thing in the world worse than being talked about, and that is not being talked about. A portrait like this would set you far above all the young men in England, and make the old men quite jealous, if old men are ever capable of any emotion."

"I know you will laugh at me," he replied, "but I really can't exhibit it. I have put too much of myself into it."

Lord Henry stretched himself out on the divan and laughed.

"Yes, I knew you would; but it is quite true, all the same."

"Too much of yourself in it! Upon my word, Basil, I didn't know you were so vain; and I really can't see any resemblance between you, with your rugged strong face and your coal-black hair, and this young Adonis,[6] who looks as if he was made out of ivory and rose-leaves. Why, my dear Basil, he is a Narcissus,[7] and you—well, of course you have an intellectual expression, and all that. But beauty, real beauty, ends where an intellectual expression begins. Intellect is in itself a mode of exaggeration, and destroys the harmony of any face. The moment one sits down to think, one becomes all nose, or all forehead, or something horrid. Look at the successful men in any of the learned professions. How perfectly hideous they are! Except, of course, in the Church. But then in the Church they don't think. A bishop keeps on saying at the age of eighty what he was told to say when he was a boy of eighteen, and as a natural consequence he always looks absolutely delightful. Your mysterious young friend, whose name you have never told me, but whose picture really fascinates me, never thinks. I feel quite sure of that. He is some brainless, beautiful creature, who should be always here in winter when we have no flowers to look at, and always here in summer when we want something to chill our intelligence. Don't flatter yourself, Basil, you are not in the least like him."

"You don't understand me, Harry," answered the artist. "Of course I am not like him. I know that perfectly well. Indeed, I should be sorry to look like him. You shrug your shoulders? I am telling you the truth. There is a fatality about all physical and intellectual distinction, the sort of fatality that seems to dog through history the faltering steps of kings. It is better not to be different from one's fellows. The ugly and the stupid have the best of it in this world. They can sit at their ease and gape at the play. If they know nothing of victory, they are at least spared the knowledge of defeat. They live as we all should live, undisturbed, indifferent, and without disquiet. They neither bring ruin upon others, nor ever receive it, from alien hands. Your rank and wealth, Harry; my brains, such as they are—my art, whatever it may be worth; Dorian Gray's good looks—we shall all suffer for what the gods have given us, suffer terribly."

"Dorian Gray? Is that his name?" asked Lord Henry, walking across the studio towards Basil Hallward.

"Yes, that is his name. I didn't intend to tell it to you."

"But why not?"

"Oh, I can't explain. When I like people immensely I never tell their names to anyone. It is like surrendering a part of them. I have grown to love secrecy. It seems to be the one thing that can make modern life mysterious or marvellous to us. The commonest thing is delightful if one only hides it. When I leave town now I never tell my people where I am going. If I did, I would lose all my pleasure. It is a silly habit, I dare say, but somehow it seems to bring a great deal of romance into one's life. I suppose you think me awfully foolish about it?"

"Not at all," answered Lord Henry, "not at all, my dear Basil. You seem to forget that I am married, and the one charm of marriage is that it makes a life of deception absolutely necessary for both parties. I never know where my wife is, and my wife never knows what I am doing. When we meet—we do meet occasionally, when we dine out together, or go down to the Duke's—we tell each other the most absurd stories with the most serious faces. My wife is very good at it—much better, in fact, than I am. She never gets confused over her dates, and I always do. But when she does find me out, she makes no row at all. I sometimes wish she would; but she merely laughs at me."

"I hate the way you talk about your married life, Harry," said Basil Hallward, strolling towards the door that led into the garden. "I ⬛⬛⬛⬛⬛⬛ really a very good husband, but that y⬛⬛⬛⬛⬛ ashamed of your own virtues. You are a⬛⬛⬛⬛⬛ fellow. You never say a moral thing, and yo⬛⬛⬛⬛⬛ wrong thing. Your cynicism is simply a pose."

"Being natural is simply a pose, and the most irritating pose I know," cried Lord Henry, laughing; and the two young men went out into the garden together, and ensconced themselves on a long bamboo seat that stood in the shade of a tall laurel bush. The sunlight slipped over the polished leaves. In the grass, white daisies were tremulous.

After a pause, Lord Henry pulled out his watch. "I am afraid I must be going, Basil," he murmured, "and before I go, I insist on your answering a question I put to you some time ago."

"What is that?" said the painter, keeping his eyes fixed on the ground.

"You know quite well."

"I do not, Harry."

"Well, I will tell you what it is. I want you to explain to me why you won't exhibit Dorian Gray's picture. I want the real reason."

"I told you the real reason."

"No, you did not. You said it was because there was too much of yourself in it. Now, that is childish."

"Harry," said Basil Hallward, looking him straight in the face, "every portrait that is painted with feeling is a portrait of the artist, not of the sitter. The sitter is merely the accident, the occasion. It is not he who is revealed by the painter; it is rather the painter who, on the coloured canvas, reveals himself. The reason I will not exhibit this picture is that I am afraid that I have shown in it the secret of my own soul."

Lord Henry laughed. "And what is that?" he asked.

"I will tell you," said Hallward; but an expression of perplexity came over his face.

"I am all expectation, Basil," continued his companion, glancing at him.

"Oh, there is really v⬛⬛⬛⬛⬛⬛⬛⬛⬛⬛⬛⬛ answered the painter; "and I am afrai⬛⬛⬛⬛⬛⬛⬛⬛⬛derstand it. Perhaps you will hardly beli⬛

Lord Henry smiled, an⬛⬛⬛⬛⬛⬛n, plucked a pink-petalled daisy from the grass, ⬛⬛⬛amined it. "I am quite sure I shall understand it," he replied, gazing intently at the little golden white-feathered disk, "and as for believing things, I can believe anything, provided that it is quite incredible."

The wind shook some blossoms from the trees, and the heavy lilac-blooms, with their clustering stars, moved to and fro in the languid air. A grasshopper began to chirrup by the wall, and like a blue thread a long thin dragon-fly floated past on its brown gauze wings. Lord Henry felt as if he could hear Basil Hallward's heart beating, and wondered what was coming.

"The story is simply this," said the painter after some time. "Two months ago I went to a crush[8] at Lady Brandon's. You know we poor artists have to show ourselves in society from time to time, just to remind the public that we are not savages. With an evening coat and a white tie, as you told me once, anybody, even a stock-broker, can gain a reputation for being civilized. Well, after I had been in the room about ten minutes, talking to huge overdressed dowagers and tedious Academicians, I suddenly became conscious that someone was looking at me. I turned half-way round, and saw Dorian Gray for the first time. When our eyes met, I felt that I was growing pale. A curious sensation of terror came over me. I knew that I had come face to face with someone whose mere personality was so fascinating that, if I allowed it to do so, it would absorb my whole nature, my whole soul, my very art itself. I did not want any external influence in my life. You know yourself, Harry, how independent I am by nature. I have always been my own master; had at least always been so, till I met Dorian Gray. Then—but I don't know how to explain it to you. Something seemed to tell me that I was on the verge of a terrible crisis in my life. I had a strange feeling that

Fate had in store for me exquisite joys and exquisite sorrows. I grew afraid, and turned to quit the room. It was not conscience that made me do it: it was a sort of cowardice. I take no credit to myself for trying to escape."

"Conscience and cowardice are really the same things, Basil. Conscience is the trade-name of the firm. That is all."

"I don't believe that, Harry, and I don't believe you do either. However, whatever was my motive—and it may have been pride, for I used to be very proud—I certainly struggled to the door. There, of course, I stumbled against Lady Brandon. 'You are not going to run away so soon, Mr. Hallward?' she screamed out. You know her curiously shrill voice?"

"Yes; she is a peacock in everything but beauty," said Lord Henry, pulling the daisy to bits with his long, nervous fingers.

"I could not get rid of her. She brought me up to Royalties, and people with Stars and Garters,[9] and elderly ladies with gigantic tiaras and parrot noses. She spoke of me as her dearest friend. I had only met her once before, but she took it into her head to lionize me. I believe some picture of mine had made a great success at that time, at least had been chattered about in the penny newspapers, which is the nineteenth-century standard of immortality. Suddenly I found myself face to face with the young man whose personality had so strangely stirred me. We were quite close, almost touching. Our eyes met again. It was reckless of me, but I asked Lady Brandon to introduce me to him. Perhaps it was not so reckless, after all. It was simply inevitable. We would have spoken to each other without any introduction. I am sure of that. Dorian told me so afterwards. He, too, felt that we were destined to know each other."

"And how did Lady Brandon describe this wonderful young man?" asked his companion. "I know she goes in for giving a rapid précis[10] of all her guests. I remember her bringing me up to a truculent and red-faced old gentleman covered all over with orders and ribbons, and hissing into my ear, in a tragic whisper which must have been perfectly audible to everybody in the room, the most astounding details. I simply fled. I like to find out people for myself. But Lady Brandon treats her guests exactly as an auctioneer treats his goods. She either explains them entirely away, or tells one everything about them except what one wants to know."

"Poor Lady Brandon! You are hard on her, Harry!" said Hallward, listlessly.

"My dear fellow, she tried to found a *salon*,[11] and only succeeded in opening a restaurant. How could I admire her? But tell me, what did she say about Mr. Dorian Gray?"

"Oh, something like 'Charming boy—poor dear mother and I absolutely inseparable. Quite forget what he does— afraid he—doesn't do anything—oh, yes, plays the piano—or is it the violin, dear Mr. Gray?' Neither of us could help laughing, and we became friends at once."

"Laughter is not at all a bad beginning for a friendship, and it is far the best ending for one," said the young lord, plucking another daisy.

Hallward shook his head. "You don't understand what friendship is, Harry," he murmured—"or what enmity is, for that matter. You like everyone; that is to say, you are indifferent to everyone."

"How horribly unjust of you!" cried Lord Henry, tilting his hat back, and looking up at the little clouds that, like ravelled skeins of glossy white silk, were drifting across the hollowed turquoise of the summer sky. "Yes, horribly unjust of you. I make a great difference between people. I choose my friends for their good looks, my acquaintances for their good characters, and my enemies for their good intellects. A man cannot be too careful in the choice of his enemies. I have not got one who is a fool, they are all men of some intellectual power, and consequently they all appreciate me. Is that very vain of me? I think it is rather vain."

"I should think it was, Harry. But according to your category I must be merely an acquaintance."

"My dear old Basil, you are much more than an acquaintance."

"And much less than a friend. A sort of brother, I suppose?"

"Oh, brothers! I don't care for brothers. My elder brother won't die, and my younger brothers seem never to do anything else."

"Harry!" exclaimed Hallward, frowning.

"My dear fellow, I am not quite serious. But I can't help detesting my relations. I suppose it comes from the fact that none of us can stand other people having the same faults as ourselves. I quite sympathize with the rage of the English democracy against what they call the vices of the upper orders. The masses feel that drunkenness, stupidity, and immorality should be their own special property, and that if anyone of us makes an ass of himself he is poaching on their preserves. When poor Southwark got into the Divorce Court, their indignation was quite magnificent. And yet I don't suppose that ten per cent of the proletariat live correctly."

"I don't agree with a single word that you have said, and, what is more, Harry, I feel sure you don't either."

Lord Henry stroked his pointed brown beard, and tapped the toe of his patent-leather boot with a tasselled ebony cane. "How English you are, Basil! That is the second time you have made that observation. If one puts forward an idea to a true Englishman—always a rash thing to do—he never dreams of considering whether the idea is right or wrong. The only thing he considers of any importance is whether one believes it oneself. Now, the value of an idea has nothing whatsoever to do with the sincerity of the man who expresses it. Indeed, the probabilities are that the more insincere the man is, the more purely intellectual will the idea be, as in that case it will not be coloured by either his wants, his desires, or his prejudices. However, I don't propose to discuss politics, sociology, or metaphysics with you. I like persons better than principles, and I like persons with no principles better than anything else in the world. Tell me more about Mr. Dorian Gray. How often do you see him?"

"Every day. I couldn't be happy if I didn't see him every day. He is absolutely necessary to me."

"How extraordinary! I thought you would never care for anything but your art."

"He is all my art to me now," said the painter, gravely. "I sometimes think, Harry, that there are only two eras of any importance in the world's history. The first is the appearance of a new medium for art, and the second is the appearance of a new personality for art also. What the invention of oil-painting was to the Venetians, the face of Antinous[12] was to late Greek sculpture, and the face of Dorian Gray will some day be to me. It is not merely that I paint from him, draw from him, sketch from him. Of course I have done all that. But he is much more to me than a model or a sitter. I won't tell you that I am dissatisfied with what I have done of him, or that his beauty is such that art cannot express it. There is nothing that art cannot express, and I know that the work I have done, since I met Dorian Gray, is good work, is the best work of my life. But in some curious way—I wonder will you understand me?—his personality has suggested to me an entirely new manner in art, an entirely new mode of style. I see things differently, I think of them differently. I can now re-create life in a way that was hidden from me before. 'A dream of form in days of thought':—who is it who says that? I forget; but it is what Dorian Gray has been to me. The merely visible presence of this lad—for he seems to me little more than a lad, though he is really over twenty—his merely visible presence—ah! I wonder can you realize all that that means? Unconsciously he defines for me the lines of a fresh school, a school that is to have in it all the passion of the romantic spirit, all the perfection of the spirit that is Greek. The harmony of soul and body—how much that is! We in our madness have separated the two, and have invented a realism that is vulgar, an ideality that is void. Harry! if you only knew what Dorian Gray is to me! You remember that landscape of mine, for which Agnew offered me such a huge price, but which I would not part with? It is one of the best things I have ever done. And why is it so? Because, while I was painting it, Dorian Gray sat beside me. Some subtle influence passed from him to me, and for the first time in my life I saw in the plain woodland the wonder I had always looked for, and always missed."

"Basil, this is extraordinary! I must see Dorian Gray."

Hallward got up from his seat, and walked up and down the garden. After some time he came back. "Harry," he said, "Dorian Gray is to me simply a motive in art. You might see nothing in him. I see everything in him. He is never more present in my work than when no image of him is there. He is a suggestion, as I have said, of a new manner. I find him in the curves of certain lines, in the loveliness and subtleties of certain colours. That is all."

"Then why won't you exhibit his portrait?" asked Lord Henry.

"Because, without intending it, I have put into it some expression of all this curious artistic idolatry, of which, of course, I have never cared to speak to him. He knows nothing about it. He shall never know anything about it. But the world might guess it; and I will not bare my soul to their shallow, prying eyes. My heart shall never be put under their microscope. There is too much of myself in the thing, Harry—too much of myself!"

"Poets are not so scrupulous as you are. They know how useful passion is for publication. Nowadays a broken heart will run to many editions."

"I hate them for it," cried Hallward. "An artist should create beautiful things, but should put nothing of his own life into them. We live in an age when men treat art as if it were meant to be a form of autobiography. We have lost the abstract sense of beauty. Some day I will show the world what it is; and for that reason the world shall never see my portrait of Dorian Gray."

"I think you are wrong, Basil, but I won't argue with you. It is only the intellectually lost who ever argue. Tell me, is Dorian Gray very fond of you?"

The painter considered for a few moments. "He likes me," he answered, after a pause; "I know he likes me. Of course I flatter him dreadfully. I find a strange pleasure in saying things to him that I know I shall be sorry for having said. As a rule, he is charming to me, and we sit in the studio and talk of a thousand things. Now and then, however, he is horribly thoughtless, and seems to take a real delight in giving me pain. Then I feel, Harry, that I have given away my whole soul to someone who treats it as if it were a flower to put in his coat, a bit of decoration to charm his vanity, an ornament for a summer's day."

"Days in summer, Basil, are apt to linger," murmured Lord Henry. "Perhaps you will tire sooner than he will. It is a sad thing to think of, but there is no doubt that genius lasts longer than beauty. That accounts for the fact that we all take such pains to overeducate ourselves. In the wild struggle for existence, we want to have something that endures, and so we fill our minds with rubbish and facts, in the silly hope of keeping our place. The thoroughly well-informed man—that is the modern ideal. And the mind of the thoroughly well-informed man is a dreadful thing. It is like a bric-à-brac shop, all monsters and dust, with everything priced above its proper value. I think you will tire first, all the same. Some day you will look at your friend and he will seem to you to be a little out of drawing, or you won't like his tone of colour, or something. You will bitterly reproach him in your own heart, and seriously think that he has behaved very badly to you. The next time he calls, you will be perfectly cold and indifferent. It will be a great pity, for it will alter you. What you have told me is quite a romance, a romance of art one might call it, and the worst of having a romance of any kind is that it leaves one so unromantic."

"Harry, don't talk like that. As long as I live, the personality of Dorian Gray will dominate me. You can't feel what I feel. You change too often."

"Ah, my dear Basil, that is exactly why I can feel it. Those who are faithful know only the trivial side of love: it is the faithless who know love's tragedies." And Lord Henry struck a light on a dainty silver case, and began to smoke a cigarette with a self-conscious and satisfied air, as if he had summed up the world in a phrase. There was a rustle of chirruping sparrows in the green lacquer leaves of the ivy, and the blue cloud-shadows chased themselves across the grass like swallows. How pleasant it was in the garden! And how delightful other people's emotions were!—much more delightful than their ideas, it seemed to him. One's own soul, and the passions of one's friends—those were the fascinating things in life. He pictured to himself with silent amusement the tedious luncheon that he had missed by staying so long with Basil Hallward. Had he gone to his aunt's, he would have been sure to have met Lord Goodbody there, and the whole conversation would have been about the feeding of the poor, and the necessity for model lodging-houses. Each class would have preached the importance of those virtues, for whose exercise there was no necessity in their own lives. The rich would have spoken on the value of thrift, and the idle grown eloquent over the dignity of labour. It was charming to have escaped all that! As he thought of his aunt, an idea seemed to strike him. He turned to Hallward, and said, "My dear fellow, I have just remembered."

"Remembered what, Harry?"

"Where I heard the name of Dorian Gray."

"Where was it?" asked Hallward, with a slight frown.

"Don't look so angry, Basil. It was at my aunt, Lady Agatha's. She told me she had discovered a wonderful young man, who was going to help her in the East End,[13] and that his name was Dorian Gray. I am bound to state that she never told me he was good-looking. Women have no appreciation of good looks; at least, good women have not. She said that he was very earnest, and had a beautiful nature. I at once pictured to myself a creature with spectacles and lank hair, horribly freckled, and tramping about on huge feet. I wish I had known it was your friend."

"I am very glad you didn't, Harry."

"Why?"

"I don't want you to meet him."

"You don't want me to meet him?"

"No."

"Mr. Dorian Gray is in the studio, sir," said the butler, coming into the garden.

"You must introduce me now," cried Lord Henry, laughing.

The painter turned to his servant, who stood blinking in the sunlight. "Ask Mr. Gray to wait, Parker: I shall be in in a few moments." The man bowed, and went up the walk.

Then he looked at Lord Henry. "Dorian Gray is my dearest friend," he said. "He has a simple and a beautiful nature. Your aunt was quite right in what she said of him. Don't spoil him. Don't try to influence him. Your influence would be bad. The world is wide, and has many marvellous people in it. Don't take away from me the one person who gives to my art whatever charm it possesses; my life as an artist depends on him. Mind, Harry, I trust you." He spoke very slowly, and the words seemed wrung out of him almost against his will.

"What nonsense you talk!" said Lord Henry, smiling, and, taking Hallward by the arm, he almost led him into the house.

II

As they entered they saw Dorian Gray. He was seated at the piano, with his back to them, turning over the pages of a volume of Schumann's[1] *Forest Scenes*. "You must lend me these, Basil," he cried. "I want to learn them. They are perfectly charming."

"That entirely depends on how you sit today, Dorian."

"Oh, I am tired of sitting, and I don't want a life-sized portrait of myself," answered the lad, swinging round on the music-stool, in a wilful, petulant manner. When he caught sight of Lord Henry, a faint blush coloured his cheeks for a moment, and he started up. "I beg your pardon, Basil, but I didn't know you had anyone with you."

"This is Lord Henry Wotton, Dorian, an old Oxford friend of mine. I have just been telling him what a capital sitter you were, and now you have spoiled everything."

"You have not spoiled my pleasure in meeting you, Mr. Gray," said Lord Henry, stepping forward and extending his hand. "My aunt has often spoken to me about you. You are one of her favourites, and, I am afraid, one of her victims, also."

"I am in Lady Agatha's black books at present," answered

Dorian, with a funny look of penitence. "I promised to go to a club in Whitechapel with her last Tuesday, and I really forgot all about it. We were to have played a duet together—three duets, I believe. I don't know what she will say to me. I am far too frightened to call."

"Oh, I will make your peace with my aunt. She is quite devoted to you. And I don't think it really matters about your not being there. The audience probably thought it was a duet. When Aunt Agatha sits down to the piano she makes quite enough noise for two people."

"That is very horrid to her, and not very nice to me," answered Dorian, laughing.

Lord Henry looked at him. Yes, he was certainly wonderfully handsome, with his finely-curved scarlet lips, his frank blue eyes, his crisp gold hair. There was something in his face that made one trust him at once. All the candour of youth was there, as well as all youth's passionate purity. One felt that he had kept himself unspotted from the world. No wonder Basil Hallward worshipped him.

"You are too charming to go in for philanthropy, Mr. Gray—far too charming." And Lord Henry flung himself down on the divan, and opened his cigarette-case.

The painter had been busy mixing his colours and getting his brushes ready. He was looking worried, and when he heard Lord Henry's last remark he glanced at him, hesitated for a moment, and then said, "Harry, I want to finish this picture today. Would you think it awfully rude of me if I asked you to go away?"

Lord Henry smiled, and looked at Dorian Gray. "Am I to go, Mr. Gray?" he asked.

"Oh, please don't, Lord Henry. I see that Basil is in one of his sulky moods; and I can't bear him when he sulks. Besides, I want you to tell me why I should not go in for philanthropy."

"I don't know that I shall tell you that, Mr. Gray. It is so tedious a subject that one would have to talk seriously about it.

But I certainly shall not run away, now that you have asked me to stop. You don't really mind, Basil, do you? You have often told me that you liked your sitters to have someone to chat to."

Hallward bit his lip. "If Dorian wishes it, of course you must stay. Dorian's whims are laws to everybody, except himself."

Lord Henry took up his hat and gloves. "You are very pressing, Basil, but I am afraid I must go. I have promised to meet a man at the Orleans.[2] Good-bye, Mr. Gray. Come and see me some afternoon in Curzon[3] Street. I am nearly always at home at five o'clock. Write to me when you are coming. I should be sorry to miss you."

"Basil," cried Dorian Gray, "if Lord Henry Wotton goes I shall go too. You never open your lips while you are painting, and it is horribly dull standing on a platform and trying to look pleasant. Ask him to stay. I insist upon it."

"Stay, Harry, to oblige Dorian, and to oblige me," said Hallward, gazing intently at his picture. "It is quite true, I never talk when I am working, and never listen either, and it must be dreadfully tedious for my unfortunate sitters. I beg you to stay."

"But what about my man at the Orleans?"

The painter laughed. "I don't think there will be any difficulty about that. Sit down again, Harry. And now, Dorian, get up on the platform, and don't move about too much, or pay any attention to what Lord Henry says. He has a very bad influence over all his friends, with the single exception of myself."

Dorian Gray stepped up on the dais, with the air of a young Greek martyr, and made a little *moue*[4] of discontent to Lord Henry, to whom he had rather taken a fancy. He was so unlike Basil. They made a delightful contrast. And he had such a beautiful voice. After a few moments he said to him, "Have you really a very bad influence, Lord Henry? As bad as Basil says?"

"There is no such thing as a good influence, Mr. Gray. All influence is immoral—immoral from the scientific point of view."

"Why?"

"Because to influence a person is to give him one's own soul. He does not think his natural thoughts, or burn with his natural passions. His virtues are not real to him. His sins, if there are such things as sins, are bor̲ ̲̲̲ed. He becomes an echo of someone else's music, an actor ̲ ̲ ̲ part that has not been written for him. The aim of life is self-development. To realize one's nature perfectly—that is what each of us is here for. People are afraid of themselves, nowadays. They have forgotten the highest of all duties, the duty that one owes to oneself. Of course they are charitable. They feed the hungry, and clothe the beggar. But their own souls starve, and are naked. Courage has gone out of our race. Perhaps we never really had it. The terror of society, which is the basis of morals, the terror of God, which is the secret of religion—these are the two things that govern us. And yet—"

"Just turn your head a little more to the right, Dorian, like a good boy," said the painter, deep in his work, and conscious only that a look had come into the lad's face that he had never seen there before.

"And yet," continued Lord Henry, in his low, musical voice, and with that graceful wave of the hand that was always so characteristic of him, and that he had even in his Eton[5] days, "I believe that if one man were to live out his life fully and completely, were to give form to every feeling, expression to every thought, reality to every dream—I believe that the world would gain such a fresh impulse of joy that we would forget all the maladies of mediaevalism, and return to the Hellenic ideal—to something finer, richer, than the Hellenic ideal, it may be. But the bravest man amongst us is afraid of himself. The mutilation of the savage has its tragic survival in the self-denial that mars our lives. We are punished for our refusals. Every impulse that we strive to strangle broods in the mind, and poisons us. The body sins once, and has done with its sin, for action is a mode of purification. Nothing remains then but the recollection of a pleasure, or the luxury of a regret. The only way to get rid of a temptation is to yield to it. Resist it, and your soul grows sick with longing for the things it has forbidden to itself, with desire for what its monstrous laws have made monstrous and unlawful. It has been said that the great events of the world take place in the brain. It is in the brain, and the brain only, that the great sins of the world take place also. You, Mr. Gray, you yourself, with your rose-red youth and your rose-white boyhood, you have had passions that have made you afraid, thoughts that have filled you with terror, day-dreams and sleeping dreams whose mere memory might stain your cheek with shame—"

"Stop!" faltered Dorian Gray, "stop! you bewilder me. I don't know what to say. There is some answer to you, but I cannot find it. Don't speak. Let me think. Or, rather, let me try not to think."

For nearly ten minutes he stood there, motionless, with parted lips, and eyes strangely bright. He was dimly conscious that entirely fresh influences were at work within him. Yet they seemed to him to have come really from himself. The few words that Basil's friend had said to him—words spoken by chance, no doubt, and with wilful paradox in them—had touched some secret chord that had never been touched before, but that he felt was now vibrating and throbbing to curious pulses.

Music had stirred him like that. Music had troubled him many times. But music was not articulate. It was not a new world, but rather another chaos, that it created in us. Words! Mere words! How terrible they were! How clear, and vivid, and cruel. One could not escape from them. And yet what a subtle magic there was in them! They seemed to be able to give a plastic form to formless things, and to have a music of their own as sweet as that of viol[6] or of lute.[7] Mere words! Was there anything so real as words?

Yes, there had been things in his boyhood that he had not

understood. He understood them now. Life suddenly became fiery-coloured to him. It seemed to him that he had
been walking in fire. Why had he not known it?

With his subtle smile, Lord Henry watched him. He knew
the precise psychological moment when to say nothing. He
felt intensely interested. He was amazed at the sudden impression that his words had produced, and, remembering a
book that he had read when he was sixteen, a book which had
revealed to him much that he had not known before, he wondered whether Dorian Gray was passing through a similar experience. He had merely shot an arrow into the air. Had it hit
the mark? How fascinating the lad was!

Hallward painted away with that marvellous bold touch of
his, that had the true refinement and perfect delicacy that in
art, at any rate, comes only from strength. He was unconscious of the silence.

"Basil, I am tired of standing," cried Dorian Gray, suddenly. "I must go out and sit in the garden. The air is stifling
here."

"My dear fellow, I am so sorry. When I am painting, I can't
think of anything else. But you never sat better. You were
perfectly still. And I have caught the effect I wanted—the
half-parted lips and the bright look in the eyes. I don't know
what Harry has been saying to you, but he has certainly made
you have the most wonderful expression. I suppose he has
been paying you compliments. You mustn't believe a word
that he says."

"He has certainly not been paying me compliments. Perhaps that is the reason that I don't believe anything he has
told me."

"You know you believe it all," said Lord Henry, looking at
him with his dreamy, languorous eyes. "I will go out to the
garden with you. It is horribly hot in the studio. Basil, let us
have something iced to drink, something with strawberries
in it."

"Certainly, Harry. Just touch the bell, and when Parker
comes I will tell him what you want. I have got to work up

this background, so I will join you later on. Don't keep Dorian too long. I have never been in better form for painting than I am today. This is going to be my masterpiece. It is my masterpiece as it stands."

Lord Henry went out to the garden, and found Dorian Gray burying his face in the great cool lilac blossoms, feverishly drinking in their perfume as if it had been wine. He came close to him, and put his hand upon his shoulder. "You are quite right to do that," he murmured. "Nothing can cure the soul but the senses, just as nothing can cure the senses but the soul."

The lad started and drew back. He was bare-headed, and the leaves had tossed his rebellious curls and tangled all their gilded threads. There was a look of fear in his eyes, such as people have when they are suddenly awakened. His finely-chiselled nostrils quivered, and some hidden nerve shook the scarlet of his lips and left them trembling.

"Yes," continued Lord Henry, "that is one of the great secrets of life—to cure the soul by means of the senses, and the senses by means of the soul. You are a wonderful creation. You know more than you think you know, just as you know less than you want to know."

Dorian Gray frowned and turned his head away. He could not help liking the tall, graceful young man who was standing by him. His romantic olive-coloured face and worn expression interested him. There was something in his low, languid voice that was absolutely fascinating. His cool, white, flower-like hands, even, had a curious charm. They moved, as he spoke, like music, and seemed to have a language of their own. But he felt afraid of him, and ashamed of being afraid. Why had it been left for a stranger to reveal him to himself? He had known Basil Hallward for months, but the friendship between them had never altered him. Suddenly there had come someone across his life who seemed to have disclosed to him life's mystery. And, yet, what was there to be afraid of? He was not a schoolboy or a girl. It was absurd to be frightened.

"Let us go and sit in the shade," said Lord Henry. "Parker has brought out the drinks, and if you stay any longer in this glare you will be quite spoiled, and Basil will never paint you again. You really must not allow yourself to become sunburnt. It would be unbecoming."

"What can it matter?" cried Dorian Gray, laughing, as he sat down on the seat at the end of the garden.

"It should matter everything to you, Mr. Gray."

"Why?"

"Because you have the most marvellous youth, and youth is the one thing worth having."

"I don't feel that, Lord Henry."

"No, you don't feel it now. Some day, when you are old and wrinkled and ugly, when thought has seared your forehead with its lines, and passion branded your lips with its hideous fires, you will feel it, you will feel it terribly. Now, wherever you go, you charm the world. Will it always be so? . . . You have a wonderfully beautiful face, Mr. Gray. Don't frown. You have. And beauty is a form of genius—is higher, indeed, than genius, as it needs no explanation. It is of the great facts of the world, like sunlight, or springtime, or the reflection in dark waters of that silver shell we call the moon. It cannot be questioned. It has its divine right of sovereignty. It makes princes of those who have it. You smile? Ah! when you have lost it you won't smile. . . . People say sometimes that beauty is only superficial. That may be so. But at least it is not so superficial as thought is. To me, beauty is the wonder of wonders. It is only shallow people who do not judge by appearances. The true mystery of the world is the visible, not the invisible. . . . Yes, Mr. Gray, the gods have been good to you. But what the gods give they quickly take away. You have only a few years in which to live really, perfectly, and fully. When your youth goes, your beauty will go with it, and then you will suddenly discover that there are no triumphs left for you, or have to content yourself with those mean triumphs that the memory of your past will make more bitter than defeats. Every month as it wanes brings you nearer to something dreadful. Time is jealous of you, and wars against your lilies and your roses. You will become sallow, and hollow-cheeked, and dull-eyed. You will suffer horribly. . . . Ah! realize your youth while you have it. Don't squander the gold of your days, listening to the tedious, trying to improve the hopeless failure, or giving away your life to the ignorant, the common, and the vulgar. These are the sickly aims, the false ideals, of our age. Live! Live the wonderful life that is in you! Let nothing be lost upon you. Be always searching for new sensations. Be afraid of nothing. . . . A new Hedonism—that is what our century wants. You might be its visible symbol. With your personality there is nothing you could not do. The world belongs to you for a season. . . . The moment I met you I saw that you were quite unconscious of what you really are, of what you really might be. There was so much in you that charmed me that I felt I must tell you something about yourself. I thought how tragic it would be if you were wasted. For there is such a little time that your youth will last—such a little time. The common hill-flowers wither, but they blossom again. The laburnum will be as yellow next June as it is now. In a month there will be purple stars on the clematis, and year after year the green night of its leaves will hold its purple stars. But we never get back our youth. The pulse of joy that beats in us at twenty, becomes sluggish. Our limbs fail, our senses rot. We degenerate into hideous puppets, haunted by the memory of the passions of which we were too much afraid, and the exquisite temptations that we had not the courage to yield to. Youth! Youth! There is absolutely nothing in the world but youth!"

Dorian Gray listened, open-eyed and wondering. The spray of lilac fell from his hand upon the gravel. A furry bee came and buzzed round it for a moment. Then it began to scramble all over the oval stellated globe of the tiny blossoms. He watched it with that strange interest in trivial things that we try to develop when things of high import make us afraid, or when we are stirred by some new emotion for which we cannot find expression, or when some thought that terrifies us lays sudden siege to the brain and calls on us to yield. After a time the bee flew away. He saw it creeping into the stained trumpet of a Tyrian convolvulus.[8] The flower seemed to quiver, and then swayed gently to and fro.

Suddenly the painter appeared at the door of the studio, and made staccato signs for them to come in. They turned to each other, and smiled.

"I am waiting," he cried. "Do come in. The light is quite perfect, and you can bring your drinks."

They rose up, and sauntered down the walk together. Two green-and-white butterflies fluttered past them, and in the pear tree at the corner of the garden a thrush began to sing.

"You are glad you have met me, Mr. Gray," said Lord Harry, looking at him.

"Yes, I am glad now. I wonder shall I always be glad?"

"Always! That is a dreadful word. It makes me shudder when I hear it. Women are so fond of using it. They spoil every romance by trying to make it last for ever. It is a meaningless word, too. The only difference between a caprice and a life-long passion is that the caprice lasts a little longer."

As they entered the studio, Dorian Gray put his hand upon Lord Henry's arm. "In that case, let our friendship be a caprice," he murmured, flushing at his own boldness, then stepped up on the platform and resumed his pose.

Lord Henry flung himself into a large wicker arm-chair, and watched him. The sweep and dash of the brush on the canvas made the only sound that broke the stillness, except when, now and then, Hallward stepped back to look at his work from a distance. In the slanting beams that streamed through the open doorway the dust danced and was golden. The heavy scent of the roses seemed to brood over everything.

After about a quarter of an hour Hallward stopped painting, looked for a long time at Dorian Gray, and then for a long time at the picture, biting the end of one of his huge brushes, and frowning. "It is quite finished," he cried at last, and stooping down he wrote his name in long vermilion letters on the left-hand corner of the canvas.

Lord Henry came over and examined the picture. It was certainly a wonderful work of art, and a wonderful likeness as well.

"My dear fellow, I congratulate you most warmly," he said. "It is the finest portrait of modern times. Mr. Gray, come over and look at yourself."

The lad started, as if awakened from some dream. "Is it really finished?" he murmured, stepping down from the platform.

"Quite finished," said the painter. "And you have sat splendidly today. I am awfully obliged to you."

"That is entirely due to me," broke in Lord Henry. "Isn't it, Mr. Gray?"

Dorian made no answer, but passed listlessly in front of his picture and turned towards it. When he saw it he drew back, and his cheeks flushed for a moment with pleasure. A look of joy came into his eyes, as if he had recognized himself for the first time. He stood there motionless and in wonder, dimly conscious that Hallward was speaking to him, but not catching the meaning of his words. The sense of his own beauty came on him like a revelation. He had never felt it before. Basil Hallward's compliments had seemed to him to be merely the charming exaggerations of friendship. He had listened to them, laughed at them, forgotten them. They had not influenced his nature. Then had come Lord Henry Wotton with his strange panegyric on youth, his terrible warning of its brevity. That had stirred him at the time, and now, as he stood gazing at the shadow of his own loveliness, the full reality of the description flashed across him. Yes, there would be a day when his face would be wrinkled and wizen, his eyes dim and colourless, the grace of his figure broken and deformed. The scarlet would pass away from his lips, and the gold steal from his hair. The life that was to make his soul would mar his body. He would become dreadful, hideous, and uncouth.

As he thought of it, a sharp pang of pain struck through him like a knife, and made each delicate fibre of his nature quiver. His eyes deepened into amethyst, and across them came a mist of tears. He felt as if a hand of ice had been laid upon his heart.

"Don't you like it?" cried Hallward at last, stung a little by the lad's silence, not understanding what it meant.

"Of course he likes it," said Lord Henry. "Who wouldn't like it? It is one of the greatest things in modern art. I will give you anything you like to ask for it. I must have it."

"It is not my property, Harry."

"Whose property is it?"

"Dorian's, of course," answered the painter.

"He is a very lucky fellow."

"How sad it is!" murmured Dorian Gray, with his eyes still fixed upon his own portrait. "How sad it is! I shall grow old, and horrible, and dreadful. But this picture will remain always young. It will never be older than this particular day of June. . . . If it were only the other way! If it were I who was to be always young, and the picture that was to grow old! For that—for that—I would give everything! Yes, there is nothing in the whole world I would not give! I would give my soul for that!"

"You would hardly care for such an arrangement, Basil," cried Lord Henry, laughing. "It would be rather hard lines on your work."

"I should object very strongly, Harry," said Hallward.

Dorian Gray turned and looked at him. "I believe you would, Basil. You like your art better than your friends. I am no more to you than a green bronze figure. Hardly as much, I dare say."

The painter stared in amazement. It was so unlike Dorian to speak like that. What had happened? He seemed quite angry. His face was flushed and his cheeks burning.

"Yes," he continued, "I am less to you than your ivory Hermes[9] or your silver Faun.[10] You will like them always. How long will you like me? Till I have my first wrinkle, I suppose. I know, now, that when one loses one's good looks, whatever they may be, one loses everything. Your picture has taught me that. Lord Henry Wotton is perfectly right. Youth is the only thing worth having. When I find that I am growing old, I shall kill myself."

Hallward turned pale, and caught his hand. "Dorian! Dorian!" he cried, "don't talk like that. I have never had such a friend as you, and I shall never have such another. You are not jealous of material things, are you?—you who are finer than any of them!"

"I am jealous of everything whose beauty does not die. I am jealous of the portrait you have painted of me. Why should it keep what I must lose? Every moment that passes takes something from me, and gives something to it. Oh, if it were only the other way! If the picture could change, and I could be always what I am now! Why did you paint it? It will mock me some day—mock me horribly!" The hot tears welled into his eyes; he tore his hand away, and, flinging himself on the divan, he buried his face in the cushions, as though he was praying.

"This is your doing, Harry," said the painter, bitterly.

Lord Henry shrugged his shoulders. "It is the real Dorian Gray—that is all."

"It is not."

"If it is not, what have I to do with it?"

"You should have gone away when I asked you," he muttered.

"I stayed when you asked me," was Lord Henry's answer.

"Harry, I can't quarrel with my two best friends at once, but between you both you have made me hate the finest piece of work I have ever done, and I will destroy it. What is it but canvas and colour? I will not let it come across our three lives and mar them."

Dorian Gray lifted his golden head from the pillow, and with pallid face and tear-stained eyes looked at him, as he walked over to the deal[11] painting-table that was set beneath the high curtained window. What was he doing there? His fingers were straying about among the litter of tin tubes and dry brushes, seeking for something. Yes, it was for the long palette knife, with its thin blade of lithe steel. He had found it at last. He was going to rip up the canvas.

With a stifled sob the lad leaped from the couch, and, rushing over to Hallward, tore the knife out of his hand, and flung it to the end of the studio. "Don't, Basil, don't!" he cried. "It would be murder!"

"I am glad you appreciate my work at last, Dorian," said the painter, coldly, when he had recovered from his surprise. "I never thought you would."

"Appreciate it? I am in love with it, Basil. It is part of myself. I feel that."

"Well, as soon as you are dry, you shall be varnished, and framed, and sent home. Then you can do what you like with yourself." And he walked across the room and rang the bell for tea. "You will have tea, of course, Dorian? And so will you, Harry? Or do you object to such simple pleasures?"

"I adore simple pleasures," said Lord Henry. "They are the last refuge of the complex. But I don't like scenes, except on the stage. What absurd fellows you are, both of you! I wonder who it was defined man as a rational animal. It was the most premature definition ever given. Man is many things, but he is not rational. I am glad he is not, after all: though I wish you chaps would not squabble over the picture. You had much better let me have it, Basil. This silly boy doesn't really want it, and I really do."

"If you let anyone have it but me, Basil, I shall never forgive you!" cried Dorian Gray; "and I don't allow people to call me a silly boy."

"You know the picture is yours, Dorian. I gave it to you before it existed."

"And you know you have been a little silly, Mr. Gray, and that you don't really object to being reminded that you are extremely young."

"I should have objected very strongly this morning, Lord Henry."

"Ah! this morning! You have lived since then."

There came a knock at the door, and the butler entered with a laden tea tray and set it down upon a small Japanese table. There was a rattle of cups and saucers and the hissing of a fluted Georgian[12] urn. Two globe-shaped china dishes were brought in by a page. Dorian Gray went over and poured out the tea. The two men sauntered languidly to the table, and examined what was under the covers.

"Let us go to the theatre tonight," said Lord Henry. "There is sure to be something on, somewhere. I have promised to dine at White's,[13] but it is only with an old friend, so I can send him a wire to say that I am ill, or that I am prevented from coming in consequence of a subsequent engagement. I think that would be a rather nice excuse: it would have all the surprise of candour."

"It is such a bore putting on one's dress-clothes," muttered Hallward. "And, when one has them on, they are so horrid."

"Yes," answered Lord Henry, dreamily, "the costume of the nineteenth century is detestable. It is so sombre, so depressing. Sin is the only real colour element left in modern life."

"You really must not say things like that before Dorian, Harry."

"Before which Dorian? The one who is pouring out tea for us, or the one in the picture?"

"Before either."

"I should like to come to the theatre with you, Lord Henry," said the lad.

"Then you shall come; and you will come too, Basil, won't you?"

"I can't, really. I would sooner not. I have a lot of work to do."

"Well, then, you and I will go, Mr. Gray."

"I should like that awfully."

The painter bit his lip and walked over, cup in hand, to the picture. "I shall stay with the real Dorian," he said, sadly.

"Is it the real Dorian?" cried the original of the portrait, strolling across to him. "Am I really like that?"

"Yes; you are just like that."

"How wonderful, Basil!"

"At least you are like it in appearance. But it will never alter," sighed Hallward. "That is something."

"What a fuss people make about fidelity!" exclaimed Lord Henry. "Why, even in love it is purely a question for physiology. It has nothing to do with our own will. Young men want to be faithful, and are not; old men want to be faithless, and cannot: that is all one can say."

"Don't go to the theatre tonight, Dorian," said Hallward. "Stop and dine with me."

"I can't, Basil."

"Why?"

"Because I have promised Lord Henry Wotton to go with him."

"He won't like you the better for keeping your promises. He always breaks his own. I beg you not to go."

Dorian Gray laughed and shook his head.

"I entreat you."

The lad hesitated, and looked over at Lord Henry, who was watching them from the tea table with an amused smile.

"I must go, Basil," he answered.

"Very well," said Hallward; and he went over and laid down his cup on the tray. "It is rather late, and, as you have to dress, you had better lose no time. Good-bye, Harry. Good-bye, Dorian. Come and see me soon. Come tomorrow."

"Certainly."

"You won't forget?"

"No, of course not," cried Dorian.

"And . . . Harry!"

"Yes, Basil?"

"Remember what I asked you, when we were in the garden this morning."

"I have forgotten it."

"I trust you."

"I wish I could trust myself," said Lord Henry, laughing. "Come, Mr. Gray, my hansom[14] is outside, and I can drop you at your own place. Good-bye, Basil. It has been a most interesting afternoon."

As the door closed behind them, the painter flung himself down on a sofa, and a look of pain came into his face.

III

A T HALF-PAST TWELVE next day Lord Henry Wotton strolled from Curzon Street over to the Albany to call on his uncle, Lord Fermor, a genial if somewhat rough-mannered old bachelor, whom the outside world called self-ish because it derived no particular benefit from him, but who was considered generous by Society as he fed the people who amused him. His father had been our ambassador at Madrid when Isabella was young, and Prim[1] unthought of, but had retired from the Diplomatic Service in a capricious moment of annoyance on not being offered the Embassy at Paris, a post to which he considered that he was fully enti-tled by reason of his birth, his indolence, the good English of his despatches, and his inordinate passion for pleasure. The son, who had been his father's secretary, had resigned along with his chief, somewhat foolishly as was thought at the time, and on succeeding some months later to the title, had set himself to the serious study of the great aristocratic art of doing absolutely nothing. He had two large town houses, but preferred to live in chambers as it was less trouble, and took most of his meals at his club. He paid some attention to the management of his collieries[2] in the Midland counties, excusing himself for this taint of industry on the ground that the one advantage of having coal was that it enabled a gentleman to afford the decency of burning wood on his own hearth. In politics he was a Tory,[3] except when the Tories were in office, during which period he roundly abused them for being a pack of Radicals. He was a hero to his valet, who bullied him, and a terror to most of his relations, whom he bullied in turn. Only England could have produced him, and he always said that the country was going to the dogs. His principles were out of date, but there was a good deal to be said for his prejudices.

When Lord Henry entered the room, he found his uncle sitting in a rough shooting coat, smoking a cheroot and grumbling over *The Times*. "Well, Harry," said the old gentleman, "what brings you out so early? I thought you dandies never got up until two, and were not visible till five."

"Pure family affection, I assure you, Uncle George. I want to get something out of you."

"Money, I suppose," said Lord Fermor, making a wry face. "Well, sit down and tell me all about it. Young people, nowadays, imagine that money is everything."

"Yes," murmured Lord Henry, settling his buttonhole[4] in his coat; "and when they grow older they know it. But I don't want money. It is only people who pay their bills who want that, Uncle George, and I never pay mine. Credit is the capital of a younger son, and one lives charmingly upon it. Besides, I always deal with Dartmoor's tradesmen, and consequently they never bother me. What I want is information; not useful information, of course; useless information."

"Well, I can tell you anything that is in an English Blue book,[5] Harry, although those fellows nowadays write a lot of nonsense. When I was in the Diplomatic, things were much better. But I hear they let them in now by examination. What can you expect? Examinations, sir, are pure humbug from beginning to end. If a man is a gentleman, he knows quite enough, and if he is not a gentleman, whatever he knows is bad for him."

"Mr. Dorian Gray does not belong to Blue books, Uncle George," said Lord Henry, languidly.

"Mr. Dorian Gray? Who is he?" asked Lord Fermor, knitting his bushy white eyebrows.

"That is what I have come to learn, Uncle George. Or rather, I know who he is. He is the last Lord Kelso's grandson. His mother was a Devereux, Lady Margaret Devereux. I want you to tell me about his mother. What was she like? Whom did she marry? You have known nearly everybody in your time, so you might have known her. I am very much interested in Mr. Gray at present. I have only just met him."

"Kelso's grandson!" echoed the old gentleman—"Kelso's grandson! . . . Of course. . . . I knew his mother intimately. I believe I was at her christening. She was an extraordinarily beautiful girl, Margaret Devereux, and made all the men frantic by running away with a penniless young fellow, a mere nobody, sir, a subaltern in a foot regiment, or something of that kind. Certainly. I remember the whole thing as if it happened yesterday. The poor chap was killed in a duel at Spa a few months after the marriage. There was an ugly story about it. They said Kelso got some rascally adventurer, some Belgian brute, to insult his son-in-law in public, paid him, sir, to do it, paid him, and that the fellow spitted his man as if he had been a pigeon. The thing was hushed up, but, egad, Kelso ate his chop alone at the club for some time afterwards. He brought his daughter back with him, I was told, and she never spoke to him again. Oh, yes; it was a bad business. The girl died too, died within a year. So she left a son, did she? I had forgotten that. What sort of boy is he? If he is like his mother he must be a good-looking chap."

"He is very good-looking," assented Lord Henry.

"I hope he will fall into proper hands," continued the old man. "He should have a pot of money waiting for him if Kelso did the right thing by him. His mother had money too. All the Selby property came to her, through her grandfather. Her grandfather hated Kelso, thought him a mean dog. He was, too. Came to Madrid once when I was there. Egad, I was ashamed of him. The Queen used to ask me about the English noble who was always quarrelling with the cabmen about their fares. They made quite a story of it. I didn't dare show my face at Court for a month. I hope he treated his grandson better than he did the jarvies."

"I don't know," answered Lord Henry. "I fancy that the boy will be well off. He is not of age yet. He has Selby, I know. He told me so. And . . . his mother was very beautiful?"

"Margaret Devereux was one of the loveliest creatures I ever saw, Harry. What on earth induced her to behave as she did, I never could understand. She could have married anybody she chose. Carlington was mad after her. She was romantic, though. All the women of that family were. The men were a poor lot, but, egad! the women were wonderful. Carlington went on his knees to her. Told me so himself. She laughed at him, and there wasn't a girl in London at the time who wasn't after him. And by the way, Harry, talking about silly marriages, what is this humbug your father tells me about Dartmoor wanting to marry an American? Ain't English girls good enough for him?"

"It is rather fashionable to marry Americans just now, Uncle George."

"I'll back English women against the world, Harry," said Lord Fermor, striking the table with his fist.

"The betting is on the Americans."

"They don't last, I am told," muttered his uncle.

"A long engagement exhausts them, but they are capital at a steeplechase. They take things flying. I don't think Dartmoor has a chance."

"Who are her people?" grumbled the old gentleman. "Has she got any?"

Lord Henry shook his head. "American girls are as clever at concealing their parents, as English women are at concealing their past," he said, rising to go.

"They are pork-packers, I suppose?"

"I hope so, Uncle George, for Dartmoor's sake. I am told that pork-packing is the most lucrative profession in America, after politics."

"Is she pretty?"

"She behaves as if she was beautiful. Most American women do. It is the secret of their charm."

"Why can't these American women stay in their own country? They are always telling us that it is the Paradise for women."

"It is. That is the reason why, like Eve, they are so excessively anxious to get out of it," said Lord Henry. "Good-bye, Uncle George. I shall be late for lunch, if I stop any longer. Thanks for giving me the information I wanted. I always like to know everything about my new friends, and nothing about my old ones."

"Where are you lunching, Harry?"

"At Aunt Agatha's. I have asked myself and Mr. Gray. He is her latest protégé."

"Humph! Tell your Aunt Agatha, Harry, not to bother me any more with her charity appeals. I am sick of them. Why, the good woman thinks that I have nothing to do but to write cheques for her silly fads."

"All right, Uncle George, I'll tell her, but it won't have any effect. Philanthropic people lose all sense of humanity. It is their distinguishing characteristic."

The old gentleman growled approvingly, and rang the bell for his servant. Lord Henry passed up the low arcade[6] into Burlington Street,[7] and turned his steps in the direction of Berkeley Square.

So that was the story of Dorian Gray's parentage. Crudely as it had been told to him, it had yet stirred him by its suggestion of a strange, almost modern romance. A beautiful woman risking everything for a mad passion. A few wild weeks of happiness cut short by a hideous, treacherous crime. Months of voiceless agony, and then a child born in pain. The mother snatched away by death, the boy left to solitude and the tyranny of an old and loveless man. Yes; it was an interesting background. It posed the lad, made him more perfect as it were. Behind every exquisite thing that existed, there was something tragic. Worlds had to be in travail, that the meanest flower might blow. . . . And how charming he had been at dinner the night before, as with startled eyes and lips parted in frightened pleasure he had sat opposite to him at the club, the red candle-shades staining to a richer rose the wakening wonder of his face. Talking to him was like playing upon an exquisite violin. He answered to every touch and thrill of the bow. . . . There was something terribly enthralling in the exercise of influence. No other activity was like it. To project one's soul into some gracious form, and let it tarry there for a moment; to hear one's own intellectual views echoed back to one with all the added music of passion and youth; to convey one's temperament into another as though it were a subtle fluid or a strange perfume: there was a real joy in that—perhaps the most satisfying joy left to us in an age so limited and vulgar as our own, an age grossly carnal in its pleasures, and grossly common in its aims. . . . He was a marvellous type, too, this lad, whom by so curious a chance he had met in Basil's studio, or could be fashioned into a marvellous type, at any rate. Grace was his, and the white purity of boyhood, and beauty such as old Greek marbles kept for us. There was nothing that one could not do with him. He could be made a Titan or a toy. What a pity it was that such beauty was destined to fade! . . And Basil? From a psychological point of view, how interesting he was! The new manner in art, the fresh mode of looking at life, suggested so strangely by the merely visible presence of one who was unconscious of it all; the silent spirit that dwelt in dim woodland, and walked unseen in open field, suddenly showing herself, dryad-like and not afraid, because in his soul who sought for her there had been wakened that wonderful vision to which alone are wonderful things revealed; the mere shapes and patterns of things becoming, as it were, refined, and gaining a kind of symbolical value, as though they were themselves patterns of some other and more perfect form whose shadow they made real: how strange it all was! He remembered something like it in history. Was it not Plato, that artist in thought, who had first analysed it? Was it not Buonaroti[8] who had carved it in the coloured marbles of a sonnet sequence? But in our own country it was strange. . . . Yes; he would try to be to Dorian Gray what, without knowing it, the lad was to the painter who had fashioned the wonderful portrait. He would seek to dominate him—had already, indeed, half done so. He would make that wonderful spirit his own. There was something fascinating in this son of love and death.

Suddenly he stopped, and glanced up at the houses. He found that he had passed his aunt's some distance, and, smiling to himself, turned back. When he entered the somewhat sombre hall the butler told him that they had gone in to lunch. He gave one of the footmen his hat and stick and passed into the dining-room.

"Late as usual, Harry," cried his aunt, shaking her head at him.

He invented a facile excuse, and having taken the vacant seat next to her, looked round to see who was there. Dorian bowed to him shyly from the end of the table, a flush of pleasure stealing into his cheek. Opposite was the Duchess of Harley, a lady of admirable good nature and good temper, much liked by everyone who knew her, and of those ample architectural proportions that in women who are not Duchesses are described by contemporary historians as stoutness. Next to her sat, on her right, Sir Thomas Burdon, a Radical member of Parliament, who followed his leader in public life and in private life followed the best cooks, dining with the Tories, and thinking with the Liberals, in accordance with a wise and well-known rule. The post on her left was occupied by Mr. Erskine of Treadley, an old gentleman of considerable charm and culture, who had fallen, however, into bad habits of silence, having, as he explained once to Lady Agatha, said everything that he had to say before he was thirty. His own neighbour was Mrs. Vandeleur, one of his aunt's oldest friends, a perfect saint amongst women, but so dreadfully dowdy that she reminded one of a badly bound hymn-book. Fortunately for him she had on the other side Lord Faudel, a most intelligent middle-aged mediocrity, as bald as a Ministerial statement in the House of Commons, with whom she was conversing in that intensely earnest manner which is the one unpardonable error, as he remarked once himself, that all really good people fall into, and from which none of them ever quite escape.

"We are talking about poor Dartmoor, Lord Henry," cried the Duchess, nodding pleasantly to him across the table. "Do you think he will really marry this fascinating young person?"

"I believe she has made up her mind to propose to him, Duchess."

"How dreadful!" exclaimed Lady Agatha. "Really, someone should interfere."

"I am told, on excellent authority, that her father keeps an American dry-goods store," said Sir Thomas Burden, looking supercilious.

"My uncle has already suggested pork-packing, Sir Thomas."

"Dry-goods! What are American dry-goods?" asked the Duchess, raising her large hands in wonder, and accentuating the verb.

"American novels," answered Lord Henry, helping himself to some quail.

The Duchess looked puzzled.

"Don't mind him, my dear," whispered Lady Agatha. "He never means anything that he says."

"When America was discovered," said the Radical member, and he began to give some wearisome facts. Like all people who try to exhaust a subject, he exhausted his listeners. The Duchess sighed, and exercised her privilege of interruption. "I wish to goodness it never had been discovered at all!" she exclaimed. "Really, our girls have no chance nowadays. It is most unfair."

"Perhaps, after all, America never has been discovered,"

said Mr. Erskine; "I myself would say that it had merely been detected."

"Oh! but I have seen specimens of the inhabitants," answered the Duchess, vaguely. "I must confess that most of them are extremely pretty. And they dress well, too. They get all their dresses in Paris. I wish I could afford to do the same."

"They say that when good Americans die they go to Paris," chuckled Sir Thomas, who had a large wardrobe of Humour's cast-off clothes.

"Really! And where do bad Americans go to when they die?" inquired the Duchess.

"They go to America," murmured Lord Henry.

Sir Thomas frowned. "I am afraid that your nephew is prejudiced against that great country," he said to Lady Agatha. "I have travelled all over it, in cars provided by the directors, who, in such matters, are extremely civil. I assure you that it is an education to visit it."

"But must we really see Chicago in order to be educated?" asked Mr. Erskine, plaintively. "I don't feel up to the journey."

Sir Thomas waved his hand. "Mr. Erskine of Treadley has the world on his shelves. We practical men like to see things, not to read about them. The Americans are an extremely interesting people. They are absolutely reasonable. I think that is their distinguishing characteristic. Yes, Mr. Erskine, an absolutely reasonable people. I assure you there is no nonsense about the Americans."

"How dreadful!" cried Lord Henry. "I can stand brute force, but brute reason is quite unbearable. There is something unfair about its use. It is hitting below the intellect."

"I do not understand you," said Sir Thomas, growing rather red.

"I do, Lord Henry," murmured Mr. Erskine, with a smile.

"Paradoxes are all very well in their way . . ." rejoined the Baronet.

"Was that a paradox?" asked Mr. Erskine. "I did not think

so. Perhaps it was. Well, the way of paradoxes is the way of truth. To test reality we must see it on the tight-rope. When the verities become acrobats we can judge them."

"Dear me!" said Lady Agatha, "how you men argue! I am sure I never can make out what you are talking about. Oh! Harry, I am quite vexed with you. Why do you try to persuade our nice Mr. Dorian Gray to give up the East End? I assure you he would be quite invaluable. They would love his playing."

"I want him to play to me," cried Lord Henry, smiling, and he looked down the table and caught a bright answering glance.

"But they are so unhappy in Whitechapel,⁹" continued Lady Agatha.

"I can sympathize with everything, except suffering," said Lord Henry, shrugging his shoulders. "I cannot sympathize with that. It is too ugly, too horrible, too distressing. There is something terribly morbid in the modern sympathy with pain. One should sympathize with the colour, the beauty, the joy of life. The less said about life's sores the better."

"Still, the East End is a very important problem," remarked Sir Thomas, with a grave shake of the head.

"Quite so," answered the young lord. "It is the problem of slavery, and we try to solve it by amusing the slaves."

The politician looked at him keenly. "What change do you propose, then?" he asked.

Lord Henry laughed. "I don't desire to change anything in England except the weather," he answered. "I am quite content with philosophic contemplation. But, as the nineteenth century has gone bankrupt through an overexpenditure of sympathy, I would suggest that we should appeal to science to put us straight. The advantage of the emotions is that they lead us astray, and the advantage of science is that it is not emotional."

"But we have such grave responsibilities," ventured Mrs. Vandeleur, timidly.

"Terribly grave," echoed Lady Agatha.

Lord Henry looked over at Mr. Erskine. "Humanity takes itself too seriously. It is the world's original sin. If the caveman had known how to laugh, history would have been different."

"You are really very comforting," warbled the Duchess. "I have always felt rather guilty when I came to see your dear aunt, for I take no interest at all in the East End. For the future I shall be able to look her in the face without a blush."

"A blush is very becoming, Duchess," remarked Lord Henry.

"Only when one is young," she answered. "When an old woman like myself blushes, it is a very bad sign. Ah! Lord Henry, I wish you would tell me how to become young again."

He thought for a moment. "Can you remember any great error that you committed in your early days, Duchess?" he asked, looking at her across the table.

"A great many, I fear," she cried.

"Then commit them over again," he said, gravely. "To get back one's youth, one has merely to repeat one's follies."

"A delightful theory!" she exclaimed. "I must put it into practice."

"A dangerous theory," came from Sir Thomas's tight lips. Lady Agatha shook her head, but could not help being amused. Mr. Erskine listened.

"Yes," he continued, "that is one of the great secrets of life. Nowadays most people die of a sort of creeping common sense, and discover when it is too late that the only things one never regrets are one's mistakes."

A laugh ran round the table.

He played with the idea, and grew wilful; tossed it into the air and transformed it; let it escape and recaptured it; made it iridescent with fancy, and winged it with paradox. The praise of folly, as he went on, soared into a philosophy, and Philosophy herself became young, and catching the mad music of Pleasure, wearing, one might fancy, her wine-stained robe and wreath of ivy, danced like a bacchante over the hills of life, and mocked the slow Silenus[10] for being sober. Facts fled before her like frightened forest things. Her white feet trod the huge press at which wise Omar sits, till the seething grape-juice rose round her bare limbs in waves of purple bubbles, or crawled in red foam over the vat's black, dripping, sloping sides. It was an extraordinary improvisation. He felt that the eyes of Dorian Gray were fixed on him, and the consciousness that amongst his audience there was one whose temperament he wished to fascinate, seemed to give his wit keenness, and to lend colour to his imagination. He was brilliant, fantastic, irresponsible. He charmed his listeners out of themselves, and they followed his pipe laughing. Dorian Gray never took his gaze off him, but sat like one under a spell, smiles chasing each other over his lips, and wonder growing grave in his darkening eyes.

At last, liveried in the costume of the age, reality entered the room in the shape of a servant to tell the Duchess that her carriage was waiting. She wrung her hands in mock despair. "How annoying!" she cried. "I must go. I have to call for my husband at the club, to take him to some absurd meeting at Willis's Rooms, where he is going to be in the chair. If I am late he is sure to be furious, and I couldn't have a scene in this bonnet. It is far too fragile. A harsh word would ruin it. No, I must go, dear Agatha. Good-bye, Lord Henry, you are quite delightful, and dreadfully demoralizing. I am sure I don't know what to say about your views. You must come and dine with us some night. Tuesday? Are you disengaged Tuesday?"

"For you I would throw over anybody, Duchess," said Lord Henry, with a bow.

"Ah! that is very nice, and very wrong of you," she cried; "so mind you come;" and she swept out of the room, followed by Lady Agatha and the other ladies.

When Lord Henry had sat down again, Mr. Erskine moved round, and taking a chair close to him, placed his hand upon his arm.

"You talk books away," he said; "why don't you write one?"

"I am too fond of reading books to care to write them, Mr. Erskine. I should like to write a novel certainly, a novel that would be as lovely as a Persian carpet and as unreal. But there is no literary public in England for anything except newspapers, primers, and encyclopaedias. Of all people in the world the English have the least sense of the beauty of literature."

"I fear you are right," answered Mr. Erskine. "I myself used to have literary ambitions, but I gave them up long ago. And now, my dear young friend, if you will allow me to call you so, may I ask if you really meant all that you said to us at lunch?"

"I quite forget what I said," smiled Lord Henry. "Was it all very bad?"

"Very bad indeed. In fact I consider you extremely dangerous, and if anything happens to our good Duchess we shall all look on you as being primarily responsible. But I should like to talk to you about life. The generation into which I was born was tedious. Some day, when you are tired of London, come down to Treadley, and expound to me your philosophy of pleasure over some admirable Burgundy I am fortunate enough to possess."

"I shall be charmed. A visit to Treadley would be a great privilege. It has a perfect host, and a perfect library."

"You will complete it," answered the old gentleman, with a courteous bow. "And now I must bid good-bye to your excellent aunt. I am due at the Athenaeum.[11] It is the hour when we sleep there."

"All of you, Mr. Erskine?"

"Forty of us, in forty arm-chairs. We are practising for an English Academy of Letters."

Lord Henry laughed, and rose. "I am going to the Park," he cried.

As he was passing out of the door Dorian Gray touched him on the arm. "Let me come with you," he murmured.

"But I thought you had promised Basil Hallward to go and see him," answered Lord Henry.

"I would sooner come with you; yes, I feel I must come with you. Do let me. And you will promise to talk to me all the time? No one talks so wonderfully as you do."

"Ah! I have talked quite enough for today," said Lord Henry, smiling. "All I want now is to look at life. You may come and look at it with me, if you care to."

IV

ONE AFTERNOON, a month later, Dorian Gray was reclining in a luxurious arm-chair, in the little library of Lord Henry's house in Mayfair. It was, in its way, a very charming room, with its high panelled wainscoting of olive-stained oak, its cream-coloured frieze and ceiling of raised plaster-work, and its brick-dust felt carpet strewn with silk long-fringed Persian rugs. On a tiny satinwood table stood a statuette by Clodion,[1] and beside it lay a copy of *Les Cent Nouvelles*,[2] bound for Margaret of Valois[3] by Clovis Eve,[4] and powdered with the gilt daisies that Queen had selected for her device. Some large blue china jars and parrot-tulips were ranged on the mantelshelf, and through the small leaded panes of the window streamed the apricot-coloured light of a summer day in London.

Lord Henry had not yet come in. He was always late on principle, his principle being that punctuality is the thief of time. So the lad was looking rather sulky, as with listless fingers he turned over the pages of an elaborately illustrated edition of *Manon Lescaut*[5] that he had found in one of the bookcases. The formal monotonous ticking of the Louis-Quatorze[6] clock annoyed him. Once or twice he thought of going away.

At last he heard a step outside, and the door opened. "How late you are, Harry!" he murmured.

"I am afraid it is not Harry, Mr. Gray," answered a shrill voice.

He glanced quickly round, and rose to his feet. "I beg your pardon. I thought—"

"You thought it was my husband. It is only his wife. You must let me introduce myself. I know you quite well by your photographs. I think my husband has got seventeen of them."

"Not seventeen, Lady Henry?"

"Well, eighteen, then. And I saw you with him the other night at the Opera." She laughed nervously as she spoke, and watched him with her vague forget-me-not eyes. She was a curious woman, whose dresses always looked as if they had been designed in a rage and put on in a tempest. She was usually in love with somebody, and, as her passion was never returned, she had kept all her illusions. She tried to look picturesque, but only succeeded in being untidy. Her name was Victoria, and she had a perfect mania for going to church.

"That was at *Lohengrin,*[7] Lady Henry, I think?"

"Yes; it was at dear *Lohengrin.* I like Wagner's music better than anybody's. It is so loud that one can talk the whole time without other people hearing what one says. That is a great advantage: don't you think so, Mr. Gray?"

The same nervous staccato laugh broke from her thin lips, and her fingers began to play with a long tortoise-shell paper-knife.

Dorian smiled, and shook his head: "I am afraid I don't think so, Lady Henry. I never talk during music—at least, during good music. If one hears bad music, it is one's duty to drown it in conversation."

"Ah! that is one of Harry's views, isn't it, Mr. Gray? I always hear Harry's views from his friends. It is the only way I get to know of them. But you must not think I don't like good music. I adore it, but I am afraid of it. It makes me too romantic. I have simply worshipped pianists—two at a time, sometimes, Harry tells me. I don't know what it is about them. Perhaps it is that they are foreigners. They all are, ain't they? Even those that are born in England become foreigners after a time, don't they? It is so clever of them, and such a compliment to art. Makes it quite cosmopolitan, doesn't it? You have never been to any of my parties, have you, Mr. Gray? You must come. I can't afford orchids, but I spare no expense in foreigners. They make one's rooms look so picturesque. But here is Harry!—Harry, I came in to look for you, to ask you something—I forget what it was—and I found Mr. Gray here. We have had such a pleasant chat about music. We have quite the same ideas. No; I think our ideas are quite different. But he has been most pleasant. I am so glad I've seen him."

"I am charmed, my love, quite charmed," said Lord Henry, elevating his dark crescent-shaped eyebrows and looking at them both with an amused smile. "So sorry I am late, Dorian. I went to look after a piece of old brocade in Wardour Street, and had to bargain for hours for it. Nowadays people know the price of everything, and the value of nothing."

"I am afraid I must be going," exclaimed Lady Henry, breaking an awkward silence with her silly sudden laugh. "I have promised to drive with the Duchess. Good-bye, Mr. Gray. Good-bye, Harry. You are dining out, I suppose? So am I. Perhaps I shall see you at Lady Thornbury's."

"I dare say, my dear," said Lord Henry, shutting the door behind her, as, looking like a bird of paradise that had been out all night in the rain, she flitted out of the room, leaving a faint odour of frangipanni.[8] Then he lit a cigarette, and flung himself down on the sofa.

"Never marry a woman with straw-coloured hair, Dorian," he said, after a few puffs.

"Why, Harry?"

"Because they are so sentimental."

"But I like sentimental people."

"Never marry at all, Dorian. Men marry because they are

tired; women, because they are curious: both are disappointed."

"I don't think I am likely to marry, Harry. I am too much in love. That is one of your aphorisms. I am putting it into practise, as I do everything that you say."

"Who are you in love with?" asked Lord Henry, after a pause.

"With an actress," said Dorian Gray, blushing.

Lord Henry shrugged his shoulders. "That is a rather commonplace début."

"You would not say so if you saw her, Harry."

"Who is she?"

"Her name is Sibyl Vane."

"Never heard of her."

"No one has. People will some day, however. She is a genius."

"My dear boy, no woman is a genius. Women are a decorative sex. They never have anything to say, but they say it charmingly. Women represent the triumph of matter over mind, just as men represent the triumph of mind over morals."

"Harry, how can you?"

"My dear Dorian, it is quite true. I am analysing women at present, so I ought to know. The subject is not so abstruse as I thought it was. I find that, ultimately, there are only two kinds of women, the plain and the coloured. The plain women are very useful. If you want to gain a reputation for respectability, you have merely to take them down to supper. The other women are very charming. They commit one mistake, however. They paint in order to try and look young. Our grandmothers painted in order to try and talk brilliantly. *Rouge* and *esprit* used to go together. That is all over now. As long as a woman can look ten years younger than her own daughter, she is perfectly satisfied. As for conversation, there are only five women in London worth talking to and two of these can't be admitted into decent society. However, tell me about your genius. How long have you known her?"

"Ah! Harry, your views terrify me."

"Never mind that. How long have you known her?"

"About three weeks."

"And where did you come across her?"

"I will tell you, Harry; but you mustn't be unsympathetic about it. After all, it never would have happened if I had not met you. You filled me with a wild desire to know everything about life. For days after I met you, something seemed to throb in my veins. As I lounged in the Park,[9] or strolled down Piccadilly,[10] I used to look at everyone who passed me, and wonder, with a mad curiosity, what sort of lives they led. Some of them fascinated me. Others filled me with terror. There was an exquisite poison in the air. I had a passion for sensations. . . . Well, one evening about seven o'clock, I determined to go out in search of some adventure. I felt that this grey, monstrous London of ours, with its myriads of people, its sordid sinners, and its splendid sins, as you once phrased it, must have something in store for me. I fancied a thousand things. The mere danger gave me a sense of delight. I remembered what you had said to me on that wonderful evening when we first dined together, about the search for beauty being the real secret of life. I don't know what I expected, but I went out and wandered eastward, soon losing my way in a labyrinth of grimy streets and black, grassless squares. About half-past eight I passed by an absurd little theatre, with great flaring gas-jets and gaudy play-bills. A hideous Jew, in the most amazing waistcoat I ever beheld in my life, was standing at the entrance, smoking a vile cigar. He had greasy ringlets, and an enormous diamond blazed in the centre of a soiled shirt. 'Have a box, my Lord?' he said, when he saw me, and he took off his hat with an air of gorgeous servility. There was something about him, Harry, that amused me. He was such a monster. You will laugh at me, I know, but I really went in and paid a whole guinea for the stage-box. To the present day I can't make out why I did so; and yet if I hadn't—my dear Harry, if I hadn't, I should have missed the greatest romance of my life. I see you are laughing. It is horrid of you!"

"I am not laughing, Dorian; at least I am not laughing at you. But you should not say the greatest romance of your life. You should say the first romance of your life. You will always be loved, and you will always be in love with love. A *grande passion* is the privilege of people who have nothing to do. That is the one use of the idle classes of a country. Don't be afraid. There are exquisite things in store for you. This is merely the beginning."

"Do you think my nature so shallow?" cried Dorian Gray, angrily.

"No; I think your nature so deep."

"How do you mean?"

"My dear boy, the people who love only once in their lives are really the shallow people. What they call their loyalty, and their fidelity, I call either the lethargy of custom or their lack of imagination. Faithfulness is to the emotional life what consistency is to the life of the intellect—simply a confession of failure. Faithfulness! I must analyse it some day. The passion for property is in it. There are many things that we would throw away if we were not afraid that others might pick them up. But I don't want to interrupt you. Go on with your story."

"Well, I found myself seated in a horrid little private box, with a vulgar drop-scene staring me in the face. I looked out from behind the curtain, and surveyed the house. It was a tawdry affair, all Cupids and cornucopias, like a third-rate wedding-cake. The gallery and pit were fairly full, but the two rows of dingy stalls were quite empty, and there was hardly a person in what I suppose they called the dress-circle. Women went about with oranges and ginger-beer, and there was a terrible consumption of nuts going on."

"It must have been just like the palmy days of the British Drama."

"Just like, I should fancy, and very depressing. I began to wonder what on earth I should do, when I caught sight of the play-bill. What do you think the play was, Harry?"

"I should think 'The Idiot Boy, or Dumb but Innocent.' Our fathers used to like that sort of piece, I believe. The longer I live, Dorian, the more keenly I feel that whatever was good enough for our fathers is not good enough for us. In art, as in politics, *les grandpères ont toujours tort.*"[11]

"This play was good enough for us, Harry. It was *Romeo and Juliet.* I must admit that I was rather annoyed at the idea of seeing Shakespeare done in such a wretched hole of a place. Still, I felt interested, in a sort of way. At any rate, I determined to wait for the first act. There was a dreadful orchestra, presided over by a young Hebrew who sat at a cracked piano, that nearly drove me away, but at last the drop-scene was drawn up, and the play began. Romeo[12] was a stout elderly gentleman, with corked eyebrows, a husky tragedy voice, and a figure like a beer-barrel. Mercurio[12] was almost as bad. He was played by the low-comedian, who had introduced gags of his own and was on most friendly terms with the pit. They were both as grotesque as the scenery, and that looked as if it had come out of a country-booth. But, Juliet![12] Harry, imagine a girl, hardly seventeen years of age, with a little flower-like face, a small Greek head with plaited coils of dark-brown hair, eyes that were violet wells of passion, lips that were like the petals of a rose. She was the loveliest thing I had ever seen in my life. You said to me once that pathos left you unmoved, but that beauty, mere beauty, could fill your eyes with tears. I tell you, Harry, I could hardly see this girl for the mist of tears that came across me. And her voice—I never heard such a voice. It was very low at first, with deep mellow notes, that seemed to fall singly upon one's ear. Then it became a little louder, and sounded like a flute or a distant hautbois.[13] In the garden scene it had all the tremulous ecstasy that one hears just before dawn when nightingales are singing. There were moments, later on, when it had the wild passion of violins. You know how a voice can stir one. Your voice and the voice of Sibyl Vane are two things that I shall never forget. When I close my eyes, I hear them, and each of them says something different. I don't know which to follow. Why should I not love her? Harry, I do love her. She is everything to me in life. Night after night I go to see her play.

One evening she is Rosalind,[14] and the next evening she is
Imogen.[15] I have seen her die in the gloom of an Italian tomb,
sucking the poison from her lover's lips. I have watched her
wandering through the forest of Arden,[16] disguised as a pretty
boy in hose and doublet and dainty cap. She has been mad,
and has come into the presence of a guilty king, and given
him rue to wear, and bitter herbs to taste of. She has been innocent, and the black hands of jealousy have crushed her
reed-like throat. I have seen her in every age and in every
costume. Ordinary women never appeal to one's imagination.
They are limited to their century. No glamour ever transfig-
ures them. One knows their minds as easily as one knows
their bonnets. One can always find them. There is no mystery
in any of them: They ride in the Park in the morning, and
chatter at tea parties in the afternoon. They have their stereotyped smile, and their fashionable manner. They are quite
obvious. But an actress! How different an actress is! Harry!
why didn't you tell me that the only thing worth loving is an
actress?"

"Because I have loved so many of them, Dorian."

"Oh, yes, horrid people with dyed hair and painted faces."

"Don't run down dyed hair and painted faces. There is an
extraordinary charm in them, sometimes," said Lord Henry.

"I wish now I had not told you about Sibyl Vane."

"You could not have helped telling me, Dorian. All
through your life you will tell me everything you do."

"Yes, Harry, I believe that is true. I cannot help telling you
things. You have a curious influence over me. If I ever did a
crime, I would come and confess it to you. You would understand me."

"People like you—the wilful sunbeams of life—don't commit crimes, Dorian. But I am much obliged for the compliment, all the same. And now tell me—reach me the matches,
like a good boy: thanks:—what are your actual relations with
Sibyl Vane?"

Dorian Gray leaped to his feet, with flushed cheeks and
burning eyes. "Harry! Sibyl Vane is sacred!"

"It is only the sacred things that are worth touching, Dorian," said Lord Henry, with a strange touch of pathos in his voice. "But why should you be annoyed? I suppose she will belong to you some day. When one is in love, one always begins by deceiving oneself, and one always ends by deceiving others. That is what the world calls a romance. You know her, at any rate, I suppose?"

"Of course I know her. On the first night I was at the theatre, the horrid old Jew came round to the box after the performance was over, and offered to take me behind the scenes and introduce me to her. I was furious with him, and told him that Juliet had been dead for hundreds of years, and that her body was lying in a marble tomb in Verona. I think, from his blank look of amazement, that he was under the impression that I had taken too much champagne, or something."

"I am not surprised."

Then he asked me if I wrote for any of the newspapers. I told him I never even read them. He seemed terribly disappointed at that, and confided to me that all the dramatic critics were in a conspiracy against him, and that they were everyone of them to be bought."

"I should not wonder if he was quite right there. But, on the other hand, judging from their appearance, most of them cannot be at all expensive."

"Well, he seemed to think they were beyond his means," laughed Dorian. "By this time, however, the lights were being put out in the theatre, and I had to go. He wanted me to try some cigars that he strongly recommended. I declined. The next night, of course, I arrived at the place again. When he saw me he made me a low bow, and assured me that I was a munificent patron of art. He was a most offensive brute, though he had an extraordinary passion for Shakespeare. He told me once, with an air of pride, that his five bankruptcies were entirely due to 'The Bard,' as he insisted on calling him. He seemed to think it a distinction."

"It was a distinction, my dear Dorian—a great distinction. Most people become bankrupt through having invested too heavily in the prose of life. To have ruined oneself over poetry is an honour. But when did you first speak to Miss Sibyl Vane?"

"The third night. She had been playing Rosalind. I could not help going round. I had thrown her some flowers, and she had looked at me; at least I fancied that she had. The old Jew was persistent. He seemed determined to take me behind, so I consented. It was curious my not wanting to know her, wasn't it?"

"No; I don't think so."

"My dear Harry, why?"

"I will tell you some other time. Now I want to know about the girl."

"Sibyl? Oh, she was so shy, and so gentle. There is something of a child about her. Her eyes opened wide in exquisite wonder when I told her what I thought of her performance, and she seemed quite unconscious of her power. I think we were both rather nervous. The old Jew stood grinning at the doorway of the dusty greenroom, making elaborate speeches about us both, while we stood looking at each other like children. He would insist on calling me 'My Lord,' so I had to assure Sibyl that I was not anything of the kind. She said quite simply to me, 'You look more like a prince. I must call you Prince Charming.' "

"Upon my word, Dorian, Miss Sibyl knows how to pay compliments."

"You don't understand her, Harry. She regarded me merely as a person in a play. She knows nothing of life. She lives with her mother, a faded tired woman who played Lady Capulet in a sort of magenta dressing-wrapper on the first night, and looks as if she had seen better days."

"I know that look. It depresses me," murmured Lord Henry, examining his rings.

"The Jew wanted to tell me her history, but I said it did not interest me."

"You were quite right. There is always something infinitely mean about other people's tragedies."

"Sibyl is the only thing I care about. What is it to me where she came from? From her little head to her little feet, she is absolutely and entirely divine. Every night of my life I go to see her act, and every night she is more marvellous."

"That is the reason, I suppose, that you never dine with me now. I thought you must have some curious romance on hand. You have; but it is not quite what I expected."

"My dear Harry, we either lunch or sup together every day, and I have been to the Opera with you several times," said Dorian, opening his blue eyes in wonder.

"You always come dreadfully late."

"Well, I can't help going to see Sibyl play," he cried, "even if it is only for a single act. I get hungry for her presence; and when I think of the wonderful soul that is hidden away in that little ivory body, I am filled with awe."

"You can dine with me tonight, Dorian, can't you?"

He shook his head. "Tonight she is Imogen," he answered, "and tomorrow night she will be Juliet."

"When is she Sibyl Vane?"

"Never."

"I congratulate you."

"How horrid you are! She is all the great heroines of the world in one. She is more than an individual. You laugh, but I tell you she has genius. I love her, and I must make her love me. You, who know all the secrets of life, tell me how to charm Sibyl Vane to love me! I want to make Romeo jealous. I want the dead lovers of the world to hear our laughter, and grow sad. I want a breath of our passion to stir their dust into consciousness, to wake their ashes into pain. My God, Harry, how I worship her!" He was walking up and down the room as he spoke. Hectic spots of red burned on his cheeks. He was terribly excited.

Lord Henry watched him with a subtle sense of pleasure. How different he was now from the shy, frightened boy he had met in Basil Hallward's studio! His nature had developed like a flower, had borne blossoms of scarlet flame. Out of its secret hiding-place had crept his soul, and desire had come to meet it on the way.

"And what do you propose to do?" said Lord Henry, at last.

"I want you and Basil to come with me some night and see her act. I have not the slightest fear of the result. You are certain to acknowledge her genius. Then we must get her out of the Jew's hands. She is bound to him for three years—at least for two years and eight months—from the present time. I shall have to pay him something, of course. When all that is settled, I shall take a West End theatre and bring her out properly. She will make the world as mad as she has made me."

"That would be impossible, my dear boy."

"Yes, she will. She has not merely art, consummate art instinct, in her, but she has personality also; and you have often told me that it is personalities, not principles, that move the age."

"Well, what night shall we go?"

"Let me see. Today is Tuesday. Let us fix tomorrow. She plays Juliet tomorrow."

"All right. The Bristol at eight o'clock; and I will get Basil."

"Not eight, Harry, please. Half-past six. We must be there before the curtain rises. You must see her in the first act, where she meets Romeo."

"Half-past six! What an hour! It will be like having a meat-tea, or reading an English novel. It must be seven. No gentleman dines before seven. Shall you see Basil between this and then? Or shall I write to him?"

"Dear Basil! I have not laid eyes on him for a week. It is rather horrid of me, as he has sent me my portrait in the most wonderful frame, specially designed by himself, and, though I am a little jealous of the picture for being a whole month younger than I am, I must admit that I delight in it. Perhaps you had better write to him. I don't want to see him alone. He says things that annoy me. He gives me good advice."

Lord Henry smiled. "People are very fond of giving away what they need most themselves. It is what I call the depth of generosity."

"Oh, Basil is the best of fellows, but he seems to me to be just a bit of a Philistine. Since I have known you, Harry, I have discovered that."

"Basil, my dear boy, puts everything that is charming in him into his work. The consequence is that he has nothing left for life but his prejudices, his principles, and his common sense. The only artists I have ever known, who are personally delightful, are bad artists. Good artists exist simply in what they make, and consequently are perfectly uninteresting in what they are. A great poet, a really great poet, is the most unpoetical of all creatures. But inferior poets are absolutely fascinating. The worse their rhymes are, the more picturesque they look. The mere fact of having published a book of second-rate sonnets makes a man quite irresistible. He lives the poetry that he cannot write. The others write the poetry that they dare not realize."

"I wonder is that really so, Harry?" said Dorian Gray, putting some perfume on his handkerchief out of a large gold-topped bottle that stood on the table. "It must be, if you say it. And now I am off. Imogen is waiting for me. Don't forget about tomorrow. Good-bye."

As he left the room Lord Henry's heavy eyelids drooped, and he began to think. Certainly few people had ever interested him so much as Dorian Gray, and yet the lad's mad adoration of someone else caused him not the slightest pang of annoyance or jealousy. He was pleased by it. It made him a more interesting study. He had been always enthralled by the methods of natural science, but the ordinary subject matter of that science had seemed to him trivial and of no import. And so he had begun by vivisecting himself, as he had ended by vivisecting others. Human life—that appeared to him the one thing worth investigating. Compared to it there was nothing else of any value. It was true that as one watched life in its curious crucible of pain and pleasure, one could not wear over one's face a mask of glass, nor keep the sulphurous fumes from troubling the brain and making the imagination turbid with monstrous fancies and misshapen dreams. There were poisons so subtle that to know their properties one had to sicken of them. There were maladies so strange that one had to pass through them if one sought to understand their nature. And, yet, what a great reward one received! How wonderful the whole world became to one! To note the curious hard logic of passion, and the emotional coloured life of the intellect—to observe where they met, and where they separated, at what point they were in unison, and at what point they were at discord—there was a delight in that! What matter what the cost was? One could never pay too high a price for any sensation.

He was conscious—and the thought brought a gleam of pleasure into his brown agate eyes—that it was through certain words of his, musical words said with musical utterance, that Dorian Gray's soul had turned to this white girl and bowed in worship before her. To a large extent the lad was his own creation. He had made him premature. That was something. Ordinary people waited till life disclosed to them its secrets, but to the few, to the elect, the mysteries of life were revealed before the veil was drawn away. Sometimes this was the effect of art, and chiefly of the art of literature, which dealt immediately with the passions and the intellect. But now and then a complex personality took the place and assumed the office of art, was indeed, in its way, a real work of art, Life having its elaborate masterpieces, just as poetry has, or sculpture, or painting.

Yes, the lad was premature. He was gathering his harvest while it was yet spring. The pulse and passion of youth were in him, but he was becoming self-conscious. It was delightful to watch him. With his beautiful face, and his beautiful soul, he was a thing to wonder at. It was no matter how it all ended, or was destined to end. He was like one of those gracious figures in a pageant or a play, whose joys seem to be remote from one, but whose sorrows stir one's sense of beauty, and whose wounds are like red roses.

Soul and body, body and soul—how mysterious they were! There was animalism in the soul, and the body had its moments of spirituality. The senses could refine, and the intellect could degrade. Who could say where the fleshly impulse ceased, or the psychical impulse began? How shallow were the arbitrary definitions of ordinary psychologists! And yet how difficult to decide between the claims of the various schools! Was the soul a shadow seated in the house of sin? Or was the body really in the soul, as Giordano Bruno[17] thought? The separation of spirit from matter was a mystery, and the union of spirit with matter was a mystery also.

He began to wonder whether we could ever make psychology so absolute a science that each little spring of life would be revealed to us. As it was, we always misunderstood ourselves, and rarely understood others. Experience was of no ethical value. It was merely the name men gave to their mistakes. Moralists had, as a rule, regarded it as a mode of warning, had claimed for it a certain ethical efficacy in the formation of character, had praised it as something that taught us what to follow and showed us what to avoid. But there was no motive power in experience. It was as little of an active cause as conscience itself. All that it really demonstrated was that our future would be the same as our past, and that the sin we had done once, and with loathing, we would do many times, and with joy.

It was clear to him that the experimental method was the only method by which one could arrive at any scientific analysis of the passions; and certainly Dorian Gray was a subject made to his hand, and seemed to promise rich and fruitful results. His sudden mad love for Sibyl Vane was a psychological phenomenon of no small interest. There was no doubt that curiosity had much to do with it, curiosity and the desire for new experiences; yet it was not a simple but rather a very complex passion. What there was in it of the purely sensuous instinct of boyhood had been transformed by the workings of the imagination, changed into something that seemed to the lad himself to be remote from sense, and was for that very reason all the more dangerous. It was the passions about whose origin we deceived ourselves that tyrannized most strongly over us. Our weakest motives were those of whose nature we were conscious. It often happened that when we thought we were experimenting on others we were really experimenting on ourselves.

While Lord Henry sat dreaming on these things, a knock came to the door, and his valet entered, and reminded him it was time to dress for dinner. He got up and looked out into the street. The sunset had smitten into scarlet gold the upper windows of the houses opposite. The panes glowed like plates of heated metal. The sky above was like a faded rose. He thought of his friend's young fiery-coloured life, and wondered how it was all going to end.

When he arrived home, about half-past twelve o'clock, he saw a telegram lying on the hall table. He opened it, and found it was from Dorian Gray. It was to tell him that he was engaged to be married to Sibyl Vane.

V

"MOTHER, Mother, I am so happy!" whispered the girl, bury-ing her face in the lap of the faded, tired-looking woman who, with back turned to the shrill intrusive light, was sitting in the one arm-chair that their dingy sitting-room contained. "I am so happy!" she repeated, "and you must be happy too!"

Mrs. Vane winced, and put her thin bismuth-whitened[1] hands on her daughter's head. "Happy!" she echoed, "I am only happy, Sibyl, when I see you act. You must not think of anything but your acting. Mr. Isaacs has been very good to us, and we owe him money."

The girl looked up and pouted. "Money, Mother?" she cried, "what does money matter? Love is more than money."

"Mr. Isaacs has advanced us fifty pounds to pay off our debts, and to get a proper outfit for James. You must not for-get that, Sibyl. Fifty pounds is a very large sum. Mr. Isaacs has been most considerate."

"He is not a gentleman, Mother, and I hate the way he talks to me," said the girl, rising to her feet, and going over to the window.

"I don't know how we could manage without him," an-swered the elder woman, querulously.

Sibyl Vane tossed her head and laughed. "We don't want him any more, Mother. Prince Charming rules life for us now." Then she paused. A rose shook in her blood, and shadowed her cheeks. Quick breath parted the petals of her lips. They trembled. Some southern wind of passion swept over her, and stirred the dainty folds of her dress. "I love him," she said, simply.

"Foolish child! foolish child!" was the parrot-phrase flung in answer. The waving of crooked, false-jewelled fingers gave grotesqueness to the words.

The girl laughed again. The joy of a caged bird was in her voice. Her eyes caught the melody, and echoed it in radiance: then closed for a moment, as though to hide their secret. When they opened, the mist of a dream had passed across them.

Thin-lipped wisdom spoke at her from the worn chair, hinted at prudence, quoted from that book of cowardice whose author apes the name of common sense. She did not listen. She was free in her prison of passion. Her prince, Prince Charming, was with her. She had called on memory to remake him. She had sent her soul to search for him, and it had brought him back. His kiss burned again upon her mouth. Her eyelids were warm with his breath.

Then wisdom altered its method and spoke of espial and discovery. This young man might be rich. If so, marriage should be thought of. Against the shell of her ear broke the waves of worldly cunning. The arrows of craft shot by her. She saw the thin lips moving, and smiled.

Suddenly she felt the need to speak. The wordy silence troubled her. "Mother, Mother," she cried, "why does he love me so much? I know why I love him. I love him because he is like what Love himself should be. But what does he see in me? I am not worthy of him. And yet—why, I cannot tell—though I feel so much beneath him, I don't feel humble. I feel proud, terribly proud. Mother, did you love my father as I love Prince Charming?"

The elder woman grew pale beneath the coarse powder

that daubed her cheeks, and her dry lips twitched with a spasm of pain. Sibyl rushed to her, flung her arms round her neck, and kissed her. "Forgive me, Mother. I know it pains you to talk about our father. But it only pains you because you loved him so much. Don't look so sad. I am as happy today as you were twenty years ago. Ah! let me be happy for ever!"

"My child, you are far too young to think of falling in love. Besides, what do you know of this young man? You don't even know his name. The whole thing is most inconvenient, and really, when James is going away to Australia, and I have so much to think of, I must say that you should have shown more consideration. However, as I said before, if he is rich. . . ."

"Ah! Mother, Mother, let me be happy!"

Mrs. Vane glanced at her, and with one of those false theatrical gestures that so often become a mode of second nature to a stage-player, clasped her in her arms. At this moment the door opened, and a young lad with rough brown hair came into the room. He was thick-set of figure, and his hands and feet were large, and somewhat clumsy in movement. He was not so finely bred as his sister. One would hardly have guessed the close relationship that existed between them. Mrs. Vane fixed her eyes on him, and intensified her smile. She mentally elevated her son to the dignity of an audience. She felt sure that the *tableau*[2] was interesting.

"You might keep some of your kisses for me, Sibyl, I think," said the lad, with a good-natured grumble.

"Ah! but you don't like being kissed, Jim," she cried. "You are a dreadful old bear." And she ran across the room and hugged him.

James Vane looked into his sister's face with tenderness. "I want you to come out with me for a walk, Sibyl. I don't suppose I shall ever see this horrid London again. I am sure I don't want to."

"My son, don't say such dreadful things," murmured Mrs. Vane, taking up a tawdry theatrical dress, with a sigh, and beginning to patch it. She felt a little disappointed that he had not joined the group. It would have increased the theatrical picturesqueness of the situation.

"Why not, Mother? I mean it."

"You pain me, my son. I trust you will return from Australia in a position of affluence. I believe there is no society of any kind in the Colonies, nothing that I would call society; so when you have made your fortune you must come back and assert yourself in London."

"Society!" muttered the lad. "I don't want to know anything about that. I should like to make some money to take you and Sibyl off the stage. I hate it."

"Oh, Jim!" said Sibyl, laughing, "how unkind of you! But are you really going for a walk with me? That will be nice! I was afraid you were going to say good-bye to some of your friends—to Tom Hardy, who gave you that hideous pipe, or Ned Langton, who makes fun of you for smoking it. It is very sweet of you to let me have your last afternoon. Where shall we go? Let us go to the Park."

"I am too shabby," he answered, frowning. "Only swell people go to the Park."

"Nonsense, Jim," she whispered, stroking the sleeve of his coat.

He hesitated for a moment. "Very well," he said at last, "but don't be too long dressing." She danced out of the door. One could hear her singing as she ran upstairs. Her little feet pattered overhead.

He walked up and down the room two or three times. Then he turned to the still figure in the chair. "Mother, are my things ready?" he asked.

"Quite ready, James," she answered, keeping her eyes on her work. For some months past she had felt ill at ease when she was alone with this rough, stern son of hers. Her shallow secret nature was troubled when their eyes met. She used to wonder if he suspected anything. The silence, for he made no other observation, became intolerable to her. She began to complain. Women defend themselves by attacking, just as they attack by sudden and strange surrenders. "I hope you will be contented, James, with your sea-faring life," she said. "You must remember that it is your own choice. You might have entered a solicitor's office. Solicitors are a very respectable class, and in the country often dine with the best families."

"I hate offices, and I hate clerks," he replied. "But you are quite right. I have chosen my own life. All I say is, watch over Sibyl. Don't let her come to any harm. Mother, you must watch over her."

"James, you really talk very strangely. Of course I watch over Sibyl."

"I hear a gentleman comes every night to the theatre, and goes behind to talk to her. Is that right? What about that?"

"You are speaking about things you don't understand, James. In the profession we are accustomed to receive a great deal of most gratifying attention. I myself used to receive many bouquets at one time. That was when acting was really understood. As for Sibyl, I do not know at present whether her attachment is serious or not. But there is no doubt that the young man in question is a perfect gentleman. He is always most polite to me. Besides, he has the appearance of being rich, and the flowers he sends are lovely."

"You don't know his name, though," said the lad, harshly.

"No," answered his mother, with a placid expression in her face. "He has not yet revealed his real name. I think it is quite romantic of him. He is probably a member of the aristocracy."

James Vane bit his lip. "Watch over Sibyl, Mother," he cried, "watch over her."

"My son, you distress me very much. Sibyl is always under my special care. Of course, if this gentleman is wealthy, there is no reason why she should not contract an alliance with him. I trust he is one of the aristocracy. He has all the appearance of it, I must say. It might be a most brilliant marriage for Sibyl. They would make a charming couple. His good looks are really quite remarkable; everybody notices them."

The lad muttered something to himself, and drummed on the windowpane with his coarse fingers. He had just turned round to say something, when the door opened, and Sibyl ran in.

"How serious you both are!" she cried. "What is the matter?"

"Nothing," he answered. "I suppose one must be serious sometimes. Good-bye, Mother; I will have my dinner at five o'clock. Everything is packed, except my shirts, so you need not trouble."

"Good-bye, my son," she answered, with a bow of strained stateliness.

She was extremely annoyed at the tone he had adopted with her, and there was something in his look that had made her feel afraid.

"Kiss me, Mother," said the girl. Her flower-like lips touched the withered cheek, and warmed its frost.

"My child! my child!" cried Mrs. Vane, looking up to the ceiling in search of an imaginary gallery.

"Come, Sibyl," said her brother, impatiently. He hated his mother's affectations.

They went out into the flickering wind-blown sunlight, and strolled down the dreary Euston Road. The passers-by glanced in wonder at the sullen, heavy youth, who, in coarse, ill-fitting clothes, was in the company of such a graceful, refined-looking girl. He was like a common gardener walking with a rose.

Jim frowned from time to time when he caught the inquisitive glance of some stranger. He had that dislike of being stared at which comes on geniuses late in life, and never leaves the commonplace. Sibyl, however, was quite unconscious of the effect she was producing. Her love was trembling in laughter on her lips. She was thinking of Prince Charming, and, that she might think of him all the more, she did not talk of him, but prattled on about the ship in which Jim was going to sail, about the gold he was certain to find, about the wonderful heiress whose life he was to save from the wicked, red-shirted bushrangers. For he was not to remain a sailor, or a super-cargo, or whatever he was going to be. Oh, no! A sailor's existence was dreadful. Fancy being cooped up in a horrid ship, with the hoarse, hump-backed waves trying to get in, and a black wind blowing the masts down, and tearing the sails into long screaming ribands! He was to leave the vessel at Melbourne, bid a polite good-bye to the captain, and go off at once to the goldfields. Before a week was over he was to come across a large nugget of pure gold, the largest nugget that had ever been discovered, and bring it down to the coast in a wagon guarded by six mounted policemen. The bushrangers were to attack them three times, and be defeated with immense slaughter. Or, no. He was not to go to the goldfields at all. They were horrid places, where men got intoxicated, and shot each other in barrooms, and used bad language. He was to be a nice sheep-farmer, and one evening, as he was riding home, he was to see the beautiful heiress being carried off by a robber on a black horse, and give chase, and rescue her. Of course she would fall in love with him, and he with her, and they would get married, and come home, and live in an immense house in London. Yes, there were delightful things in store for him. But he must be very good, and not lose his temper, or spend his money foolishly. She was only a year older than he was, but she knew so much more of life. He must be sure, also, to write to her by every mail, and to say his prayers each night before he went to sleep. God was very good, and would watch over him. She would pray for him, too, and in a few years he would come back quite rich and happy.

The lad listened sulkily to her, and made no answer. He was heart-sick at leaving home.

Yet it was not this alone that made him gloomy and morose. Inexperienced though he was, he had still a strong sense of the danger of Sibyl's position. This young dandy who was making love to her could mean her no good. He was a gentleman, and he hated him for that, hated him through some curious race instinct for which he could not account, and which for that reason was all the more dominant within him. He was conscious also of the shallowness and vanity of his mother's nature, and in that saw infinite peril for Sibyl and Sibyl's happiness. Children begin by loving their parents; as they grow older they judge them; sometimes they forgive them.

His mother! He had something on his mind to ask of her, something that he had brooded on for many months of silence. A chance phrase that he had heard at the theatre, a whispered sneer that had reached his ears one night as he waited at the stage door, had set loose a train of horrible thoughts. He remembered it as if it had been the lash of a hunting crop across his face. His brows knit together into a wedge-like furrow, and with a twitch of pain he bit his underlip.

"You are not listening to a word I am saying, Jim," cried Sibyl, "and I am making the most delightful plans for your future. Do say something."

"What do you want me to say?"

"Oh! that you will be a good boy, and not forget us," she answered, smiling at him.

He shrugged his shoulders. "You are more likely to forget me, than I am to forget you, Sibyl."

She flushed. "What do you mean, Jim?" she asked.

"You have a new friend, I hear. Who is he? Why have you not told me about him? He means you no good."

"Stop, Jim!" she exclaimed. "You must not say anything against him. I love him."

"Why, you don't even know his name," answered the lad. "Who is he? I have a right to know."

"He is called Prince Charming. Don't you like the name? Oh! you silly boy! you should never forget it. If you only saw him, you would think him the most wonderful person in the world. Some day you will meet him: when you come back from Australia. You will like him so much. Everybody likes him, and I . . . love him. I wish you could come to the theatre tonight. He is going to be there, and I am to play Juliet. Oh!

how I shall play it! Fancy, Jim, to be in love and play Juliet! To
have him sitting there! To play for his delight! I am afraid I
may frighten the company, frighten or enthrall them. To be in
love is to surpass one's self. Poor dreadful Mr. Isaacs will be
shouting 'genius' to his loafers at the bar. He has preached
me as a dogma; tonight he will announce me as a revelation.
I feel it. And it is all his, his only, Prince Charming, my wonderful lover, my god of graces. But I am poor beside him.
Poor? What does that matter? When poverty creeps in at the
door, love flies in through the window. Our proverbs want
rewriting. They were made in winter, and it is summer now;
springtime for me, I think, a very dance of blossoms in blue
skies."

"He is a gentleman," said the lad, sullenly.

"A prince!" she cried, musically. "What more do you
want?"

"He wants to enslave you."

"I shudder at the thought of being free."

"I want you to beware of him."

"To see him is to worship him, to know him is to trust
him."

"Sibyl, you are mad about him."

She laughed, and took his arm. "You dear old Jim, you talk
as if you were a hundred. Some day you will be in love yourself. Then you will know what it is. Don't look so sulky. Surely
you should be glad to think that, though you are going away,
you leave me happier than I have ever been before. Life has
been hard for us both, terribly hard and difficult. But it will
be different now. You are going to a new world, and I have
found one. Here are two chairs; let us sit down and see the
smart[3] people go by."

They took their seats amidst a crowd of watchers. The
tulip beds across the road flamed like throbbing rings of fire.
A white dust, tremulous cloud of orris-root[4] it seemed, hung
in the panting air. The brightly coloured parasols danced and
dipped like monstrous butterflies.

She made her brother talk of himself, his hopes, his

prospects. He spoke slowly and with effort. They passed words to each other as players at a game pass counters. Sibyl felt oppressed. She could not communicate her joy. A faint smile curving that sullen mouth was all the echo she could win. After some time she became silent. Suddenly she caught a glimpse of golden hair and laughing lips, and in an open carriage with two ladies Dorian Gray drove past.

She started to her feet. "There he is!" she cried.

"Who?" said Jim Vane.

"Prince Charming," she answered, looking after the victoria.

He jumped up, and seized her roughly by the arm. "Show him to me. Which is he? Point him out. I must see him!" he exclaimed; but at that moment the Duke of Berwick's four-in-hand came between, and when it had left the space clear, the carriage had swept out of the Park.

"He is gone," murmured Sibyl, sadly. "I wish you had seen him."

"I wish I had, for as sure as there is a God in heaven, if he ever does you any wrong, I shall kill him."

She looked at him in horror. He repeated his words. They cut the air like a dagger. The people round began to gape. A lady standing close to her tittered.

"Come away, Jim; come away," she whispered. He followed her doggedly, as she passed through the crowd. He felt glad at what he had said.

When they reached the Achilles Statue[5] she turned round. There was pity in her eyes that became laughter on her lips. She shook her head at him. "You are foolish, Jim, utterly foolish; a bad-tempered boy, that is all. How can you say such horrible things? You don't know what you are talking about. You are simply jealous and unkind. Ah! I wish you would fall in love. Love makes people good, and what you said was wicked."

"I am sixteen," he answered, "and I know what I am about. Mother is no help to you. She doesn't understand how to look after you. I wish now that I was not going to Australia at all. I have a great mind to chuck the whole thing up. I would, if my articles hadn't been signed."

"Oh, don't be so serious, Jim. You are like one of the heroes of those silly melodramas mother used to be so fond of acting in. I am not going to quarrel with you. I have seen him, and oh! to see him is perfect happiness. We won't quarrel. I know you would never harm anyone I love, would you?"

"Not as long as you love him, I suppose," was the sullen answer.

"I shall love him for ever!" she cried.

"And he?"

"For ever, too!"

"He had better."

She shrank from him. Then she laughed and put her hand on his arm. He was merely a boy.

At the Marble Arch[6] they hailed an omnibus,[7] which left them close to their shabby home in the Euston Road. It was after five o'clock, and Sibyl had to lie down for a couple of hours before acting. Jim insisted that she should do so. He said that he would sooner part with her when their mother was not present. She would be sure to make a scene, and he detested scenes of every kind.

In Sibyl's own room they parted. There was jealousy in the lad's heart, and a fierce, murderous hatred of the stranger who, as it seemed to him, had come between them. Yet, when her arms were flung round his neck, and her fingers strayed through his hair, he softened, and kissed her with real affection. There were tears in his eyes as he went downstairs.

His mother was waiting for him below. She grumbled at his unpunctuality, as he entered. He made no answer, but sat down to his meagre meal. The flies buzzed round the table, and crawled over the stained cloth. Through the rumble of omnibuses, and the clatter of street-cabs, he could hear the droning voice devouring each minute that was left to him.

After some time, he thrust away his plate, and put his head in his hands. He felt that he had a right to know. It should have been told to him before, if it was as he suspected. Leaden with fear, his mother watched him. Words dropped mechanically from her lips. A tattered lace handkerchief twitched in her fingers. When the clock struck six, he got up, and went to the door. Then he turned back, and looked at her. Their eyes met. In hers he saw a wild appeal for mercy. It enraged him.

"Mother, I have something to ask you," he said. Her eyes wandered vaguely about the room. She made no answer. "Tell me the truth. I have a right to know. Were you married to my father?"

She heaved a deep sigh. It was a sigh of relief. The terrible moment, the moment that night and day, for weeks and months, she had dreaded, had come at last, and yet she felt no terror. Indeed in some measure it was a disappointment to her. The vulgar directness of the question called for a direct answer. The situation had not been gradually led up to. It was crude. It reminded her of a bad rehearsal.

"No," she answered, wondering at the harsh simplicity of life.

"My father was a scoundrel then!" cried the lad, clenching his fists.

She shook her head. "I knew he was not free. We loved each other very much. If he had lived, he would have made provision for us. Don't speak against him, my son. He was your father, and a gentleman. Indeed he was highly connected."

An oath broke from his lips. "I don't care for myself," he exclaimed, "but don't let Sibyl. . . . It is a gentleman, isn't it, who is in love with her, or says he is? Highly connected, too, I suppose."

For a moment a hideous sense of humiliation came over the woman. Her head drooped. She wiped her eyes with shaking hands. "Sibyl has a mother," she murmured; "I had none."

The lad was touched. He went towards her, and stooping down he kissed her. "I am sorry if I have pained you by asking about my father," he said, "but I could not help it. I must go now. Good-bye. Don't forget that you will have only one child now to look after, and believe me that if this man wrongs my sister, I will find out who he is, track him down, and kill him like a dog. I swear it."

The exaggerated folly of the threat, the passionate gesture that accompanied it, the mad melodramatic words, made life seem more vivid to her. She was familiar with the atmosphere. She breathed more freely, and for the first time for many months she really admired her son. She would have liked to have continued the scene on the same emotional scale, but he cut her short. Trunks had to be carried down, and mufflers looked for. The lodging-house drudge bustled in and out. There was the bargaining with the cabman. The moment was lost in vulgar details. It was with a renewed feeling of disappointment that she waved the tattered lace handkerchief from the window, as her son drove away. She was conscious that a great opportunity had been wasted. She consoled herself by telling Sibyl how desolate she felt her life would be, now that she had only one child to look after. She remembered the phrase. It had pleased her. Of the threat she said nothing. It was vividly and dramatically expressed. She felt that they would all laugh at it some day.

VI

I SUPPOSE you have heard the news, Basil?" said Lord Henry that evening, as Hallward was shown into a little private room at the Bristol where dinner had been laid for three.

"No, Harry," answered the artist, giving his hat and coat to the bowing waiter. "What is it? Nothing about politics, I hope? They don't interest me. There is hardly a single person in the House of Commons worth painting; though many of them would be the better for a little whitewashing.¹"

"Dorian Gray is engaged to be married," said Lord Henry, watching him as he spoke.

Hallward started, and then frowned. "Dorian engaged to be married!" he cried. "Impossible!"

"It is perfectly true."

"To whom?"

"To some little actress or other."

"I can't believe it. Dorian is far too sensible."

"Dorian is far too wise not to do foolish things now and then, my dear Basil."

"Marriage is hardly a thing that one can do now and then, Harry."

"Except in America," rejoined Lord Henry, languidly.

"But I didn't say he was married. I said he was engaged to be married. There is a great difference. I have a distinct remembrance of being married, but I have no recollection at all of being engaged. I am inclined to think that I never was engaged."

"But think of Dorian's birth, and position, and wealth. It would be absurd for him to marry so much beneath him."

"If you want to make him marry this girl tell him that, Basil. He is sure to do it, then. Whenever a man does a thoroughly stupid thing, it is always from the noblest motives."

"I hope the girl is good, Harry. I don't want to see Dorian tied to some vile creature, who might degrade his nature and ruin his intellect."

"Oh, she is better than good—she is beautiful," murmured Lord Henry, sipping a glass of vermouth and orange-bitters. "Dorian says she is beautiful; and he is not often wrong about things of that kind. Your portrait of him has quickened his appreciation of the personal appearance of other people. It has had that excellent effect, amongst others. We are to see her tonight, if that boy doesn't forget his appointment."

"Are you serious?"

"Quite serious, Basil. I should be miserable if I thought I should ever be more serious than I am at the present moment."

"But do you approve of it, Harry?" asked the painter, walking up and down the room, and biting his lip. "You can't approve of it, possibly. It is some silly infatuation."

"I never approve, or disapprove, of anything now. It is an absurd attitude to take towards life. We are not sent into the world to air our moral prejudices. I never take any notice of what common people say, and I never interfere with what charming people do. If a personality fascinates me, whatever mode of expression that personality selects is absolutely delightful to me. Dorian Gray falls in love with a beautiful girl who acts Juliet, and proposes to marry her. Why not? If he wedded Messalina[2] he would be none the less interesting.

You know I am not a champion of marriage. The real drawback to marriage is that it makes one unselfish. And unselfish people are colourless. They lack individuality. Still, there are certain temperaments that marriage makes more complex. They retain their egotism, and add to it many other egos. They are forced to have more than one life. They become more highly organized, and to be highly organized is, I should fancy, the object of man's existence. Besides, every experience is of value, and, whatever one may say against marriage, it is certainly an experience. I hope that Dorian Gray will make this girl his wife, passionately adore her for six months, and then suddenly become fascinated by someone else. He would be a wonderful study."

"You don't mean a single word of all that, Harry; you know you don't. If Dorian Gray's life were spoiled, no one would be sorrier than yourself. You are much better than you pretend to be."

Lord Henry laughed. "The reason we all like to think so well of others is that we are all afraid for ourselves. The basis of optimism is sheer terror. We think that we are generous because we credit our neighbour with the possession of those virtues that are likely to be a benefit to us. We praise the banker that we may overdraw our account, and find good qualities in the highwayman in the hope that he may spare our pockets. I mean everything that I have said. I have the greatest contempt for optimism. As for a spoiled life, no life is spoiled but one whose growth is arrested. If you want to mar a nature, you have merely to reform it. As for marriage, of course that would be silly, but there are other and more interesting bonds between men and women. I will certainly encourage them. They have the charm of being fashionable. But here is Dorian himself. He will tell you more than I can."

"My dear Harry, my dear Basil, you must both congratulate me!" said the lad, throwing off his evening cape with its satin-lined wings, and shaking each of his friends by the hand in turn. "I have never been so happy. Of course it is sudden: all really delightful things are. And yet it seems to me to be the one thing I have been looking for all my life." He was flushed with excitement and pleasure, and looked extraordinarily handsome.

"I hope you will always be very happy, Dorian," said Hallward, "but I don't quite forgive you for not having let me know of your engagement. You let Harry know."

"And I don't forgive you for being late for dinner," broke in Lord Henry, putting his hand on the lad's shoulder, and smiling as he spoke. "Come, let us sit down and try what the new chef here is like, and then you will tell us how it all came about."

"There is really not much to tell," cried Dorian, as they took their seats at the small round table. "What happened was simply this. After I left you yesterday evening, Harry, I dressed, had some dinner at that little Italian restaurant in Rupert Street you introduced me to, and went down at eight o'clock to the theatre. Sibyl was playing Rosalind. Of course the scenery was dreadful, and the Orlando³ absurd. But Sibyl! You should have seen her! When she came on in her boy's clothes she was perfectly wonderful. She wore a moss-coloured velvet jerkin with cinnamon sleeves, slim brown cross-gartered hose, a dainty little green cap with a hawk's feather caught in a jewel, and a hooded cloak lined with dull red. She had never seemed to me more exquisite. She had all the delicate grace of that Tanagra figurine⁴ that you have in your studio, Basil. Her hair clustered round her face like dark leaves round a pale rose. As for her acting—well, you shall see her tonight. She is simply a born artist. I sat in the dingy box absolutely enthralled. I forgot that I was in London and in the nineteenth century. I was away with my love in a forest that no man had ever seen. After the performance was over I went behind, and spoke to her. As we were sitting together, suddenly there came into her eyes a look that I had never seen there before. My lips moved towards hers. We kissed each other. I can't describe to you what I felt at that moment. It seemed to me that all my life had been narrowed to one perfect point of rose-coloured joy. She trembled all over, and shook like a white narcissus. Then she flung herself on her knees and kissed my hands. I feel that I should not tell you all this, but I can't help it. Of course our engagement is a dead secret. She has not even told her own mother. I don't know what my guardian will say. Lord Radley is sure to be furious. I don't care. I shall be of age in less than a year, and then I can do what I like. I have been right, Basil, haven't I, to take my love out of poetry, and to find my wife in Shakespeare's plays? Lips that Shakespeare taught to speak have whispered their secret in my ear. I have had the arms of Rosalind around me, and kissed Juliet on the mouth."

"Yes, Dorian, I suppose you were right," said Hallward, slowly.

"Have you seen her today?" asked Lord Henry.

Dorian Gray shook his head. "I left her in the forest of Arden, I shall find her in an orchard in Verona.'"

Lord Henry sipped his champagne in a meditative manner. "At what particular point did you mention the word marriage, Dorian? And what did she say in answer? Perhaps you forgot all about it."

"My dear Harry, I did not treat it as a business transaction, and I did not make any formal proposal. I told her that I loved her, and she said she was not worthy to be my wife. Not worthy! Why, the whole world is nothing to me compared with her."

"Women are wonderfully practical," murmured Lord Henry—"much more practical than we are. In situations of that kind we often forget to say anything about marriage, and they always remind us."

Hallward laid his hand upon his arm. "Don't, Harry. You have annoyed Dorian. He is not like other men. He would never bring misery upon anyone. His nature is too fine for that."

Lord Henry looked across the table. "Dorian is never annoyed with me," he answered. "I asked the question for the best reason possible, for the only reason, indeed, that excuses one for asking any question—simply curiosity. I have a theory that it is always the women who propose to us, and not we who propose to the women. Except, of course, in middle-class life. But then the middle classes are not modern."

Dorian Gray laughed, and tossed his head. "You are quite incorrigible, Harry; but I don't mind. It is impossible to be angry with you. When you see Sibyl Vane you will feel that the man who could wrong her would be a beast, a beast without a heart. I cannot understand how anyone can wish to shame the thing he loves. I love Sibyl Vane. I want to place her on a pedestal of gold, and to see the world worship the woman who is mine. What is marriage? An irrevocable vow. You mock at it for that. Ah! don't mock. It is an irrevocable vow that I want to take. Her trust makes me faithful, her belief makes me good. When I am with her, I regret all that you have taught me. I become different from what you have known me to be. I am changed, and the mere touch of Sibyl Vane's hand makes me forget you and all your wrong, fascinating, poisonous, delightful theories."

"And those are . . . ?" asked Lord Henry, helping himself to some salad.

"Oh, your theories about life, your theories about love, your theories about pleasure. All your theories, in fact, Harry."

"Pleasure is the only thing worth having a theory about," he answered, in his slow, melodious voice. "But I am afraid I cannot claim my theory as my own. It belongs to Nature, not to me. Pleasure is Nature's test, her sign of approval. When we are happy we are always good, but when we are good we are not always happy."

"Ah! but what do you mean by good?" cried Basil Hallward.

"Yes," echoed Dorian, leaning back in his chair, and looking at Lord Henry over the heavy clusters of purple-lipped irises that stood in the centre of the table, "what do you mean by good, Harry?"

"To be good is to be in harmony with one's self," he replied, touching the thin stem of his glass with his pale, fine-pointed fingers. "Discord is to be forced to be in harmony with others. One's own life—that is the important thing. As for the lives of one's neighbours, if one wishes to be a prig or a Puritan, one can flaunt one's moral views about them, but they are not one's concern. Besides, individualism has really the higher aim. Modern morality consists in accepting the standard of one's age. I consider that for any man of culture to accept the standard of his age is a form of the grossest immorality."

"But, surely, if one lives merely for one's self, Harry, one pays a terrible price for doing so," suggested the painter.

"Yes, we are overcharged for everything nowadays. I should fancy that the real tragedy of the poor is that they can afford nothing but self-denial. Beautiful sins, like beautiful things, are the privilege of the rich."

"One has to pay in other ways but money."

"What sort of ways, Basil?"

"Oh! I should fancy in remorse, in suffering, in . . . well, in the consciousness of degradation."

Lord Henry shrugged his shoulders. "My dear fellow, mediaeval art is charming, but mediaeval emotions are out of date. One can use them in fiction, of course. But then the only things that one can use in fiction are the things that one has ceased to use in fact. Believe me, no civilized man ever regrets a pleasure, and no uncivilized man ever knows what a pleasure is."

"I know what pleasure is," cried Dorian Gray. "It is to adore someone."

"That is certainly better than being adored," he answered, toying with some fruits. "Being adored is a nuisance. Women treat us just as humanity treats its gods. They worship us, and are always bothering us to do something for them."

"I should have said that whatever they ask for they had first given to us," murmured the lad, gravely. "They create love in our natures. They have a right to demand it back."

"That is quite true, Dorian," cried Hallward.

"Nothing is ever quite true," said Lord Henry.

"This is," interrupted Dorian. "You must admit, Harry, that women give to men the very gold of their lives."

"Possibly," he sighed, "but they invariably want it back in such very small change. That is the worry. Women, as some witty Frenchman once put it, inspire us with the desire to do masterpieces, and always prevent us from carrying them out."

"Harry, you are dreadful! I don't know why I like you so much."

"You will always like me, Dorian," he replied. "Will you have some coffee, you fellows?— Waiter, bring coffee, and *fine-champagne*,[6] and some cigarettes. No; don't mind the cigarettes; I have some. Basil, I can't allow you to smoke cigars. You must have a cigarette. A cigarette is the perfect type of a perfect pleasure. It is exquisite, and it leaves one unsatisfied. What more can one want? Yes, Dorian, you will always be fond of me. I represent to you all the sins you have never had the courage to commit."

"What nonsense you talk, Harry!" cried the lad, taking a light from a fire-breathing silver dragon that the waiter had placed on the table. "Let us go down to the theatre. When Sibyl comes on the stage you will have a new ideal of life. She will represent something to you that you have never known."

"I have known everything," said Lord Henry, with a tired look in his eyes, "but I am always ready for a new emotion. I am afraid, however, that, for me at any rate, there is no such thing. Still, your wonderful girl may thrill me. I love acting. It is so much more real than life. Let us go. Dorian, you will come with me. I am so sorry, Basil, but there is only room for two in the brougham.[7] You must follow us in a hansom."

They got up and put on their coats, sipping their coffee standing. The painter was silent and preoccupied. There was a gloom over him. He could not bear this marriage, and yet it seemed to him to be better than many other things that might have happened. After a few minutes, they all passed downstairs. He drove off by himself, as had been arranged, and watched the flashing lights of the little brougham in front of him. A strange sense of loss came over him. He felt that Dorian Gray would never again be to him all that he had been in the past. Life had come between them. . . . His eyes darkened, and the crowded, flaring streets became blurred to his eyes. When the cab drew up at the theatre, it seemed to him that he had grown years older.

VII

For some reason or other, the house was crowded that night, and the fat Jew manager who met them at the door was beaming from ear to ear with an oily, tremulous smile. He escorted them to their box with a sort of pompous humility, waving his fat jewelled hands, and talking at the top of his voice. Dorian Gray loathed him more than ever. He felt as if he had come to look for Miranda[1] and had been met by Caliban.[1] Lord Henry, upon the other hand, rather liked him. At least he declared he did, and insisted on shaking him by the hand, and assuring him that he was proud to meet a man who had discovered a real genius and gone bankrupt over a poet. Hallward amused himself with watching the faces in the pit. The heat was terribly oppressive, and the huge sunlight flamed like a monstrous dahlia with petals of yellow fire. The youths in the gallery had taken off their coats and waistcoats and hung them over the side. They talked to each other across the theatre, and shared their oranges with the tawdry girls who sat beside them. Some women were laughing in the pit. Their voices were horribly shrill and discordant. The sound of the popping of corks came from the bar.

"What a place to find one's divinity in!" said Lord Henry.

"Yes!" answered Dorian Gray. "It was here I found her, and she is divine beyond all living things. When she acts you will forget everything. These common, rough people, with their coarse faces and brutal gestures, become quite different when she is on the stage. They sit silently and watch her. They weep and laugh as she wills them to do. She makes them as responsive as a violin. She spiritualizes them, and one feels that they are of the same flesh and blood as oneself."

"The same flesh and blood as oneself! Oh, I hope not!" exclaimed Lord Henry, who was scanning the occupants of the gallery through his opera-glass.

"Don't pay any attention to him, Dorian," said the painter. "I understand what you mean, and I believe in this girl. Anyone you love must be marvellous, and any girl that has the effect you describe must be fine and noble. To spiritualize one's age—that is something worth doing. If this girl can give a soul to those who have lived without one, if she can create the sense of beauty in people whose lives have been sordid and ugly, if she can strip them of their selfishness and lend them tears for sorrows that are not their own, she is worthy of all your adoration, worthy of the adoration of the world. This marriage is quite right. I did not think so at first, but I admit it now. The gods made Sibyl Vane for you. Without her you would have been incomplete."

"Thanks, Basil," answered Dorian Gray, pressing his hand. "I knew that you would understand me. Harry is so cynical, he terrifies me. But here is the orchestra. It is quite dreadful, but it only lasts for about five minutes. Then the curtain rises, and you will see the girl to whom I am going to give all my life, to whom I have given everything that is good in me."

A quarter of an hour afterwards, amidst an extraordinary turmoil of applause, Sibyl Vane stepped on to the stage. Yes, she was certainly lovely to look at—one of the loveliest creatures, Lord Henry thought, that he had ever seen. There was something of the fawn in her shy grace and startled eyes. A faint blush, like the shadow of a rose in a mirror of silver, came to her cheeks as she glanced at the crowded, enthusiastic house. She stepped back a few paces, and her lips seemed to tremble. Basil Hallward leaped to his feet and began to applaud. Motionless, and as one in a dream, sat Dorian Gray, gazing at her. Lord Henry peered through his glasses, murmuring, "Charming! charming!"

The scene was the hall of Capulet's house, and Romeo in his pilgrim's dress had entered with Mercutio and his other friends. The band, such as it was, struck up a few bars of music, and the dance began. Through the crowd of ungainly, shabbily dressed actors, Sibyl Vane moved like a creature from a finer world. Her body swayed, while she danced, as a plant sways in the water. The curves of her throat were the curves of a white lily. Her hands seemed to be made of cool ivory.

Yet she was curiously listless. She showed no sign of joy when her eyes rested on Romeo. The few words she had to speak—

> "Good pilgrim, you do wrong your hand too much,
>   Which mannerly devotion shows in this;
> For saints have hands that pilgrims' hands do touch,
>   And palm to palm is holy palmers' kiss—"

with the brief dialogue that follows, were spoken in a thoroughly artificial manner. The voice was exquisite, but from the point of view of tone it was absolutely false. It was wrong in colour. It took away all the life from the verse. It made the passion unreal.

Dorian Gray grew pale as he watched her. He was puzzled and anxious. Neither of his friends dared to say anything to him. She seemed to them to be absolutely incompetent. They were horribly disappointed.

Yet they felt that the true test of any Juliet is the balcony scene of the second act. They waited for that. If she failed there, there was nothing in her.

She looked charming as she came out in the moonlight.

That could not be denied. But the staginess of her acting was unbearable, and grew worse as she went on. Her gestures became absurdly artificial. She overemphasized everything that she had to say. The beautiful passage—

"Thou knowest the mask of night is on my face,
Else would a maiden blush bepaint my cheek
For that which thou hast heard me speak tonight—"

was declaimed with the painful precision of a schoolgirl who has been taught to recite by some second-rate professor of elocution. When she leaned over the balcony and came to those wonderful lines—

"Although I joy in thee,
I have no joy of this contract tonight;
It is too rash, too unadvised, too sudden;
Too like the lightning, which doth cease to be
Ere one can say, 'It lightens.' Sweet, good night!
This bud of love by summer's ripening breath
May prove a beauteous flower when next we meet—"

she spoke the words as though they conveyed no meaning to her. It was not nervousness. Indeed, so far from being nervous, she was absolutely self-contained. It was simply bad art. She was a complete failure.

Even the common, uneducated audience of the pit and gallery lost their interest in the play. They got restless, and began to talk loudly and to whistle. The Jew manager, who was standing at the back of the dress-circle, stamped and swore with rage. The only person unmoved was the girl herself.

When the second act was over there came a storm of hisses, and Lord Henry got up from his chair and put on his coat. "She is quite beautiful, Dorian," he said, "but she can't act. Let us go."

"I am going to see the play through," answered the lad, in a hard, bitter voice. "I am awfully sorry that I have made you waste an evening, Harry. I apologize to you both."

"My dear Dorian, I should think Miss Vane was ill," interrupted Hallward. "We will come some other night."

"I wish she were ill," he rejoined. "But she seems to me to be simply callous and cold. She has entirely altered. Last night she was a great artist. This evening she is merely a commonplace, mediocre actress."

"Don't talk like that about anyone you love, Dorian. Love is a more wonderful thing than art."

"They are both simply forms of imitation," remarked Lord Henry. "But do let us go. Dorian, you must not stay here any longer. It is not good for one's morals to see bad acting. Besides, I don't suppose you will want your wife to act. So what does it matter if she plays Juliet like a wooden doll? She is very lovely, and if she knows as little about life as she does about acting, she will be a delightful experience. There are only two kinds of people who are really fascinating—people who know absolutely everything, and people who know absolutely nothing. Good heavens, my dear boy, don't look so tragic! The secret of remaining young is never to have an emotion that is unbecoming. Come to the club with Basil and myself. We will smoke cigarettes and drink to the beauty of Sibyl Vane. She is beautiful. What more can you want?"

"Go away, Harry," cried the lad. "I want to be alone. Basil, you must go. Ah! can't you see that my heart is breaking?" The hot tears came to his eyes. His lips trembled, and rushing to the back of the box, he leaned up against the wall, hiding his face in his hands.

"Let us go, Basil," said Lord Henry, with a strange tenderness in his voice; and the two young men passed out together.

A few moments afterwards the footlights flared up, and the curtain rose on the third act. Dorian Gray went back to his seat. He looked pale, and proud, and indifferent. The play dragged on, and seemed interminable. Half of the audience went out, tramping in heavy boots, and laughing. The whole thing was a fiasco. The last act was played to almost empty benches. The curtain went down on a titter, and some groans.

As soon as it was over, Dorian Gray rushed behind the scenes into the green-room. The girl was standing there alone, with a look of triumph on her face. Her eyes were lit with an exquisite fire. There was a radiance about her. Her parted lips were smiling over some secret of their own.

When he entered, she looked at him, and an expression of infinite joy came over her. "How badly I acted tonight, Dorian!" she cried.

"Horribly!" he answered, gazing at her in amazement— "horribly! It was dreadful. Are you ill? You have no idea what it was. You have no idea what I suffered."

The girl smiled. "Dorian," she answered, lingering over his name with long-drawn music in her voice, as though it were sweeter than honey to the red petals of her mouth— "Dorian, you should have understood. But you understand now, don't you?"

"Understand what?" he asked, angrily.

"Why I was so bad tonight. Why I shall always be bad. Why I shall never act well again."

He shrugged his shoulders. "You are ill, I suppose. When you are ill you shouldn't act. You make yourself ridiculous. My friends were bored. I was bored."

She seemed not to listen to him. She was transfigured with joy. An ecstasy of happiness dominated her.

"Dorian, Dorian," she cried, "before I knew you, acting was the one reality of my life. It was only in the theatre that I lived. I thought that it was all true. I was Rosalind one night, and Portia the other. The joy of Beatrice was my joy, and the sorrows of Cordelia[2] were mine also. I believed in everything. The common people who acted with me seemed to me to be god-like. The painted scenes were my world. I knew nothing but shadows, and I thought them real. You came—oh, my beautiful love!—and you freed my soul from prison. You taught me what reality really is. Tonight, for the first time in my life, I saw through the hollowness, the sham, the silliness of the empty pageant in which I had always played. Tonight, for the first time, I became conscious that the Romeo was hideous, and old, and painted, that the moonlight in the orchard was false, that the scenery was vulgar, and that the words I had to speak were unreal, were not my words, were not what I wanted to say. You had brought me something higher, something of which all art is but a reflection. You had made me understand what love really is. My love! my love! Prince Charming! prince of life! I have grown sick of shadows. You are more to me than all art can ever be. What have I to do with the puppets of a play? When I came on tonight, I could not understand how it was that everything had gone from me. I thought that I was going to be wonderful. I found that I could do nothing. Suddenly it dawned on my soul what it all meant. The knowledge was exquisite to me. I heard them hissing, and I smiled. What could they know of love such as ours? Take me away, Dorian—take me away with you, where we can be quite alone. I hate the stage. I might mimic a passion that I do not feel, but I cannot mimic one that burns me like fire. Oh, Dorian, Dorian, you understand now what it signifies? Even if I could do it, it would be profanation for me to play at being in love. You have made me see that."

He flung himself down on the sofa, and turned away his face. "You have killed my love," he muttered.

She looked at him in wonder, and laughed. He made no answer. She came across to him, and with her little fingers stroked his hair. She knelt down and pressed his hands to her lips. He drew them away, and a shudder ran through him.

Then he leaped up, and went to the door. "Yes," he cried, "you have killed my love. You used to stir my imagination. Now you don't even stir my curiosity. You simply produce no effect. I loved you because you were marvellous, because you had genius and intellect, because you realized the dreams of great poets and gave shape and substance to the shadows of art. You have thrown it all away. You are shallow and stupid.

My God! how mad I was to love you! What a fool I have been! You are nothing to me now. I will never see you again. I will never think of you. I will never mention your name. You don't know what you were to me, once. Why, once . . . Oh, I can't bear to think of it! I wish I had never laid eyes upon you! You have spoiled the romance of my life. How little you can know of love, if you say it mars your art! Without your art you are nothing. I would have made you famous, splendid, magnificent. The world would have worshipped you, and you would have borne my name. What are you now? A third-rate actress with a pretty face."

The girl grew white, and trembled. She clenched her hands together, and her voice seemed to catch in her throat. "You are not serious, Dorian?" she murmured. "You are acting."

"Acting! I leave that to you. You do it so well," he answered, bitterly.

She rose from her knees, and, with a piteous expression of pain in her face, came across the room to him. She put her hand upon his arm, and looked into his eyes. He thrust her back. "Don't touch me!" he cried.

A low moan broke from her, and she flung herself at his feet, and lay there like a trampled flower. "Dorian, Dorian, don't leave me!" she whispered. "I am so sorry I didn't act well. I was thinking of you all the time. But I will try—indeed, I will try. It came so suddenly across me, my love for you. I think I should never have known it if you had not kissed me—if we had not kissed each other. Kiss me again, my love. Don't go away from me. I couldn't bear it. Oh! don't go away from me. My brother. . . . No, never mind. He didn't mean it. He was in jest. . . . But you, oh! can't you forgive me for tonight? I will work so hard, and try to improve. Don't be cruel to me because I love you better than anything in the world. After all, it is only once that I have not pleased you. But you are quite right, Dorian. I should have shown myself more of an artist. It was foolish of me; and yet I couldn't help it. Oh, don't leave me, don't leave me." A fit of passionate sobbing choked her. She crouched on the floor like a wounded thing, and Dorian Gray, with his beautiful eyes, looked down at her, and his chiselled lips curled in exquisite disdain. There is always something ridiculous about the emotions of people whom one has ceased to love. Sibyl Vane seemed to him to be absurdly melodramatic. Her tears and sobs annoyed him.

"I am going," he said at last, in his calm, clear voice. "I don't wish to be unkind, but I can't see you again. You have disappointed me."

She wept silently, and made no answer, but crept nearer. Her little hands stretched blindly out, and appeared to be seeking for him. He turned on his heel, and left the room. In a few moments he was out of the theatre.

Where he went to he hardly knew. He remembered wandering through dimly lit streets, past gaunt black-shadowed archways and evil-looking houses. Women with hoarse voices and harsh laughter had called after him. Drunkards had reeled by cursing, and chattering to themselves like monstrous apes. He had seen grotesque children huddled upon doorsteps, and heard shrieks and oaths from gloomy courts.

As the dawn was just breaking he found himself close to Covent Garden.³ The darkness lifted, and flushed with faint fires, the sky hollowed itself into a perfect pearl. Huge carts filled with nodding lilies rumbled slowly down the polished empty street. The air was heavy with the perfume of the flowers, and their beauty seemed to bring him an anodyne for his pain. He followed into the market, and watched the men unloading their wagons. A white-smocked carter offered him some cherries. He thanked him, wondered why he refused to accept any money for them, and began to eat them listlessly. They had been plucked at midnight, and the coldness of the moon had entered into them. A long line of boys carrying crates of striped tulips, and of yellow and red roses, defiled in front of him, threading their way through the huge jade-green piles of vegetables. Under the portico, with its grey sun-bleached pillars, loitered a troop of draggled bare-headed girls, waiting for the auction to be over. Others crowded round the swinging doors of the coffee-house in the piazza. The heavy cart-horses slipped and stamped upon the rough stones, shaking their bells and trappings. Some of the drivers were lying asleep on a pile of sacks. Iris-necked and pink-footed, the pigeons ran about picking up seeds.

After a little while, he hailed a hansom, and drove home. For a few moments he loitered upon the doorstep, looking round at the silent Square with its blank close-shuttered windows, and its staring blinds. The sky was pure opal now, and the roofs of the houses glistened like silver against it. From some chimney opposite a thin wreath of smoke was rising. It curled, a violet riband, through the nacre-coloured air.

In the huge gilt Venetian lantern, spoil of some Doge's[4] barge, that hung from the ceiling of the great oak-panelled hall of entrance, lights were still burning from three flickering jets: thin blue petals of flame they seemed, rimmed with white fire. He turned them out, and, having thrown his hat and cape on the table, passed through the library towards the door of his bedroom, a large octagonal chamber on the ground floor that, in his new-born feeling for luxury, he had just had decorated for himself, and hung with some curious Renaissance[5] tapestries that had been discovered stored in a disused attic at Selby Royal. As he was turning the handle of the door, his eye fell upon the portrait Basil Hallward had painted of him. He started back as if in surprise. Then he went on into his own room, looking somewhat puzzled. After he had taken the buttonhole out of his coat, he seemed to hesitate. Finally he came back, went over to the picture, and examined it. In the dim arrested light that struggled through the cream-coloured silk blinds, the face appeared to him to be a little changed. The expression looked different. One would have said that there was a touch of cruelty in the mouth. It was certainly strange.

He turned round, and, walking to the window, drew up the blind. The bright dawn flooded the room, and swept the fantastic shadows into dusky corners, where they lay shuddering. But the strange expression that he had noticed in the face of the portrait seemed to linger there, to be more intensified even. The quivering, ardent sunlight showed him the lines of cruelty round the mouth as clearly as if he had been looking into a mirror after he had done some dreadful thing.

He winced, and, taking up from the table an oval glass framed in ivory Cupids, one of Lord Henry's many presents to him, glanced hurriedly into its polished depths. No line like that warped his red lips. What did it mean?

He rubbed his eyes, and came close to the picture, and examined it again. There were no signs of any change when he looked into the actual painting, and yet there was no doubt that the whole expression had altered. It was not a mere fancy of his own. The thing was horribly apparent.

He threw himself into a chair, and began to think. Suddenly there flashed across his mind what he had said in Basil Hallward's studio the day the picture had been finished. Yes, he remembered it perfectly. He had uttered a mad wish that he himself might remain young, and the portrait grow old; that his own beauty might be untarnished, and the face on the canvas bear the burden of his passions and his sins; that the painted image might be seared with the lines of suffering and thought, and that he might keep all the delicate bloom and loveliness of his then just conscious boyhood. Surely his wish had not been fulfilled? Such things were impossible. It seemed monstrous even to think of them. And, yet, there was the picture before him, with the touch of cruelty in the mouth.

Cruelty! Had he been cruel? It was the girl's fault, not his. He had dreamed of her as a great artist, had given his love to her because he had thought her great. Then she had disappointed him. She had been shallow and unworthy. And, yet, a feeling of infinite regret came over him, as he thought of her lying at his feet sobbing like a little child. He remembered with what callousness he had watched her. Why had he been made like that? Why had such a soul been given to him? But he had suffered also. During the three terrible hours that the play had lasted, he had lived centuries of pain, aeon upon aeon of torture. His life was well worth hers. She had marred him for a moment, if he had wounded her for an age. Besides, women were better suited to bear sorrow than men. They lived on their emotions. They only thought of their emotions. When they took lovers, it was merely to have someone with whom they could have scenes. Lord Henry had told him that, and Lord Henry knew what women were. Why should he trouble about Sibyl Vane? She was nothing to him now.

But the picture? What was he to say of that? It held the secret of his life, and told his story. It had taught him to love his own beauty. Would it teach him to loathe his own soul? Would he ever look at it again?

No; it was merely an illusion wrought on the troubled senses. The horrible night that he had passed had left phantoms behind it. Suddenly there had fallen upon his brain that tiny scarlet speck that makes men mad. The picture had not changed. It was folly to think so.

Yet it was watching him, with its beautiful marred face and its cruel smile. Its bright hair gleamed in the early sunlight. Its blue eyes met his own. A sense of infinite pity, not for himself, but for the painted image of himself, came over him. It had altered already, and would alter more. Its gold would wither into grey. Its red and white roses would die. For every sin that he committed, a stain would fleck and wreck its fairness. But he would not sin. The picture, changed or unchanged, would be to him the visible emblem of conscience. He would resist temptation. He would not see Lord Henry any more—would not, at any rate, listen to those subtle poisonous theories that in Basil Hallward's garden had first stirred within him the passion for impossible things. He would go back to Sibyl Vane, make her amends, marry her, try to love her again. Yes, it was his duty to do so. She must have suffered more than he had. Poor child! He had been selfish and cruel to her. The fascination that she had exercised over him would return. They would be happy together. His life with her would be beautiful and pure.

He got up from his chair, and drew a large screen right in front of the portrait, shuddering as he glanced at it. "How horrible!" he murmured to himself, and he walked across to the window and opened it. When he stepped out on to the grass, he drew a deep breath. The fresh morning air seemed to drive away all his sombre passions. He thought only of Sibyl. A faint echo of his love came back to him. He repeated her name over and over again. The birds that were singing in the dew-drenched garden seemed to be telling the flowers about her.

VIII

It was long past noon when he awoke. His valet had crept several times on tiptoe into the room to see if he was stirring, and had wondered what made his young master sleep so late. Finally his bell sounded, and Victor came in softly with a cup of tea, and a pile of letters, on a small tray of old Sèvres[1] china, and drew back the olive-satin curtains, with their shimmering blue lining, that hung in front of the three tall windows.

"Monsieur has well slept this morning," he said, smiling.

"What o'clock is it, Victor?" asked Dorian Gray, drowsily.

"One hour and a quarter, Monsieur."

How late it was! He sat up, and, having sipped some tea, turned over his letters. One of them was from Lord Henry, and had been brought by hand that morning. He hesitated for a moment, and then put it aside. The others he opened listlessly. They contained the usual collection of cards, invitations to dinner, tickets for private views, programmes of charity concerts, and the like, that are showered on fashionable young men every morning during the season. There was a rather heavy bill, for a chased silver Louis-Quinze[2] toilet-set, that he had not yet had the courage to send on to his guardians, who were extremely old-fashioned people and did not realize that we live in an age when unnecessary things are our only necessities; and there were several very courteously worded communications from Jermyn Street moneylenders offering to advance any sum of money at a moment's notice and at the most reasonable rates of interest.

After about ten minutes he got up, and, throwing on an elaborate dressing gown of silk-embroidered cashmere wool, passed into the onyx-paved bathroom. The cool water refreshed him after his long sleep. He seemed to have forgotten all that he had gone through. A dim sense of having taken part in some strange tragedy came to him once or twice, but there was the unreality of a dream about it.

As soon as he was dressed, he went into the library and sat down to a light French breakfast, that had been laid out for him on a small round table close to the open window. It was an exquisite day. The warm air seemed laden with spices. A bee flew in, and buzzed round the blue-dragon bowl that, filled with sulphur-yellow roses, stood before him. He felt perfectly happy.

Suddenly his eye fell on the screen that he had placed in front of the portrait, and he started.

"Too cold for Monsieur?" asked his valet, putting an omelette on the table. "I shut the window?"

Dorian shook his head. "I am not cold," he murmured.

Was it all true? Had the portrait really changed? Or had it been simply his own imagination that had made him see a look of evil where there had been a look of joy? Surely a painted canvas could not alter? The thing was absurd. It would serve as a tale to tell Basil some day. It would make him smile.

And, yet, how vivid was his recollection of the whole thing! First in the dim twilight, and then in the bright dawn, he had seen the touch of cruelty round the warped lips. He almost dreaded his valet's leaving the room. He knew that when he was alone he would have to examine the portrait. He was afraid of certainty. When the coffee and cigarettes had been brought and the man turned to go, he felt a wild desire to tell him to remain. As the door was closing behind him he called him back. The man stood waiting for his orders. Dorian looked at him for a moment. "I am not at home to anyone, Victor," he said, with a sigh. The man bowed and retired.

Then he rose from the table, lit a cigarette and flung himself down on a luxuriously-cushioned couch that stood facing the screen. The screen was an old one, of gilt Spanish leather, stamped and wrought with a rather florid Louis-Quatorze pattern. He scanned it curiously, wondering if ever before it had concealed the secret of a man's life.

Should he move it aside, after all? Why not let it stay there? What was the use of knowing? If the thing was true, it was terrible. If it was not true, why trouble about it? But what if, by some fate or deadlier chance, eyes other than his spied behind, and saw the horrible change? What should he do if Basil Hallward came and asked to look at his own picture? Basil would be sure to do that. No; the thing had to be examined, and at once. Anything would be better than this dreadful state of doubt.

He got up, and locked both doors. At least he would be alone when he looked upon the mask of his shame. Then he drew the screen aside, and saw himself face to face. It was perfectly true. The portrait had altered.

As he often remembered afterwards, and always with no small wonder, he found himself at first gazing at the portrait with a feeling of almost scientific interest. That such a change should have taken place was incredible to him. And yet it was a fact. Was there some subtle affinity between the chemical atoms, that shaped themselves into form and colour on the canvas, and the soul that was within him? Could it be that what that soul thought, they realized?—that what it dreamed, they made true? Or was there some other, more terrible reason? He shuddered, and felt afraid, and, going back to the couch, lay there, gazing at the picture in sickened horror.

One thing, however, he felt that it had done for him. It had made him conscious how unjust, how cruel, he had been to Sibyl Vane. It was not too late to make reparation for that. She could still be his wife. His unreal and selfish love would yield to some higher influence, would be transformed into some nobler passion, and the portrait that Basil Hallward had painted of him would be a guide to him through life, would be to him what holiness is to some, and conscience to others, and the fear of God to us all. There were opiates for remorse, drugs that could lull the moral sense to sleep. But here was a visible symbol of the degradation of sin. Here was an ever-present sign of the ruin men brought upon their souls.

Three o'clock struck, and four, and the half-hour rang its double chime, but Dorian Gray did not stir. He was trying to gather up the scarlet threads of life, and to weave them into a pattern; to find his way through the sanguine labyrinth of passion through which he was wandering. He did not know what to do, or what to think. Finally, he went over to the table and wrote a passionate letter to the girl he had loved, imploring her forgiveness, and accusing himself of madness. He covered page after page with wild words of sorrow, and wilder words of pain. There is a luxury in self-reproach. When we blame ourselves we feel that no one else has a right to blame us. It is the confession, not the priest, that gives us absolution. When Dorian had finished the letter, he felt that he had been forgiven.

Suddenly there came a knock to the door, and he heard Lord Henry's voice outside. "My dear boy, I must see you. Let me in at once. I can't bear your shutting yourself up like this."

He made no answer at first, but remained quite still. The knocking still continued, and grew louder. Yes, it was better to let Lord Henry in, and to explain to him the new life he was going to lead, to quarrel with him if it became necessary to quarrel, to part if parting was inevitable. He jumped up, drew the screen hastily across the picture, and unlocked the door.

"I am so sorry for it all, Dorian," said Lord Henry, as he entered. "But you must not think too much about it."

"Do you mean about Sibyl Vane?" asked the lad.

"Yes, of course," answered Lord Henry, sinking into a chair, and slowly pulling off his yellow gloves. "It is dreadful, from one point of view, but it was not your fault. Tell me, did you go behind and see her, after the play was over?"

"Yes."

"I felt sure you had. Did you make a scene with her?"

"I was brutal, Harry—perfectly brutal. But it is all right now. I am not sorry for anything that has happened. It has taught me to know myself better."

"Ah, Dorian, I am so glad you take it in that way! I was afraid I would find you plunged in remorse, and tearing that nice curly hair of yours."

"I have got through all that," said Dorian, shaking his head, and smiling. "I am perfectly happy now. I know what conscience is, to begin with. It is not what you told me it was. It is the divinest thing in us. Don't sneer at it, Harry, any more—at least not before me. I want to be good. I can't bear the idea of my soul being hideous."

"A very charming artistic basis for ethics, Dorian! I congratulate you on it. But how are you going to begin?"

"By marrying Sibyl Vane."

"Marrying Sibyl Vane!" cried Lord Henry, standing up, and looking at him in perplexed amazement. "But, my dear Dorian—"

"Yes, Harry, I know what you are going to say. Something dreadful about marriage. Don't say it. Don't ever say things of that kind to me again. Two days ago I asked Sibyl to marry me. I am not going to break my word to her. She is to be my wife."

"Your wife! Dorian! . . . Didn't you get my letter? I wrote to you this morning, and sent the note down, by my own man."

"Your letter? Oh, yes, I remember. I have not read it yet, Harry. I was afraid there might be something in it that I wouldn't like. You cut life to pieces with your epigrams."

"You know nothing then?"

"What do you mean?"

Lord Henry walked across the room, and, sitting down by Dorian Gray, took both his hands in his own, and held them tightly. "Dorian," he said, "my letter—don't be frightened—was to tell you that Sibyl Vane is dead."

A cry of pain broke from the lad's lips, and he leaped to his feet, tearing his hands away from Lord Henry's grasp. "Dead! Sibyl dead! It is not true! It is a horrible lie! How dare you say it?"

"It is quite true, Dorian," said Lord Henry, gravely. "It is in all the morning papers. I wrote down to you to ask you not to see anyone till I came. There will have to be an inquest, of course, and you must not be mixed up in it. Things like that make a man fashionable in Paris. But in London people are so prejudiced. Here, one should never make one's début with a scandal. One should reserve that to give an interest to one's old age. I suppose they don't know your name at the theatre? If they don't, it is all right. Did anyone see you going round to her room? That is an important point."

Dorian did not answer for a few moments. He was dazed with horror. Finally he stammered, in a stifled voice, "Harry, did you say an inquest? What did you mean by that? Did Sibyl—? Oh, Harry, I can't bear it! But be quick. Tell me everything at once."

"I have no doubt it was not an accident, Dorian, though it must be put in that way to the public. It seems that as she was leaving the theatre with her mother, about half-past twelve or so, she said she had forgotten something upstairs. They waited some time for her, but she did not come down again. They ulimately found her lying dead on the floor of her dressing-room. She had swallowed something by mistake, some dreadful thing they use at theatres. I don't know what it was, but it had either prussic acid[3] or white lead in it. I should fancy it was prussic acid, as she seems to have died instantaneously."

"Harry, Harry, it is terrible!" cried the lad.

"Yes; it is very tragic, of course, but you must not get yourself mixed up in it. I see by *The Standard* that she was seventeen. I should have thought she was almost younger than that. She looked such a child, and seemed to know so little about acting. Dorian, you mustn't let this thing get on your nerves. You must come and dine with me, and afterwards we will look in at the Opera. It is a Patti⁴ night, and everybody will be there. You can come to my sister's box. She has got some smart women with her."

"So I have murdered Sibyl Vane," said Dorian Gray, half to himself—"murdered her as surely as if I had cut her little throat with a knife. Yet the roses are not less lovely for all that. The birds sing just as happily in my garden. And tonight I am to dine with you, and then go on to the Opera, and sup somewhere, I suppose, afterwards. How extraordinarily dramatic life is! If I had read all this in a book, Harry, I think I would have wept over it. Somehow, now that it has happened actually, and to me, it seems far too wonderful for tears. Here is the first passionate love letter I have ever written in my life. Strange, that my first passionate love letter should have been addressed to a dead girl. Can they feel, I wonder, those white silent people we call the dead? Sibyl! Can she feel, or know, or listen? Oh, Harry, how I loved her once! It seems years ago to me now. She was everything to me. Then came that dreadful night—was it really only last night?—when she played so badly, and my heart almost broke. She explained it all to me. It was terribly pathetic. But I was not moved a bit. I thought her shallow. Suddenly something happened that made me afraid. I can't tell you what it was, but it was terrible. I said I would go back to her. I felt I had done wrong. And now she is dead. My God! my God! Harry, what shall I do? You don't know the danger I am in, and there is nothing to keep me straight. She would have done that for me. She had no right to kill herself. It was selfish of her."

"My dear Dorian," answered Lord Henry, taking a cigarette from his case, and producing a gold-latten⁵ matchbox, "the only way a woman can ever reform a man is by boring him so completely that he loses all possible interest in life. If you had married this girl you would have been wretched. Of course you would have treated her kindly. One can always be kind to people about whom one cares nothing. But she would have soon found out that you were absolutely indifferent to her. And when a woman finds that out about her husband, she either becomes dreadfully dowdy, or wears very smart bonnets that some other woman's husband has to pay for. I say nothing about the social mistake, which would have been abject, which, of course, I would not have allowed, but I assure you that in any case the whole thing would have been an absolute failure."

"I suppose it would," muttered the lad, walking up and down the room, and looking horribly pale. "But I thought it was my duty. It is not my fault that this terrible tragedy has prevented my doing what was right. I remember your saying once that there is a fatality about good resolutions—that they are always made too late. Mine certainly were."

"Good resolutions are useless attempts to interfere with scientific laws. Their origin is pure vanity. Their result is absolutely *nil*. They give us, now and then, some of those luxurious sterile emotions that have a certain charm for the weak. That is all that can be said for them. They are simply cheques that men draw on a bank where they have no account."

"Harry," cried Dorian Gray, coming over and sitting down beside him, "why is it that I cannot feel this tragedy as much as I want to? I don't think I am heartless. Do you?"

"You have done too many foolish things during the last fortnight to be entitled to give yourself that name, Dorian," answered Lord Henry, with his sweet, melancholy smile.

The lad frowned. "I don't like that explanation, Harry," he rejoined, "but I am glad you don't think I am heartless. I am nothing of the kind. I know I am not. And yet I must admit that this thing that has happened does not affect me as it should. It seems to me to be simply like a wonderful ending to a wonderful play. It has all the terrible beauty of a Greek tragedy, a tragedy in which I took a great part, but by which I have not been wounded."

"It is an interesting question," said Lord Henry, who found an exquisite pleasure in playing on the lad's unconscious egotism—"an extremely interesting question. I fancy that the true explanation is this. It often happens that the real tragedies of life occur in such an inartistic manner that they hurt us by their crude violence, their absolute incoherence, their absurd want of meaning, their entire lack of style. They affect us just as vulgarity affects us. They give us an impression of sheer brute force, and we revolt against that. Sometimes, however, a tragedy that possesses artistic elements of beauty crosses our lives. If these elements of beauty are real, the whole thing simply appeals to our sense of dramatic effect. Suddenly we find that we are no longer the actors, but the spectators of the play. Or rather we are both. We watch ourselves, and the mere wonder of the spectacle enthralls us. In the present case, what is it that has really happened? Someone has killed herself for love of you. I wish that I had ever had such an experience. It would have made me in love with love for the rest of my life. The people who have adored me—there have not been very many, but there have been some—have always insisted on living on, long after I had ceased to care for them, or they to care for me. They have become stout and tedious, and when I meet them they go in at once for reminiscences. That awful memory of woman! What a fearful thing it is! And what an utter intellectual stagnation it reveals! One should absorb the colour of life, but one should never remember its details. Details are always vulgar."

"I must sow poppies[6] in my garden," sighed Dorian.

"There is no necessity," rejoined his companion. "Life has always poppies in her hands. Of course, now and then things linger. I once wore nothing but violets[6] all through one season, as a form of artistic mourning for a romance that would not die. Ultimately, however, it did die. I forget what killed it. I think it was her proposing to sacrifice the whole world for me. That is always a dreadful moment. It fills one with the terror of eternity. Well—would you believe it?—a week ago,

at Lady Hampshire's, I found myself seated at dinner next
to the lady in question, and she insisted on going over the
whole thing again, and digging up the past, and raking up
the future. I had buried my romance in a bed of asphodel.[6]
She dragged it out again, and assured me that I had spoiled
her life. I am bound to state that she ate an enormous dinner, so I did not feel any anxiety. But what a lack of taste she
showed! The one charm of the past is that it is the past. But
women never know when the curtain has fallen. They always want a sixth act,[7] and as soon as the interest of the play
is entirely over they propose to continue it. If they were allowed their own way, every comedy would have a tragic
ending, and every tragedy would culminate in a farce. They
are charmingly artificial, but they have no sense of art. You
are more fortunate than I am. I assure you, Dorian, that not
one of the women I have known would have done for me
what Sibyl Vane did for you. Ordinary women always console themselves. Some of them do it by going in for sentimental colours. Never trust a woman who wears mauve,
whatever her age may be, or a woman over thirty-five who is
fond of pink ribbons. It always means that they have a history. Others find a great consolation in suddenly discovering
the good qualities of their husbands. They flaunt their con-
jugal felicity in one's face, as if it were the most fascinating
of sins. Religion consoles some. Its mysteries have all the
charm of a flirtation, a woman once told me; and I can quite
understand it. Besides, nothing makes one so vain as being
told that one is a sinner. Conscience makes egotists of us all.
Yes; there is really no end to the consolations that women
find in modern life. Indeed, I have not mentioned the most
important one."

"What is that, Harry?" said the lad, listlessly.

"Oh, the obvious consolation. Taking someone else's ad-
mirer when one loses one's own. In good society that always
whitewashes a woman. But really, Dorian, how different
Sibyl Vane must have been from all the women one meets!
There is something to me quite beautiful about her death. I

am glad I am living in a century when such wonders happen. They make one believe in the reality of the things we all play with, such as romance, passion, and love."

"I was terribly cruel to her. You forget that."

"I am afraid that women appreciate cruelty, downright cruelty, more than anything else. They have wonderfully primitive instincts. We have emancipated them, but they remain slaves looking for their masters, all the same. They love being dominated. I am sure you were splendid. I have never seen you really and absolutely angry, but I can fancy how delightful you looked. And, after all, you said something to me the day before yesterday that seemed to me at the time to be merely fanciful, but that I see now was absolutely true, and it holds the key to everything."

"What was that, Harry?"

"You said to me that Sibyl Vane represented to you all the heroines of romance—that she was Desdemona[8] one night, and Ophelia[8] the other; that if she died as Juliet, she came to life as Imogen."

"She will never come to life again now," muttered the lad, burying his face in his hands.

"No, she will never come to life. She has played her last part. But you must think of that lonely death in the tawdry dressing-room simply as a strange lurid fragment from some Jacobean[9] tragedy, as a wonderful scene from Webster,[10] or Ford,[10] or Cyril Tourneur.[10] The girl never really lived, and so she has never really died. To you at least she was always a dream, a phantom that flitted through Shakespeare's plays and left them lovelier for its presence, a reed through which Shakespeare's music sounded richer and more full of joy. The moment she touched actual life, she marred it, and it marred her, and so she passed away. Mourn for Ophelia, if you like. Put ashes on your head because Cordelia was strangled. Cry out against Heaven because the daughter of Brabantio[11] died. But don't waste your tears over Sibyl Vane. She was less real than they are."

There was a silence. The evening darkened in the room.

Noiselessly, and with silver feet, the shadows crept in from the garden. The colours faded wearily out of things.

After some time Dorian Gray looked up. "You have explained me to myself, Harry," he murmured, with something of a sigh of relief. "I felt all that you have said, but somehow I was afraid of it, and I could not express it to myself. How well you know me! But we will not talk again of what has happened. It has been a marvellous experience. That is all. I wonder if life has still in store for me anything as marvellous."

"Life has everything in store for you, Dorian. There is nothing that you, with your extraordinary good looks, will not be able to do."

"But suppose, Harry, I became haggard, and old, and wrinkled? What then?"

"Ah, then," said Lord Henry, rising to go—"then, my dear Dorian, you would have to fight for your victories. As it is, they are brought to you. No, you must keep your good looks. We live in an age that reads too much to be wise, and that thinks too much to be beautiful. We cannot spare you. And now you had better dress, and drive down to the club. We are rather late, as it is."

"I think I shall join you at the Opera, Harry. I feel too tired to eat anything. What is the number of your sister's box?"

"Twenty-seven, I believe. It is on the grand tier. You will see her name on the door. But I am sorry you won't come and dine."

"I don't feel up to it," said Dorian, listlessly. "But I am awfully obliged to you for all that you have said to me. You are certainly my best friend. No one has ever understood me as you have."

"We are only at the beginning of our friendship, Dorian," answered Lord Henry, shaking him by the hand. "Good-bye. I shall see you before nine-thirty, I hope. Remember, Patti is singing."

As he closed the door behind him, Dorian Gray touched the bell, and in a few minutes Victor appeared with the lamps and drew the blinds down. He waited impatiently for him to go. The man seemed to take an interminable time over everything.

As soon as he had left, he rushed to the screen, and drew it back. No, there was no further change in the picture. It had received the news of Sibyl Vane's death before he had known of it himself. It was conscious of the events of life as they occurred. The vicious cruelty that marred the fine lines of the mouth had, no doubt, appeared at the very moment that the girl had drunk the poison, whatever it was. Or was it indifferent to results? Did it merely take cognizance of what passed within the soul? He wondered, and hoped that some day he would see the change taking place before his very eyes, shuddering as he hoped it.

Poor Sibyl! what a romance it had all been! She had often mimicked death on the stage. Then Death himself had touched her, and taken her with him. How had she played that dreadful last scene? Had she cursed him, as she died? No; she had died for love of him, and love would always be a sacrament to him now. She had atoned for everything, by the sacrifice she had made of her life. He would not think any more of what she had made him go through, on that horrible night at the theatre. When he thought of her, it would be as a wonderful tragic figure sent on to the world's stage to show the supreme reality of love. A wonderful tragic figure? Tears came to his eyes as he remembered her child-like look and winsome fanciful ways and shy tremulous grace. He brushed them away hastily, and looked again at the picture.

He felt that the time had really come for making his choice. Or had his choice already been made? Yes, life had decided that for him—life, and his own infinite curiosity about life. Eternal youth, infinite passion, pleasure subtle and secret, wild joys and wilder sins—he was to have all these things. The portrait was to bear the burden of his shame: that was all.

A feeling of pain crept over him as he thought of the desecration that was in store for the fair face on the canvas. Once, in boyish mockery of Narcissus, he had kissed, or feigned to kiss, those painted lips that now smiled so cruelly at him. Morning after morning he had sat before the portrait wondering at its beauty, almost enamoured of it, as it seemed to him at times. Was it to alter now with every mood to which he yielded? Was it to become a monstrous and loathsome thing, to be hidden away in a locked room, to be shut out from the sunlight that had so often touched to brighter gold the waving wonder of its hair? The pity of it! the pity of it!

For a moment he thought of praying that the horrible sympathy that existed between him and the picture might cease. It had changed in answer to a prayer; perhaps in answer to a prayer it might remain unchanged. And, yet, who, that knew anything about life, would surrender the chance of remaining always young, however fantastic that chance might be, or with what fateful consequences it might be fraught? Besides, was it really under his control? Had it indeed been prayer that had produced the substitution? Might there not be some curious scientific reason for it all? If thought could exercise its influence upon a living organism, might not thought exercise an influence upon dead and inorganic things? Nay, without thought or conscious desire, might not things external to ourselves vibrate in unison with our moods and passions, atom calling to atom in secret love or strange affinity? But the reason was of no importance. He would never again tempt by a prayer any terrible power. If the picture was to alter, it was to alter. That was all. Why inquire too closely into it?

For there would be a real pleasure in watching it. He would be able to follow his mind into its secret places. This portrait would be to him the most magical of mirrors. As it had revealed to him his own body, so it would reveal to him his own soul. And when winter came upòn it, he would still be standing where spring trembles on the verge of summer. When the blood crept from its face, and left behind a pallid mask of chalk with leaden eyes, he would keep the glamour of boyhood. Not one blossom of his loveliness would ever fade. Not one pulse of his life would ever weaken. Like the gods of the Greeks, he would be strong, and fleet, and joyous. What did it matter what happened to the coloured image on the canvas? He would be safe. That was everything.

He drew the screen back into its former place in front of the picture, smiling as he did so, and passed into his bedroom, where his valet was already waiting for him. An hour later he was at the Opera, and Lord Henry was leaning over his chair.

IX

As he was sitting at breakfast next morning, Basil Hall-ward was shown into the room.

"I am so glad I have found you, Dorian," he said, gravely. "I called last night, and they told me you were at the Opera. Of course I knew that was impossible. But I wish you had left word where you had really gone to. I passed a dreadful evening, half afraid that one tragedy might be followed by an-other. I think you might have telegraphed for me when you heard of it first. I read of it quite by chance in a late edition of *The Globe*, that I picked up at the club. I came here at once, and was miserable at not finding you. I can't tell you how heartbroken I am about the whole thing. I know what you must suffer. But where were you? Did you go down and see the girl's mother? For a moment I thought of following you there. They gave the address in the paper. Somewhere in the Euston Road, isn't it? But I was afraid of intruding upon a sorrow that I could not lighten. Poor woman! What a state she must be in! And her only child, too! What did she say about it all?"

"My dear Basil, how do I know?" murmured Dorian Gray, sipping some pale-yellow wine from a delicate gold-beaded bubble of Venetian glass, and looking dreadfully bored. "I was at the Opera. You should have come on there. I met Lady Gwendolen, Harry's sister, for the first time. We were in her box. She is perfectly charming; and Patti sang divinely. Don't talk about horrid subjects. If one doesn't talk about a thing, it has never happened. It is simply expression, as Harry says, that gives reality to things. I may mention that she was not the woman's only child. There is a son, a charming fellow, I believe. But he is not on the stage. He is a sailor, or something. And now, tell me about yourself and what you are painting."

"You went to the Opera?" said Hallward, speaking very slowly, and with a strained touch of pain in his voice. "You went to the Opera while Sibyl Vane was lying dead in some sordid lodging? You can talk to me of other women being charming, and of Patti singing divinely, before the girl you loved has even the quiet of a grave to sleep in? Why, man, there are horrors in store for that little white body of hers!"

"Stop, Basil! I won't hear it!" cried Dorian leaping to his feet. "You must not tell me about things. What is done is done. What is past is past."

"You call yesterday the past?"

"What has the actual lapse of time got to do with it? It is only shallow people who require years to get rid of an emotion. A man who is master of himself can end a sorrow as easily as he can invent a pleasure. I don't want to be at the mercy of my emotions. I want to use them, to enjoy them, and to dominate them."

"Dorian, this is horrible! Something has changed you completely. You look exactly the same wonderful boy who, day after day, used to come down to my studio to sit for his picture. But you were simple, natural, and affectionate then. You were the most unspoiled creature in the whole world. Now, I don't know what has come over you. You talk as if you had no heart, no pity in you. It is all Harry's influence. I see that."

The lad flushed up, and, going to the window, looked out

for a few moments on the green, flickering, sun-lashed garden. "I owe a great deal to Harry, Basil," he said, at last—"more than I owe to you. You only taught me to be vain."

"Well, I am punished for that, Dorian—or shall be some day."

"I don't know what you mean, Basil," he exclaimed, turning round. "I don't know what you want. What do you want?"

"I want the Dorian Gray I used to paint," said the artist, sadly.

"Basil," said the lad, going over to him, and putting his hand on his shoulder, "you have come too late. Yesterday when I heard that Sibyl Vane had killed herself—"

"Killed herself! Good heavens! is there no doubt about that?" cried Hallward, looking up at him with an expression of horror.

"My dear Basil! Surely you don't think it was a vulgar accident? Of course she killed herself."

The elder man buried his face in his hands. "How fearful," he muttered, and a shudder ran through him.

"No," said Dorian Gray, "there is nothing fearful about it. It is one of the great romantic tragedies of the age. As a rule, people who act lead the most commonplace lives. They are good husbands, or faithful wives, or something tedious. You know what I mean—middle-class virtue, and all that kind of thing. How different Sibyl was! She lived her finest tragedy. She was always a heroine. The last night she played—the night you saw her—she acted badly because she had known the reality of love. When she knew its unreality, she died, as Juliet might have died. She passed again into the sphere of art. There is something of the martyr about her. Her death has all the pathetic uselessness of martyrdom, all its wasted beauty. But, as I was saying, you must not think I have not suffered. If you had come in yesterday at a particular moment—about half-past five, perhaps, or a quarter to six—you would have found me in tears. Even Harry, who was here, who brought me the news, in fact, had no idea what I was going through. I suffered immensely. Then it passed away. I

cannot repeat an emotion. No one can, except sentimental-
ists. And you are awfully unjust, Basil. You come down here
to console me. That is charming of you. You find me consoled, and you are furious. How like a sympathetic person!
You remind me of a story Harry told me about a certain philanthropist who spent twenty years of his life in trying to get
some grievance redressed, or some unjust law altered—I forget exactly what it was. Finally he succeeded, and nothing
could exceed his disappointment. He had absolutely nothing
to do, almost died of ennui, and became a confirmed misan-
thrope. And besides, my dear old Basil, if you really want to
console me, teach me rather to forget what has happened, or
to see it from a proper artistic, point of view. Was it not Gau-
tier¹ who used to write about *la consolation des arts*? I remember picking up a little vellum-covered book in your
studio one day and chancing on that delightful phrase. Well,
I am not like that young man you told me of when we were
down at Marlow together, the young man who used to say
that yellow satin could console one for all the miseries of life.
I love beautiful things that one can touch and handle. Old
brocades, green bronzes, lacquer-work, carved ivories, exquisite surroundings, luxury, pomp, there is much to be got
from all these. But the artistic temperament that they create,
or at any rate reveal, is still more to me. To become the spectator of one's own life, as Harry says, is to escape the suffering
of life. I know you are surprised at my talking to you like this.
You have not realized how I have developed. I was a schoolboy when you knew me. I am a man now. I have new passions, new thoughts, new ideas. I am different, but you must
not like me less. I am changed, but you must always be my
friend. Of course I am very fond of Harry. But I know that
you are better than he is. You are not stronger—you are too
much afraid of life—but you are better. And how happy we
used to be together! Don't leave me, Basil, and don't quarrel
with me. I am what I am. There is nothing more to be said."

  The painter felt strangely moved. The lad was infinitely
dear to him, and his personality had been the great turning-

point in his art. He could not bear the idea of reproaching
him any more. After all, his indifference was probably merely
a mood that would pass away. There was so much in him that
was good, so much in him that was noble.

"Well, Dorian," he said, at length, with a sad smile, "I
won't speak to you again about this horrible thing, after today.
I only trust your name won't be mentioned in connection
with it. The inquest is to take place this afternoon. Have they
summoned you?"

Dorian shook his head, and a look of annoyance passed
over his face at the mention of the word "inquest." There was
something so crude and vulgar about everything of the kind.
"They don't know my name," he answered.

"But surely she did?"

"Only my Christian name, and that I am quite sure she
never mentioned to anyone. She told me once that they were
all rather curious to learn who I was, and that she invariably
told them my name was Prince Charming. It was pretty of
her. You must do me a drawing of Sibyl, Basil. I should like to
have something more of her than the memory of a few kisses
and some broken pathetic words."

"I will try and do something, Dorian, if it would please
you. But you must come and sit to me yourself again. I can't
get on without you."

"I can never sit to you again, Basil. It is impossible!" he exclaimed, starting back.

The painter stared at him. "My dear boy, what nonsense!"
he cried. "Do you mean to say you don't like what I did for
you? Where is it? Why have you pulled the screen in front of
it? Let me look at it. It is the best thing I have ever done. Do
take the screen away, Dorian. It is simply disgraceful of your
servant hiding my work like that. I felt the room looked different as I came in."

"My servant has nothing to do with it, Basil. You don't
imagine I let him arrange my room for me? He settles my
flowers for me sometimes—that is all. No, I did it myself.
The light was too strong on the portrait."

"Too strong! Surely not, my dear fellow? It is an admirable place for it. Let me see it." And Hallward walked towards the corner of the room.

A cry of terror broke from Dorian Gray's lips, and he rushed between the painter and the screen. "Basil," he said, looking very pale, "you must not look at it. I don't wish you to."

"Not look at my own work! you are not serious. Why shouldn't I look at it?" exclaimed Hallward, laughing.

"If you try to look at it, Basil, on my word of honour I will never speak to you again as long as I live. I am quite serious. I don't offer any explanation, and you are not to ask for any. But, remember, if you touch this screen, everything is over between us."

Hallward was thunderstruck. He looked at Dorian Gray in absolute amazement. He had never seen him like this before. The lad was actually pallid with rage. His hands were clenched, and the pupils of his eyes were like disks of blue fire. He was trembling all over.

"Dorian!"

"Don't speak!"

"But what is the matter? Of course I won't look at it if you don't want me to," he said, rather coldly, turning on his heel, and going over towards the window. "But, really, it seems rather absurd that I shouldn't see my own work, especially as I am going to exhibit it in Paris in the autumn. I shall probably have to give it another coat of varnish before that, so I must see it some day, and why not today?"

"To exhibit it! You want to exhibit it?" exclaimed Dorian Gray, a strange sense of terror creeping over him. Was the world going to be shown his secret? Were people to gape at the mystery of his life? That was impossible. Something—he did not know what—had to be done at once.

"Yes, I don't suppose you will object to that. Georges Petit is going to collect all my best pictures for a special exhibition in the Rue de Sèze, which will open the first week in October. The portrait will only be away a month. I should think you could easily spare it for that time. In fact, you are sure to be out of town. And if you keep it always behind a screen, you can't care much about it."

Dorian Gray passed his hand over his forehead. There were beads of perspiration there. He felt that he was on the brink of a horrible danger. "You told me a month ago that you would never exhibit it," he cried. "Why have you changed your mind? You people who go in for being consistent have just as many moods as others have. The only difference is that your moods are rather meaningless. You can't have forgotten that you assured me most solemnly that nothing in the world would induce you to send it to any exhibition. You told Harry exactly the same thing." He stopped suddenly, and a gleam of light came into his eyes. He remembered that Lord Henry had said to him once, half seriously and half in jest, "If you want to have a strange quarter of an hour, get Basil to tell you why he won't exhibit your picture. He told me why he wouldn't, and it was a revelation to me." Yes, perhaps, Basil, too, had his secret. He would ask him and try.

"Basil," he said, coming over quite close, and looking him straight in the face, "we have each of us a secret. Let me know yours, and I shall tell you mine. What was your reason for refusing to exhibit my picture"

The painter shuddered in spite of himself. "Dorian, if I told you, you might like me less than you do, and you would certainly laugh at me. I could not bear your doing either of those two things. If you wish me never to look at your picture again, I am content. I have always you to look at. If you wish the best work I have ever done to be hidden from the world, I am satisfied. Your friendship is dearer to me than any fame or reputation."

"No, Basil, you must tell me," insisted Dorian Gray. "I think I have a right to know." His feeling of terror had passed away, and curiosity had taken its place. He was determined to find out Basil Hallward's mystery.

"Let us sit down, Dorian," said the painter, looking troubled. "Let us sit down. And just answer me one question.

Have you noticed in the picture something curious?—something that probably at first did not strike you, but that revealed itself to you suddenly?"

"Basil!" cried the lad, clutching the arms of his chair with trembling hands, and gazing at him with wild, startled eyes.

"I see you did. Don't speak. Wait till you hear what I have to say. Dorian, from the moment I met you, your personality had the most extraordinary influence over me. I was dominated, soul, brain, and power by you. You became to me the visible incarnation of that unseen ideal whose memory haunts us artists like an exquisite dream. I worshipped you. I grew jealous of everyone to whom you spoke. I wanted to have you all to myself. I was only happy when I was with you. When you were away from me you were still present in my art. . . . Of course I never let you know anything about this. It would have been impossible. You would not have understood it. I hardly understood it myself. I only knew that I had seen perfection face to face, and that the world had become wonderful to my eyes—too wonderful, perhaps, for in such mad worships there is peril, the peril of losing them, no less than the peril of keeping them. . . . Weeks and weeks went on, and I grew more and more absorbed in you. Then came a new development. I had drawn you as Paris[2] in dainty armour, and as Adonis with huntsman's cloak and polished boar spear. Crowned with heavy lotus blossoms you had sat on the prow of Adrian's barge,[3] gazing across the green turbid Nile. You had leant over the still pool of some Greek woodland, and seen in the water's silent silver the marvel of your own face. And it had all been what art should be, unconscious, ideal, and remote. One day, a fatal day I sometimes think, I determined to paint a wonderful portrait of you as you actually are, not in the costume of dead ages, but in your own dress and in your own time. Whether it was the realism of the method or the mere wonder of your own personality, thus directly presented to me without mist or veil, I cannot tell. But I know that as I worked at it, every flake and film of colour seemed to me to reveal my secret. I grew afraid that others would know of my idolatry. I felt, Dorian, that I had told too much, that I had put too much of myself into it. Then it was that I resolved never to allow the picture to be exhibited. You were a little annoyed; but then you did not realize all that it meant to me. Harry, to whom I talked about it, laughed at me. But I did not mind that. When the picture was finished, and I sat alone with it, I felt that I was right. . . . Well, after a few days the thing left my studio, and as soon as I had got rid of the intolerable fascination of its presence it seemed to me that I had been foolish in imagining that I had seen anything in it, more than that you were extremely good-looking and that I could paint. Even now I cannot help feeling that it is a mistake to think that the passion one feels in creation is ever really shown in the work one creates. Art is always more abstract than we fancy. Form and colour tell us of form and colour—that is all. It often seems to me that art conceals the artist far more completely than it ever reveals him. And so when I got this offer from Paris I determined to make your portrait the principal thing in my exhibition. It never occurred to me that you would refuse. I see now that you were right. The picture cannot be shown. You must not be angry with me, Dorian, for what I have told you. As I said to Harry, once, you are made to be worshipped."

Dorian Gray drew a long breath. The colour came back to his cheeks, and a smile played about his lips. The peril was over. He was safe for the time. Yet he could not help feeling infinite pity for the painter who had just made this strange confession to him, and wondered if he himself would ever be so dominated by the personality of a friend. Lord Henry had the charm of being very dangerous. But that was all. He was too clever and too cynical to be really fond of. Would there ever be someone who would fill him with a strange idolatry? Was that one of the things that life had in store?

"It is extraordinary to me, Dorian," said Hallward, "that you should have seen this in the portrait. Did you really see it?"

"I saw something in it," he answered, "something that seemed to me very curious."

"Well, you don't mind my looking at the thing now?"

Dorian shook his head. "You must not ask me that, Basil. I could not possibly let you stand in front of that picture."

"You will some day, surely?"

"Never."

"Well, perhaps you are right. And now good-bye, Dorian. You have been the one person in my life who has really influenced my art. Whatever I have done that is good, I owe to you. Ah! you don't know what it cost me to tell you all that I have told you."

"My dear Basil," said Dorian, "what have you told me? Simply that you felt that you admired me too much. That is not even a compliment."

"It was not intended as a compliment. It was a confession. Now that I have made it, something seems to have gone out of me. Perhaps one should never put one's worship into words."

"It was a disappointing confession."

"Why, what did you expect, Dorian? You didn't see anything else in the picture, did you? There was nothing else to see?"

"No; there was nothing else to see. Why do you ask? But you mustn't talk about worship. It is foolish. You and I are friends, Basil, and we must always remain so."

"You have got Harry," said the painter, sadly.

"Oh, Harry?" cried the lad, with a ripple of laughter. "Harry spends his days in saying what is incredible, and his evenings in doing what is improbable. Just the sort of life I would like to lead. But still I don't think I would go to Harry if I were in trouble. I would sooner go to you, Basil."

"You will sit to me again?"

"Impossible!"

"You spoil my life as an artist by refusing, Dorian. No man came across two ideal things. Few come across one."

"I can't explain it to you, Basil, but I must never sit to you again. There is something fatal about a portrait. It has a life of its own. I will come and have tea with you. That will be just as pleasant."

"Pleasanter for you, I am afraid," murmured Hallward, regretfully. "And now good-bye. I am sorry you won't let me look at the picture once again. But that can't be helped. I quite understand what you feel about it."

As he left the room, Dorian Gray smiled to himself. Poor Basil! how little he knew of the true reason! And how strange it was that, instead of having been forced to reveal his own secret, he had succeeded, almost by chance, in wresting a secret from his friend! How much that strange confession explained to him! The painter's absurd fits of jealousy, his wild devotion, his extravagant panegyrics, his curious reticences—he understood them all now, and he felt sorry. There seemed to him to be something tragic in a friendship so coloured by romance.

He sighed, and touched the bell. The portrait must be hidden away at all costs. He could not run such a risk of discovery again. It had been mad of him to have allowed the thing to remain, even for an hour, in a room to which any of his friends had access.

X

WHEN HIS servant entered, he looked at him steadfastly, and wondered if he had thought of peering behind the screen. The man was quite impassive, and waited for his orders. Dorian lit a cigarette, and walked over to the glass and glanced into it. He could see the reflection of Victor's face perfectly. It was like a placid mask of servility. There was nothing to be afraid of, there. Yet he thought it best to be on his guard.

Speaking very slowly, he told him to tell the housekeeper that he wanted to see her, and then to go to the frame-maker and ask him to send two of his men round at once. It seemed to him that as the man left the room his eyes wandered in the direction of the screen. Or was that merely his own fancy?

After a few moments, in her black silk dress with old-fashioned thread mittens on her wrinkled hands, Mrs. Leaf bustled into the library. He asked her for the key of the schoolroom.

"The old schoolroom, Mr. Dorian?" she exclaimed. "Why, it is full of dust. I must get it arranged, and put straight before you go into it. It is not fit for you to see, sir. It is not, indeed."

127

"I don't want it put straight, Leaf. I only want the key."

"Well, sir, you'll be covered with cobwebs if you go into it. Why, it hasn't been opened for nearly five years, not since his lordship died."

He winced at the mention of his grandfather. He had hateful memories of him. "That does not matter," he answered. "I simply want to see the place—that is all. Give me the key."

"And here is the key, sir," said the old lady, going over the contents of her bunch with tremulously uncertain hands. "Here is the key. I'll have it off the bunch in a moment. But you don't think of living up there, sir, and you so comfortable here?"

"No, no," he cried, petulantly. "Thank you, Leaf. That will do."

She lingered for a few moments, and was garrulous over some detail of the household. He sighed, and told her to manage things as she thought best. She left the room, wreathed in smiles.

As the door closed, Dorian put the key in his pocket, and looked round the room. His eye fell on a large purple satin coverlet heavily embroidered with gold, a splendid piece of late seventeenth-century Venetian work that his grandfather had found in a convent near Bologna. Yes, that would serve to wrap the dreadful thing in. It had perhaps served often as a pall for the dead. Now it was to hide something that had a corruption of its own, worse than the corruption of death itself—something that would breed horrors and yet would never die. What the worm was to the corpse, his sins would be to the painted image on the canvas. They would mar its beauty, and eat away its grace. They would defile it, and make it shameful. And yet the thing would still live on. It would be always alive.

He shuddered, and for a moment he regretted that he had not told Basil the true reason why he had wished to hide the picture away. Basil would have helped him to resist Lord Henry's influence, and the still more poisonous influences that came from his own temperament. The love that he bore him—for it was really love—had nothing in it that was not noble and intellectual. It was not that mere physical admiration of beauty that is born of the senses, and that dies when the senses tire. It was such love as Michelangelo[1] had known, and Montaigne,[1] and Winckelmann,[1] and Shakespeare[1] himself. Yes, Basil could have saved him. But it was too late now. The past could always be annihilated. Regret, denial, or forgetfulness could do that. But the future was inevitable. There were passions in him that would find their terrible outlet, dreams that would make the shadow of their evil real.

He took up from the couch the great purple-and-gold texture that covered it, and, holding it in his hands, passed behind the screen. Was the face on the canvas viler than before? It seemed to him that it was unchanged; and yet his loathing of it was intensified. Gold hair, blue eyes, and rose-red lips—they all were there. It was simply the expression that had altered. That was horrible in its cruelty. Compared to what he saw in it of censure or rebuke, how shallow Basil's reproaches about Sibyl Vane had been!—how shallow, and of what little account! His own soul was looking out at him from the canvas and calling him to judgment. A look of pain came across him, and he flung the rich pall over the picture. As he did so, a knock came to the door. He passed out as his servant entered.

"The persons are here, Monsieur."

He felt that the man must be got rid of at once. He must not be allowed to know where the picture was being taken to. There was something sly about him, and he had thoughtful, treacherous eyes. Sitting down at the writing-table, he scribbled a note to Lord Henry, asking him to send him round something to read, and reminding him that they were to meet at eight-fifteen that evening.

"Wait for an answer," he said, handing it to him, "and show the men in here."

In two or three minutes there was another knock, and Mr. Hubbard himself, the celebrated frame-maker of South Audley Street, came in with a somewhat rough-looking young assistant. Mr. Hubbard was a florid, red-whiskered little man, whose admiration for art was considerably tempered by the inveterate impecuniosity of most of the artists who dealt with him. As a rule, he never left his shop. He waited for people to come to him. But he always made an exception in favour of Dorian Gray. There was something about Dorian that charmed everybody. It was a pleasure even to see him.

"What can I do for you, Mr. Gray?" he said, rubbing his fat freckled hands. "I thought I would do myself the honour of coming round in person. I have just got a beauty of a frame, sir. Picked it up at a sale. Came from Fonthill,[2] I believe. Admirably suited for a religious subject, Mr. Gray."

"I am so sorry you have given yourself the trouble of coming round, Mr. Hubbard. I shall certainly drop in and look at the frame—though I don't go in much at present for religious art—but today I only want a picture carried to the top of the house for me. It is rather heavy, so I thought I would ask you to lend me a couple of your men."

"No trouble at all, Mr. Gray. I am delighted to be of any service to you. Which is the work of art, sir?"

"This," replied Dorian, moving the screen back. "Can you move it, covering and all, just as it is? I don't want it to get scratched going upstairs."

"There will be no difficulty, sir," said the genial framemaker, beginning, with the aid of his assistant, to unhook the picture from the long brass chains by which it was suspended. "And, now, where shall we carry it to, Mr. Gray?"

"I will show you the way, Mr. Hubbard, if you will kindly follow me. Or perhaps you had better go in front. I am afraid it is right at the top of the house. We will go up by the front staircase, as it is wider."

He held the door open for them, and they passed out into the hall and began the ascent. The elaborate character of the frame had made the picture extremely bulky, and now and then, in spite of the obsequious protests of Mr. Hubbard, who had the true tradesman's spirited dislike of seeing a gentleman doing anything useful, Dorian put his hand to it so as to help them.

"Something of a load to carry, sir," gasped the little man, when they reached the top landing. And he wiped his shiny forehead.

"I am afraid it is rather heavy," murmured Dorian, as he unlocked the door that opened into the room that was to keep for him the curious secret of his life and hide his soul from the eyes of men.

He had not entered the place for more than four years—not, indeed, since he had used it first as a play-room when he was a child, and then as a study when he grew somewhat older. It was a large, well-proportioned room, which had been specially built by the last Lord Kelso for the use of the little grandson whom, for his strange likeness to his mother, and also for other reasons, he had always hated and desired to keep at a distance. It appeared to Dorian to have but little changed. There was the huge Italian *cassone*,[3] with its fantastically painted panels and its tarnished gilt mouldings, in which he had so often hidden himself as a boy. There the satinwood bookcase filled with his dog-eared schoolbooks. On the wall behind it was hanging the same ragged Flemish tapestry where a faded king and queen were playing chess in a garden, while a company of hawkers rode by, carrying hooded birds on their gauntleted wrists. How well he remembered it all! Every moment of his lonely childhood came back to him as he looked round. He recalled the stainless purity of his boyish life, and it seemed horrible to him that it was here the fatal portrait was to be hidden away. How little he had thought, in those dead days, of all that was in store for him!

But there was no other place in the house so secure from prying eyes as this. He had the key, and no one else could enter it. Beneath its purple pall, the face painted on the canvas could grow bestial, sodden, and unclean. What did it matter? No one could see it. He himself would not see it. Why should he watch the hideous corruption of his soul? He kept his youth—that was enough. And, besides, might not his nature grow finer, after all? There was no reason that the future should be so full of shame. Some love might come across his life, and purify him, and shield him from those sins that seemed to be already stirring in spirit and in flesh—those curious unpictured sins whose very mystery lent them their subtlety and their charm. Perhaps, some day, the cruel look would have passed away from the scarlet sensitive mouth, and he might show to the world Basil Hallward's masterpiece.

No, that was impossible. Hour by hour, and week by week, the thing upon the canvas was growing old. It might escape the hideousness of sin, but the hideousness of age was in store for it. The cheeks would become hollow or flaccid. Yellow crow's-feet would creep round the fading eyes and make them horrible. The hair would lose its brightness, the mouth would gape or droop, would be foolish or gross, as the mouths of old men are. There would be the wrinkled throat, the cold, blue-veined hands, the twisted body, that he remembered in the grandfather who had been so stern to him in his boyhood. The picture had to be concealed. There was no help for it.

"Bring it in, Mr. Hubbard, please," he said, wearily, turning round. "I am sorry I kept you so long. I was thinking of something else."

"Always glad to have a rest, Mr. Gray," answered the frame-maker, who was still gasping for breath. "Where shall we put it, sir?"

"Oh, anywhere. Here: this will do. I don't want to have it hung up. Just lean it against the wall. Thanks."

"Might one look at the work of art, sir?"

Dorian started. "It would not interest you, Mr. Hubbard," he said, keeping his eye on the man. He felt ready to leap upon him and fling him to the ground if he dared to lift the gorgeous hanging that concealed the secret of his life. "I shan't trouble you any more now. I am much obliged for your kindness in coming round."

"Not at all, not at all, Mr. Gray. Ever ready to do anything

for you, sir." And Mr. Hubbard tramped downstairs, followed
by the assistant, who glanced back at Dorian with a look of
shy wonder in his rough, uncomely face. He had never seen
anyone so marvellous.

When the sound of their footsteps had died away, Dorian
locked the door, and put the key in his pocket. He felt safe
now. No one would ever look upon the horrible thing. No eye
but his would ever see his shame.

On reaching the library he found that it was just after five
o'clock, and that the tea had been already brought up. On a
little table of dark perfumed wood thickly incrusted with
nacre,[4] a present from Lady Radley, his guardian's wife, a
pretty professional invalid, who had spent the preceding winter in Cairo, was lying a note from Lord Henry, and beside it
was a book bound in yellow paper, the cover slightly torn and
the edges soiled. A copy of the third edition of *The St. James's
Gazette* had been placed on the tea tray. It was evident that
Victor had returned. He wondered if he had met the men in
the hall as they were leaving the house, and had wormed out
of them what they had been doing. He would be sure to miss
the picture—had no doubt missed it already, while he had
been laying the tea-things. The screen had not been set back,
and a blank space was visible on the wall. Perhaps some night
he might find him creeping upstairs and trying to force the
door of the room. It was a horrible thing to have a spy in one's
house. He had heard of rich men who had been blackmailed
all their lives by some servant who had read a letter, or over-
heard a conversation, or picked up a card with an address, or
found beneath a pillow a withered flower or a shred of crum-
pled lace.

He sighed, and, having poured himself out some tea,
opened Lord Henry's note. It was simply to say that he sent
him round the evening paper, and a book that might interest
him, and that he would be at the club at eight-fifteen. He
opened *The St. James's* languidly, and looked through it. A
red pencil-mark on the fifth page caught his eye. It drew attention to the following paragraph:—

"INQUEST ON AN ACTRESS.—An inquest was held this morning at the Bell Tavern, Hoxton Road, by Mr. Danby, the District Coroner, on the body of Sibyl Vane, a young actress recently engaged at the Royal Theatre, Holborn. A verdict of death by misadventure was returned. Considerable sympathy was expressed for the mother of the deceased, who was greatly affected during the giving of her own evidence, and that of Dr. Birrell, who had made the post-mortem examination of the deceased."

He frowned, and, tearing the paper in two went across the room and flung the pieces away. How ugly it all was! And how horribly real ugliness made things! He felt a little annoyed with Lord Henry for having sent him the report. And it was certainly stupid of him to have marked it with red pencil. Victor might have read it. The man knew more than enough English for that.

Perhaps he had read it, and had begun to suspect something. And, yet, what did it matter? What had Dorian Gray to do with Sibyl Vane's death? There was nothing to fear. Dorian Gray had not killed her.

His eye fell on the yellow book[5] that Lord Henry had sent him. What was it, he wondered. He went towards the little pearl-coloured octagonal stand, that had always looked to him like the work of some strange Egyptian bees that wrought in silver, and taking up the volume, flung himself into an arm-chair, and began to turn over the leaves. After a few minutes he became absorbed. It was the strangest book that he had ever read. It seemed to him that in exquisite raiment, and to the delicate sound of flutes, the sins of the world were passing in dumb show before him. Things that he had dimly dreamed of were suddenly made real to him. Things of which he had never dreamed were gradually revealed.

It was a novel without a plot, and with only one character, being indeed, simply a psychological study of a certain young Parisian, who spent his life trying to realize in the nineteenth century all the passions and modes of thought that belonged to every century except his own, and to sum up, as it were, in himself the various moods through which the world-spirit had ever passed, loving for their mere artificiality those renunciations that men have unwisely called virtue, as much as those natural rebellions that wise men still call sin. The style in which it was written was that curious jewelled style, vivid and obscure at once, full of argot and of archaisms, of technical expressions and of elaborate paraphrases, that characterizes the work of some of the finest artists of the French school of *Symbolistes*.[6] There were in it metaphors as monstrous as orchids, and as subtle in colour. The life of the senses was described in the terms of mystical philosophy. One hardly knew at times whether one was reading the spiritual ecstasies of some mediaeval saint or the morbid confessions of a modern sinner. It was a poisonous book. The heavy odour of incense seemed to cling about its pages and to trouble the brain. The mere cadence of the sentences, the subtle monotony of their music, so full as it was of complex refrains and movements elaborately repeated, produced in the mind of the lad, as he passed from chapter to chapter, a form of reverie, a malady of dreaming, that made him unconscious of the falling day and creeping shadows.

Cloudless, and pierced by one solitary star, a copper-green sky gleamed through the windows. He read on by its wan light till he could read no more. Then, after his valet had reminded him several times of the lateness of the hour, he got up, and, going into the next room, placed the book on the little Florentine table that always stood at his bedside, and began to dress for dinner.

It was almost nine o'clock before he reached the club, where he found Lord Henry sitting alone, in the morning-room, looking very much bored.

"I am so sorry, Harry," he cried, "but really it is entirely your fault. That book you sent me so fascinated me that I forgot how the time was going."

"Yes; I thought you would like it," replied his host, rising from his chair.

"I didn't say I liked it, Harry. I said it fascinated me. There is a great difference."

"Ah, you have discovered that?" murmured Lord Henry. And they passed into the dining-room.

XI[1]

❧

FOR YEARS, Dorian Gray could not free himself from the influence of this book. Or perhaps it would be more accurate to say that he never sought to free himself from it. He procured from Paris no less than nine large-paper copies of the first edition, and had them bound in different colours, so that they might suit his various moods and the changing fancies of a nature over which he seemed, at times, to have almost entirely lost control. The hero, the wonderful young Parisian, in whom the romantic and the scientific temperaments were so strangely blended, became to him a kind of prefiguring type of himself. And, indeed, the whole book seemed to him to contain the story of his own life, written before he had lived it.

In one point he was more fortunate than the novel's fantastic hero. He never knew—never, indeed, had any cause to know—that somewhat grotesque dread of mirrors, and polished metal surfaces, and still water, which came upon the young Parisian so early in his life, and was occasioned by the sudden decay of a beauty that had once, apparently, been so remarkable. It was with an almost cruel joy—and perhaps in nearly every joy, as certainly in every pleasure, cruelty has its

137

place—that he used to read the latter part of the book, with its really tragic, if somewhat overemphasized, account of the sorrow and despair of one who had himself lost what in others, and in the world, he had most dearly valued.

For the wonderful beauty that had so fascinated Basil Hallward, and many others besides him, seemed never to leave him. Even those who had heard the most evil things against him, and from time to time strange rumours about his mode of life crept through London and became the chatter of the clubs, could not believe anything to his dishonour when they saw him. He had always the look of one who had kept himself unspotted from the world. Men who talked grossly became silent when Dorian Gray entered the room. There was something in the purity of his face that rebuked them. His mere presence seemed to recall to them the memory of the innocence that they had tarnished. They wondered how one so charming and graceful as he was could have escaped the stain of an age that was at once sordid and sensual.

Often, on returning home from one of those mysterious and prolonged absences that gave rise to such strange conjecture among those who were his friends, or thought that they were so, he himself would creep upstairs to the locked room, open the door with the key that never left him now, and stand, with a mirror, in front of the portrait that Basil Hallward had painted of him, looking now at the evil and aging face on the canvas, and now at the fair young face that laughed back at him from the polished glass. The very sharpness of the contrast used to quicken his sense of pleasure. He grew more and more enamoured of his own beauty, more and more interested in the corruption of his own soul. He would examine with minute care, and sometimes with a monstrous and terrible delight, the hideous lines that seared the wrinkling forehead or crawled around the heavy sensual mouth, wondering sometimes which were the more horrible, the signs of sin or the signs of age. He would place his white hands beside the coarse bloated hands of the picture, and smile. He mocked the misshapen body and the failing limbs.

There were moments, indeed, at night, when, lying sleepless in his own delicately scented chamber, or in the sordid room of the little ill-famed tavern near the Docks, which, under an assumed name, and in disguise, it was his habit to frequent, he would think of the ruin he had brought upon his soul, with a pity that was all the more poignant because it was purely selfish. But moments such as these were rare. That curiosity about life which Lord Henry had first stirred in him, as they sat together in the garden of their friend, seemed to increase with gratification. The more he knew, the more he desired to know. He had mad hungers that grew more ravenous as he fed them.

Yet he was not really reckless, at any rate in his relations to society. Once or twice every month during the winter, and on each Wednesday evening while the season lasted, he would throw open to the world his beautiful house and have the most celebrated musicians of the day to charm his guests with the wonders of their art. His little dinners, in the settling of which Lord Henry always assisted him, were noted as much for the careful selection and placing of those invited, as for the exquisite taste shown in the decoration of the table, with its subtle symphonic arrangements of exotic flowers, and embroidered cloths, and antique plate of gold and silver. Indeed, there were many, especially among the very young men, who saw, or fancied that they saw, in Dorian Gray the true realization of a type of which they had often dreamed in Eton or Oxford days, a type that was to combine something of the real culture of the scholar with all the grace and distinction and perfect manner of a citizen of the world. To them he seemed to be of the company of those whom Dante describes as having sought to "make themselves perfect by the worship of beauty." Like Gautier, he was one for whom "the visible world existed."

And certainly, to him life itself was the first, the greatest, of the arts, and for it all the other arts seemed to be but a preparation. Fashion, by which what is really fantastic becomes for a moment universal, and dandyism, which, in its own way, is an attempt to assert the absolute modernity of beauty, had, of course their fascination for him. His mode of dressing, and the particular styles that from time to time he affected, had their marked influence on the young exquisites of the Mayfair balls and Pall Mall Club windows, who copied him in everything that he did, and tried to reproduce the accidental charm of his graceful, though to him only half-serious, fopperies.

For, while he was but too ready to accept the position that was almost immediately offered to him on his coming of age, and found, indeed, a subtle pleasure in the thought that he might really become to the London of his own day what to imperial Neronian Rome the author of the *Satyricon* once had been, yet in his inmost heart he desired to be something more than a mere *arbiter elegantiarum,* to be consulted on the wearing of a jewel, or the knotting of a necktie, or the conduct of a cane. He sought to elaborate some new scheme of life that would have its reasoned philosophy and its ordered principles, and find in the spiritualizing of the senses its highest realization.

The worship of the senses has often, and with much justice, been decried, men feeling a natural instinct of terror about passions and sensations that seem stronger than themselves, and that they are conscious of sharing with the less highly organized forms of existence. But it appeared to Dorian Gray that the true nature of the senses had never been understood, and that they had remained savage and animal merely because the world had sought to starve them into submission or to kill them by pain, instead of aiming at making them elements of a new spirituality, of which a fine instinct for beauty was to be the dominant characteristic. As he looked back upon man moving through history, he was haunted by a feeling of loss. So much had been surrendered! and to such little purpose! There had been mad wilful rejections, monstrous forms of self-torture and self-denial, whose origin was fear, and whose result was a degradation infinitely more terrible than that fancied degradation from which, in their ignorance, they had sought to escape, nature, in her wonderful irony, driving out the anchorite to feed with the wild animals of the desert and giving to the hermit the beasts of the field as his companions.

Yes; there was to be, as Lord Henry had prophesied, a new Hedonism that was to re-create life, and to save it from that harsh, uncomely Puritanism that is having, in our own day, its curious revival. It was to have its service of the intellect, certainly; yet, it was never to accept any theory or system that would involve the sacrifice of any mode of passionate experience. Its aim, indeed, was to be experience itself, and not the fruits of experience, sweet or bitter as they might be. Of the asceticism that deadens the senses, as of the vulgar profligacy that dulls them, it was to know nothing. But it was to teach man to concentrate himself upon the moments of a life that is itself but a moment.

There are few of us who have not sometimes wakened before dawn, either after one of those dreamless nights that make us almost enamoured of death, or one of those nights of horror and misshapen joy, when through the chambers of the brain sweep phantoms more terrible than reality itself, and instinct with that vivid life that lurks in all grotesques, and that lends to Gothic art its enduring vitality, this art being, one might fancy, especially the art of those whose minds have been troubled with the malady of reverie. Gradually white fingers creep through the curtains, and they appear to tremble. In black fantastic shapes, dumb shadows crawl into the corners of the room, and crouch there. Outside, there is the stirring of birds among the leaves, or the sound of men going forth to their work, or the sigh and sob of the wind coming down from the hills, and wandering round the silent house, as though it feared to wake the sleepers, and yet must needs call forth sleep from her purple cave. Veil after veil of thin dusky gauze is lifted, and by degrees the forms and colours of things are restored to them, and we watch the dawn remaking the world in its antique pattern. The wan mirrors get back their mimic life. The flameless tapers stand where we had left them, and beside them lies the half-cut book that we had been studying, or the wired flower that we had worn at the ball, or the letter that we had been afraid to read, or that we had read too often. Nothing seems to us changed. Out of the unreal shadows of the night comes back the real life that we had known. We have to resume it where we had left off and there steals over us a terrible sense of the necessity for the continuance of energy in the same wearisome round of stereotyped habits, or a wild longing, it may be, that our eyelids might open some morning upon a world that had been re-fashioned anew in the darkness for our pleasure, a world in which things would have fresh shapes and colours, and be changed, or have other secrets, a world in which the past would have little or no place, or survive, at any rate, in no conscious form of obligation or regret, the remembrance even of joy having its bitterness, and the memories of pleasure their pain.

It was the creation of such worlds as these that seemed to Dorian Gray to be the true object, or amongst the true objects, of life; and in his search for sensations that would be at once new and delightful, and possess that element of strangeness that is so essential to romance, he would often adopt certain modes of thought that he knew to be really alien to his nature, abandon himself to their subtle influences, and then, having, as it were, caught their colour and satisfied his intellectual curiosity, leave them with that curious indifference that is not incompatible with a real ardour of temperament, and that indeed, according to certain modern psychologists, is often a condition of it.

It was rumoured of him once that he was about to join the Roman Catholic communion; and certainly the Roman ritual had always a great attraction for him. The daily sacrifice, more awful really than all the sacrifices of the antique world, stirred him as much by its superb rejection of the evidence of the senses as by the primitive simplicity of its elements and the eternal pathos of the human tragedy that it sought to symbolize. He loved to kneel down on the cold marble pavement, and watch the priest, in his stiff flowered dalmatic, slowly and with white hands moving aside the veil of the tabernacle, or raising aloft the jewelled lantern-shaped monstrance with that pallid wafer that at times, one would fain think, is indeed the *"panis caelestis,"* the bread of angels, or, robed in the garments of the Passion of Christ, breaking the Host into the chalice, and smiting his breast for his sins. The fuming censers, that the grave boys, in their lace and scarlet, tossed into the air like great gilt flowers, had their subtle fascination for him. As he passed out, he used to look with wonder at the black confessionals, and long to sit in the dim shadow of one of them and listen to men and women whispering through the worn grating the true story of their lives.

But he never fell into the error of arresting his intellectual development by any formal acceptance of creed or system, or of mistaking, for a house in which to live, an inn that is but suitable for the sojourn of a night, or for a few hours of a night in which there are no stars and the moon is in travail. Mysticism, with its marvellous power of making common things strange to us, and the subtle antinomianism[2] that always seems to accompany it, moved him for a season; and for a season he inclined to the materialistic doctrines of the *Darwinismus* movement in Germany, and found a curious pleasure in tracing the thoughts and passions of men to some pearly cell in the brain, or some white nerve in the body, delighting in the conception of the absolute dependence of the spirit on certain physical conditions, morbid or healthy, normal or diseased. Yet, as has been said of him before, no theory of life seemed to him to be of any importance compared with life itself. He felt keenly conscious of how barren all intellectual speculation is when separated from action and experiment. He knew that the senses, no less than the soul, have their spiritual mysteries to reveal.

And so he would now study perfumes, and the secrets of their manufacture, distilling heavily scented oils, and burning odorous gums from the East. He saw that there was no mood of the mind that had not its counterpart in the sensuous life, and set himself to discover their true relations, wondering what there was in frankincense that made one mystical, and in ambergris that stirred one's passions, and in violets that woke the memory of dead romances, and in musk that troubled the brain, and in champak that stained the imagination; and seeking often to elaborate a real psychology of perfumes, and to estimate the several influences of sweet-smelling roots, and scented pollen-laden flowers, of aromatic balms, and of dark and fragrant woods, of spikenard that sickens, of hovenia that makes men mad, and of aloes that are said to be able to expel melancholy from the soul.

At another time he devoted himself entirely to music, and in a long latticed room, with a vermilion-and-gold ceiling and walls of olive-green lacquer, he used to give curious concerts in which mad gypsies tore wild music from little zithers, or grave yellow-shawled Tunisians plucked at the strained strings of monstrous lutes, while grinning negroes beat monotonously upon copper drums, and, crouching upon scarlet mats, slim turbaned Indians blew through long pipes of reed or brass, and charmed, or feigned to charm, great hooded snakes and horrible horned adders. The harsh intervals and shrill discords of barbaric music stirred him at times when Schubert's grace, and Chopin's beautiful sorrows, and the mighty harmonies of Beethoven himself, fell unheeded on his ear. He collected together from all parts of the world the strangest instruments that could be found, either in the tombs of dead nations or among the few savage tribes that have survived contact with Western civilizations, and loved to touch and try them. He had the mysterious *juruparis* of the Rio Negro Indians, that women are not allowed to look at, and that even youths may not see till they have been subjected to fasting and scourging, and the earthen jars of the Peruvians that have the shrill cries of birds, and flutes of human bones such as Alfonso de Ovalle heard in Chili, and the sonorous green jaspers that are found near Cuzco and give forth a note of singular sweetness. He had painted gourds filled with pebbles that rattled when they were shaken; the long *clarin* of the Mexicans, into which the performer does not blow, but through which he inhales the air; the harsh *ture* of the Amazon tribes, that is sounded by the sentinels who sit all day long in high trees, and can be heard, it is said, at a distance of three leagues; the *teponaztli,* that has two vibrating tongues of wood, has her monsters, things of bestial shape and with an elastic gum obtained from the milky juice of plants; the *yotl* bells of the Aztecs, that are hung in clusters like grapes; and a huge cylindrical drum, covered with the skins of great serpents, like the one that Bernal Díaz saw when he went with Cortés into the Mexican temple, and of whose doleful sound he has left us so vivid a description. The fantastic character of these instruments fascinated him, and he felt a curious delight in the thought that art, like nature, has her monsters, things of bestial shape and with hideous voices. Yet, after some time, he wearied of them, and would sit in his box at the Opera, either alone or with Lord Henry, listening in rapt pleasure to *Tannhäuser,* and seeing in the prelude to that great work of art a presentation of the tragedy of his own soul.

On one occasion he took up the study of jewels, and appeared at a costume ball as Anne de Joyeuse, Admiral of France, in a dress covered with five hundred and sixty pearls. This taste enthralled him for years, and, indeed, may be said never to have left him. He would often spend a whole day settling and resettling in their cases the various stones that he had collected, such as the olive-green chrysoberyl that turns red by lamplight, the cymophane with its wire-like line of silver, the pistachio-coloured peridot, rose-pink and wine-yellow topazes, carbuncles of fiery scarlet with tremulous four-rayed stars, flame-red cinnamon-stones, orange and violet spinels, and amethysts with their alternate layers of ruby and sapphire. He loved the red gold of the sunstone, and the moonstone's pearly whiteness, and the broken rainbow of the milky opal. He procured from Amsterdam three emeralds of extraordinary size and richness of colour, and had a turquoise *de la vieille roche* that was the envy of all the connoisseurs.

He discovered wonderful stories, also, about jewels. In Alphonso's *Clericalis disciplina* a serpent was mentioned with eyes of real jacinth, and in the romantic history of Alexander, the Conqueror of Emathia was said to have found in the vale of Jordan, snakes "with collars of real emeralds growing on their backs." There was a gem in the brain of the dragon, Philostratus told us, and "by the exhibition of golden letters and a scarlet robe" the monster could be thrown into a magical sleep, and slain. According to the great alchemist, Pierre de Boniface, the diamond rendered a man invisible, and the agate of India made him eloquent. The cornelian appeased anger, and the hyacinth provoked sleep, and the amethyst drove away the fumes of wine. The garnet cast out demons, and the hydropicus deprived the moon of her colour. The selenite waxed and waned with the moon, and the meloceus, that discovers thieves, could be affected only by the blood of kids. Leonardus Camillus had seen a white stone taken from the brain of a newly killed toad, that was a certain antidote against poison. The bezoar, that was found in the heart of the Arabian deer, was a charm that could cure the plague. In the nests of Arabian birds was the aspilates, that, according to Democritus, kept the wearer from any danger by fire.

The King of Ceylon rode through his city with a large ruby in his hand, at the ceremony of his coronation. The gates of the palace of John the Priest were "made of sardius, with the horn of the horned snake inwrought, so that no man might bring poison within." Over the gable were "two golden apples, in which were two carbuncles," so that the gold might shine by day, and the carbuncles by night. In Lodge's strange romance *A Margarite of America* it was stated that in the chamber of the queen one could behold "all the chaste ladies of the world, inchased out of silver, looking through fair mirrors of chrysolites, carbuncles, sapphires, and greene emeraults." Marco Polo had seen the inhabitants of Zipangu place rose-coloured pearls in the mouths of the dead. A sea monster had been enamoured of the pearl that the diver brought to King Perozes, and had slain the thief, and mourned for seven moons over its loss. When the Huns lured the king into the great pit, he flung it away—Procopius tells the story—nor was it ever found again, though the Emperor Anastasius offered five hundred-weight of gold pieces for it. The King of Malabar had shown to a certain Venetian a rosary of three hundred and four pearls, one for every god that he worshipped.

When the Duke de Valentinois, son of Alexander VI, visited Louis XII of France, his horse was loaded with gold leaves, according to Brantôme, and his cap had double rows of rubies that threw out a great light. Charles of England had ridden in stirrups hung with four hundred and twenty-one diamonds. Richard II had a coat, valued at thirty thousand marks, which was covered with balas rubies. Hall described Henry VIII, on his way to the Tower previous to his coronation, as wearing "a jacket of raised gold, the placard embroidered with diamonds and other rich stones, and a great bauderike about his neck of large balasses." The favourites of James I wore ear-rings of emeralds set in gold filigrane. Edward II gave to Piers Gaveston a suit of red-gold armour studded with jacinths, a collar of gold roses set with turquoise-stones, and a skull-cap *parsemé* with pearls. Henry II wore jewelled gloves reaching to the elbow, and had a hawk-glove sewn with twelve rubies and fifty-two great orients. The ducal hat of Charles the Rash, the last Duke of Burgundy of his race, was hung with pear-shaped pearls, and studded with sapphires.

How exquisite life had once been! How gorgeous in its pomp and decoration! Even to read of the luxury of the dead was wonderful.

Then he turned his attention to embroideries, and to the tapestries that performed the office of frescoes in the chill rooms of the Northern nations of Europe. As he investigated the subject—and he always had an extraordinary faculty of becoming absolutely absorbed for the moment in whatever he took up—he was almost saddened by the reflection of the ruin that time brought on beautiful and wonderful things.

He, at any rate, had escaped that. Summer followed summer, and the yellow jonquils bloomed and died many times, and nights of horror repeated the story of their shame, but he was unchanged. No winter marred his face or stained his flower-like bloom. How different it was with material things! Where had they passed to? Where was the great crocus-coloured robe, on which the gods fought against the giants, that had been worked by brown girls for the pleasure of Athena? Where, the huge velarium that Nero had stretched across the Colosseum at Rome, that Titan sail of purple on which was represented the starry sky, and Apollo driving a chariot drawn by white gilt-reined steeds? He longed to see the curious table-napkins wrought for the Priest of the Sun, on which were displayed all the dainties and viands that could be wanted for a feast; the mortuary cloth of King Chilperic, with its three hundred golden bees; the fantastic robes that excited the indignation of the Bishop of Pontus, and were figured with "lions, panthers, bears, dogs, forests, rocks, hunters—all, in fact, that a painter can copy from nature"; and the coat that Charles of Orleans once wore, on the sleeves of which were embroidered the verses of a song beginning *"Madame, je suis tout joyeux,"* the musical accompaniment of the words being wrought in gold thread, and each note, of square shape in those days, formed with four pearls. He read of the room that was prepared at the palace at Reims for the use of Queen Joan of Burgundy, and was decorated with "thirteen hundred and twenty-one parrots, made in broidery, and blazoned with the king's arms, and five hundred and sixty-one butterflies, whose wings were similarly ornamented with the arms of the queen, the whole worked in gold." Catherine de' Medici had a mourning-bed made for her of black velvet powdered with crescents and suns. Its curtains were of damask, with leafy wreaths and garlands, figured upon a gold and silver ground, and fringed along the edges with broideries of pearls, and it stood in a room hung with rows of the queen's devices in cut black velvet upon cloth of silver. Louis XIV had gold embroidered caryatides fifteen feet high in his apartment. The state bed of Sobieski, King of Poland, was made of Smyrna gold brocade embroidered in turquoises with verses from the Koran. Its supports were of silver gilt, beautifully chased, and profusely set with enamelled and jewelled medallions. It had been taken from the Turkish camp before Vienna, and the standard of Mohammed had stood beneath the tremulous gilt of its canopy.

And so, for a whole year, he sought to accumulate the most exquisite specimens that he could find of textile and embroidered work, getting the dainty Delhi muslins, finely wrought with gold-thread palmates, and stitched over with iridescent beetles' wings; the Dacca gauzes, that from their transparency are known in the East as "woven air," and "running water," and "evening dew"; strange figured cloths from Java; elaborate yellow Chinese hangings; books bound in tawny satins or fair blue silks, and wrought with fleurs-de-lis, birds and images; veils of *lacis* worked in Hungary point; Sicilian brocades, and stiff Spanish velvets; Georgian work with its gilt coins, and Japanese *Foukousas* with their green-toned golds and their marvellously plumaged birds.

He had a special passion, also, for ecclesiastical vestments, as indeed he had for everything connected with the service of the Church. In the long cedar chests that lined the west gallery of his house he had stored away many rare and beautiful specimens of what is really the raiment of the Bride of Christ, who must wear purple and jewels and fine linen that she may hide the pallid macerated body that is worn by the suffering that she seeks for, and wounded by self-inflicted pain. He possessed a gorgeous cope of crimson silk and gold-thread damask, figured with a repeating pattern of golden pomegranates set in six-petalled formal blossoms, beyond which on either side was the pine-apple device wrought in seed-pearls. The orphreys were divided into panels representing scenes from the life of the Virgin, and the coronation of the Virgin was figured in coloured silks upon the hood. This was Italian work of the fifteenth century. Another cope was of green velvet, embroidered with heart-shaped groups of acanthus-leaves, from which spread long-stemmed white blossoms, the details of which were picked out with silver thread and coloured crystals. The morse bore a seraph's head in gold-thread raised work. The orphreys were woven in a diaper of red and gold silk, and were starred with medallions of many saints and martyrs, among whom was St. Sebastian. He had chasubles, also, of amber-coloured silk, and blue silk and gold brocade, and yellow silk damask and cloth of gold, figured with representations of the Passion and Crucifixion of Christ, and embroidered with lions and peacocks and other emblems; dalmatics of white satin and pink silk damask, decorated with tulips and dolphins and fleurs-de-lis; altar frontals of crimson velvet and blue linen; and many corporals, chalice-veils, and sudaria. In the mystic offices to which such things were put, there was something that quickened his imagination.

For these treasures, and everything that he collected in his lovely house, were to be to him means of forgetfulness, modes by which he could escape, for a season, from the fear that seemed to him at times to be almost too great to be borne. Upon the walls of the lonely locked room where he had spent so much of his boyhood, he had hung with his own hands the terrible portrait whose changing features showed him the real degradation of his life, and in front of it had draped the purple-and-gold pall as a curtain. For weeks he would not go there, would forget the hideous painted thing, and get back his light heart, his wonderful joyousness, his passionate absorption in mere existence. Then, suddenly, some night he would creep out of the house, go down to dreadful places near Blue Gate Fields, and stay there, day after day, until he was driven away. On his return he would sit in front of the picture, sometimes loathing it and himself, but filled, at other times, with that pride of individualism that is half the fascination of sin, and smiling, with secret pleasure, at the misshapen shadow that had to bear the burden that should have been his own.

After a few years he could not endure to be long out of

England, and gave up the villa that he had shared at Trouville with Lord Henry, as well as the little white walled-in house at Algiers where they had more than once spent the winter. He hated to be separated from the picture that was such a part of his life, and was also afraid that during his absence someone might gain access to the room, in spite of the elaborate bars that he had caused to be placed upon the door.

He was quite conscious that this would tell them nothing. It was true that the portrait still preserved, under all the foulness and ugliness of the face, its masked likeness to himself; but what could they learn from that? He would laugh at anyone who tried to taunt him. He had not painted it. What was it to him how vile and full of shame it looked? Even if he told them, would they believe it?

Yet he was afraid. Sometimes when he was down at his great house in Nottinghamshire, entertaining the fashionable young men of his own rank who were his chief companions, and astounding the county by the wanton luxury and gorgeous splendour of his mode of life, he would suddenly leave his guests and rush back to town to see that the door had not been tampered with, and that the picture was still there. What if it should be stolen? The mere thought made him cold with horror. Surely the world would know his secret then. Perhaps the world already suspected it.

For, while he fascinated many, there were not a few who distrusted him. He was very nearly blackballed at a West End club of which his birth and social position fully entitled him to become a member, and it was said that on one occasion, when he was brought by a friend into the smoking-room of the Churchill, the Duke of Berwick and another gentleman got up in a marked manner and went out. Curious stories became current about him after he had passed his twenty-fifth year. It was rumoured that he had been seen brawling with foreign sailors in a low den in the distant parts of Whitechapel, and that he consorted with thieves and coiners and knew the mysteries of their trade. His extraordinary absences became notorious, and, when he used to reappear again in society, men would whisper to each other in corners, or pass him with a sneer, or look at him with cold searching eyes, as though they were determined to discover his secret.

Of such insolences and attempted slights he, of course, took no notice, and in the opinion of most people his frank debonair manner, his charming boyish smile, and the infinite grace of that wonderful youth that seemed never to leave him, were in themselves a sufficient answer to the calumnies, for so they termed them, that were circulated about him. It was remarked, however, that some of those who had been most intimate with him appeared, after a time, to shun him. Women who had wildly adored him, and for his sake had braved all social censure and set convention at defiance, were seen to grow pallid with shame or horror if Dorian Gray entered the room.

Yet these whispered scandals only increased, in the eyes of many, his strange and dangerous charm. His great wealth was a certain element of security. Society, civilized society at least, is never very ready to believe anything to the detriment of those who are both rich and fascinating. It feels instinctively that manners are of more importance than morals, and, in its opinion, the highest respectability is of much less value than the possession of a good chef. And, after all, it is a very poor consolation to be told that the man who has given one a bad dinner, or poor wine, is irreproachable in his private life. Even the cardinal virtues cannot atone for half-cold entrées, as Lord Henry remarked once, in a discussion on the subject; and there is possibly a good deal to be said for his view. For the canons of good society are, or should be, the same as the canons of art. Form is absolutely essential to it. It should have the dignity of a ceremony, as well as its unreality, and should combine the insincere character of a romantic play with the wit and beauty that makes such plays delightful to us. Is insincerity such a terrible thing? I think not. It is merely a method by which we can multiply our personalities.

Such, at any rate, was Dorian Gray's opinion. He used to wonder at the shallow psychology of those who conceive the

Ego in man as a thing simple, permanent, reliable, and of one essence. To him, man was a being with myriad lives and myriad sensations, a complex multiform creature that bore within itself strange legacies of thought and passion, and whose very flesh was tainted with the monstrous maladies of the dead. He loved to stroll through the gaunt cold picture-gallery of his country house and look at the various portraits of those whose blood flowed in his veins. Here was Philip Herbert, described by Francis Osborne, in his *Memoires on the Reigns of Queen Elizabeth and King James,* as one who was "caressed by the Court for his handsome face, which kept him not long company." Was it young Herbert's life that he sometimes led? Had some strange poisonous germ crept from body to body till it had reached his own? Was it some dim sense of that ruined grace that had made him so suddenly, and almost without cause, give utterance, in Basil Hallward's studio, to the mad prayer that had so changed his life? Here, in gold-embroidered red doublet, jeweled surcoat, and gilt-edged ruff and wrist-bands, stood Sir Anthony Sherard, with his silver-and-black armour piled at his feet. What had this man's legacy been? Had the lover of Giovanna of Naples bequeathed him some inheritance of sin and shame? Were his own actions merely the dreams that the dead man had not dared to realize? Here, from the fading canvas, smiled Lady Elizabeth Devereux, in her gauze hood, pearl stomacher, and pink slashed sleeves. A flower was in her right hand, and her left clasped an enamelled collar of white and damask roses. On a table by her side lay a mandolin and an apple. There were large green rosettes upon her little pointed shoes. He knew her life, and the strange stories that were told about her lovers. Had he something of her temperament in him? These oval heavy-lidded eyes seemed to look curiously at him. What of George Willoughby, with his powdered hair and fantastic patches? How evil he looked! The face was saturnine and swarthy, and the sensual lips seemed to be twisted with disdain. Delicate lace ruffles fell over the lean yellow hands that were so overladen with rings. He had been a macaroni[3] of the eighteenth century, and the friend, in his youth, of Lord Ferrars. What of the second Lord Beckenham, the companion of the Prince Regent in his wildest days, and one of the witnesses at the secret marriage with Mrs. Fitzherbert? How proud and handsome he was, with his chestnut curls and insolent pose! What passions had he bequeathed? The world had looked upon him as infamous. He had led the orgies at Carlton House. The star of the Garter glittered upon his breast. Beside him hung the portrait of his wife, a pallid, thin-lipped woman in black. Her blood, also, stirred within him. How curious it all seemed! And his mother with her Lady Hamilton face, and her moist wine-dashed lips—he knew what he had got from her. He had got from her his beauty, and his passion for the beauty of others. She laughed at him in her loose bacchante dress. There were vine leaves in her hair. The purple spilled from the cup she was holding. The carnations of the painting had withered, but the eyes were still wonderful in their depth and brilliancy of colour. They seemed to follow him wherever he went.

Yet one had ancestors in literature, as well as in one's own race, nearer perhaps in type and temperament, many of them, and certainly with an influence of which one was more absolutely conscious. There were times when it appeared to Dorian Gray that the whole of history was merely the record of his own life, not as he had lived it in act and circumstance, but as his imagination had created it for him, as it had been in his brain and in his passions. He felt that he had known them all, those strange terrible figures that had passed across the stage of the world and made sin so marvellous and evil so full of subtlety. It seemed to him that in some mysterious way their lives had been his own.

The hero of the wonderful novel that had so influenced his life had himself known this curious fancy. In the seventh chapter he tells how, crowned with laurel, lest lightning might strike him, he had sat, as Tiberius, in a garden at Capri reading the shameful books of Elephantis, while dwarfs and peacocks strutted round him and the flute-player mocked the swinger of the censer; and, as Caligula, had caroused with the green-shirted jockeys in their stables, and supped in an ivory manger with a jewel-frontleted horse; and, as Domitian, had wandered through a corridor lined with marble mirrors, looking round with haggard eyes for the reflection of the dagger that was to end his days, and sick with that ennui, that terrible *taedium vitae*, that comes on those to whom life denies nothing: and had peered through a clear emerald at the red shambles of the Circus, and then, in a litter of pearl and purple drawn by silver-shod mules, been carried through the Street of Pomegranates to a House of Gold, and heard men cry on Nero Caesar as he passed by; and, as Elagabalus, had painted his face with colours, and plied the distaff among the women, and brought the Moon from Carthage, and given her in mystic marriage to the Sun.

Over and over again Dorian used to read this fantastic chapter, and the two chapters immediately following, in which, as in some curious tapestries or cunningly wrought enamels, were pictured the awful and beautiful forms of those whom vice and blood and weariness had made monstrous or mad: Filippo, Duke of Milan, who slew his wife, and painted her lips with a scarlet poison that her lover might suck death from the dead thing he fondled; Pietro Barbi, the Venetian, known as Paul the Second, who sought in his vanity to assume the title of Formosus, and whose tiara, valued at two hundred thousand florins, was bought at the price of a terrible sin; Gian Maria Visconti, who used hounds to chase living men, and whose murdered body was covered with roses by a harlot who had loved him; the Borgia on his white horse, with fratricide riding beside him, and his mantle stained with the blood of Perotto; Pietro Riario, the young Cardinal Archbishop of Florence, child and minion of Sixtus IV, whose beauty was equalled only by his debauchery, and who received Leonora of Aragon in a pavilion of white and crimson silk, filled with nymphs and centaurs, and gilded a boy that he might serve at the feast as Ganymede or Hylas; Ezzelin, whose melancholy could be cured only by the spectacle of death, and who had a passion for red blood, as other men have for red wine—the son of the Fiend, as was reported, and one who had cheated his father at dice when gambling with him for his own soul; Giambattista Cibo, who in mockery took the name of Innocent, and into whose torpid veins the blood of three lads was infused by a Jewish doctor; Sigismondo Malatesta, the lover of Isotta, and the lord of Rimini, whose effigy was burned at Rome as the enemy of God and man, who strangled Polyssena with a napkin, and gave poison to Ginevra d'Este in a cup of emerald, and in honour of a shameful passion built a pagan church for Christian worship; Charles VI, who had so wildly adored his brother's wife that a leper had warned him of the insanity that was coming on him, and who, when his brain had sickened and grown strange, could only be soothed by Saracen cards painted with the images of love and death and madness; and, in his trimmed jerkin and jewelled cap and acanthus-like curls, Grifonetto Baglioni, who slew Astorre with his bride, and Simonetto with his page, and whose comeliness was such that, as he lay dying in the yellow piazza of Perugia, those who had hated him could not choose but weep, and Atalanta, who had cursed him, blessed him.

There was a horrible fascination in them all. He saw them at night, and they troubled his imagination in the day. The Renaissance knew of strange manners of poisoning—poisoning by a helmet and a lighted torch, by an embroidered glove and a jewelled fan, by a gilded pomander and by an amber chain. Dorian Gray had been poisoned by a book. There were moments when he looked on evil simply as a mode through which he could realize his conception of the beautiful.

XII

IT WAS on the ninth of November, the eve of his own thirty-eighth birthday as he often remembered afterwards.

He was walking home about eleven o'clock from Lord Henry's, where he had been dining, and was wrapped in heavy furs, as the night was cold and foggy. At the corner of Grosvenor Square and South Audley Street a man passed him in the mist, walking very fast, and with the collar of his grey ulster turned up. He had a bag in his hand. Dorian recognized him. It was Basil Hallward. A strange sense of fear, for which he could not account, came over him. He made no sign of recognition, and went on quickly, in the direction of his own house.

But Hallward had seen him. Dorian heard him first stopping on the pavement and then hurrying after him. In a few moments his hand was on his arm.

"Dorian! What an extraordinary piece of luck! I have been waiting for you in your library ever since nine o'clock. Finally I took pity on your tired servant, and told him to go to bed, as he let me out. I am off to Paris by the midnight train, and I particularly wanted to see you before I left. I thought it was you, or rather your fur coat, as you passed me. But I wasn't quite sure. Didn't you recognize me?"

"In this fog, my dear Basil? Why, I can't even recognize Grosvenor Square. I believe my house is somewhere about here, but I don't feel at all certain about it. I am sorry you are going away, as I have not seen you for ages. But I suppose you will be back soon?"

"No; I am going to be out of England for six months. I intend to take a studio in Paris, and shut myself up till I have finished a great picture I have in my head. However, it wasn't about myself I wanted to talk. Here we are at your door. Let me come in for a moment. I have something to say to you."

"I shall be charmed. But won't you miss your train?" said Dorian Gray, languidly, as he passed up the steps and opened the door with his latch-key.

The lamplight struggled out through the fog, and Hallward looked at his watch. "I have heaps of time," he answered. "The train doesn't go till twelve-fifteen, and it is only just eleven. In fact, I was on my way to the club to look for you, when I met you. You see, I shan't have any delay about luggage, as I have sent on my heavy things. All I have with me is in this bag, and I can easily get to Victoria in twenty minutes."

Dorian looked at him and smiled. "What a way for a fashionable painter to travel! A Gladstone bag,[1] and an ulster![2] Come in, or the fog will get into the house. And mind you don't talk about anything serious. Nothing is serious nowadays. At least nothing should be."

Hallward shook his head, as he entered, and followed Dorian into the library. There was a bright wood fire blazing in the large open hearth. The lamps were lit, and an open Dutch silver spirit-case stood, with some siphons of soda-water and large cut-glass tumblers, on a little marqueterie[3] table.

"You see your servant made me quite at home, Dorian. He gave me everything I wanted, including your best gold-tipped cigarettes. He is a most hospitable creature. I like him much better than the Frenchman you used to have. What has become of the Frenchman, by the bye?"

Dorian shrugged his shoulders. "I believe he married Lady Radley's maid, and has established her in Paris as an English dressmaker. *Anglomanie*⁴ is very fashionable over there now, I hear. It seems silly of the French, doesn't it? But—do you know?—he was not at all a bad servant. I never liked him, but I had nothing to complain about. One often imagines things that are quite absurd. He was really very devoted to me, and seemed quite sorry when he went away. Have another brandy-and-soda? Or would you like hock-and-selzer?⁵ I always take hock-and-selzer myself. There is sure to be some in the next room."

"Thanks, I won't have anything more," said the painter, taking his cap and coat off, and throwing them on the bag that he had placed in the corner. "And now, my dear fellow, I want to speak to you seriously. Don't frown like that. You make it so much more difficult for me."

"What is it all about?" cried Dorian, in his petulant way, flinging himself down on the sofa. "I hope it is not about myself. I am tired of myself tonight. I should like to be somebody else."

"It is about yourself," answered Hallward, in his grave, deep voice, "and I must say it to you. I shall only keep you half an hour."

Dorian sighed, and lit a cigarette. "Half an hour!" he murmured.

"It is not much to ask of you, Dorian, and it is entirely for your own sake that I am speaking. I think it right that you should know that the most dreadful things are being said against you in London."

"I don't wish to know anything about them. I love scandals about other people, but scandals about myself don't interest me. They have not got the charm of novelty."

"They must interest you, Dorian. Every gentleman is interested in his good name. You don't want people to talk of you as something vile and degraded. Of course you have your position, and your wealth, and all that kind of thing. But position and wealth are not everything. Mind you, I don't believe these rumours at all. At least, I can't believe them when I see you. Sin is a thing that writes itself across a man's face. It cannot be concealed. People talk sometimes of secret vices. There are no such things. If a wretched man has a vice, it shows itself in the lines of his mouth, the droop of his eyelids, the moulding of his hands even. Somebody—I won't mention his name, but you know him—came to me last year to have his portrait done. I had never seen him before, and had never heard anything about him at the time, though I have heard a good deal since. He offered an extravagant price. I refused him. There was something in the shape of his fingers that I hated. I know now that I was quite right in what I fancied about him. His life is dreadful. But you, Dorian, with your pure, bright, innocent face, and your marvellous untroubled youth—I can't believe anything against you. And yet I see you very seldom, and you never come down to the studio now, and when I am away from you, and I hear all these hideous things that people are whispering about you, I don't know what to say. Why is it, Dorian, that a man like the Duke of Berwick leaves the room of a club when you enter it? Why is it that so many gentlemen in London will neither go to your house nor invite you to theirs? You used to be a friend of Lord Staveley. I met him at dinner last week. Your name happened to come up in conversation, in connection with the miniatures you have lent to the exhibition at the Dudley. Staveley curled his lip, and said that you might have the most artistic tastes, but that you were a man whom no pure-minded girl should be allowed to know, and whom no chaste woman should sit in the same room with. I reminded him that I was a friend of yours, and asked him what he meant. He told me. He told me right out before everybody. It was horrible! Why is your friendship so fatal to young men? There was that wretched boy in the Guards who committed suicide. You were his great friend. There was Sir Henry Ashton, who had to leave England, with a tarnished name. You and he were inseparable. What about Adrian Singleton, and his dreadful end? What about Lord Kent's only son, and his career? I met his father yesterday in St. James's Street. He seemed broken with shame and sorrow. What about the young Duke of Perth? What sort of life has he got now? What gentleman would associate with him?"

"Stop, Basil. You are talking about things of which you know nothing," said Dorian Gray, biting his lip, and with a note of infinite contempt in his voice. "You ask me why Berwick leaves a room when I enter it. It is because I know everything about his life, not because he knows anything about mine. With such blood as he has in his veins, how could his record be clean? You ask me about Henry Ashton and young Perth. Did I teach the one his vices, and the other his debauchery? If Kent's silly son takes his wife from the streets, what is that to me? If Adrian Singleton writes his friend's name across a bill, am I his keeper? I know how people chatter in England. The middle classes air their moral prejudices over their gross dinner-tables, and whisper about what they call the profligacies of their betters in order to try and pretend that they are in smart society, and on intimate terms with the people they slander. In this country it is enough for a man to have distinction and brains for every common tongue to wag against him. And what sort of lives do these people, who pose as being moral, lead themselves? My dear fellow, you forget that we are in the native land of the hypocrite."

"Dorian," cried Hallward, "that is not the question. England is bad enough I know, and English society is all wrong. That is the reason why I want you to be fine. You have not been fine. One has a right to judge of a man by the effect he has over his friends. Yours seem to lose all sense of honour, of goodness, of purity. You have filled them with a madness for pleasure. They have gone down into the depths. You led them there. Yes, you led them there, and yet you can smile, as you are smiling now. And there is worse behind. I know you and Harry are inseparable. Surely for that reason, if for none other, you should not have made his sister's name a by-word."

"Take care, Basil. You go too far."

"I must speak, and you must listen. You shall listen. When you met Lady Gwendolen, not a breath of scandal had ever touched her. Is there a single decent woman in London now who would drive with her in the Park? Why, even her children are not allowed to live with her. Then there are other stories—stories that you have been seen creeping at dawn out of dreadful houses and slinking in disguise into the foulest dens in London. Are they true? Can they be true? When I first heard them, I laughed. I hear them now, and they make me shudder. What about your country house, and the life that is led there? Dorian, you don't know what is said about you. I won't tell you that I don't want to preach to you. I remember Harry saying once that every man who turned himself into an amateur curate for the moment always began by saying that, and then proceeded to break his word. I do want to preach to you. I want you to lead such a life as will make the world respect you. I want you to have a clean name and a fair record. I want you to get rid of the dreadful people you associate with. Don't shrug your shoulders like that. Don't be so indifferent. You have a wonderful influence. Let it be for good, not for evil. They say that you corrupt everyone with whom you become intimate, and that it is quite sufficient for you to enter a house, for shame of some kind to follow after. I don't know whether it is so or not. How should I know? But it is said of you. I am told things that it seems impossible to doubt. Lord Gloucester was one of my greatest friends at Oxford. He showed me a letter that his wife had written to him when she was dying alone in her villa at Mentone.[6] Your name was implicated in the most terrible confession I ever read. I told him that it was absurd—that I knew you thoroughly, and that you were incapable of anything of the kind. Know you? I wonder do I know you? Before I could answer that, I should have to see your soul."

"To see my soul!" muttered Dorian Gray, starting up from the sofa and turning almost white from fear.

"Yes," answered Hallward, gravely, and with deep-toned

sorrow in his voice—"to see your soul. But only God can do that."

A bitter laugh of mockery broke from the lips of the younger man. "You shall see it yourself, tonight!" he cried, seizing a lamp from the table. "Come: it is your own handiwork. Why shouldn't you look at it? You can tell the world all about it afterwards, if you choose. Nobody would believe you. If they did believe you, they would like me all the better for it. I know the age better than you do, though you will prate about it so tediously. Come, I tell you. You have chattered enough about corruption. Now you shall look on it face to face."

There was the madness of pride in every word he uttered. He stamped his foot upon the ground in his boyish insolent manner. He felt a terrible joy at the thought that someone else was to share his secret, and that the man who had painted the portrait that was the origin of all his shame was to be burdened for the rest of his life with the hideous memory of what he had done.

"Yes," he continued, coming closer to him, and looking steadfastly into his stern eyes, "I shall show you my soul. You shall see the thing that you fancy only God can see."

Hallward started back. "This is blasphemy, Dorian!" he cried. "You must not say things like that. They are horrible, and they don't mean anything."

"You think so?" he laughed again.

"I know so. As for what I said to you tonight, I said it for your good. You know I have been always a staunch friend to you."

"Don't touch me. Finish what you have to say."

A twisted flash of pain shot across the painter's face. He paused for a moment, and a wild feeling of pity came over him. After all, what right had he to pry into the life of Dorian Gray? If he had done a tithe of what was rumoured about him, how much he must have suffered! Then he straightened himself up, and walked over to the fireplace, and stood there, looking at the burning logs with their frost-like ashes and their throbbing cores of flame.

"I am waiting, Basil," said the young man, in a hard, clear voice.

He turned round. "What I have to say is this," he cried. "You must give me some answer to these horrible charges that are made against you. If you tell me that they are absolutely untrue from beginning to end, I shall believe you. Deny them, Dorian, deny them! Can't you see what I am going through? My God! don't tell me that you are bad, and corrupt, and shameful."

Dorian Gray smiled. There was a curl of contempt in his lips. "Come upstairs, Basil," he said, quietly. "I keep a diary of my life from day to day, and it never leaves the room in which it is written. I shall show it to you if you come with me."

"I shall come with you, Dorian, if you wish it. I see I have missed my train. That makes no matter. I can go tomorrow. But don't ask me to read anything tonight. All I want is a plain answer to my question."

"That shall be given to you upstairs. I could not give it here. You will not have to read long."

XIII

H<small>E PASSED</small> out of the room, and began the ascent, Basil Hallward following close behind. They walked softly, as men do instinctively at night. The lamp cast fantastic shadows on the wall and staircase. A rising wind made some of the windows rattle.

When they reached the top landing, Dorian set the lamp down on the floor, and taking out the key turned it in the lock. "You insist on knowing, Basil?" he asked, in a low voice.

"Yes."

"I am delighted," he answered, smiling. Then he added, somewhat harshly, "You are the one man in the world who is entitled to know everything about me. You have had more to do with my life than you think": and, taking up the lamp, he opened the door and went in. A cold current of air passed them, and the light shot up for a moment in a flame of murky orange. He shuddered. "Shut the door behind you," he whispered, as he placed the lamp on the table.

Hallward glanced around him, with a puzzled expression. The room looked as if it had not been lived in for years. A faded Flemish tapestry, a curtained picture, an old Italian *cassone*, and an almost empty bookcase—that was all that it seemed to contain, besides a chair and a table. As Dorian Gray was lighting a half-burned candle that was standing on the mantelshelf, he saw that the whole place was covered with dust, and that the carpet was in holes. A mouse ran scuffling behind the wainscoting. There was a damp odour of mildew.

"So you think that it is only God who sees the soul, Basil? Draw that curtain back, and you will see mine."

The voice that spoke was cold and cruel. "You are mad, Dorian, or playing a part," muttered Hallward, frowning.

"You won't? Then I must do it myself," said the young man; and he tore the curtain from its rod, and flung it on the ground.

An exclamation of horror broke from the painter's lips as he saw in the dim light the hideous face on the canvas grinning at him. There was something in its expression that filled him with disgust and loathing. Good heavens! it was Dorian Gray's own face that he was looking at! The horror, whatever it was, had not yet entirely spoiled that marvellous beauty. There was still some gold in the thinning hair and some scarlet on the sensual mouth. The sodden eyes had kept something of the loveliness of their blue, the noble curves had not yet completely passed away from chiselled nostrils and from plastic throat. Yes; it was Dorian himself. But who had done it? He seemed to recognize his own brush-work, and the frame was his own design. The idea was monstrous, yet he felt afraid. He seized the lighted candle, and held it to the picture. In the left-hand corner was his own name, traced in long letters of bright vermilion.

It was some foul parody, some infamous, ignoble satire. He had never done that. Still, it was his own picture. He knew it, and he felt as if his blood had changed in a moment from fire to sluggish ice. His own picture! What did it mean? Why had it altered? He turned, and looked at Dorian Gray with the eyes of a sick man. His mouth twitched, and his parched tongue seemed unable to articulate. He passed his hand across his forehead. It was dank with clammy sweat.

The young man was leaning against the mantelshelf, watching him with that strange expression that one sees on the faces of those who are absorbed in a play when some great artist is acting. There was neither real sorrow in it nor real joy. There was simply the passion of the spectator, with perhaps a flicker of triumph in his eyes. He had taken the flower out of his coat, and was smelling it, or pretending to do so.

"What does this mean?" cried Hallward, at last. His own voice sounded shrill and curious in his ears.

"Years ago, when I was a boy," said Dorian Gray, crushing the flower in his hand, "you met me, flattered me, and taught me to be vain of my good looks. One day you introduced me to a friend of yours, who explained to me the wonder of youth, and you finished a portrait of me that revealed to me the wonder of beauty. In a mad moment, that, even now, I don't know whether I regret or not, I made a wish, perhaps you would call it a prayer. . . ."

"I remember it! Oh, how well I remember it! No! the thing is impossible. The room is damp. Mildew has got into the canvas. The paints I used had some wretched mineral poison in them. I tell you the thing is impossible."

"Ah, what is impossible?" murmured the young man, going over to the window, and leaning his forehead against the cold, mist-stained glass.

"You told me you had destroyed it."

"I was wrong. It has destroyed me."

"I don't believe it is my picture."

"Can't you see your ideal in it?" said Dorian, bitterly.

"My ideal, as you call it. . . ."

"As you called it."

"There was nothing evil in it, nothing shameful. You were to me such an ideal as I shall never meet again. This is the face of a satyr."[1]

"It is the face of my soul."

"Christ! what a thing I must have worshipped! It has the eyes of a devil."

"Each of us has heaven and hell in him,[2] Basil," cried Dorian, with a wild gesture of despair.

Hallward turned again to the portrait, and gazed at it. "My God! if it is true," he exclaimed, "and this is what you have done with your life, why, you must be worse even than those who talk against you fancy you to be!" He held the light up again to the canvas, and examined it. The surface seemed to be quite undisturbed, and as he had left it. It was from within, apparently, that the foulness and horror had come. Through some strange quickening of inner life the leprosies of sin were slowly eating the thing away. The rotting of a corpse in a watery grave was not so fearful.

His hand shook, and the candle fell from its socket on the floor, and lay there sputtering. He placed his foot on it and put it out. Then he flung himself into the rickety chair that was standing by the table and buried his face in his hands.

"Good God, Dorian, what a lesson! What an awful lesson!" There was no answer, but he could hear the young man sobbing at the window. "Pray, Dorian, pray," he murmured. "What is it that one was taught to say in one's boyhood? 'Lead us not into temptation. Forgive us our sins. Wash away our iniquities.' Let us say that together. The prayer of your pride has been answered. The prayer of your repentance will be answered also. I worshipped you too much. I am punished for it. You worshipped yourself too much. We are both punished."

Dorian Gray turned slowly around, and looked at him with tear-dimmed eyes. "It is too late, Basil," he faltered.

"It is never too late, Dorian. Let us kneel down and try if we cannot remember a prayer. Isn't there a verse somewhere, 'Though your sins be as scarlet, yet I will make them as white as snow'?"[3]

"Those words mean nothing to me now."

"Hush! don't say that. You have done enough evil in your life. My God! Don't you see that accursed thing leering at us?"

Dorian Gray glanced at the picture, and suddenly an uncontrollable feeling of hatred for Basil Hallward came over him, as though it had been suggested to him by the image on the canvas, whispered into his ear by those grinning lips. The mad passions of a hunted animal stirred within him, and he loathed the man who was seated at the table, more than in his whole life he had ever loathed anything. He glanced wildly around. Something glimmered on the top of the painted chest that faced him. His eye fell on it. He knew what it was. It was a knife that he had brought up some days before, to cut a piece of cord, and had forgotten to take away with him. He moved slowly towards it, passing Hallward as he did so. As soon as he got behind him, he seized it, and turned round. Hallward stirred in his chair as if he was going to rise. He rushed at him, and dug the knife into the great vein that is behind the ear, crushing the man's head down on the table, and stabbing again and again.

There was a stifled groan, and the horrible sound of some-one choking with blood. Three times the outstretched arms shot up convulsively, waving grotesque stiff-fingered hands in the air. He stabbed him twice more, but the man did not move. Something began to trickle on the floor. He waited for a moment, still pressing the head down. Then he threw the knife on the table, and listened.

He could hear nothing, but the drip, drip on the thread-bare carpet. He opened the door and went out on the land-ing. The house was absolutely quiet. No one was about. For a few seconds he stood bending over the balustrade, and peer-ing down into the black seething well of darkness. Then he took out the key and returned to the room, locking himself in as he did so.

The thing was still seated in the chair, straining over the table with bowed head, and humped back, and long fantastic arms. Had it not been for the red jagged tear in the neck, and the clotted black pool that was slowly widening on the table, one would have said that the man was simply asleep.

How quickly it had all been done! He felt strangely calm, and, walking over to the window, opened it, and stepped out on the balcony. The wind had blown the fog away, and the sky was like a monstrous peacock's tail, starred with myriads of golden eyes. He looked down, and saw the policeman going his rounds and flashing the long beam of his lantern on the doors of the silent houses. The crimson spot of a prowling hansom gleamed at the corner, and then vanished. A woman in a fluttering shawl was creeping slowly by the railings, staggering as she went. Now and then she stopped, and peered back. Once, she began to sing in a hoarse voice. The policeman strolled over and said something to her. She stumbled away, laughing. A bitter blast swept across the Square. The gas lamps flickered, and became blue, and the leafless trees shook their black iron branches to and fro. He shivered, and went back, closing the window behind him.

Having reached the door, he turned the key, and opened it. He did not even glance at the murdered man. He felt that the secret of the whole thing was not to realize the situation. The friend who had painted the fatal portrait to which all his misery had been due, had gone out of his life. That was enough.

Then he remembered the lamp. It was a rather curious one of Moorish workmanship, made of dull silver inlaid with arabesques of burnished steel, and studded with coarse turquoises. Perhaps it might be missed by his servant, and questions would be asked. He hesitated for a moment, then he turned back and took it from the table. He could not help seeing the dead thing. How still it was! How horribly white the long hands looked! It was like a dreadful wax image.

Having locked the door behind him, he crept quietly downstairs. The woodwork creaked, and seemed to cry out as if in pain. He stopped several times, and waited. No, everything was still. It was merely the sound of his own footsteps.

When he reached the library, he saw the bag and coat in the corner. They must be hidden away somewhere. He unlocked a secret press that was in the wainscoting, a press in which he kept his own curious disguises, and put them into it.

He could easily burn them afterwards. Then he pulled out his watch. It was twenty minutes to two.

He sat down and began to think. Every year—every month, almost—men were strangled in England for what he had done. There had been a madness of murder in the air. Some red star had come too close to the earth. . . . And yet what evidence was there against him? Basil Hallward had left the house at eleven. No one had seen him come in again. Most of the servants were at Selby Royal. His valet had gone to bed. . . . Paris? Yes. It was to Paris that Basil had gone, and by the midnight train, as he had intended. With his curious reserved habits, it would be months before any suspicions would be aroused. Months! Everything could be destroyed long before then.

A sudden thought struck him. He put on his fur coat and hat, and went out into the hall. There he paused, hearing the slow, heavy tread of the policeman on the pavement outside, and seeing the flash of the bull's-eye⁴ reflected in the window. He waited, and held his breath.

After a few moments he drew back the latch, and slipped out, shutting the door very gently behind him. Then he began ringing the bell. In about five minutes his valet appeared, half dressed, and looking very drowsy.

"I am sorry to have had to wake you up, Francis," he said, stepping in; "but I had forgotten my latch-key. What time is it?"

"Ten minutes past two, sir," answered the man, looking at the clock and blinking.

"Ten minutes past two? How horribly late! You must wake me at nine tomorrow. I have some work to do."

"All right, sir."

"Did anyone call this evening?"

"Mr. Hallward, sir. He stayed here till eleven, and then he went away to catch his train."

"Oh! I am sorry I didn't see him. Did he leave any message?"

"No, sir, except that he would write to you from Paris, if he did not find you at the club."

"That will do, Francis. Don't forget to call me at nine to-morrow."

"No, sir."

The man shambled down the passage in his slippers.

Dorian Gray threw his hat and coat upon the table, and passed into the library. For a quarter of an hour he walked up and down the room biting his lip, and thinking. Then he took down the Blue book[5] from one of the shelves, and began to turn over the leaves. "Alan Campbell, 152 Hertford Street, Mayfair." Yes; that was the man he wanted.

XIV

A T NINE O'CLOCK the next morning his servant came in with a cup of chocolate on a tray, and opened the shutters. Dorian was sleeping quite peacefully, lying on his right side, with one hand underneath his cheek. He looked like a boy who had been tired out with play, or study.

The man had to touch him twice on the shoulder before he woke, and as he opened his eyes a faint smile passed across his lips, as though he had been lost in some delightful dream. Yet he had not dreamed at all. His night had been untroubled by any images of pleasure or of pain. But youth smiles without any reason. It is one of its chiefest charms.

He turned round, and, leaning upon his elbow, began to sip his chocolate. The mellow November sun came streaming into the room. The sky was bright, and there was a genial warmth in the air. It was almost like a morning in May.

Gradually the events of the preceding night crept with silent blood-stained feet into his brain and reconstructed themselves there with terrible distinctness. He winced at the memory of all that he had suffered, and for a moment the same curious feeling of loathing for Basil Hallward, that had made him kill him as he sat in the chair, came back to him, and he grew cold with passion. The dead man was still sitting there, too, and in the sunlight now. How horrible that was! Such hideous things were for the darkness, not for the day.

He felt that if he brooded on what he had gone through he would sicken or grow mad. There were sins whose fascination was more in the memory than in the doing of them, strange triumphs that gratified the pride more than the passions, and gave to the intellect a quickened sense of joy, greater than any joy they brought, or could ever bring, to the senses. But this was not one of them. It was a thing to be driven out of the mind, to be drugged with poppies, to be strangled lest it might strangle one itself.

When the half-hour struck, he passed his hand across his forehead, and then got up hastily, and dressed himself with even more than his usual care, giving a good deal of attention to the choice of his necktie and scarf-pin, and changing his rings more than once. He spent a long time also over breakfast, tasting the various dishes, talking to his valet about some new liveries that he was thinking of getting made for the servants at Selby, and going through his correspondence. At some of the letters he smiled. Three of them bored him. One he read several times over, and then tore up with a slight look of annoyance in his face. "That awful thing, a woman's memory!" as Lord Henry had once said.

After he had drunk his cup of black coffee, he wiped his lips slowly with a napkin, motioned to his servant to wait, and going over to the table sat down and wrote two letters. One he put in his pocket, the other he handed to the valet.

"Take this round to 152 Hertford Street, Francis, and if Mr. Campbell is out of town, get his address."

As soon as he was alone, he lit a cigarette, and began sketching upon a piece of paper, drawing first flowers, and bits of architecture, and then human faces. Suddenly he remarked that every face that he drew seemed to have a fantastic likeness to Basil Hallward. He frowned, and, getting up, went over to the bookcase and took out a volume at haz-ard. He was determined that he would not think about what had happened until it became absolutely necessary that he should do so.

When he had stretched himself on the sofa, he looked at the title-page of the book. It was Gautier's *Emaux et Camées*,[1] Charpentier's[2] Japanese-paper edition, with the Jacquemart[3] etching. The binding was of citron-green leather, with a de-sign of gilt trellis-work and dotted pomegranates. It had been given to him by Adrian Singleton. As he turned over the pages his eye fell on the poem about the hand of Lacenaire,[4] the cold yellow hand *"du supplice encore mal lavée,"*[5] with its downy red hairs and its *"doigts de faune."*[6] He glanced at his own white taper fingers, shuddering slightly in spite of him-self, and passed on, till he came to those lovely stanzas upon Venice:

Sur une gamme chromatique,
    Le sein de perles ruisselant,
La Vénus de l'Adriatique
    Sort de l'eau son corps rose et blanc.

Les dômes, sur l'azur des ondes
    Suivant la phrase au pur contour,
S'enflent comme des gorges rondes
    Que soulève un soupir d'amour.

L'esquif aborde et me dépose,
    Jetant son amarre au pilier,
Devant une façade rose,
    Sur le marbre d'un escalier.

How exquisite they were! As one read them, one seemed to be floating down the green waterways of the pink and pearl city, seated in a black gondola with silver prow and trail-ing curtains. The mere lines looked to him like those straight lines of turquoise-blue that follow one as one pushes out to the Lido.[7] The sudden flashes of colour reminded him of the gleam of the opal-and-iris-throated birds that flutter round the tall honey-combed Campanile,[8] or stalk, with such stately grace, through the dim, dust-stained arcades. Leaning back with half-closed eyes, he kept saying over and over to himself:—

> Devant une façade rose,
>   Sur le marbre d'un escalier.

The whole of Venice was in those two lines. He remembered the autumn that he had passed there, and a wonderful love that had stirred him to mad, delightful follies. There was romance in every place. But Venice, like Oxford, had kept the background for romance, and, to the true romantic, background was everything, or almost everything. Basil had been with him part of the time, and had gone wild over Tintoretto.[9] Poor Basil! what a horrible way for a man to die!

He sighed, and took up the volume again, and tried to forget. He read of the swallows that fly in and out of the little café at Smyrna[10] where the Hadjis[11] sit counting their amber beads and the turbaned merchants smoke their long tasselled pipes and talk gravely to each other; he read of the Obelisk in the Place de la Concorde that weeps tears of granite in its lonely sunless exile, and longs to be back by the hot lotus-covered Nile, where there are Sphinxes, and rose-red ibises, and white vultures with gilded claws, and crocodiles, with small beryl eyes, that crawl over the green steaming mud; he began to brood over those verses which, drawing music from kiss-stained marble, tell of that curious statue that Gautier compares to a contralto voice, the *"monstre charmant"*[12] that couches in the porphyry-room of the Louvre.[13] But after a time the book fell from his hand. He grew nervous, and a horrible fit of terror came over him. What if Alan Campbell should be out of England? Days would elapse before he could come back. Perhaps he might refuse to come. What could he do then? Every moment was of vital importance.

They had been great friends once, five years before—almost inseparable, indeed. Then the intimacy had come suddenly to an end. When they met in society now, it was only Dorian Gray who smiled; Alan Campbell never did.

He was an extremely clever young man, though he had no real appreciation of the visible arts, and whatever little sense of the beauty of poetry he possessed he had gained entirely from Dorian. His dominant intellectual passion was for science. At Cambridge he had spent a great deal of his time working in the Laboratory, and had taken a good class[14] in the Natural Science Tripos[15] of his year. Indeed, he was still devoted to the study of chemistry, and had a laboratory of his own, in which he used to shut himself up all day long, greatly to the annoyance of his mother, who had set her heart on his standing for Parliament and had a vague idea that a chemist was a person who made up prescriptions. He was an excellent musician, however, as well, and played both the violin and the piano better than most amateurs. In fact, it was music that had first brought him and Dorian Gray together—music and that indefinable attraction that Dorian seemed to be able to exercise whenever he wished, and indeed exercised often without being conscious of it. They had met at Lady Berkshire's the night that Rubinstein[16] played there, and after that used to be always seen together at the Opera, and wherever good music was going on. For eighteen months their intimacy lasted. Campbell was always either at Selby Royal or in Grosvenor Square. To him, as to many others, Dorian Gray was the type of everything that is wonderful and fascinating in life. Whether or not a quarrel had taken place between them no one ever knew. But suddenly people remarked that they scarcely spoke when they met, and that Campbell seemed always to go away early from any party at which Dorian Gray was present. He had changed, too—was strangely melancholy at times, appeared almost to dislike hearing music, and would never himself play, giving as his excuse, when he was called upon, that he was so absorbed in science that he had no time left in which to practise. And this was certainly true. Every day he seemed to become more interested in biology, and his name appeared once or twice in some of the scientific reviews, in connection with certain curious experiments.

This was the man Dorian Gray was waiting for. Every second he kept glancing at the clock. As the minutes went by he became horribly agitated. At last he got up, and began to pace up and down the room, looking like a beautiful caged thing. He took long stealthy strides. His hands were curiously cold.

The suspense became unbearable. Time seemed to him to be crawling with feet of lead, while he by monstrous winds was being swept towards the jagged edge of some black cleft of precipice. He knew what was waiting for him there; saw it indeed, and, shuddering, crushed with dank hands his burning lids as though he would have robbed the very brain of sight, and driven the eyeballs back into their cave. It was useless. The brain had its own food on which it battened, and the imagination, made grotesque by terror, twisted and distorted as a living thing by pain, danced like some foul puppet on a stand, and grinned through moving masks. Then, suddenly, time stopped for him. Yes; that blind, slow-breathing thing crawled no more, and horrible thoughts, time being dead, raced nimbly on in front, and dragged a hideous future from its grave, and showed it to him. He stared at it. Its very horror made him stone.

At last the door opened, and his servant entered. He turned glazed eyes upon him.

"Mr. Campbell, sir," said the man.

A sigh of relief broke from his parched lips, and the colour came back to his cheeks.

"Ask him to come in at once, Francis." He felt that he was himself again. His mood of cowardice had passed away.

The man bowed, and retired. In a few moments Alan

Campbell walked in, looking very stern and rather pale, his pallor being intensified by his coal-black hair and dark eyebrows.

"Alan! this is kind of you. I thank you for coming."

"I had intended never to enter your house again, Gray. But you said it was a matter of life and death." His voice was hard and cold. He spoke with slow deliberation. There was a look of contempt in the steady searching gaze that he turned on Dorian. He kept his hands in the pockets of his Astrakhan[17] coat, and seemed not to have noticed the gesture with which he had been greeted.

"Yes; it is a matter of life and death, Alan, and to more than one person. Sit down."

Campbell took a chair by the table, and Dorian sat opposite to him. The two men's eyes met. In Dorian's there was infinite pity. He knew that what he was going to do was dreadful.

After a strained moment of silence, he leaned across and said, very quietly, but watching the effect of each word upon the face of him he had sent for, "Alan, in a locked room at the top of this house, a room to which nobody but myself has access, a dead man is seated at a table. He has been dead ten hours now. Don't stir, and don't look at me like that. Who the man is, why he died, how he died, are matters that do not concern you. What you have to do is this—"

"Stop, Gray. I don't want to know anything further. Whether what you have told me is true or not true, doesn't concern me. I entirely decline to be mixed up in your life. Keep your horrible secrets to yourself. They don't interest me any more."

"Alan, they will have to interest you. This one will have to interest you. I am awfully sorry for you, Alan. But I can't help myself. You are the one man who is able to save me. I am forced to bring you into the matter. I have no option. Alan, you are scientific. You know about chemistry, and things of that kind. You have made experiments. What you have got to do is to destroy the thing that is upstairs—to destroy it so that not a vestige of it will be left. Nobody saw this person come into the house. Indeed, at the present moment he is supposed to be in Paris. He will not be missed for months. When he is missed, there must be no trace of him found here. You, Alan, you must change him, and everything that belongs to him, into a handful of ashes that I may scatter in the air."

"You are mad, Dorian."

"Ah! I was waiting for you to call me Dorian."

"You are mad, I tell you—mad to imagine that I would raise a finger to help you, mad to make this monstrous confession. I will have nothing to do with this matter, whatever it is. Do you think I am going to peril my reputation for you? What is it to me what devil's work you are up to?"

"It was suicide, Alan."

"I am glad of that. But who drove him to it? You, I should fancy."

"Do you still refuse to do this for me?"

"Of course I refuse. I will have absolutely nothing to do with it. I don't care what shame comes on you. You deserve it all. I should not be sorry to see you disgraced, publicly disgraced. How dare you ask me, of all men in the world, to mix myself up in this horror? I should have thought you knew more about people's characters. Your friend Lord Henry Wotton can't have taught you much about psychology, whatever else he has taught you. Nothing will induce me to stir a step to help you. You have come to the wrong man. Go to some of your friends. Don't come to me."

"Alan, it was murder. I killed him. You don't know what he had made me suffer. Whatever my life is, he had more to do with the making or the marring of it than poor Harry has had. He may not have intended it, the result was the same."

"Murder! Good God, Dorian, is that what you have come to? I shall not inform upon you. It is not my business. Besides, without my stirring in the matter, you are certain to be arrested. Nobody ever commits a crime without doing something stupid. But I will have nothing to do with it."

"You must have something to do with it. Wait, wait a moment; listen to me. Only listen, Alan. All I ask of you is to perform a certain scientific experiment. You go to hospitals and dead-houses, and the horrors that you do there don't affect you. If in some hideous dissecting-room or fetid laboratory you found this man lying on a leaden table with red gutters scooped out in it for the blood to flow through, you would simply look upon him as an admirable subject. You would not turn a hair. You would not believe that you were doing anything wrong. On the contrary, you would probably feel that you were benefiting the human race, or increasing the sum of knowledge in the world, or gratifying intellectual curiosity, or something of that kind. What I want you to do is merely what you have often done before. Indeed, to destroy a body must be far less horrible than what you are accustomed to work at. And, remember, it is the only piece of evidence against me. If it is discovered, I am lost; and it is sure to be discovered unless you help me."

"I have no desire to help you. You forget that. I am simply indifferent to the whole thing. It has nothing to do with me."

"Alan, I entreat you. Think of the position I am in. Just before you came I almost fainted with terror. You may know terror yourself some day. No! don't think of that. Look at the matter purely from the scientific point of view. You don't inquire where the dead things on which you experiment come from. Don't inquire now. I have told you too much as it is. But I beg of you to do this. We were friends once, Alan."

"Don't speak about those days, Dorian: they are dead."

"The dead linger sometimes. The man upstairs will not go away. He is sitting at the table with bowed head and outstretched arms. Alan! Alan! if you don't come to my assistance I am ruined. Why, they will hang me, Alan! Don't you understand? They will hang me for what I have done."

"There is no good in prolonging this scene. I absolutely refuse to do anything in the matter. It is insane of you to ask me."

"You refuse?"

"Yes."

"I entreat you, Alan."

"It is useless."

The same look of pity came into Dorian Gray's eyes. Then he stretched out his hand, took a piece of paper, and wrote something on it. He read it over twice, folded it carefully, and pushed it across the table. Having done this, he got up, and went over to the window.

Campbell looked at him in surprise, and then took up the paper, and opened it. As he read it, his face became ghastly pale, and he fell back in his chair. A horrible sense of sickness came over him. He felt as if his heart was beating itself to death in some empty hollow.

After two or three minutes of terrible silence, Dorian turned round, and came and stood behind him, putting his hand upon his shoulder.

"I am so sorry for you, Alan," he murmured, "but you leave me no alternative. I have a letter written already. Here it is. You see the address. If you don't help me, I must send it. If you don't help me, I will send it. You know what the result will be. But you are going to help me. It is impossible for you to refuse now. I tried to spare you. You will do me the justice to admit that. You were stern, harsh, offensive. You treated me as no man has ever dared to treat me—no living man, at any rate. I bore it all. Now it is for me to dictate terms."

Campbell buried his face in his hands, and a shudder passed through him.

"Yes, it is my turn to dictate terms, Alan. You know what they are. The thing is quite simple. Come, don't work yourself into this fever. The thing has to be done. Face it, and do it."

A groan broke from Campbell's lips, and he shivered all over. The ticking of the clock on the mantelpiece seemed to him to be dividing time into separate atoms of agony, each of which was too terrible to be borne. He felt as if an iron ring was being slowly tightened round his forehead, as if the disgrace with which he was threatened had already come upon him. The hand upon his shoulder weighed like a band of lead. It was intolerable. It seemed to crush him.

"Come, Alan, you must decide at once."

"I cannot do it," he said, mechanically, as though words could alter things.

"You must. You have no choice. Don't delay."

He hesitated a moment. "Is there a fire in the room upstairs?"

"Yes, there is a gas-fire with asbestos."

"I shall have to go home and get some things from the laboratory."

"No, Alan, you must not leave the house. Write out on a sheet of note-paper what you want, and my servant will take a cab and bring the things back to you."

Campbell scrawled a few lines, blotted them, and addressed an envelope to his assistant. Dorian took the note up and read it carefully. Then he rang the bell, and gave it to his valet, with orders to return as soon as possible, and to bring the things with him.

As the hall door shut, Campbell started nervously, and, having got up from the chair, went over to the chimney-piece. He was shivering with a kind of ague.[18] For nearly twenty minutes, neither of the men spoke. A fly buzzed noisily about the room, and the ticking of the clock was like the beat of a hammer.

As the chime struck one, Campbell turned round, and, looking at Dorian Gray, saw that his eyes were filled with tears. There was something in the purity and refinement of that sad face that seemed to enrage him. "You are infamous, absolutely infamous!" he muttered.

"Hush, Alan: you have saved my life," said Dorian.

"Your life? Good heavens! what a life that is! You have gone from corruption to corruption, and you have culminated in crime. In doing what I am going to do, what you force me to do, it is not of your life that I am thinking."

"Ah, Alan," murmured Dorian, with a sigh, "I wish you had a thousandth part of the pity for me that I have for you." He turned away as he spoke, and stood looking out at the garden. Campbell made no answer.

After about ten minutes a knock came to the door, and the servant entered, carrying a large mahogany chest of chemicals, with a long coil of steel and platinum wire and two rather curiously shaped iron clamps.

"Shall I leave the things here, sir?" he asked Campbell.

"Yes," said Dorian. "And I am afraid, Francis, that I have another errand for you. What is the name of the man at Richmond who supplies Selby with orchids?"

"Harden, sir."

"Yes—Harden. You must go down to Richmond at once, see Harden personally, and tell him to send twice as many orchids as I ordered, and to have as few white ones as possible. In fact, I don't want any white ones. It is a lovely day, Francis, and Richmond is a very pretty place, otherwise I wouldn't bother you about it."

"No trouble, sir. At what time shall I be back?"

Dorian looked at Campbell. "How long will your experiment take, Alan?" he said, in a calm, indifferent voice. The presence of a third person in the room seemed to give him extraordinary courage.

Campbell frowned, and bit his lip. "It will take about five hours," he answered.

"It will be time enough, then, if you are back at half-past seven, Francis. Or stay: just leave my things out for dressing. You can have the evening to yourself. I am not dining at home, so I shall not want you."

"Thank you, sir," said the man, leaving the room.

"Now, Alan, there is not a moment to be lost. How heavy this chest is! I'll take it for you. You bring the other things." He spoke rapidly, and in an authoritative manner. Campbell felt dominated by him. They left the room together.

When they reached the top landing, Dorian took out the key and turned it in the lock. Then he stopped, and a troubled look came into his eyes. He shuddered. "I don't think I can go in, Alan," he murmured.

"It is nothing to me. I don't require you," said Campbell, coldly.

Dorian half opened the door. As he did so, he saw the face of his portrait leering in the sunlight. On the floor in front of it the torn curtain was lying. He remembered that the night before he had forgotten, for the first time in his life, to hide the fatal canvas, and was about to rush forward, when he drew back with a shudder.

What was that loathsome red dew that gleamed, wet and glistening, on one of the hands, as though the canvas had sweated blood? How horrible it was!—more horrible, it seemed to him for the moment, than the silent thing that he knew was stretched across the table, the thing whose grotesque misshapen shadow on the spotted carpet showed him that it had not stirred, but was still there, as he had left it.

He heaved a deep breath, opened the door a little wider, and with half-closed eyes and averted head walked quickly in, determined that he would not look even once upon the dead man. Then, stooping down, and taking up the gold-and-purple hanging, he flung it right over the picture.

There he stopped, feeling afraid to turn round, and his eyes fixed themselves on the intricacies of the pattern before him. He heard Campbell bringing in the heavy chest, and the irons, and the other things that he had required for his dreadful work. He began to wonder if he and Basil Hallward had ever met, and, if so, what they had thought of each other.

"Leave me now," said a stern voice behind him.

He turned and hurried out, just conscious that the dead man had been thrust back into the chair, and that Campbell was gazing into a glistening yellow face. As he was going downstairs he heard the key being turned in the lock.

It was long after seven when Campbell came back into the library. He was pale, but absolutely calm. "I have done what you asked me to do," he muttered. "And now, good-bye. Let us never see each other again."

"You have saved me from ruin, Alan. I cannot forget that," said Dorian, simply.

As soon as Campbell had left, he went upstairs. There was a horrible smell of nitric acid in the room. But the thing that had been sitting at the table was gone.

XV

❧

THAT EVENING, at eight-thirty, exquisitely dressed, and wearing a large buttonhole of Parma violets, Dorian Gray was ushered into Lady Narborough's drawing-room by bowing servants. His forehead was throbbing with maddened nerves, and he felt wildly excited, but his manner as he bent over his hostess's hand was as easy and graceful as ever. Perhaps one never seems so much at one's ease as when one has to play a part. Certainly no one looking at Dorian Gray that night could have believed that he had passed through a tragedy as horrible as any tragedy of our age. Those finely shaped fingers could never have clutched a knife of sin, nor those smiling lips have cried out on God and goodness. He himself could not help wondering at the calm of his demeanour, and for a moment felt keenly the terrible pleasure of a double life.

It was a small party, got up rather in a hurry by Lady Narborough, who was a very clever woman, with what Lord Henry used to describe as the remains of really remarkable ugliness. She had proved an excellent wife to one of our most tedious ambassadors, and having buried her husband properly in a marble mausoleum, which she had herself designed, and

married off her daughters to some rich, rather elderly men,
she devoted herself now to the pleasures of French fiction,
French cookery, and French *esprit* when she could get it.

Dorian was one of her especial favourites, and she always
told him that she was extremely glad she had not met him in
early life. "I know, my dear, I should have fallen madly in love
with you," she used to say, "and thrown my bonnet right over
the mills for your sake. It is most fortunate that you were not
thought of at the time. As it was, our bonnets were so unbecoming, and the mills were so occupied in trying to raise the
wind, that I never had even a flirtation with anybody. However, that was all Narborough's fault. He was dreadfully short-
sighted, and there is no pleasure in taking in a husband who
never sees anything."

Her guests this evening were rather tedious. The fact was,
as she explained to Dorian, behind a very shabby fan, one of
her married daughters had come up quite suddenly to stay
with her, and, to make matters worse, had actually brought
her husband with her. "I think it is most unkind of her, my
dear," she whispered. "Of course I go and stay with them
every summer after I come from Homburg, but then an old
woman like me must have fresh air sometimes, and besides, I
really wake them up. You don't know what an existence they
lead down there. It is pure unadulterated country life. They
get up early, because they have so much to do, and go to bed
early because they have so little to think about. There has not
been a scandal in the neighbourhood since the time of
Queen Elizabeth,[1] and consequently they all fall asleep after
dinner. You shan't sit next to either of them. You shall sit by
me, and amuse me."

Dorian murmured a graceful compliment, and looked
round the room. Yes, it was certainly a tedious party. Two of
the people he had never seen before, and the others consisted of Ernest Harrowden, one of those middle-aged mediocrities so common in London clubs who have no enemies,
but are thoroughly disliked by their friends; Lady Roxton, an
overdressed woman of forty-seven, with a hooked nose, who

was always trying to get herself compromised, but was so peculiarly plain that to her great disappointment no one would ever believe anything against her; Mrs. Erlynne, a pushing nobody, with a delightful lisp, and Venetian-red hair; Lady Alice Chapman, his hostess's daughter, a dowdy dull girl, with one of those characteristic British faces that, once seen, are never remembered; and her husband, a red-cheeked, white-whiskered creature who, like so many of his class, was under the impression that inordinate joviality can atone for an entire lack of ideas.

He was rather sorry he had come, till Lady Narborough, looking at the great ormolu[2] gilt clock that sprawled in gaudy curves on the mauve-draped mantelshelf, exclaimed: "How horrid of Henry Wotton to be so late! I sent round to him this morning on chance, and he promised faithfully not to disappoint me."

It was some consolation that Harry was to be there, and when the door opened and he heard his slow musical voice lending charm to some insincere apology, he ceased to feel bored.

But at dinner he could not eat anything. Plate after plate went away untasted. Lady Narborough kept scolding him for what she called "an insult to poor Adolphe, who invented the menu specially for you," and now and then Lord Henry looked across at him, wondering at his silence and abstracted manner. From time to time the butler filled his glass with champagne. He drank eagerly, and his thirst seemed to increase.

"Dorian," said Lord Henry, at last, as the *chaudfroid*[3] was being handed round, "what is the matter with you tonight? You are quite out of sorts."

"I believe he is in love," cried Lady Narborough, "and that he is afraid to tell me for fear I should be jealous. He is quite right. I certainly should."

"Dear Lady Narborough," murmured Dorian, smiling, "I have not been in love for a whole week—not, in fact, since Madame de Ferrol left town."

"How you men can fall in love with that woman!" exclaimed the old lady. "I really cannot understand it."

"It is simply because she remembers you when you were a little girl, Lady Narborough," said Lord Henry. "She is the one link between us and your short frocks."

"She does not remember my short frocks at all, Lord Henry. But I remember her very well at Vienna thirty years ago, and how *décolletée*[4] she was then."

"She is still *décolletée*," he answered, taking an olive in his long fingers; "and when she is in a very smart gown she looks like an *édition de luxe*[5] of a bad French novel. She is really wonderful, and full of surprises. Her capacity for family affection is extraordinary. When her third husband died, her hair turned quite gold from grief."

"How can you, Harry!" cried Dorian.

"It is a most romantic explanation," laughed the hostess. "But her third husband, Lord Henry! You don't mean to say Ferrol is the fourth?"

"Certainly, Lady Narborough."

"I don't believe a word of it."

"Well, ask Mr. Gray. He is one of her most intimate friends."

"Is it true, Mr. Gray?"

"She assures me so, Lady Narborough," said Dorian. "I asked her whether, like Marguerite de Navarre,[6] she had their hearts embalmed and hung at her girdle. She told me she didn't, because none of them had had any hearts at all."

"Four husbands! Upon my word that is *trop de zèle*."[7]

"*Trop d'audace*,[8] I tell her," said Dorian.

"Oh! she is audacious enough for anything, my dear. And what is Ferrol like? I don't know him."

"The husbands of very beautiful women belong to the criminal classes," said Lord Henry, sipping his wine.

Lady Narborough hit him with her fan. "Lord Henry, I am not at all surprised that the world says that you are extremely wicked."

"But what world says that?" asked Lord Henry, elevating

his eyebrows. "It can only be the next world. This world and I are on excellent terms."

"Everybody I know says you are very wicked," cried the old lady, shaking her head.

Lord Henry looked serious for some moments. "It is perfectly monstrous," he said, at last, "the way people go about nowadays saying things against one behind one's back that are absolutely and entirely true."

"Isn't he incorrigible?" cried Dorian, leaning forward in his chair.

"I hope so," said his hostess, laughing. "But really if you all worship Madame de Ferrol in this ridiculous way, I shall have to marry again so as to be in the fashion."

"You will never marry again, Lady Narborough," broke in Lord Henry. "You were far too happy. When a woman marries again it is because she detested her first husband. When a man marries again, it is because he adored his first wife. Women try their luck; men risk theirs."

"Narborough wasn't perfect," cried the old lady.

"If he had been, you would not have loved him, my dear lady," was the rejoinder. "Women love us for our defects. If we have enough of them they will forgive us everything, even our intellects. You will never ask me to dinner again, after saying this, I am afraid, Lady Narborough; but it is quite true."

"Of course it is true, Lord Henry. If we women did not love you for your defects, where would you all be? Not one of you would ever be married. You would be a set of unfortunate bachelors. Not, however, that that would alter you much. Nowadays all the married men live like bachelors, and all the bachelors like married men."

"Fin de siècle,"[9] murmured Lord Henry.

"Fin du globe,"[10] answered his hostess.

"I wish it were *fin du globe,"* said Dorian, with a sigh. "Life is a great disappointment."

"Ah, my dear," cried Lady Narborough, putting on her gloves, "don't tell me that you have exhausted life. When a man says that one knows that life has exhausted him. Lord Henry is very wicked, and I sometimes wish that I had been; but you are made to be good—you look so good. I must find you a nice wife. Lord Henry, don't you think that Mr. Gray should get married?"

"I am always telling him so, Lady Narborough," said Lord Henry, with a bow.

"Well, we must look out for a suitable match for him. I shall go through Debrett[11] carefully tonight, and draw out a list of all the eligible young ladies."

"With their ages, Lady Narborough?" asked Dorian.

"Of course, with their ages, slightly edited. But nothing must be done in a hurry. I want it to be what *The Morning Post* calls a suitable alliance, and I want you both to be happy."

"What nonsense people talk about happy marriages!" exclaimed Lord Henry. "A man can be happy with any woman, as long as he does not love her."

"Ah! what a cynic you are!" cried the old lady, pushing back her chair, and nodding to Lady Ruxton. "You must come and dine with me soon again. You are really an admirable tonic, much better than what Sir Andrew prescribes for me. You must tell me what people you would like to meet, though. I want it to be a delightful gathering."

"I like men who have a future, and women who have a past," he answered. "Or do you think that would make it a petticoat party?"

"I fear so," she said, laughing, as she stood up. "A thousand pardons, my dear Lady Ruxton," she added, "I didn't see you hadn't finished your cigarette."

"Never mind, Lady Narborough. I smoke a great deal too much. I am going to limit myself, for the future."

"Pray don't, Lady Ruxton," said Lord Henry. "Moderation is a fatal thing. Enough is as bad as a meal. More than enough is as good as a feast."

Lady Ruxton glanced at him curiously. "You must come

and explain that to me some afternoon, Lord Henry. It sounds a fascinating theory," she murmured, as she swept out of the room.

"Now, mind you don't stay too long over your politics and scandal," cried Lady Narborough from the door. "If you do, we are sure to squabble upstairs."

The men laughed, and Mr. Chapman got up solemnly from the foot of the table and came up to the top. Dorian Gray changed his seat, and went and sat by Lord Henry. Mr. Chapman began to talk in a loud voice about the situation in the House of Commons. He guffawed at his adversaries. The word *doctrinaire*[12]—a word full of terror to the British mind—reappeared from time to time between his explosions. An alliterative prefix served as an ornament of oratory. He hoisted the Union Jack[13] on the pinnacles of thought. The inherited stupidity of the race—sound English common sense he jovially termed it—was shown to be the proper bulwark for society.

A smile curved Lord Henry's lips, and he turned round and looked at Dorian.

"Are you better, my dear fellow?" he asked. "You seemed rather out of sorts at dinner."

"I am quite well, Harry. I am tired. That is all."

"You were charming last night. The little Duchess is quite devoted to you. She tells me she is going down to Selby."

"She has promised to come on the twentieth."

"Is Monmouth to be there too?"

"Oh, yes, Harry."

"He bores me dreadfully, almost as much as he bores her. She is very clever, too clever for a woman. She lacks the indefinable charm of weakness. It is the feet of clay that makes the gold of the image precious. Her feet are very pretty, but they are not feet of clay. White porcelain feet, if you like. They have been through the fire, and what fire does not destroy, it hardens. She has had experiences."

"How long has she been married?" asked Dorian.

"An eternity, she tells me. I believe, according to the peerage, it is ten years, but ten years with Monmouth must have been like eternity, with time thrown in. Who else is coming?"

"Oh, the Willoughbys, Lord Rugby and his wife, our hostess, Geoffrey Clouston, the usual set. I have asked Lord Grotrian."

"I like him," said Lord Henry. "A great many people don't, but I find him charming. He atones for being occasionally somewhat overdressed, by being always absolutely overeducated. He is a very modern type."

"I don't know if he will be able to come, Harry. He may have to go to Monte Carlo with his father."

"Ah! what a nuisance people's people are! Try and make him come. By the way, Dorian, you ran off very early last night. You left before eleven. What did you do afterwards? Did you go straight home?"

Dorian glanced at him hurriedly, and frowned. "No, Harry," he said at last, "I did not get home till nearly three."

"Did you go to the club?"

"Yes," he answered. Then he bit his lip. "No, I don't mean that. I didn't go to the club. I walked about. I forget what I did. . . . How inquisitive you are, Harry! You always want to know what one has been doing. I always want to forget what I have been doing. I came in at half-past two, if you wish to know the exact time. I had left my latch-key at home, and my servant had to let me in. If you want any corroborative evidence on the subject you can ask him."

Lord Henry shrugged his shoulders. "My dear fellow, as if I cared! Let us go up to the drawing-room. No sherry, thank you, Mr. Chapman. Something has happened to you, Dorian. Tell me what it is. You are not yourself tonight."

"Don't mind me, Harry. I am irritable, and out of temper. I shall come round and see you tomorrow, or next day. Make my excuses to Lady Narborough. I shan't go upstairs. I shall go home. I must go home."

"All right, Dorian. I dare say I shall see you tomorrow at teatime. The Duchess is coming."

"I will try to be there, Harry," he said, leaving the room. As he drove back to his own house he was conscious that the sense of terror he thought he had strangled had come back to him. Lord Henry's casual questioning had made him lose his nerve for the moment, and he wanted his nerve still. Things that were dangerous had to be destroyed. He winced. He hated the idea of even touching them.

Yet it had to be done. He realized that, and when he had locked the door of his library, he opened the secret press into which he had thrust Basil Hallward's coat and bag. A huge fire was blazing. He piled another log on it. The smell of the singeing clothes and burning leather was horrible. It took him three-quarters of an hour to consume everything. At the end he felt faint and sick, and having lit some Algerian pastilles[14] in a pierced copper brazier, he bathed his hands and forehead with a cool musk-scented vinegar.

Suddenly he started. His eyes grew strangely bright and he gnawed nervously at his underlip. Between two of the windows stood a large Florentine cabinet, made out of ebony, and inlaid with ivory and blue lapis. He watched it as though it were a thing that could fascinate and make afraid, as though it held something that he longed for and yet almost loathed. His breath quickened. A mad craving came over him. He lit a cigarette and then threw it away. His eyelids drooped till the long fringed lashes almost touched his cheek. But he still watched the cabinet. At last he got up from the sofa on which he had been lying, went over to it, and, having unlocked it, touched some hidden spring. A triangular drawer passed slowly out. His fingers moved instinctively to-wards it, dipped in, and closed on something. It was a small Chinese box of black and gold-dust lacquer, elaborately wrought, the sides patterned with curved waves, and the silken cords hung with round crystals and tasselled in plaited metal threads. He opened it. Inside was a green paste[15] waxy in lustre, the odour curiously heavy and persistent.

He hesitated for some moments, with a strangely immo-bile smile upon his face. Then shivering, though the atmos phere of the room was terribly hot, he drew himself up, and glanced at the clock. It was twenty minutes to twelve. He put the box back, shutting the cabinet doors as he did so, and went into his bedroom.

As midnight was striking bronze blows upon the dusky air, Dorian Gray, dressed commonly, and with a muffler wrapped round his throat, crept quietly out of his house. In Bond Street he found a hansom with a good horse. He hailed it, and in a low voice gave the driver an address.

The man shook his head. "It is too far for me," he muttered.

"Here is a sovereign for you," said Dorian. "You shall have another if you drive fast."

"All right, sir," answered the man, "you will be there in an hour," and after his fare had got in he turned his horse round, and drove rapidly towards the river.

XVI

A COLD RAIN began to fall, and the blurred street lamps looked ghastly in the dripping mist. The public-houses were just closing, and dim men and women were clustering in broken groups round their doors. From some of the bars came the sound of horrible laughter. In others, drunkards brawled and screamed.

Lying back in the hansom, with his hat pulled over his forehead, Dorian Gray watched with listless eyes the sordid shame of the great city, and now and then he repeated to himself the words that Lord Henry had said to him on the first day they had met, "To cure the soul by means of the senses, and the senses by means of the soul." Yes, that was the secret. He had often tried it, and would try it again now. There were opium dens, where one could buy oblivion, dens of horror where the memory of old sins could be destroyed by the madness of sins that were new.

The moon hung low in the sky like a yellow skull. From time to time a huge misshapen cloud stretched a long arm across and hid it. The gas lamps grew fewer, and the streets more narrow and gloomy. Once the man lost his way, and had to drive back half a mile. A steam rose from the horse as it splashed up the puddles. The side-windows of the hansom were clogged with a grey-flannel mist.

"To cure the soul by means of the senses, and the senses by means of the soul!" How the words rang in his ears! His soul, certainly, was sick to death. Was it true that the senses could cure it? Innocent blood had been spilt. What could atone for that? Ah! for that there was no atonement; but though forgiveness was impossible, forgetfulness was possible still, and he was determined to forget, to stamp the thing out, to crush it as one would crush the adder that had stung one. Indeed, what right had Basil to have spoken to him as he had done? Who had made him a judge over others? He had said things that were dreadful, horrible, not to be endured.

On and on plodded the hansom, going slower, it seemed to him, at each step. He thrust up the trap, and called to the man to drive faster. The hideous hunger for opium began to gnaw at him. His throat burned, and his delicate hands twitched nervously together. He struck at the horse madly with his stick. The driver laughed, and whipped up. He laughed in answer, and the man was silent.

The way seemed interminable, and the streets like the black web of some sprawling spider. The monotony became unbearable, and, as the mist thickened, he felt afraid.

Then they passed by lonely brickfields. The fog was lighter here, and he could see the strange bottle-shaped kilns with their orange fan-like tongues of fire. A dog barked as they went by, and far away in the darkness some wandering seagull screamed. The horse stumbled in a rut, then swerved aside, and broke into a gallop.

After some time they left the clay road, and rattled again over rough-paven streets. Most of the windows were dark, but now and then fantastic shadows were silhouetted against some lamp-lit blind. He watched them curiously. They moved like monstrous marionettes, and made gestures like live things. He hated them. A dull rage was in his heart. As they turned a corner a woman yelled something at them from an open door, and two men ran after the hansom for about a hundred yards. The driver beat at them with his whip.

It is said that passion makes one think in a circle. Certainly with hideous iteration the bitten lips of Dorian Gray shaped and reshaped those subtle words that dealt with soul and sense, till he had found in them the full expression, as it were, of his mood, and justified, by intellectual approval, passions that without such justification would still have dominated his temper. From cell to cell of his brain crept the one thought; and the wild desire to live, most terrible of all man's appetites, quickened into force each trembling nerve and fibre. Ugliness that had once been hateful to him because it made things real, became dear to him now for that very reason. Ugliness was the one reality. The coarse brawl, the loathsome den, the crude violence of disordered life, the very vileness of thief and outcast, were more vivid, in their intense actuality of impression, than all the gracious shapes of art, the dreamy shadows of song. They were what he needed for forgetfulness. In three days he would be free.

Suddenly the man drew up with a jerk at the top of a dark lane. Over the low roofs and jagged chimney-stacks of the houses rose the black masts of ships. Wreaths of white mist clung like ghostly sails to the yards.

"Somewhere about here, sir, ain't it?" he asked huskily through the trap.

Dorian started, and peered round. "This will do," he answered, and, having got out hastily, and given the driver the extra fare he had promised him, he walked quickly in the direction of the quay. Here and there a lantern gleamed at the stern of some huge merchantman. The light shook and splintered in the puddles. A red glare came from an outward-bound steamer that was coaling. The slimy pavement looked like a wet mackintosh.

He hurried on towards the left, glancing back now and then to see if he was being followed. In about seven or eight

minutes he reached a small shabby house, that was wedged
in between two gaunt factories. In one of the top windows
stood a lamp. He stopped, and gave a peculiar knock.

After a little time he heard steps in the passage, and the
chain being unhooked. The door opened quietly, and he went
in without saying a word to the squat misshapen figure that
flattened itself into the shadow as he passed. At the end of
the hall hung a tattered green curtain that swayed and shook
in the gusty wind which had followed him in from the street.
He dragged it aside, and entered a long, low room which
looked as if it had once been a third-rate dancing-saloon.
Shrill flaring gas jets, dulled and distorted in the fly-blown
mirrors that faced them, were ranged round the walls.
Greasy reflectors of ribbed tin backed them, making quivering disks of light. The floor was covered with ochre-coloured
sawdust, trampled here and there into mud, and stained with
rings of spilt liquor. Some Malays[1] were crouching by a little
charcoal stove playing with bone counters, and showing their
white teeth as they chattered. In one corner with his head
buried in his arms, a sailor sprawled over a table, and by the
tawdrily painted bar that ran across one complete side stood
two haggard women mocking an old man who was brushing
the sleeves of his coat with an expression of disgust. "He
thinks he's got red ants on him," laughed one of them, as Dorian passed by. The man looked at her in terror, and began to
whimper.

At the end of the room there was a little staircase, leading
to a darkened chamber. As Dorian hurried up its three rickety steps, the heavy odour of opium met him. He heaved a
deep breath, and his nostrils quivered with pleasure. When
he entered, a young man with smooth yellow hair, who was
bending over a lamp lighting a long thin pipe, looked up at
him, and nodded in a hesitating manner.

"You here, Adrian?" muttered Dorian.

"Where else should I be?" he answered, listlessly. "None
of the chaps will speak to me now."

"I thought you had left England."

"Darlington is not going to do anything. My brother paid the bill at last. George doesn't speak to me either. . . . I don't care," he added, with a sigh. "As long as one has this stuff, one doesn't want friends. I think I have had too many friends."

Dorian winced, and looked round at the grotesque things that lay in such fantastic postures on the ragged mattresses. The twisted limbs, the gaping mouths, the staring lustreless eyes, fascinated him. He knew in what strange heavens they were suffering, and what dull hells were teaching them the secret of some new joy. They were better off than he was. He was prisoned in thought. Memory, like a horrible malady, was eating his soul away. From time to time he seemed to see the eyes of Basil Hallward looking at him. Yet he felt he could not stay. The presence of Adrian Singleton troubled him. He wanted to be where no one would know who he was. He wanted to escape from himself.

"I am going on to the other place," he said, after a pause.

"On the wharf?"

"Yes."

"That mad-cat is sure to be there. They won't have her in this place now."

Dorian shrugged his shoulders. "I am sick of women who love one. Women who hate one are much more interesting. Besides, the stuff is better."

"Much the same."

"I like it better. Come and have something to drink. I must have something."

"I don't want anything," murmured the young man.

"Never mind."

Adrian Singleton rose up wearily, and followed Dorian to the bar. A half-caste,[2] in a ragged turban and a shabby ulster, grinned a hideous greeting as he thrust a bottle of brandy and two tumblers in front of them. The women sidled up, and began to chatter. Dorian turned his back on them, and said something in a low voice to Adrian Singleton.

A crooked smile, like a Malay crease, writhed across the

face of one of the women. "We are very proud tonight," she sneered.

"For God's sake don't talk to me," cried Dorian, stamping his foot on the ground. "What do you want? Money? Here it is. Don't ever talk to me again."

Two red sparks flashed for a moment in the woman's sodden eyes, then flickered out, and left them dull and glazed. She tossed her head, and raked the coins off the counter with greedy fingers. Her companion watched her enviously.

"It's no use," sighed Adrian Singleton. "I don't care to go back. What does it matter? I am quite happy here."

"You will write to me if you want anything, won't you?" said Dorian, after a pause.

"Perhaps."

"Good night, then."

"Good night," answered the young man, passing up the steps, and wiping his parched mouth with a handkerchief.

Dorian walked to the door with a look of pain in his face. As he drew the curtain aside a hideous laugh broke from the painted lips of the woman who had taken the money. "There goes the devil's bargain!" she hiccoughed, in a hoarse voice.

"Curse you," he answered, "don't call me that."

She snapped her fingers. "Prince Charming is what you like to be called, ain't it?" she yelled after him.

The drowsy sailor leapt to his feet as she spoke, and looked wildly round. The sound of the shutting of the hall door fell on his ear. He rushed out as if in pursuit.

Dorian Gray hurried along the quay through the drizzling rain. His meeting with Adrian Singleton had strangely moved him, and he wondered if the ruin of that young life was really to be laid at his door, as Basil Hallward had said to him with such infamy of insult. He bit his lip, and for a few seconds his eyes grew sad. Yet, after all, what did it matter to him? One's days were too brief to take the burden of another's errors on one's shoulders. Each man lived his own life, and paid his own price for living it. The only pity was one had to pay so often for a single fault. One had to pay over and over again, indeed. In her dealings with man Destiny never closed her accounts.

There are moments, psychologists tell us, when the passion for sin, or for what the world calls sin, so dominates a nature, that every fibre of the body, as every cell of the brain, seems to be instinct with fearful impulses. Men and women at such moments lose the freedom of their will. They move to their terrible end as automatons move. Choice is taken from them, and conscience is either killed, or, if it lives at all, lives but to give rebellion its fascination, and disobedience its charm. For all sins, as theologians weary not of reminding us, are sins of disobedience. When that high spirit, that morning star of evil, fell from heaven, it was as a rebel that he fell.

Callous, concentrated on evil, with stained mind, and soul hungry for rebellion, Dorian Gray hastened on, quickening his step as he went, but as he darted aside into a dim archway, that had served him often as a short cut to the ill-famed place where he was going, he felt himself suddenly seized from behind, and before he had time to defend himself he was thrust back against the wall, with a brutal hand round his throat.

He struggled madly for life, and by a terrible effort wrenched the tightening fingers away. In a second he heard the click of a revolver, and saw the gleam of a polished barrel pointing straight at his head, and the dusky form of a short thick-set man facing him.

"What do you want?" he gasped.

"Keep quiet," said the man. "If you stir, I shoot you."

"You are mad. What have I done to you?"

"You wrecked the life of Sibyl Vane," was the answer, "and Sibyl Vane was my sister. She killed herself. I know it. Her death is at your door. I swore I would kill you in return. For years I have sought you. I had no clue, no trace. The two people who could have described you were dead. I knew nothing of you but the pet name she used to call you. I heard it tonight by chance. Make your peace with God, for tonight you are going to die."

Dorian Gray grew sick with fear. "I never knew her," he stammered. "I never heard of her. You are mad."

"You had better confess your sin, for as sure as I am James Vane, you are going to die." There was a horrible moment. Dorian did not know what to say or do. "Down on your knees!" growled the man. "I give you one minute to make your peace—no more. I go on board tonight for India, and I must do my job first. One minute. That's all."

Dorian's arms fell to his side. Paralyzed with terror, he did not know what to do. Suddenly a wild hope flashed across his brain. "Stop," he cried. "How long ago is it since your sister died? Quick, tell me!"

"Eighteen years," said the man. "Why do you ask me? What do years matter?"

"Eighteen years," laughed Dorian Gray, with a touch of triumph in his voice. "Eighteen years! Set me under the lamp and look at my face."

James Vane hesitated for a moment, not understanding what was meant. Then he seized Dorian Gray and dragged him from the archway.

Dim and wavering as was the windblown light, yet it served to show him the hideous error, as it seemed, into which he had fallen, for the face of the man he had sought to kill had all the bloom of boyhood, all the unstained purity of youth. He seemed little more than a lad of twenty summers, hardly older, if older indeed at all, than his sister had been when they had parted so many years ago. It was obvious that this was not the man who had destroyed her life.

He loosened his hold and reeled back. "My God! my God!" he cried, "and I would have murdered you!"

Dorian Gray drew a long breath. "You have been on the brink of committing a terrible crime, my man," he said, looking at him sternly. "Let this be a warning to you not to take vengeance into your own hands."

"Forgive me, sir," muttered James Vane. "I was deceived. A chance word I heard in that damned den set me on the wrong track."

"You had better go home, and put that pistol away, or you may get into trouble," said Dorian, turning on his heel, and going slowly down the street.

James Vane stood on the pavement in horror. He was trembling from head to foot. After a little while a black shadow that had been creeping along the dripping wall, moved out into the light and came close to him with stealthy footsteps. He felt a hand laid on his arm and looked round with a start. It was one of the women who had been drinking at the bar.

"Why didn't you kill him?" she hissed out, putting her haggard face quite close to his. "I knew you were following him when you rushed out from Daly's.³ You fool! You should have killed him. He has lots of money, and he's as bad as bad."

"He is not the man I am looking for," he answered, "and I want no man's money. I want a man's life. The man whose life I want must be nearly forty now. This one is little more than a boy. Thank God, I have not got his blood upon my hands."

The woman gave a bitter laugh. "Little more than a boy!" she sneered. "Why, man, it's nigh on eighteen years since Prince Charming made me what I am."

"You lie!" cried James Vane.

She raised her hand up to heaven. "Before God I am telling the truth," she cried.

"Before God?"

"Strike me dumb if it ain't so. He is the worst one that comes here. They say he has sold himself to the devil for a pretty face. It's nigh on eighteen years since I met him. He hasn't changed much since then. I have though," she added, with a sickly leer.

"You swear this?"

"I swear it," came in hoarse echo from her flat mouth. "But don't give me away to him," she whined; "I am afraid of him. Let me have some money for my night's lodging."

He broke from her with an oath, and rushed to the corner of the street, but Dorian Gray had disappeared. When he looked back, the woman had vanished also.

XVII

A WEEK LATER Dorian Gray was sitting in the conservatory at Selby Royal talking to the pretty Duchess of Monmouth, who with her husband, a jaded-looking man of sixty, was amongst his guests. It was teatime, and the mellow light of the huge lace-covered lamp that stood on the table lit up the delicate china and hammered silver of the service at which the Duchess was presiding. Her white hands were moving daintily among the cups, and her full red lips were smiling at something that Dorian had whispered to her. Lord Henry was lying back in a silk-draped wicker chair looking at them. On a peach-coloured divan sat Lady Narborough pretending to listen to the Duke's description of the last Brazilian beetle that he had added to his collection. Three young men in elaborate smoking-suits were handing tea-cakes to some of the women. The house party consisted of twelve people, and there were more expected to arrive on the next day.

"What are you two talking about?" said Lord Henry, strolling over to the table, and putting his cup down. "I hope Dorian has told you about my plan for rechristening everything, Gladys. It is a delightful idea."

"But I don't want to be rechristened, Harry," rejoined the Duchess, looking up at him with her wonderful eyes. "I am quite satisfied with my own name, and I am sure Mr. Gray should be satisfied with his."

"My dear Gladys, I would not alter either name for the world. They are both perfect. I was thinking chiefly of flowers. Yesterday I cut an orchid, for my buttonhole. It was a marvellous spotted thing, as effective as the seven deadly sins. In a thoughtless moment I asked one of the gardeners what it was called. He told me it was a fine specimen of *Robinsoniana*, or something dreadful of that kind. It is a sad truth, but we have lost the faculty of giving lovely names to things. Names are everything. I never quarrel with actions. My one quarrel is with words. That is the reason I hate vulgar realism in literature.[1] The man who could call a spade a spade should be compelled to use one. It is the only thing he is fit for."

"Then what should we call you, Harry?" she asked.

"His name is Prince Paradox," said Dorian.

"I recognize him in a flash," exclaimed the Duchess.

"I won't hear of it," laughed Lord Henry, sinking into a chair. "From a label there is no escape! I refuse the title."

"Royalties may not abdicate," fell as a warning from pretty lips.

"You wish me to defend my throne, then?"

"Yes."

"I give the truths of tomorrow."

"I prefer the mistakes of today," she answered.

"You disarm me, Gladys," he cried, catching the wilfulness of her mood.

"Of your shield, Harry: not of your spear."

"I never tilt against beauty," he said, with a wave of his hand.

"That is your error, Harry, believe me. You value beauty far too much."

"How can you say that? I admit that I think that it is better to be beautiful than to be good. But on the other hand no one is more ready than I am to acknowledge that it is better to be good than to be ugly."

"Ugliness is one of the seven deadly sins, then?" cried the Duchess. "What becomes of your simile about the orchid?"

"Ugliness is one of the seven deadly virtues, Gladys. You, as a good Tory, must not underrate them. Beer, the Bible, and the seven deadly virtues have made our England what she is."

"You don't like your country, then?" she asked.

"I live in it."

"That you may censure it the better."

"Would you have me take the verdict of Europe on it?" he enquired.

"What do they say of us?"

"That Tartuffe[2] has emigrated to England and opened a shop."

"Is that yours, Harry?"

"I give it to you."

"I could not use it. It is too true."

"You need not be afraid. Our countrymen never recognize a description."

"They are practical."

"They are more cunning than practical. When they make up their ledger, they balance stupidity by wealth, and vice by hypocrisy."

"Still, we have done great things."

"Great things have been thrust on us, Gladys."

"We have carried their burden."

"Only as far as the Stock Exchange."

She shook her head. "I believe in the race," she cried.

"It represents the survival of the pushing."[3]

"It has development."

"Decay fascinates me more."

"What of art?" she asked.

"It is a malady."

"Love?"

"An illusion."

"Religion?"

"The fashionable substitute for belief."

"You are a sceptic."

"Never! Scepticism is the beginning of faith."

"What are you?"

"To define is to limit."

"Give me a clue."

"Threads snap. You would lose your way in the labyrinth."

"You bewilder me. Let us talk of someone else."

"Our host is a delightful topic. Years ago he was christened Prince Charming."

"Ah! don't remind me of that," cried Dorian Gray.

"Our host is rather horrid this evening," answered the Duchess, colouring. "I believe he thinks that Monmouth married me on purely scientific principles as the best specimen he could find of a modern butterfly."

"Well, I hope he won't stick pins into you, Duchess," laughed Dorian.

"Oh! my maid does that already, Mr. Gray, when she is annoyed with me."

"And what does she get annoyed with you about, Duchess?"

"For the most trivial things, Mr. Gray, I assure you. Usually because I come in at ten minutes to nine and tell her that I must be dressed by half-past eight."

"How unreasonable of her! You should give her warning."

"I daren't, Mr. Gray. Why, she invents hats for me. You remember the one I wore at Lady Hilstone's garden party? You don't, but it is nice of you to pretend that you do. Well, she made it out of nothing. All good hats are made out of nothing."

"Like all good reputations, Gladys," interrupted Lord Henry. "Every effect that one produces gives one an enemy. To be popular one must be a mediocrity."

"Not with women," said the Duchess, shaking her head;

"and women rule the world. I assure you we can't bear mediocrities. We women, as someone says, love with our ears, just as you men love with your eyes, if you ever love at all."

"It seems to me that we never do anything else," murmured Dorian.

"Ah! then, you never really love, Mr. Gray," answered the Duchess, with mock sadness.

"My dear Gladys!" cried Lord Henry. "How can you say that? Romance lives by repetition, and repetition converts an appetite into an art. Besides, each time that one loves is the only time one has ever loved. Difference of object does not alter singleness of passion. It merely intensifies it. We can have in life but one great experience at best, and the secret of life is to reproduce that experience as often as possible."

"Even when one has been wounded by it, Harry?" asked the Duchess, after a pause.

"Especially when one has been wounded by it," answered Lord Henry.

The Duchess turned and looked at Dorian Gray with a curious expression in her eyes. "What do you say to that, Mr. Gray?" she enquired.

Dorian hesitated for a moment. Then he threw his head back and laughed. "I always agree with Harry, Duchess."

"Even when he is wrong?"

"Harry is never wrong, Duchess."

"And does his philosophy make you happy?"

"I have never searched for happiness. Who wants happiness? I have searched for pleasure."

"And found it, Mr. Gray?"

"Often. Too often."

The Duchess sighed. "I am searching for peace," she said, "and if I don't go and dress, I shall have none this evening."

"Let me get you some orchids, Duchess," cried Dorian, starting to his feet, and walking down the conservatory.

"You are flirting disgracefully with him," said Lord Henry to his cousin. "You had better take care. He is very fascinating."

"If he were not, there would be no battle."

"Greek meets Greek, then?"

"I am on the side of the Trojans.⁴ They fought for a woman."

"They were defeated."

"There are worse things than capture," she answered.

"You gallop with a loose rein."

"Pace gives life," was the ripost.

"I shall write it in my diary tonight."

"What?"

"That a burnt child loves the fire."

"I am not even singed. My wings are untouched."

"You use them for everything, except flight."

"Courage has passed from men to women. It is a new experience for us."

"You have a rival."

"Who?"

He laughed. "Lady Narborough," he whispered. "She perfectly adores him."

"You fill me with apprehension. The appeal to Antiquity is fatal to us who are romanticists."

"Romanticists! You have all the methods of science."

"Men have educated us."

"But not explained you."

"Describe us as a sex," was her challenge.

"Sphinxes without secrets."

She looked at him, smiling. "How long Mr. Gray is!" she said. "Let us go and help him. I have not yet told him the colour of my frock."

"Ah! you must suit your frock to his flowers, Gladys."

"That would be a premature surrender."

"Romantic art begins with its climax."

"I must keep an opportunity for retreat."

"In the Parthian⁵ manner?"

"They found safety in the desert. I could not do that."

"Women are not always allowed a choice," he answered, but hardly had he finished the sentence before from the far end of the conservatory came a stifled groan, followed by the dull sound of a heavy fall. Everybody started up. The Duchess stood motionless in horror. And with fear in his eyes Lord Henry rushed through the flapping palms, to find Dorian Gray lying face downwards on the tiled floor in a deathlike swoon.

He was carried at once into the blue drawing-room, and laid upon one of the sofas. After a short time he came to himself, and looked round with a dazed expression.

"What has happened?" he asked. "Oh! I remember. Am I safe here, Harry?" He began to tremble.

"My dear Dorian," answered Lord Henry, "you merely fainted. That was all. You must have overtired yourself. You had better not come down to dinner. I will take your place."

"No, I will come down," he said, struggling to his feet. "I would rather come down. I must not be alone."

He went to his room and dressed. There was a wild recklessness of gaiety in his manner as he sat at table, but now and then a thrill of terror ran through him when he remembered that, pressed against the window of the conservatory, like a white handkerchief, he had seen the face of James Vane watching him.

XVIII

THE NEXT DAY he did not leave the house, and, indeed, spent most of the time in his own room, sick with a wild terror of dying, and yet indifferent to life itself. The consciousness of being hunted, snared, tracked down, had begun to dominate him. If the tapestry did but tremble in the wind, he shook. The dead leaves that were blown against the leaded panes seemed to him like his own wasted resolutions and wild regrets. When he closed his eyes, he saw again the sailor's face peering through the mist-stained glass, and horror seemed once more to lay its hand upon his heart.

But perhaps it had been only his fancy that had called vengeance out of the night, and set the hideous shapes of punishment before him. Actual life was chaos, but there was something terribly logical in the imagination. It was the imagination that set remorse to dog the feet of sin. It was the imagination that made each crime bear its misshapen brood. In the common world of fact the wicked were not punished, nor the good rewarded. Success was given to the strong, failure thrust upon the weak. That was all. Besides, had any stranger been prowling round the house he would have been seen by the servants or the keepers. Had any footmarks been found on the flower-beds, the gardeners would have reported it. Yes, it had been merely fancy. Sibyl Vane's brother had not come back to kill him. He had sailed away in his ship to founder in some winter sea. From him, at any rate, he was safe. Why, the man did not know who he was, could not know who he was. The mask of youth had saved him.

And yet if it had been merely an illusion, how terrible it was to think that conscience could raise such fearful phantoms, and give them visible form, and make them move before one! What sort of life would his be if, day and night, shadows of his crime were to peer at him from silent corners, to mock him from secret places, to whisper in his ear as he sat at the feast, to wake him with icy fingers as he lay asleep! As the thought crept through his brain, he grew pale with terror, and the air seemed to him to have become suddenly colder. Oh! in what a wild hour of madness he had killed his friend! How ghastly the mere memory of the scene! He saw it all again. Each hideous detail came back to him with added horror. Out of the black cave of time, terrible and swathed in scarlet, rose the image of his sin. When Lord Henry came in at six o'clock, he found him crying as one whose heart will break.

It was not till the third day that he ventured to go out. There was something in the clear, pine-scented air of that winter morning that seemed to bring him back his joyousness and his ardour for life. But it was not merely the physical conditions of environment that had caused the change. His own nature had revolted against the excess of anguish that had sought to maim and mar the perfection of its calm. With subtle and finely wrought temperaments it is always so. Their strong passions must either bruise or bend. They either slay the man, or themselves die. Shallow sorrows and shallow loves live on. The loves and sorrows that are great are destroyed by their own plenitude. Besides, he had convinced himself that he had been the victim of a terror-stricken imagination, and looked back now on his fears with something of pity and not a little of contempt.

After breakfast he walked with the Duchess for an hour in the garden, and then drove across the park to join the shooting party. The crisp frost lay like salt upon the grass. The sky was an inverted cup of blue metal. A thin film of ice bordered the flat reed-grown lake.

At the corner of the pine wood he caught sight of Sir Geoffrey Clouston, the Duchess's brother, jerking two spent cartridges out of his gun. He jumped from the cart, and having told the groom to take the mare home, made his way towards his guest through the withered bracken and rough undergrowth.

"Have you had good sport, Geoffrey?" he asked.

"Not very good, Dorian. I think most of the birds have gone to the open. I dare say it will be better after lunch, when we get to new ground."

Dorian strolled along by his side. The keen aromatic air, the brown and red lights that glimmered in the wood, the hoarse cries of the beaters ringing out from time to time, and the sharp snaps of the guns that followed, fascinated him, and filled him with a sense of delightful freedom. He was dominated by the carelessness of happiness, by the high indifference of joy.

Suddenly from a lumpy tussock of old grass, some twenty yards in front of them, with black-tipped ears erect, and long hinder limbs throwing it forward, started a hare. It bolted for a thicket of alders. Sir Geoffrey put his gun to his shoulder, but there was something in the animal's grace of movement that strangely charmed Dorian Gray, and he cried out at once, "Don't shoot it, Geoffrey. Let it live."

"What nonsense, Dorian!" laughed his companion, and as the hare bounded into the thicket he fired. There were two cries heard, the cry of a hare in pain, which is dreadful, the cry of a man in agony, which is worse.

"Good heavens! I have hit a beater!" exclaimed Sir Geoffrey. "What an ass the man was to get in front of the guns! Stop shooting there!" he called out at the top of his voice. "A man is hurt."

The head-keeper came running up with a stick in his hand.

"Where, sir? Where is he?" he shouted. At the same time the firing ceased along the line.

"Here," answered Sir Geoffrey, angrily, hurrying towards the thicket. "Why on earth don't you keep your men back? Spoiled my shooting for the day."

Dorian watched them as they plunged into the alder-clump, brushing the lithe, swinging branches aside. In a few moments they emerged, dragging a body after them into the sunlight. He turned away in horror. It seemed to him that misfortune followed wherever he went. He heard Sir Geoffrey ask if the man was really dead, and the affirmative answer of the keeper. The wood seemed to him to have become suddenly alive with faces. There was the trampling of myriad feet, and the low buzz of voices. A great copper-breasted pheasant came beating through the boughs overhead.

After a few moments, that were to him, in his perturbed state, like endless hours of pain, he felt a hand laid on his shoulder. He started, and looked round.

"Dorian," said Lord Henry, "I had better tell them that the shooting is stopped for today. It would not look well to go on."

"I wish it were stopped for ever, Harry," he answered, bitterly. "The whole thing is hideous and cruel. Is the man . . . ?"

He could not finish the sentence.

"I am afraid so," rejoined Lord Henry. "He got the whole charge of shot in his chest. He must have died almost instantaneously. Come; let us go home."

They walked side by side in the direction of the avenue for nearly fifty yards without speaking. Then Dorian looked at Lord Henry, and said, with a heavy sigh, "It is a bad omen, Harry, a very bad omen."

"What is?" asked Lord Henry. "Oh! this accident, I suppose. My dear fellow, it can't be helped. It was the man's own fault. Why did he get in front of the guns? Besides, it is nothing to us. It is rather awkward for Geoffrey, of course. It does not do to pepper beaters. It makes people think that one is a wild shot. And Geoffrey is not; he shoots very straight. But there is no use talking about the matter."

Dorian shook his head. "It is a bad omen, Harry. I feel as if something horrible were going to happen to some of us. To myself, perhaps," he added, passing his hand over his eyes, with a gesture of pain.

The elder man laughed. "The only horrible thing in the world is ennui, Dorian. That is the one sin for which there is no forgiveness. But we are not likely to suffer from it, unless these fellows keep chattering about this thing at dinner. I must tell them that the subject is to be tabooed. As for omens, there is no such thing as an omen. Destiny does not send us heralds. She is too wise or too cruel for that. Besides, what on earth could happen to you, Dorian? You have everything in the world that a man can want. There is no one who would not be delighted to change places with you."

"There is no one with whom I would not change places, Harry. Don't laugh like that. I am telling you the truth. The wretched peasant who has just died is better off than I am. I have no terror of death. It is the coming of death that terrifies me. Its monstrous wings seem to wheel in the leaden air around me. Good heavens! don't you see a man moving behind the trees there, watching me, waiting for me?"

Lord Henry looked in the direction in which the trembling gloved hand was pointing. "Yes," he said, smiling, "I see the gardener waiting for you. I suppose he wants to ask you what flowers you wish to have on the table tonight. How absurdly nervous you are, my dear fellow! You must come and see my doctor, when we get back to town."

Dorian heaved a sigh of relief as he saw the gardener approaching. The man touched his hat, glanced for a moment at Lord Henry in a hesitating manner, and then produced a letter, which he handed to his master. "Her Grace told me to wait for an answer," he murmured.

Dorian put the letter into his pocket. "Tell her Grace that

I am coming in," he said, coldly. The man turned round, and went rapidly in the direction of the house.

"How fond women are of doing dangerous things!" laughed Lord Henry. "It is one of the qualities in them that I admire most. A woman will flirt with anybody in the world as long as other people are looking on."

"How fond you are of saying dangerous things, Harry! In the present instance you are quite astray. I like the Duchess very much, but I don't love her."

"And the Duchess loves you very much, but she likes you less, so you are excellently matched."

"You are talking scandal, Harry, and there is never any basis for scandal."

"The basis of every scandal is an immoral certainty," said Lord Henry, lighting a cigarette.

"You would sacrifice anybody, Harry, for the sake of an epigram."

"The world goes to the altar of its own accord," was the answer.

"I wish I could love," cried Dorian Gray, with a deep note of pathos in his voice. "But I seem to have lost the passion, and forgotten the desire. I am too much concentrated on myself. My own personality has become a burden to me. I want to escape, to go away, to forget. It was silly of me to come down here at all. I think I shall send a wire to Harvey to have the yacht got ready. On a yacht one is safe."

"Safe from what, Dorian? You are in some trouble. Why not tell me what it is? You know I would help you."

"I can't tell you, Harry," he answered, sadly. "And I dare say it is only a fancy of mine. This unfortunate accident has upset me. I have a horrible presentiment that something of the kind may happen to me."

"What nonsense!"

"I hope it is, but I can't help feeling it. Ah! here is the Duchess, looking like Artemis[1] in a tailor-made gown. You see we have come back, Duchess."

"I have heard all about it, Mr. Gray," she answered. "Poor Geoffrey is terribly upset. And it seems that you asked him not to shoot the hare. How curious!"

"Yes, it was very curious. I don't know what made me say it. Some whim, I suppose. It looked the loveliest of little live things. But I am sorry they told you about the man. It is a hideous subject."

"It is an annoying subject," broke in Lord Henry. "It has no psychological value at all. Now if Geoffrey had done the thing on purpose, how interesting he would be! I should like to know someone who had committed a real murder."

"How horrid of you, Harry!" cried the Duchess. "Isn't it, Mr. Gray? Harry, Mr. Gray is ill again. He is going to faint."

Dorian drew himself up with an effort, and smiled. "It is nothing, Duchess," he murmured; "my nerves are dreadfully out of order. That is all. I am afraid I walked too far this morning. I didn't hear what Harry said. Was it very bad? You must tell me some other time. I think I must go and lie down. You will excuse me, won't you?"

They had reached the great flight of steps that led from the conservatory onto the terrace. As the glass door closed behind Dorian, Lord Henry turned and looked at the Duchess with his slumberous eyes. "Are you very much in love with him?" he asked.

She did not answer for some time, but stood gazing at the landscape. "I wish I knew," she said at last.

He shook his head. "Knowledge would be fatal. It is the uncertainty that charms one. A mist makes things wonderful."

"One may lose one's way."

"All ways end at the same point, my dear Gladys."

"What is that?"

"Disillusion."

"It was my début in life," she sighed.

"It came to you crowned."

"I am tired of strawberry leaves."[2]

"They become you."

"Only in public."

"You would miss them," said Lord Henry.

"I will not part with a petal."

"Monmouth has ears."

"Old age is dull of hearing."

"Has he never been jealous?"

"I wish he had been."

He glanced about as if in search of something. "What are you looking for?" she enquired.

"The button³ from your foil," he answered. "You have dropped it."

She laughed. "I have still the mask."³

"It makes your eyes lovelier," was his reply.

She laughed again. Her teeth showed like white seeds in a scarlet fruit.

Upstairs, in his own room, Dorian Gray was lying on a sofa, with terror in every tingling fibre of his body. Life had suddenly become too hideous a burden for him to bear. The dreadful death of the unlucky beater, shot in the thicket like a wild animal, had seemed to him to prefigure death for himself also. He had nearly swooned at what Lord Henry had said in a chance mood of cynical jesting.

At five o'clock he rang his bell for his servant, and gave him orders to pack his things for the night-express to town, and to have the brougham at the door by eight-thirty. He was determined not to sleep another night at Selby Royal. It was an ill-omened place. Death walked there in the sunlight. The grass of the forest had been spotted with blood.

Then he wrote a note to Lord Henry, telling him that he was going up to town to consult his doctor, and asking him to entertain his guests in his absence. As he was putting it into the envelope, a knock came to the door, and his valet informed him that the head-keeper wished to see him. He frowned, and bit his lip. "Send him in," he muttered, after some moments' hesitation.

As soon as the man entered Dorian pulled his cheque-book out of a drawer, and spread it out before him.

"I suppose you have come about the unfortunate accident of this morning, Thornton?" he said, taking up a pen.

"Yes, sir," answered the gamekeeper.

"Was the poor fellow married? Had he any people dependent on him?" asked Dorian, looking bored. "If so, I should not like them to be left in want, and will send them any sum of money you may think necessary."

"We don't know who he is, sir. That is what I took the liberty of coming to you about."

"Don't know who he is?" said Dorian, listlessly. "What do you mean? Wasn't he one of your men?"

"No, sir. Never saw him before. Seems like a sailor, sir."

The pen dropped from Dorian Gray's hand, and he felt as if his heart had suddenly stopped beating. "A sailor?" he cried out. "Did you say a sailor?"

"Yes, sir. He looks as if he had been a sort of sailor; tattooed on both arms, and that kind of thing."

"Was there anything found on him?" said Dorian, leaning forward and looking at the man with startled eyes. "Anything that would tell his name?"

"Some money, sir—not much, and a six-shooter. There was no name of any kind. A decent-looking man, sir, but rough-like. A sort of sailor we think."

Dorian started to his feet. A terrible hope fluttered past him. He clutched at it madly. "Where is the body?" he exclaimed. "Quick! I must see it at once."

"It is in an empty stable in the Home Farm, sir. The folk don't like to have that sort of thing in their houses. They say a corpse brings bad luck."

"The Home Farm! Go there at once and meet me. Tell one of the grooms to bring my horse round. No. Never mind. I'll go to the stables myself. It will save time."

In less than a quarter of an hour Dorian Gray was galloping down the long avenue as hard as he could go. The trees seemed to sweep past him in spectral procession, and wild shadows to fling themselves across his path. Once the mare swerved at a white gate-post and nearly threw him. He lashed her across the neck with his crop. She cleft the dusky air like an arrow. The stones flew from her hoofs.

At last he reached the Home Farm. Two men were loitering in the yard. He leapt from the saddle and threw the reins to one of them. In the farthest stable a light was glimmering. Something seemed to tell him that the body was there, and he hurried to the door, and put his hand upon the latch.

There he paused for a moment, feeling that he was on the brink of a discovery that would either make or mar his life. Then he thrust the door open, and entered.

On a heap of sacking in the far corner was lying the dead body of a man dressed in a coarse shirt and a pair of blue trousers. A spotted handkerchief had been placed over the face. A coarse candle, stuck in a bottle, sputtered beside it.

Dorian Gray shuddered. He felt that his could not be the hand to take the handkerchief away, and called out to one of the farm servants to come to him.

"Take that thing off the face. I wish to see it," he said, clutching at the doorpost for support.

When the farm servant had done so, he stepped forward. A cry of joy broke from his lips. The man who had been shot in the thicket was James Vane.

He stood there for some minutes looking at the dead body. As he rode home, his eyes were full of tears, for he knew he was safe.

XIX

"THERE IS no use your telling me that you are going to be good," cried Lord Henry, dipping his white fingers into a red copper bowl filled with rose-water. "You are quite perfect. Pray, don't change."

Dorian Gray shook his head. "No, Harry, I have done too many dreadful things in my life. I am not going to do any more. I began my good actions yesterday."

"Where were you yesterday?"

"In the country, Harry. I was staying at a little inn by myself."

"My dear boy," said Lord Henry, smiling, "anybody can be good in the country. There are no temptations there. That is the reason why people who live out of town are so absolutely uncivilized. Civilization is not by any means an easy thing to attain to. There are only two ways by which man can reach it. One is by being cultured, the other by being corrupt. Country people have no opportunity of being either, so they stagnate."

"Culture and corruption," echoed Dorian. "I have known something of both. It seems terrible to me now that they should ever be found together. For I have a new ideal, Harry. I am going to alter. I think I have altered."

"You have not yet told me what your good action was. Or did you say you had done more than one?" asked his companion, as he spilt into his plate a little crimson pyramid of seeded strawberries, and through a perforated shell-shaped spoon snowed white sugar upon them.

"I can tell you, Harry. It is not a story I could tell to anyone else. I spared somebody. It sounds vain, but you understand what I mean. She was quite beautiful and wonderfully like Sibyl Vane. I think it was that which first attracted me to her. You remember Sibyl, don't you? How long ago that seems! Well, Hetty was not one of our own class, of course. She was simply a girl in a village. But I really loved her. I am quite sure that I loved her. All during this wonderful May that we have been having, I used to run down and see her two or three times a week. Yesterday she met me in a little orchard. The apple-blossoms kept tumbling down on her hair, and she was laughing. We were to have gone away together this morning at dawn. Suddenly I determined to leave her as flower-like as I had found her."

"I should think the novelty of the emotion must have given you a thrill of real pleasure, Dorian," interrupted Lord Henry. "But I can finish your idyll for you. You gave her good advice, and broke her heart. That was the beginning of your reformation."

"Harry, you are horrible! You mustn't say these dreadful things. Hetty's heart is not broken. Of course she cried, and all that. But there is no disgrace upon her. She can live, like Perdita,[1] in her garden of mint and marigold."

"And weep over a faithless Florizel,"[1] said Lord Henry, laughing, as he leant back in his chair. "My dear Dorian, you have the most curiously boyish moods. Do you think this girl will ever be really contented now with anyone of her own rank? I suppose she will be married some day to a rough carter or a grinning ploughman. Well, the fact of having met you, and loved you, will teach her to despise her husband, and she will be wretched. From a moral point of view, I cannot say that I think much of your great renunciation. Even as a beginning, it is poor. Besides, how do you know that Hetty isn't floating at the present moment in some star-lit millpond, with lovely water-lilies round her, like Ophelia?"

"I can't bear this, Harry! You mock at everything, and then suggest the most serious tragedies. I am sorry I told you now. I don't care what you say to me. I know I was right in acting as I did. Poor Hetty! As I rode past the farm this morning, I saw her white face at the window, like a spray of jasmine. Don't let us talk about it any more, and don't try to persuade me that the first good action I have done for years, the first little bit of self-sacrifice I have ever known, is really a sort of sin. I want to be better. I am going to be better. Tell me something about yourself. What is going on in town? I have not been to the club for days."

"The people are still discussing poor Basil's disappearance."

"I should have thought they had got tired of that by this time," said Dorian, pouring himself out some wine, and frowning slightly.

"My dear boy, they have only been talking about it for six weeks, and the British public are really not equal to the mental strain of having more than one topic every three months. They have been very fortunate lately, however. They have had my own divorce-case, and Alan Campbell's suicide. Now they have got the mysterious disappearance of an artist. Scotland Yard still insists that the man in the grey ulster who left for Paris by the midnight train on the ninth of November was poor Basil, and the French police declare that Basil never arrived in Paris at all. I suppose in about a fortnight we shall be told that he has been seen in San Francisco. It is an odd thing, but everyone who disappears is said to be seen at San Francisco. It must be a delightful city, and possess all the attractions of the next world."

"What do you think has happened to Basil?" asked Dorian, holding up his Burgundy against the light, and wondering how it was that he could discuss the matter so calmly.

"I have not the slightest idea. If Basil chooses to hide himself, it is no business of mine. If he is dead, I don't want to think about him. Death is the only thing that ever terrifies me. I hate it."

"Why?" said the younger man, wearily.

"Because," said Lord Henry, passing beneath his nostrils the gilt trellis of an open vinaigrette box,[2] "one can survive everything nowadays except that. Death and vulgarity are the only two facts in the nineteenth century that one cannot explain away. Let us have our coffee in the music-room, Dorian. You must play Chopin[3] to me. The man with whom my wife ran away played Chopin exquisitely. Poor Victoria! I was very fond of her. The house is rather lonely without her. Of course married life is merely a habit, a bad habit. But then one regrets the loss even of one's worst habits. Perhaps one regrets them the most. They are such an essential part of one's personality."

Dorian said nothing, but rose from the table, and, passing into the next room, sat down to the piano and let his fingers stray across the white and black ivory of the keys. After the coffee had been brought in, he stopped, and, looking over at Lord Henry, said, "Harry, did it ever occur to you that Basil was murdered?"

Lord Henry yawned. "Basil was very popular, and always wore a Waterbury[4] watch. Why should he have been murdered? He was not clever enough to have enemies. Of course he had a wonderful genius for painting. But a man can paint like Velásquez[5] and yet be as dull as possible. Basil was really rather dull. He only interested me once, and that was when he told me, years ago, that he had a wild adoration for you, and that you were the dominant motive of his art."

"I was very fond of Basil," said Dorian, with a note of sadness in his voice. "But don't people say that he was murdered?"

"Oh, some of the papers do. It does not seem to me to be at all probable. I know there are dreadful places in Paris, but Basil was not the sort of man to have gone to them. He had no curiosity. It was his chief defect."

"What would you say, Harry, if I told you that I had murdered Basil?" said the younger man. He watched him intently after he had spoken.

"I would say, my dear fellow, that you were posing for a character that doesn't suit you. All crime is vulgar, just as all vulgarity is crime. It is not in you, Dorian, to commit a murder. I am sorry if I hurt your vanity by saying so, but I assure you it is true. Crime belongs exclusively to the lower orders. I don't blame them in the smallest degree. I should fancy that crime was to them what art is to us, simply a method of procuring extraordinary sensations."

"A method of procuring sensations? Do you think, then, that a man who has once committed a murder could possibly do the same crime again? Don't tell me that."

"Oh! anything becomes a pleasure if one does it too often," cried Lord Henry, laughing. "That is one of the most important secrets of life. I should fancy, however, that murder is always a mistake. One should never do anything that one cannot talk about after dinner. But let us pass from poor Basil. I wish I could believe that he had come to such a really romantic end as you suggest; but I can't. I dare say he fell into the Seine off an omnibus, and that the conductor hushed up the scandal. Yes, I should fancy that was his end. I see him lying now on his back under those dull-green waters with the heavy barges floating over him, and long weeds catching in his hair. Do you know, I don't think he would have done much more good work. During the last ten years his painting had gone off very much."

Dorian heaved a sigh, and Lord Henry strolled across the room and began to stroke the head of a curious Java parrot, a large grey-plumaged bird, with pink crest and tail, that was balancing itself upon a bamboo perch. As his pointed fingers touched it, it dropped the white scurf of crinkled lids over black glass-like eyes, and began to sway backwards and forwards.

"Yes," he continued, turning round, and taking his handkerchief out of his pocket; "his painting had quite gone off. It seemed to me to have lost something. It had lost an ideal. When you and he ceased to be great friends, he ceased to be a great artist. What was it separated you? I suppose he bored you. If so, he never forgave you. It's a habit bores have. By the way, what has become of that wonderful portrait he did of you? I don't think I have ever seen it since he finished it. Oh! I remember your telling me years ago that you had sent it down to Selby, and that it had got mislaid or stolen on the way. You never got it back? What a pity! It was really a masterpiece. I remember I wanted to buy it. I wish I had now. It belonged to Basil's best period. Since then, his work was that curious mixture of bad painting and good intentions that always entitles a man to be called a representative British artist. Did you advertise for it? You should."

"I forget," said Dorian. "I suppose I did. But I never really liked it. I am sorry I sat for it. The memory of the thing is hateful to me. Why do you talk of it? It used to remind me of those curious lines in some play—*Hamlet*, I think—how do they run?—

> 'Like the painting of a sorrow,
> A face without a heart.'[6]

Yes, that is what it was like."

Lord Henry laughed. "If a man treats life artistically, his brain is his heart," he answered, sinking into an arm-chair.

Dorian Gray shook his head, and struck some soft chords on the piano. " 'Like the painting of a sorrow,' " he repeated, " 'a face without a heart.' "

The elder man lay back and looked at him with half-closed eyes. "By the way, Dorian," he said, after a pause, " 'what does it profit a man if he gain the whole world and lose'— how does the quotation run?—'his own soul?' "[7]

The music jarred and Dorian Gray started, and stared at his friend. "Why do you ask me that, Harry?"

"My dear fellow," said Lord Henry, elevating his eyebrows in surprise, "I asked you because I thought you might be able to give me an answer. That is all. I was going through the Park last Sunday, and close by the Marble Arch there stood a little crowd of shabby-looking people listening to some vulgar street-preacher. As I passed by, I heard the man yelling out that question to his audience. It struck me as being rather dramatic. London is very rich in curious effects of that kind. A wet Sunday, an uncouth Christian in a mackintosh, a ring of sickly white faces under a broken roof of dripping umbrellas, and a wonderful phrase flung into the air by shrill, hysterical lips—it was really very good in its way, quite a suggestion. I thought of telling the prophet that art had a soul, but that man had not. I am afraid, however, he would not have understood me."

"Don't, Harry. The soul is a terrible reality. It can be bought, and sold, and bartered away. It can be poisoned, or made perfect. There is a soul in each one of us. I know it."

"Do you feel quite sure of that, Dorian?"

"Quite sure."

"Ah! then it must be an illusion. The things one feels absolutely certain about are never true. That is the fatality of faith, and the lesson of romance. How grave you are! Don't be so serious. What have you or I to do with the superstitions of our age? No, we have given up our belief in the soul. Play me something. Play me a nocturne, Dorian, and, as you play, tell me, in a low voice, how you have kept your youth. You must have some secret. I am only ten years older than you are, and I am wrinkled, and worn, and yellow. You are really wonderful, Dorian. You have never looked more charming than you do tonight. You remind me of the day I saw you first. You were rather cheeky, very shy, and absolutely extraordinary. You have changed, of course, but not in appearance. I wish you would tell me your secret. To get back my youth I would do anything in the world, except take exercise, get up early, or be respectable. Youth! There is nothing like it. It's absurd to talk of the ignorance of youth. The only people to whose opinions I listen now with any respect are people much younger than myself. They seem in front of me. Life has revealed to them her latest wonder. As for the aged, I always contradict the aged. I do it on principle. If you ask them their opinion on something that happened yesterday, they solemnly give you the opinions current in 1820, when people wore high stocks, believed in everything, and knew absolutely nothing. How lovely that thing you are playing is! I wonder did Chopin write it at Majorca,[8] with the sea weeping round the villa, and the salt spray dashing against the panes? It is marvellously romantic. What a blessing it is that there is one art left to us that is not imitative! Don't stop. I want music tonight. It seems to me that you are the young Apollo,[9] and that I am Marsyas[10] listening to you. I have sorrows, Dorian, of my own, that even you know nothing of. The tragedy of old age is not that one is old, but that one is young. I am amazed sometimes at my own sincerity. Ah, Dorian, how happy you are! What an exquisite life you have had! You have drunk deeply of everything. You have crushed the grapes against your palate. Nothing has been hidden from you. And it has all been to you no more than the sound of music. It has not marred you. You are still the same."

"I am not the same, Harry."

"Yes, you are the same. I wonder what the rest of your life will be. Don't spoil it by renunciations. At present you are a perfect type. Don't make yourself incomplete. You are quite flawless now. You need not shake your head: you know you are. Besides, Dorian, don't deceive yourself. Life is not governed by will or intention. Life is a question of nerves, and fibres, and slowly built-up cells in which thought hides itself and passion has its dreams. You may fancy yourself safe, and think yourself strong. But a chance tone of colour in a room or a morning sky, a particular perfume that you had once loved and that brings subtle memories with it, a line from a forgotten poem that you had come across again, a cadence from a piece of music that you had ceased to play—I tell you, Dorian, that it is on things like these that our lives depend. Browning[11] writes about that somewhere; but our own senses will imagine them for us. There are moments when the odour of *lilas blanc*[12] passes suddenly across me, and I have to live the strangest month of my life over again. I wish I could change places with you, Dorian. The world has cried out against us both, but it has always worshipped you. It always will worship you. You are the type of what the age is searching for, and what it is afraid it has found. I am so glad that you have never done anything, never carved a statue, or painted a picture, or produced anything outside of yourself! Life has been your art. You have set yourself to music. Your days are your sonnets."

Dorian rose up from the piano, and passed his hand through his hair. "Yes, life has been exquisite," he murmured, "but I am not going to have the same life, Harry. And you must not say these extravagant things to me. You don't know everything about me. I think that if you did, even you would turn from me. You laugh. Don't laugh."

"Why have you stopped playing, Dorian? Go back and give me the nocturne over again. Look at that great honey-coloured moon that hangs in the dusky air. She is waiting for you to charm her, and if you play she will come closer to the earth. You won't? Let us go to the club, then. It has been a charming evening, and we must end it charmingly. There is someone at White's who wants immensely to know you—young Lord Poole, Bournemouth's eldest son. He has already copied your neckties, and has begged me to introduce him to you. He is quite delightful, and rather reminds me of you."

"I hope not," said Dorian, with a sad look in his eyes. "But I am tired tonight, Harry. I shan't go to the club. It is nearly eleven, and I want to go to bed early."

"Do stay. You have never played so well as tonight. There was something in your touch that was wonderful. It had more expression than I had ever heard from it before."

"It is because I am going to be good," he answered, smiling. "I am a little changed already."

"You cannot change to me, Dorian," said Lord Henry. "You and I will always be friends."

"Yet you poisoned me with a book once. I should not forgive that. Harry, promise me that you will never lend that book to anyone. It does harm."

"My dear boy, you are really beginning to moralize. You will soon be going about like the converted, and the revivalist, warning people against all the sins of which you have grown tired. You are much too delightful to do that. Besides, it is no use. You and I are what we are, and will be what we will be. As for being poisoned by a book, there is no such thing as that. Art has no influence upon action. It annihilates the desire to act. It is superbly sterile. The books that the world calls immoral are books that show the world its own shame. That is all. But we won't discuss literature. Come round tomorrow. I am going to ride at eleven. We might go together, and I will take you to lunch afterwards with Lady Branksome. She is a charming woman, and wants to consult you about some tapestries she is thinking of buying. Mind you come. Or shall we lunch with our little Duchess? She says she never sees you now. Perhaps you are tired of Gladys? I thought you would be. Her clever tongue gets on one's nerves. Well, in any case, be here at eleven."

"Must I really come, Harry?"

"Certainly. The Park is quite lovely now. I don't think there have been such lilacs since the year I met you."

"Very well. I shall be here at eleven," said Dorian. "Good night, Harry." As he reached the door he hesitated for a moment, as if he had something more to say. Then he sighed and went out.

XX

IT WAS a lovely night, so warm that he threw his coat over his arm, and did not even put his silk scarf round his throat. As he strolled home, smoking his cigarette, two young men in evening dress passed him. He heard one of them whisper to the other, "That is Dorian Gray." He remembered how pleased he used to be when he was pointed out, or stared at, or talked about. He was tired of hearing his own name now. Half the charm of the little village where he had been so often lately was that no one knew who he was. He had often told the girl whom he had lured to love him that he was poor, and she had believed him. He had told her once that he was wicked, and she had laughed at him, and answered that wicked people were always very old and very ugly. What a laugh she had!—just like a thrush singing. And how pretty she had been in her cotton dresses and her large hats! She knew nothing, but she had everything that he had lost.

When he reached home, he found his servant waiting up for him. He sent him to bed, and threw himself down on the sofa in the library, and began to think over some of the things that Lord Henry had said to him.

Was it really true that one could never change? He felt a

wild longing for the unstained purity of his boyhood—his rose-white boyhood, as Lord Henry had once called it. He knew that he had tarnished himself, filled his mind with corruption and given horror to his fancy; that he had been an evil influence to others and had experienced a terrible joy in being so; and that of the lives that had crossed his own it had been the fairest and the most full of promise that he had brought to shame. But was it all irretrievable? Was there no hope for him?

Ah! in what a monstrous moment of pride and passion he had prayed that the portrait should bear the burden of his days, and he keep the unsullied splendour of eternal youth! All his failure had been due to that. Better for him that each sin of his life had brought its sure, swift penalty along with it. There was purification in punishment. Not "Forgive us our sins," but "Smite us for our iniquities" should be the prayer of man to a most just God.

The curiously carved mirror that Lord Henry had given to him, so many years ago now, was standing on the table, and the white-limbed Cupids laughed round it as of old. He took it up, as he had done on that night of horror, when he had first noted the change in the fatal picture, and with wild tear-dimmed eyes looked into its polished shield. Once, someone who had terribly loved him, had written to him a mad letter, ending with these idolatrous words: "The world is changed because you are made of ivory and gold. The curves of your lips rewrite history." The phrases came back to his memory, and he repeated them over and over to himself. Then he loathed his own beauty, and flinging the mirror on the floor crushed it into silver splinters beneath his heel. It was his beauty that had ruined him, his beauty and the youth that he had prayed for. But for those two things, his life might have been free from stain. His beauty had been to him but a mask, his youth but a mockery. What was youth at best? A green, an unripe time, a time of shallow moods, and sickly thoughts. Why had he worn its livery? Youth had spoiled him.

It was better not to think of the past. Nothing could alter

that. It was of himself, and of his own future, that he had to think. James Vane was hidden in a nameless grave in Selby churchyard. Alan Campbell had shot himself one night in his laboratory, but had not revealed the secret that he had been forced to know. The excitement, such as it was, over Basil Hallward's disappearance would soon pass away. It was already waning. He was perfectly safe there. Nor, indeed, was it the death of Basil Hallward that weighed most upon his mind. It was the living death of his own soul that troubled him. Basil had painted the portrait that had marred his life. He could not forgive him that. It was the portrait that had done everything. Basil had said things to him that were unbearable, and that he had yet borne with patience. The murder had been simply the madness of a moment. As for Alan Campbell, his suicide had been his own act. He had chosen to do it. It was nothing to him.

A new life! That was what he wanted. That was what he was waiting for. Surely he had begun it already. He had spared one innocent thing, at any rate. He would never again tempt innocence. He would be good.

As he thought of Hetty Merton, he began to wonder if the portrait in the locked room had changed. Surely it was not still so horrible as it had been? Perhaps if his life became pure, he would be able to expel every sign of evil passion from the face. Perhaps the signs of evil had already gone away. He would go and look.

He took the lamp from the table and crept upstairs. As he unbarred the door, a smile of joy flitted across his strangely young-looking face and lingered for a moment about his lips. Yes, he would be good, and the hideous thing that he had hidden away would no longer be a terror to him. He felt as if the load had been lifted from him already.

He went in quietly, locking the door behind him, as was his custom, and dragged the purple hanging from the portrait. A cry of pain and indignation broke from him. He could see no change, save that in the eyes there was a look of cunning, and in the mouth the curved wrinkle of the hypocrite.

The thing was still loathsome—more loathsome, if possible, than before—and the scarlet dew that spotted the hand seemed brighter, and more like blood newly spilt. Then he trembled. Had it been merely vanity that had made him do his one good deed? Or the desire for a new sensation, as Lord Henry had hinted, with his mocking laugh? Or that passion to act a part that sometimes makes us do things finer than we are ourselves? Or, perhaps, all these? And why was the red stain larger than it had been? It seemed to have crept like a horrible disease over the wrinkled fingers. There was blood on the painted feet, as though the thing had dripped—blood even on the hand that had not held the knife. Confess? Did it mean that he was to confess? To give himself up, and be put to death? He laughed. He felt that the idea was monstrous. Besides, even if he did confess, who would believe him? There was no trace of the murdered man anywhere. Everything belonging to him had been destroyed. He himself had burned what had been below-stairs. The world would simply say that he was mad. They would shut him up if he persisted in his story. . . . Yet it was his duty to confess, to suffer public shame, and to make public atonement. There was a God who called upon men to tell their sins to earth as well as to heaven. Nothing that he could do would cleanse him till he had told his own sin. His sin? He shrugged his shoulders. The death of Basil Hallward seemed very little to him. He was thinking of Hetty Merton. For it was an unjust mirror, this mirror of his soul that he was looking at. Vanity? Curiosity? Hypocrisy? Had there been nothing more in his renunciation than that? There had been something more. At least he thought so. But who could tell? . . . No. There had been nothing more. Through vanity he had spared her. In hypocrisy he had worn the mask of goodness. For curiosity's sake he had tried the denial of self. He recognized that now.

But this murder—was it to dog him all his life? Was he always to be burdened by his past? Was he really to confess? Never. There was only one bit of evidence left against him. The picture itself—that was evidence. He would destroy it.

Why had he kept it so long? Once it had given him pleasure to watch it changing and growing old. Of late he had felt no such pleasure. It had kept him awake at night. When he had been away, he had been filled with terror lest other eyes should look upon it. It had brought melancholy across his passions. Its mere memory had marred many moments of joy. It had been like conscience to him. Yes, it had been conscience. He would destroy it.

He looked round, and saw the knife that had stabbed Basil Hallward. He had cleaned it many times, till there was no stain left upon it. It was bright, and glistened. As it had killed the painter, so it would kill the painter's work, and all that that meant. It would kill the past, and when that was dead he would be free. It would kill this monstrous soul-life, and without its hideous warnings, he would be at peace. He seized the thing, and stabbed the picture with it.

There was a cry heard, and a crash. The cry was so horrible in its agony that the frightened servants woke, and crept out of their rooms. Two gentlemen, who were passing in the Square below, stopped, and looked up at the great house. They walked on till they met a policeman, and brought him back. The man rang the bell several times, but there was no answer. Except for a light in one of the top windows, the house was all dark. After a time, he went away, and stood in an adjoining portico and watched.

"Whose house is that, constable?" asked the elder of the two gentlemen.

"Mr. Dorian Gray's, sir," answered the policeman.

They looked at each other, as they walked away, and sneered. One of them was Sir Henry Ashton's uncle.

Inside, in the servants' part of the house, the half-clad domestics were talking in low whispers to each other. Old Mrs. Leaf was crying, and wringing her hands. Francis was as pale as death.

After about a quarter of an hour, he got the coachman and one of the footmen and crept upstairs. They knocked, but there was no reply. They called out. Everything was still. Finally, after vainly trying to force the door, they got on the roof, and dropped down on to the balcony. The windows yielded easily: their bolts were old.

When they entered, they found hanging upon the wall a splendid portrait of their master as they had last seen him, in all the wonder of his exquisite youth and beauty. Lying on the floor was a dead man, in evening dress, with a knife in his heart. He was withered, wrinkled, and loathsome of visage. It was not till they had examined the rings that they recognized who it was.

De Profundis

Epistola: In Carcere et Vinculis

DEAR BOSIE,[1]—After long and fruitless waiting I have determined to write to you myself, as much for your sake as for mine, as I would not like to think that I had passed through two long years of imprisonment without ever having received a single line from you, or any news or message even, except such as gave me pain.

Our ill-fated and most lamentable friendship has ended in ruin and public infamy for me, yet the memory of our ancient affection is often with me, and the thought that loathing, bitterness and contempt should for ever take the place in my heart once held by love is very sad to me: and you yourself will, I think, feel in your heart that to write to me as I lie in the loneliness of prison life is better than to publish my letters without my permission or to dedicate poems to me unasked, though the world will know nothing of whatever words of grief or passion, of remorse or indifference you may choose to send as your answer or your appeal.

I have no doubt that in this letter which I have to write of your life and of mine, of the past and of the future, of sweet things changed to bitterness and of bitter things that may be turned into joy, there will be much that will wound your vanity to the quick. If it prove so, read the letter over and over again till it kills your vanity. If you find in it something of which you feel that you are unjustly accused, remember that one should be thankful that there is any fault of which one can be unjustly accused. If there be in it one single passage that brings tears to your eyes, weep as we weep in prison where the day no less than the night is set apart for tears. It is the only thing that can save you. If you go complaining to your mother, as you did with reference to the scorn of you I displayed in my letter to Robbie,[2] so that she may flatter and soothe you back into self-complacency or conceit, you will be completely lost. If you find one false excuse for yourself you will soon find a hundred, and be just what you were before. Do you still say, as you said to Robbie in your answer, that I "attribute unworthy motives to you?" Ah! you had no motives in life. You had appetites merely. A motive is an intellectual aim. That you were "very young" when our friendship began? Your defect was not that you knew so little about life, but that you knew so much. The morning dawn of boyhood with its delicate bloom, its clear pure light, its joy of innocence and expectation you had left far behind. With very swift and running feet you had passed from Romance to Realism. The gutter and the things that live in it had begun to fascinate you. That was the origin of the trouble in which you sought my aid, and I, unwisely according to the wisdom of this world, out of pity and kindness, gave it to you. You must read this letter right through, though each word may become to you as the fire or knife of the surgeon that makes the delicate flesh burn or bleed. Remember that the fool to the eyes of the gods and the fool to the eyes of man are very different. One who is entirely ignorant of the modes of art in its revelation or the mood of thought in its progress, of the pomp of the Latin line or the richer music of the vowelled Greek, of Tuscan sculpture or Elizabethan song, may yet be full of the very sweetest wisdom. The real fool, such as the gods mock or mar, is he who does not know himself. I was such a one too long. You have been such a one too long. Be so no more. Do not be afraid. The supreme vice is shallowness. Everything that is realized is right. Remember also that whatever is misery to you to read, is still greater misery to me to set down. To you the Unseen Powers have been very good. They have permitted you to see the strange and tragic shapes of life as one sees shadows in a crystal. The head of Medusa that turns living men to stone, you have been allowed to look at in a mirror merely. You yourself have walked free among the flowers. From me the beautiful world of colour and motion has been taken away.

I will begin by telling you that I blame myself terribly. As I sit here in this dark cell in convict clothes, a disgraced and ruined man, I blame myself. In the perturbed and fitful nights of anguish, in the long monotonous days of pain, it is myself I blame. I blame myself for allowing an unintellectual friendship, a friendship whose primary aim was not the creation and contemplation of beautiful things, entirely to dominate my life. From the very first there was too wide a gap between us. You had been idle at your school, worse than idle at your university. You did not realize that an artist, and especially such an artist as I am, one, that is to say, the quality of whose work depends on the intensification of personality, requires for the development of his art the companionship of ideas, and intellectual atmosphere, quiet, peace, and solitude. You admired my work when it was finished: you enjoyed the brilliant successes of my first nights, and the brilliant banquets that followed them: you were proud, and quite naturally so, of being the intimate friend of an artist so distinguished: but you could not understand the conditions requisite for the production of artistic work. I am not speaking in phrases of rhetorical exaggeration but in terms of absolute truth to actual fact when I remind you that during the whole time we were together I never wrote one single line. Whether at Torquay, Goring, London, Florence, or elsewhere, my life, as long as you were by my side, was entirely sterile and uncreative. And with but few intervals you were, I regret to say, by my side always.

I remember, for instance, in September 1893, to select merely one instance out of many, taking a set of chambers, purely in order to work undisturbed, as I had broken my contract with John Hare for whom I had promised to write a play and who was pressing me on the subject. During the first week you kept away. We had, not unnaturally indeed, differed on the question of the artistic value of your translation of *Salomé*. So you contented yourself with sending me foolish letters on the subject. In that week I wrote and completed in every detail, as it was ultimately performed, the first act of *An Ideal Husband*. The second week you returned and my work practically had to be given up. I arrived at St. James's Place every morning at 11:30 in order to have the opportunity of thinking and writing without the interruption inseparable from my own household, quiet and peaceful as that household was. But the attempt was vain. At 12 o'clock you drove up and stayed smoking cigarettes and chattering till 1:30, when I had to take you out to luncheon at the Café Royal or the Berkeley. Luncheon with its liqueurs lasted usually till 3:30. For an hour you retired to White's. At teatime you appeared again and stayed till it was time to dress for dinner. You dined with me either at the Savoy or at Tite Street. We did not separate as a rule till after midnight, as supper at Willis's had to wind up the entrancing day. That was my life for those three months, every single day, except during the four days when you went abroad. I then, of course, had to go over to Calais to fetch you back. For one of my nature and temperament it was a position at once grotesque and tragic.

You surely must realize that now. You must see now that your incapacity for being alone: your nature so exigent in its persistent claim on the attention and time of others: your lack of any power of sustained intellectual concentration: the unfortunate accident—for I like to think it was no more—that you had not yet been able to acquire the "Oxford temper" in intellectual matters, never, I mean, been one who could play gracefully with ideas but had arrived at violence of opinion merely—that all these things, combined with the fact that your desires and your interests were in Life not in Art, were as destructive to your own progress in culture as they were to my work as an artist. When I compare my friendship with you to my friendship with such still younger men as John Gray and Pierre Louÿs I feel ashamed. My real life, my higher life, was with them and such as them.

Of the appalling results of my friendship with you I don't speak at present. I am thinking merely of its quality while it lasted. It was intellectually degrading to me. You had the rudiments of an artistic temperament in its germ. But I met you either too late or too soon, I don't know which. When you were away I was all right. The moment, in the early December of the year to which I have been alluding, I had succeeded in inducing your mother to send you out of England, I collected again the torn and ravelled web of my imagination, got my life back into my own hands, and not merely finished the three remaining acts of *An Ideal Husband* but conceived and had almost completed two other plays of a completely different type, the *Florentine Tragedy* and *La Sainte Courtisane*, when suddenly, unbidden, unwelcome, and under circumstances fatal to my happiness, you returned. The two works left then imperfect I was unable to take up again. The mood that created them I could never recover. You now, having yourself published a volume of verse, will be able to recognize the truth of everything I have said here. Whether you can or not, it remains as a hideous truth in the very heart of our friendship. While you were with me you were the absolute ruin of my art, and in allowing you to stand persistently between Art and myself I give to myself shame and blame in the fullest degree. You couldn't know, you couldn't understand, you couldn't appreciate. I had no right to expect it of you at all. Your interests were merely in your meals and moods. Your desires were simply for amusements, for ordinary or less ordinary pleasures. They were what your temperament needed, or thought it needed for the moment.

I should have forbidden you my house and my chambers except when I specially invited you. I blame myself without reserve for my weakness. It was merely weakness. One half-hour with Art was always more to me than a cycle with you. Nothing really at any period of my life was ever of the smallest importance to me compared with Art. But in the case of an artist, weakness is nothing less than a crime, when it is a weakness that paralyses the imagination.

I blame myself for having allowed you to bring me to utter and discreditable financial ruin. I remember one morning in the early October of 1892 sitting in the yellowing woods at Bracknell with your mother. At that time I knew very little of your real nature. I had stayed from a Saturday to Monday with you at Oxford. You had stayed with me at Cromer for ten days and played golf. The conversation turned on you, and your mother began to speak to me about your character. She told me of your two chief faults, your vanity, and your being as she termed it "all wrong about money." I have a distinct recollection of how I laughed. I had no idea that the first would bring me to prison and the second to bankruptcy. I thought vanity a sort of graceful flower for a young man to wear: as for extravagance—for I thought she meant no more than extravagance—the virtues of prudence and thrift were not in my own nature or my own race. But before our friendship was one month older I began to see what your mother really meant. Your insistence on a life of reckless profusion, your incessant demands for money, your claim that all your pleasures should be paid for by me whether I was with you or not, brought me after some time into serious monetary difficulties, and what made the extravagance to me at any rate so monotonously uninteresting, as your persistent grasp on my life grew stronger and stronger, was that the money was really spent on little more than the pleasures of eating, drinking, and the like. Now and then it is a joy to have one's table red with wine and roses, but you outstripped all taste and temperance. You demanded without grace and received without thanks. You grew to think that you had a sort of right to live at my expense and in a profuse luxury to which you had never been accustomed, and which for that reason made your appetites all the more keen; and at the end if you lost money gambling in some Algiers Casino you simply telegraphed next morning to me in London to lodge the amount of your losses to your account at your bank, and gave the matter no further thought of any kind.

When I tell you that between the autumn of 1892 and the date of my imprisonment I spent with you and on you more than £5,000 in actual money, irrespective of the bills I incurred, you will have some idea of the sort of life on which you insisted. Do you think I exaggerate? My ordinary expenses with you for any ordinary day in London—for luncheon, dinner, supper, amusements, hansoms, and the rest of it—ranged from £12 to £20, and the week's expenses were naturally in proportion and ranged from £80 to £130. For our three months at Goring my expenses (rent of course included) were £1,340. Step by step with the Bankruptcy Receiver I had to go over every item of my life. It was horrible. "Plain living and high thinking" was, of course, an ideal you could not at that time have appreciated, but such an extravagance was a disgrace to both of us. One of the most delightful dinners I remember ever having had is one Robbie and I had together in a little Soho café, which cost about as many shillings as my dinners to you used to cost pounds. Out of my dinner with Robbie came the first and best of all my dialogues. Idea, title, treatment, mode, everything was struck out at a 3 franc 50 c. *table d'hôte*. Out of the reckless dinners with you nothing remains but the memory that too much was eaten and too much was drunk. And my yielding to your demands was bad for you. You know that now. It made you grasping often: at times not a little unscrupulous: ungracious always. There was on far too many occasions too little joy or privilege in being your host. You forgot—I will not say the formal courtesy of thanks, for formal courtesies will strain a close friendship—but simply the grace of sweet companionship, the charm of pleasant conversation, that τερπνὸν καλόν as the Greeks called it, and all those gentle humanities that make life lovely, and are an accompaniment to life as music might be, keeping things in tune and filling with melody the harsh or silent places. And though it may seem strange to you that one in the terrible position in which I am situated should find a difference between one disgrace and another, still I frankly admit that the folly of throwing away all this money on you, and letting you squander my fortune to your own hurt as well as to mine, gives to me and in my eyes a note of common profligacy to my bankruptcy and makes me doubly ashamed of it. I was made for other things.

But most of all I blame myself for the entire ethical degradation I allowed you to bring on me. The basis of character is will power, and my will power became absolutely subject to yours. It sounds a grotesque thing to say, but it is none the less true. Those incessant scenes that seemed to be almost physically necessary to you and in which your mind and body grew distorted and you became a thing as terrible to look at as to listen to: that dreadful mania you inherit from your father, the mania for writing revolting and loathsome letters: your entire lack of any control over your emotions, as displayed in your long resentful moods of sullen silence, no less than in your sudden fits of almost epileptic rage: all these things in reference to which one of my letters to you, left by you lying about at the Savoy or some other hotel and so produced in Court by your father's Counsel, contained an entreaty not devoid of pathos, had you at that time been able to recognize pathos in its elements or its expression:—these, I say, were the origin and causes of my fatal yielding to you in your daily increasing demands. You wore me out. It was the triumph of the smaller over the bigger nature. It was the case of that tyranny of the weak over the strong which somewhere in one of my plays I describe as being "the only tyranny that lasts."

And it was inevitable. In every relation of life with others one has to find some *moyen de vivre*.[3] In your case, one had either to give up to you or to give you up. There was no al-

ternative. Through deep if misplaced affection for you:
through great pity for your defects of temper and temperament: through my own proverbial good nature and Celtic
laziness: through an artistic aversion from coarse scenes and
ugly words: through that incapacity to bear resentment of any
kind which at that time characterized me: through my dislike
of seeing life made bitter and uncomely by what to me, with
my eyes really fixed on other things, seemed to be mere tri-
fles too petty for more than a moment's thought or interest:—through those reasons, simple as they may sound, I
gave up to you always. As a natural result, your claims, your
efforts at domination, your exactions grew more and more
unreasonable. Your meanest motive, your lowest appetite,
your most common passion, became to you laws by which the
lives of others were to be guided always, and to which, if necessary, they were to be without scruple sacrificed. Knowing
that by making a scene you could always have your way, it was
but natural that you should proceed, almost unconsciously I
have no doubt, to every excess of vulgar violence. At the end
you did not know to what you were hurrying, or with what
aim in view. Having made your most of my genius, my will
power and my fortune, you required, in the blindness of an
inexhaustible greed, my entire existence. You took it. At the
one supremely and tragically critical moment of all my life,
just before my lamentable step of beginning my absurd action, on the one side there was your father attacking me with
hideous cards left at my club, on the other side there was you
attacking me with no less loathsome letters. The letter I received from you on the morning of the day I let you take me
down to the Police Station to apply for the ridiculous warrant
for your father's arrest was one of the worst you ever wrote,
and for the most shameful reason. Between you both I had
lost my head. My judgement forsook me. Terror took its
place. I saw no possible escape, I may say frankly, from either
of you. Blindly I staggered as an ox to the shambles. I had
made a gigantic psychological error. I had always thought that
my giving up to you in small things meant nothing: that when

a great moment arrived I could myself re-assert my will power in its natural superiority. It was not so. At the great moment my will power completely failed me. In life there is really no great or small thing. All things are of equal value and of equal size. My habit—due to indifference chiefly at first—of giving up to you in everything had become insensibly a real part of my nature. Without my knowing it, it had stereotyped my temperament to one permanent and fatal mood. That is why, in the subtle epilogue to the first edition of his essays, Pater says that "Failure is to form habits." When he said it the dull Oxford people thought the phrase a mere wilful inversion of the somewhat wearisome text of Aristotelian Ethics, but there is a wonderful, a terrible truth hidden in it. I had allowed you to sap my strength of character, and to me the formation of a habit had proved to be not failure merely but ruin. Ethically you had been even still more destructive to me than you had been artistically.

The warrant once granted, your will of course directed everything. At the time when I should have been in London taking wise counsel and calmly considering the hideous trap in which I had allowed myself to be caught—the booby trap as your father calls it to the present day—you insisted on my taking you to Monte Carlo, of all revolting places on God's earth, that all day and all night as well you might gamble as long as the Casino remained open. As for me—baccarat having no charms for me—I was left alone outside to myself. You refused to discuss even for five minutes the position to which you and your father had brought me. My business was merely to pay your hotel expenses and your losses. The slightest allusion to the ordeal awaiting me was regarded as a bore. A new brand of champagne that was recommended to us had more interest for you.

On our return to London those of my friends who really desired my welfare implored me to retire abroad, and not to face an impossible trial. You imputed mean motives to them for giving such advice and cowardice to me for listening to it. You forced me to stay to brazen it out, if possible, in the box by absurd and silly perjuries. At the end, of course, I was arrested and your father became the hero of the hour: more indeed than the hero of the hour merely: your family now ranks strangely enough with the Immortals: for with the grotesqueness of effect that is as it were a Gothic element in history, and makes Clio the least serious of all the Muses, your father will always live among the kind pure-minded parents of Sunday school literature; your place is with the infant Samuel; and in the lowest mire of Malebolge I sit between Gilles de Retz[4] and the Marquis de Sade.[5]

Of course, I should have got rid of you. I should have shaken you out of my life as a man shakes from his raiment a thing that has stung him. In the most wonderful of all his plays Aeschylus[6] tells us of the great lord who brings up in his house the lion cub, the λέοντος ἶνιν, and loves it because it comes bright-eyed to his call and fawns on him for its food; φαιδρωπὸς ποτὶ χεῖρα σαίνων τε γαστρὸς ἀνάγκαις and the thing grows up and shows the nature of its race, ἦθος τὸ πρὸς τοκέων, and destroys the lord and his house and all that he possesses. I feel that I was such a one as he. But my fault was, not that I did not part from you, but that I parted from you far too often. As far as I can make out I ended my friendship with you every three months regularly. And each time that I did so you managed by means of entreaties, telegrams, letters, the interposition of your friends, the interposition of mine, and the like to induce me to allow you back. When at the end of March 1893 you left my house at Torquay I had determined never to speak to you again, or to allow you under any circumstances to be with me, so revolting had been the scene you made the night before your departure. You wrote and telegraphed from Bristol to beg me to forgive you and meet you. Your tutor,[7] who had stayed behind, told me that he thought that at times you were quite irresponsible for what you said and did, and that most if not all of the men at Magdalen were of the same opinion. I consented to meet you and, of course, I forgave you. On the way up to town you begged me to take you to the Savoy. That was indeed a fatal

visit to me. Three months later, in June, we were at Goring.
Some of your Oxford friends came to stay from a Saturday to
Monday. The morning of the day they went away you made a
scene so dreadful, so distressing that I told you that we must
part. I remember quite well as we stood on the level croquet
ground with the pretty lawn all round us, pointing out to you
that we were spoiling each other's lives, that you were absolutely ruining mine and that I evidently was not making you
really happy, and that an irrevocable parting and complete
separation was the one wise philosophic thing to do. You
went sullenly after luncheon, leaving one of your most offensive letters behind with the butler to be handed to me after
your departure. Before three days had elapsed you were
telegraphing from London to beg to be forgiven and allowed
to return. I had taken the place to please you. I had engaged
your own servants at your request. I was always terribly sorry
for the hideous temper to which you were really a prey. I was
fond of you. So I let you come back and forgave you. Three
months later still, in September, new scenes occurred, the occasion of them being my pointing out to you the schoolboy
faults of your attempted translation of *Salomé*. You must by
this time be a fair enough French scholar to know that the
translation was as unworthy of you, as an ordinary Oxonian,
as it was of the work it sought to render. You did not, of
course, know it then and, in one of the violent letters you
wrote to me on the point, you said you were under "no intellectual obligation of any kind" to me. I remember that when
I read that statement I felt that it was really the one true
thing you had written to me in the whole course of our
friendship. I saw that a less cultivated nature would really
have suited you much better. I am not saying this in bitterness at all, but simply as a fact of companionship. Ultimately
the bond of all companionship, whether in marriage or in
friendship, is conversation, and conversation must have a
common basis, and between two people of widely different
culture the only common basis possible is the lowest level.
The trivial in thought and action is charming. I had made it

the keystone of a very brilliant philosophy expressed in plays and paradoxes. But the froth and folly of our life grew often very wearisome to me: it was only in the mire that we met: and fascinating, terribly fascinating though the one topic round which your talk invariably centred was, still at the end it became quite monotonous to me. I was often bored to death by it, and accepted it, as I accepted your passion for going to music halls, or your mania for absurd extravagances in eating and drinking, or any other of your to me less attractive characteristics, as a thing, that is to say, that one simply had to put up with, a part of the high price one had to pay for knowing you. When after leaving Goring I went to Dinard for a fortnight you were extremely angry with me for not taking you with me, and, before my departure there, made some very unpleasant scenes on the subject at the Albemarle Hotel, and sent me some equally unpleasant telegrams to a country house where I was staying for a few days. I told you, I remember, that I thought it was your duty to be with your own people for a little, as you had passed the whole season away from them. But in reality, to be perfectly frank with you, I could not under any circumstances have let you be with me. We had been together nearly twelve weeks. I required rest and freedom from the terrible strain of your companionship. It was necessary for me to be a little by myself. It was intellectually necessary. And so I confess I saw in your letter, from which I have quoted, a very good opportunity for ending the fatal friendship that had sprung up between us, and ending it without bitterness, as I had indeed tried to do on that bright June morning at Goring three months before. It was, however, represented to me—I am bound to say candidly by one of my own friends to whom you had gone in your difficulty— that you would be much hurt, perhaps almost humiliated, at having your work sent back to you like a schoolboy's exercise; that I was expecting far too much intellectually from you; and no matter what you wrote or did, you were absolutely and entirely devoted to me. I did not want to be the first to check or discourage you in your beginnings in literature. I knew quite well that no translation, unless one done by a poet, could render the colour and cadence of my work in any adequate measure: devotion seemed to me, seems to me still, a wonderful thing not to be lightly thrown away: so I took the translation and you back. Exactly three months later, after a series of scenes culminating in one more than usually revolting, when you came one Monday evening to my rooms accompanied by two of your friends, I found myself actually flying abroad next morning to escape from you, giving my family some absurd reason for my sudden departure, and leaving a false address with my servant for fear you might follow me by the next train. And I remember that afternoon, as I was in the railway carriage whirling up to Paris, thinking into what an impossible, terrible, utterly wrong state my life had got when I, a man of world-wide reputation, was actually forced to run away from England in order to try to get rid of a friendship that was entirely destructive of everything fine in me either from the intellectual or ethical point of view: the person from whom I was flying being no terrible creature sprung from sewer or mire into modern life with whom I had entangled my days, but you yourself, a young man of my own social rank and position, who had been at my own College at Oxford and was an incessant guest at my house. The usual telegrams of entreating and remorse followed. I disregarded them. Finally you threatened that unless I consented to meet you, you would under no circumstances consent to proceed to Egypt. I had myself, with your knowledge and concurrence, begged your mother to send you to Egypt away from England, as you were wrecking your life in London. I knew that if you did not go it would be a terrible disappointment to her, and for her sake I did meet you, and under the influence of great emotion, which even you cannot have forgotten, I forgave the past; though I said nothing at all about the future. On my return to London next day I remember sitting in my room and sadly and seriously trying to make up my mind whether or not you really were what you seemed to me to be, so full of terrible defects, so utterly ruinous both to yourself and others, so fatal a one to know even or to be with. For a whole week I thought about it, and wondered if, after all, I was not unjust and mistaken in my estimate of you. At the end of the week a letter from your mother was handed in. It expressed to the full every feeling I myself had about you. In it she spoke of your blind exaggerated vanity which made you despise your home, and treat your elder brother—that *candissima anima*⁸—as "a Philistine": of your temper which made her afraid to speak to you about your life, the life she felt, she knew, you were leading: about your conduct in money matters, so distressing to her in more ways than one: of the degeneration and change that had taken place in you. She saw, of course, that heredity had burdened you with a terrible legacy, and frankly admitted it, admitted it with terror: he is "the one of my children who has inherited the fatal Douglas temperament," she wrote of you. At the end she stated that she felt bound to declare that your friendship with me, in her opinion, had so intensified your vanity that it had become the source of all your faults, and earnestly begged me not to meet you abroad. I wrote to her at once in reply, and told her that I agreed entirely with every word she had said. I added much more. I went as far as I could possibly go. I told her that the origin of our friendship was you in your undergraduate days at Oxford coming to beg me to help you in very serious trouble of a very particular character. I told her that your life had been continually in the same manner troubled. The reason of your going to Belgium you had placed to the fault of your companion in that journey, and your mother had reproached me with having introduced you to him. I replaced the fault on the right shoulders, on yours. I assured her at the end that I had not the smallest intention of meeting you abroad and begged her to try to keep you there either as an honorary attaché, if that were possible, or to learn modern languages, if it were not; or for any reason she chose, at least during two or three years and for your sake as well as for mine. In the meantime you were writing to me by every post from Egypt. I took not the smallest notice of any of your communications. I read them and tore them up. I had quite settled to have no more to do with you. My mind was made up and I gladly devoted myself to the art whose progress I had allowed you to interrupt. At the end of three months, your mother, with that unfortunate weakness of will that characterizes her, and that in the tragedy of my life has been an element no less fatal than your father's violence, actually writes to me herself—I had no doubt of course at your instigation—tells me that you are extremely anxious to hear from me, and in order that I should have no excuse for not communicating with you sends me your address in Athens, which, of course, I knew perfectly well. I confess I was absolutely astounded at her letter. I could not understand how, after what she had written to me in December, and what I in answer had written to her, she could in any way try to repair or renew my unfortunate friendship with you. I acknowledged her letter, of course, and again urged her to try to get you connected with some Embassy abroad, so as to prevent your returning to England, but I did not write to you, or take any more notice of your telegrams than I did before your mother had written to me. Finally you actually telegraphed to my wife begging her to use her influence with me to get me to write to you. Our friendship had always been a source of distress to her: not merely because she had never liked you personally, but because she saw how your continual companionship altered me, and not for the better: still, just as she has always been most gracious and hospitable to you, so she could not bear the idea of my being in any way unkind—for so it seemed to her—to any of my friends. She thought, knew indeed, that it was a thing alien to my character. At her request I did communicate with you. I remember the wording of my telegram quite well. I said that time healed every wound but that for many months to come I would neither write to you nor see you. You started without delay for Paris, sending me passionate telegrams on the road to beg me to see you once, at any rate. I declined. You arrived in Paris late on a Saturday night and found a brief letter from me waiting for you at your hotel stating that I would not see you. Next morning I received in Tite Street a telegram of some ten or eleven pages in length from you. You stated in it that no matter what you had done to me you could not believe that I would absolutely decline to see you: you reminded me that for the sake of seeing me even for one hour you had travelled six days and nights across Europe without stopping once on the way: you made what was, I must admit, a most pathetic appeal and ended with what seemed to me a threat of suicide and one not thinly veiled. You had yourself often told me how many of your race there had been who had stained their hands in their own blood; your uncle certainly, your grandfather possibly, among others in the mad, bad line from which you came. Pity, my old affection for you, regard for your mother to whom your death under such dreadful circumstances would have been a blow almost too great for her to bear, the horror of the idea that so young a life, and one that amidst all its ugly faults had still promise of beauty in it, should come to so revolting an end, merely humanity itself— all these, if excuses be necessary, must serve as my excuse for consenting to accord you one last interview. When I arrived in Paris, your tears breaking out again and again all through the evening, and falling over your cheeks like rain as we sat at dinner first at Voisin's, at supper at Paillard's afterwards: the unfeigned joy you evinced at seeing me, holding my hand whenever you could as though you were a gentle and penitent child: your contrition, so simple and sincere at the moment: made me consent to renew our friendship. Two days after we had returned to London, your father saw you having luncheon with me at the Café Royal, joined my table, drank of my wine, and that afternoon, through a letter addressed to you, began his first attack on me.

It may be strange, but I had once again, I will not say the chance, but the duty of separating from you forced upon me. I need hardly remind you that I refer to your conduct to me at Brighton from 10th to 13th October 1894. Three years is a long time for you to go back. But we who live in prison, and

in whose lives there is no event but sorrow, have to measure
time by throbs of pain, and the record of bitter moments. We
have nothing else to think of. Suffering—curious as it may
sound to you—is the means by which we exist, because it is
the only means by which we become conscious of existing;
and the remembrance of suffering in the past is necessary to
us as the warrant, the evidence, of our continued identity. Between myself and the memory of joy lies a gulf no less deep
than that between myself and joy in its actuality. Had our life
together been as the world fancied it to be, one simply of
pleasure, profligacy, and laughter, I would not be able to recall a single passage in it. It is because it was full of moments
and days tragic, bitter, sinister in their warnings, dull or
dreadful in their monotonous scenes and unseemly violences,
that I can see or hear each separate incident in its detail, can
indeed see or hear little else. So much in this place do men
live by pain that my friendship with you, in the way through
which I am forced to remember it, appears to me always as a
prelude consonant with those varying modes of anguish
which each day I have to realize; nay more, to necessitate
them even; as though my life, whatever it had seemed to myself and others, had all the while been a real symphony of
sorrow, passing through its rhythmically linked movements to
its certain resolution, with that inevitableness that in Art
characterizes the treatment of every great theme.

I spoke of your conduct to me on three successive days
three years ago, did I not? I was trying to finish my last play at
Worthing by myself. The two visits you had paid me had
ended. You suddenly appeared a third time bringing with you
a companion who you actually proposed should stay in my
house. I (you must admit now quite properly) absolutely declined. I entertained you, of course; I had no option in the
matter: but elsewhere, and not in my own house. The next
day, Monday, your companion returned to the duties of his
profession, and you stayed with me. Bored with Worthing,
and still more, I have no doubt, with my fruitless efforts to
concentrate my attention on my play, the only thing that

really interested me at the moment, you insist on being taken to the Grand Hotel at Brighton. The night we arrive you fall ill with that dreadful low fever that is foolishly called the influenza, your second if not your third attack. I need not remind you how I waited on you and tended you, not merely with every luxury of fruit, flowers, presents, books, and the like that money can procure, but with that affection, tenderness and love that whatever you may think is not to be procured for money. Except for an hour's walk in the morning, an hour's drive in the afternoon, I never left the hotel. I got special grapes from London for you as you did not care for those the hotel supplied, invented things to please you, remained either with you or in the room next to yours, sat with you every evening to quiet or amuse you. After four or five days you recover and I take lodgings in order to try to finish my play. You, of course, accompany me. The morning after the day on which we were installed I feel extremely ill. You have to go to London on business, but promise to return in the afternoon. In London you meet a friend, and do not come back to Brighton till late on the next day, by which time I am in a terrible fever, and the doctor finds I have caught the influenza from you. Nothing could have been more uncomfortable for anyone ill than the lodgings turn out to be. My sitting-room is on the first floor, my bedroom on the third. There is no manservant to wait on one, not even anyone to send out on a message, or to get what the doctor orders. But you are there. I feel no alarm. The next two days you leave me entirely alone without care, without attendance, without anything. It was not a question of grapes, flowers, and charming gifts: it was a question of mere necessaries: I could not even get the milk the doctor had ordered me: lemonade was pronounced an impossibility: and when I begged you to procure a book at the bookseller's, or if they had not got whatever I had fixed on, to choose something else, you never even take the trouble to go there. And when I was left all day without anything to read in consequence, you calmly tell me that you bought me the book and that they promised to send it down, a statement which I found by chance afterwards to have been entirely untrue from beginning to end. All the while you are, of course, living at my expense, driving about, dining at the Grand Hotel, and indeed only appearing in my room for money. On the Saturday night, you having left me completely unattended and alone since the morning, I asked you to come back after dinner, and sit with me for a little. With irritable voice and ungracious manner you promise to do so. I wait till eleven o'clock and you never appear. I then left a note for you in your room just reminding you of the promise you had made me, and how you had kept it. At three in the morning, unable to sleep, and tortured with thirst, I made my way in the dark and cold, down to the sitting-room in the hopes of finding some water there. I found you. You fell on me with every hideous word an intemperate mood, an undisciplined and untutored nature could suggest. By the terrible alchemy of egotism you converted your remorse into rage. You accused me of selfishness in expecting you to be with me when I was ill; of standing between you and your amusements: of trying to deprive you of your pleasures. You told me, and I know it was quite true, that you had come back at midnight simply in order to change your dress-clothes and go out again to where you hoped new pleasures were awaiting for you, but that by leaving for you a letter in which I had reminded you that you had neglected me the whole day and the whole evening I had really robbed you of your desire for more enjoyments, and diminished your actual capacity for fresh delights. I went back upstairs in disgust and remained sleepless till dawn, nor till long after dawn was I able to get anything to quench the thirst of the fever that was on me. At eleven o'clock you came into my room. In the previous scene I could not help observing that by my letter I had, at any rate, checked you in a night of more than usual excess. In the morning you were quite yourself. I waited naturally to hear what excuses you had to make, and in what way you were going to ask for the forgiveness that you knew in your heart was invariably waiting for you, no matter what you did; your

absolute trust that I would always forgive you being the thing
in you that I always really liked best, perhaps the best thing in
you to like. So far from doing that, you began to repeat the
same scene with renewed emphasis and more violent assertion. I told you at length to leave the room: you pretended to
do so, but when I lifted up my head from the pillow in which
I had buried it, you were still there, and with brutality of
laughter and hysteria of rage you moved suddenly towards
me. A sense of horror came over me, for what exact reason I
could not make out: but I got out of my bed at once, and
bare-footed and just as I was, made my way down the two
flights of stairs to the sitting-room, which I did not leave till
the owner of the lodgings—whom I had rung for—had assured me that you had left my bedroom, and promised to remain within call in case of necessity. After an interval of an
hour, during which time the doctor had come and found me,
of course, in a state of absolute nervous prostration, as well as
in a worse condition of fever than I had been at the outset,
you returned silently for money: took what you could find on
the dressing-table and mantelpiece, and left the house with
your luggage. Need I tell you what I thought of you during
the two lonely wretched days of illness that followed? Is it
necessary for me to state that I saw clearly that it would be a
dishonour to myself to continue even an acquaintance with
such a one as you had showed yourself to be? That I recognized that the ultimate moment had come and recognized it
as being really a great relief? And that I knew that for the future my Art and Life would be freer and better and more
beautiful in every possible way? Ill as I was, I felt at ease. The
fact that the separation was irrevocable gave me peace. By
Tuesday the fever had left me: and for the first time I dined
downstairs. Tuesday was my birthday. Amongst the telegrams
and communications on my table was a letter in your hand-
writing. I opened it with a sense of sadness on me. I knew
that the time had gone by when a pretty phrase, an expression of affection, a word of sorrow would make me take you
back. But I was entirely deceived. I had underrated you. The

letter you sent to me on my birthday was an elaborate repetition of the two scenes set cunningly and carefully down in black and white! You mocked me with common jests. Your one satisfaction in the whole affair was, you said, that you retired to the Grand Hotel, and entered your luncheon to my account before you left for town. You congratulated me on my prudence in leaving the sickbed, on my sudden flight downstairs. "It was an ugly moment for you," you said, "uglier than you imagine." Ah! I felt it but too well. What it had really meant I do not know: whether you had with you the pistol you had bought to try to frighten your father with, and that, thinking it to be unloaded, you had once fired off in a public restaurant in my company: whether your hand was moving towards a common dinner knife that by chance was lying on the table between us: whether, forgetting in your rage your low stature and inferior strength, you had thought of some specially personal insult, or attack even, as I lay ill there: I could not tell. I do not know to the present moment. All I know is that a feeling of utter horror had come over me, and that I had felt that unless I left the room at once and got away, you would have done or tried to do something that would have been, even to you, a source of lifelong shame. Only once before in my life had I experienced such a feeling of horror at any human being. It was when in my Library at Tite Street, waving his small hands in the air in epileptic fury, your father, with his bully, or his friend between us, had stood uttering every foul word his foul mind could think of, and screaming the loathsome threats he afterwards with such cunning carried out. In the latter case, he, of course, was the one who had to leave the room first. I drove him out. In your case *I* went. It was not the first time I had been obliged to save you from yourself.

You concluded your letter by saying: "When you are not on your pedestal you are not interesting. The next time you are ill I will go away at once." Ah! what coarseness of fibre does that reveal! What an entire lack of imagination! How callous, how common had the temperament by that time become! "When you are not on your pedestal you are not interesting. The next time you are ill I will go away at once." How often have those words come back to me in the wretched solitary cell of the various prisons to which I have been sent. I have said them to myself over and over again, and seen in them, I hope unjustly, some of the secret of your strange silence. For you to write this to me, when the very illness and fever from which I was suffering I had caught from tending you, was of course revolting in its coarseness and crudity; but for any human being in the whole wide world to write thus to another would be a sin for which there is no pardon, were there any sin for which there is none.

I confess that when I finished your letter I felt almost polluted, as if by associating with one of such a nature I had soiled and shamed my life irretrievably. I had, it is true, done so, but I was not to learn how fully, till just six months later in life. I settled with myself to go back to London on the Friday, and see Sir George Lewis privately and request him to write to your father to state that I had determined never under any circumstances to allow you to enter my house, to sit at my board, to talk to me, walk with me, or anywhere and at any time to be my companion at all. This done I would have written to you just to inform you of the course of action I had adopted; the reasons you would have inevitably have realized yourself. I had everything arranged on Thursday night, when on Friday morning, as I was sitting at breakfast before starting, I happened to open the newspaper and saw in it a telegram stating that your elder brother, the real head of the family, the heir to the title, the pillar of the house, had been found dead in a ditch with his gun lying discharged beside him. The horror of the circumstances of the tragedy, now known to have been an accident, but then stained with a darker suggestion, the pathos of the sudden death of one so loved by all who knew him and almost on the eve, as it were, of his marriage; my idea of what your own sorrow would be, or should be; my consciousness of the misery awaiting your mother at the loss of the one to whom she clung for comfort and joy in life, and who, as she told me once herself, had from the very day of his birth never caused her to shed a single tear; my consciousness of your own isolation, both your other brothers being out of Europe and you consequently the only one to whom your mother and sister could look not merely for companionship in their sorrow but also for those dreary responsibilities of dreadful detail that Death always brings with it; the mere sense of the *lacrimae rerum*,[9] of the tears of which the world is made, and of the sadness of all human things—out of the confluence of these thoughts and emotions crowding into my brain came infinite pity for you and your family. My own griefs and bitterness against you I forgot. What you had been to me in my sickness, I could not be to you in your bereavement. I telegraphed at once to you my deepest sympathy, and in the letter that followed invited you to come to my house as soon as you were able. I felt that to abandon you at that particular moment, and formally through a solicitor, would have been too terrible for you.

On your return to town from the actual scene of the tragedy to which you had been summoned, you came at once to me very sweetly and very simply, in your suit of woe, and with your eyes dim with tears. You sought consolation and help, as a child might seek it. I opened to you my house, my home, my heart. I made your sorrow mine also, that you might have help in bearing it. Never even by one word did I allude to your conduct towards me, to the revolting scenes and the revolting letter. Your grief which was real seemed to me to bring you nearer to me than you had ever been. The flowers you took from me to put on your brother's grave were to be a symbol not merely of the beauty of his life, but of the beauty that in all lives lies dormant and may be brought to light.

The gods are strange. It is not our vices only they make instruments to scourge us. They bring us to ruin through what in us is good, gentle, humane, loving. But for my pity and affection for you and yours, I would not now be weeping in this terrible place.

Of course, I discern in all our relations not Destiny merely, but Doom: Doom that (always) walks swiftly, because she goes to the shedding of blood. Through your father you come of a race, marriage with whom is horrible, friendship fatal, and that lays violent hands either on its own life, or on the lives of others. In every little circumstance in which the ways of our lives met; in every point of great, or seemingly trivial import in which you came to me for pleasure or for help; in the small chances, the slight accidents that look, in their relation to life, to be no more than the dust that dances in a beam, or the leaf that flutters from a tree, Ruin followed like the echo of a bitter cry, or the shadow that hunts with the beast of prey. Our friendship really begins with your begging me in a most pathetic and charming letter to assist you in a position appalling to any one, doubly so to a young man at Oxford: I do so, and ultimately through your using my name as your friend with Sir George Lewis I began to lose his esteem and friendship, a friendship of fifteen years' standing. When I was deprived of his advice and help and regard I was deprived of the one great safeguard of my life.

You send me a very nice poem of the undergraduate school of verse for my approval: I reply by a letter of fantastic literary conceits: I compare you to Hylas, or Hyacinth, Jonquil or Narcisse[10] or some one whom the great God of Poetry favoured, and honoured with his love. The letter is like a passage from one of Shakespeare's sonnets transposed to a minor key. It can be understood only by those who had read the *Symposium* of Plato, or caught the spirit of a certain grave mood made beautiful for us in Greek marbles. It was, let me say frankly, the sort of letter I would, in a happy if wilful moment, have written to any graceful young man of either University who had sent me a poem of his own making, certain that he would have sufficient wit, or culture, to interpret rightly its fantastic phrases. Look at the history of that letter! It passes from you into the hands of a loathsome companion: from him to a gang of blackmailers: copies of it are sent about London to my friends, and to the manager of the theatre where my work is being performed: every construction but the right one is put on it: Society is thrilled with the absurd rumours that I have had to pay a huge sum of money for having written an infamous letter to you: this forms the basis of your father's worst attack: I produce the original letter myself in Court to show what it really is: it is denounced by your father's Counsel as a revolting and insidious attempt to corrupt innocence: ultimately it forms part of a criminal charge: the Crown takes it up: the Judge sums up on it with little learning and much morality: I go to prison for it at last. That is the result of writing you a charming letter.

While I am staying with you at Salisbury you are terribly alarmed at a threatening communication from a former companion of yours: you beg me to see the writer and help you: I do so. The result is ruin for me. I am forced to take everything you have done on my shoulders and answer for it. When, having failed to take your degree, you have to go down from Oxford, you telegraph to me in London to beg me to come to you. I do so at once: you ask me to take you to Goring, as you did not like under the circumstances to go home: at Goring you see a house that charms you: I take it for you: the result from every point of view is ruin for me. One day you come to me and ask me as a personal favour to you, to write something for an Oxford undergraduate magazine, about to be started by some friend of yours of whom I have never heard in all my life, and knew nothing at all about. To please you—what did I not do always to please you?—I sent him a page of paradoxes destined originally for the *Saturday Review*. A few months later I find myself standing in the dock of the Old Bailey on account of the character of the magazine. It forms part of the Crown charge against me. I am called upon to defend your friend's prose and your own verse. The former I cannot palliate: the latter I, loyal to the bitter extreme, to your youthful literature as to your youthful life, do very strongly defend, and will not hear of your being a writer of indecencies. But I go to prison, all the same, for your friend's undergraduate magazine and the "Love that

dares not tell its name." At Christmas I give you a "very
pretty present"—as you described it in your letter of thanks,
on which I knew you had set your heart, worth some £40 or
£50 at most. When the crash of my life comes and I am ruined, the bailiff who seizes my library, and has it sold, does so
to pay for the "very pretty present." It was for that the execution was put into my house. At the ultimate and terrible moment when I am taunted, and spurred on by your taunts, to
take an action against your father and have him arrested, the
last straw to which I clutch in my wretched efforts to escape
is the terrible expense. I tell the solicitor in your presence
that I have no funds, that I cannot possibly afford the appalling cost, that I have no money at my disposal. What I said
was, as you know, perfectly true. On that fatal Friday instead
of being in Humphrey's office weakly consenting to my own
ruin, I would have been happy and free in France, away from
you and your father, unconscious of his loathsome card, and
indifferent to your letters, if I had been able to leave the
Avondale Hotel. But the hotel people absolutely refused to
allow me to go. You had been staying with me for ten days:
indeed you ultimately and to my great and, you will admit,
rightful indignation, brought a companion of yours to stay
with me also: my bill for the ten days was nearly £140. The
proprietor said he could not allow my luggage to be removed
from the hotel till I had paid the account in full. That is what
kept me in London. Had it not been for the hotel bill I would
have gone to Paris on Thursday morning.

When I told the solicitor I had no money to face the gigantic expense, you interposed at once. You said that your
own family would be only too delighted to pay all the necessary costs: that your father had been an incubus to them all:
that they had often discussed the possibility of getting him
put into a lunatic asylum so as to keep him out of the way:
that he was a daily source of annoyance and distress to your
mother and to everyone else: that if only I would come forward to have him shut up I would be regarded by the family
as their champion and their benefactor; and that your

mother's rich relations themselves would look on it as a real delight to be allowed to pay all costs and expenses that might be incurred in any such effort. The solicitor closed at once, and I was hurried to the Police Court. I had no excuse left for not going. I was forced into it. Of course, your family don't pay the costs, and when I am made bankrupt, it is by your father and for the costs—the meagre balance of them—some £700. At the present moment my wife, estranged from me over the important question whether I should have £3 or 10s. a week to live on, is preparing a divorce suit, for which, of course, entirely new evidence and an entirely new trial, to be followed perhaps by more serious proceedings, will be necessary. I, naturally, know nothing of the details. I merely know the name of the witness on whose evidence my wife's solicitors rely. It is your own Oxford servant, whom at your special request I took into my service for our summer at Goring.

But, indeed, I need not go on further into more instances of the strange doom you seem to have brought on me in all things big or little. It makes me feel sometimes as if you yourself had been merely a puppet worked by some secret and unseen hand to bring terrible events to a terrible issue. But puppets themselves have passions. They will bring a new plot into what they are presenting, and twist the ordered issue of vicissitude to suit some whim or appetite of their own. To be entirely free, and at the same time entirely dominated by law, is the eternal paradox of human life that we realize at every moment: and this, I often think, is the only explanation possible of your nature, if indeed for the profound and terrible mystery of a human soul there is any explanation at all, except one that makes the mystery all the more marvellous still.

Of course, you had your illusions, lived in them indeed, and through the shifting mists and coloured veils saw all things changed. You thought, I remember quite well, that your devoting yourself to me, to the entire exclusion of your family and family life, was a proof of your wonderful appreciation of me and your great affection. No doubt to you it seemed so. But recollect that with me was luxury, high living, unlimited pleasure, money without stint. Your family life bored you. The "cold cheap wine of Salisbury," to use a phrase of your own making, was distasteful to you. On my side and along with my intellectual attractions were the flesh-pots of Egypt. When you could not find me to be with, the companions whom you chose as substitutes were not flattering.

You thought again that in sending a lawyer's letter to your father to say that, rather than sever your eternal friendship with me, you will give up the allowance of £250 a year which, with, I believe, deductions for your Oxford debts, he was then making you, you were realizing the very chivalry of friendship, touching the noblest note of self-denial. But your surrender of your little allowance did not mean that you were ready to give up even one of your most superfluous luxuries, or most unnecessary extravagances. On the contrary, your appetite for luxurious living was never so keen. My expenses for eight days in Paris for myself, you and your Italian servant were nearly £150: Paillard alone absorbing £85. At the rate at which you wished to live, your entire income for a whole year, if you had taken your meals alone, and had been especially economical in your selection of the cheaper form of pleasures, would hardly have lasted you three weeks. The fact that in what was merely pretence of bravado you had surrendered your allowance, such as it was, gave you at least a plausible reason for your claim to live at my expense: or what you thought a plausible reason: and on many occasions you seriously availed yourself of it, and gave the very fullest expression to it: and the continued drain, principally of course on me, but also to a terrible extent, I know, on your mother, was never so distressing; because in my case, at any rate, never so completely unaccompanied by the smallest word of thanks, or sense of limit.

You thought again that in attacking your own father with dreadful letters, abusive telegrams, and insulting postcards, you were really fighting your mother's battles, coming forward as her champion, and avenging the no doubt terrible wrongs and sufferings of her married life. It was quite an illusion on your part, one of your worst indeed. The way for you to have avenged your mother's wrongs on your father, if you considered it part of a son's duty to do so, was by being a better son to your mother than you had been: by not making her afraid to speak to you on serious things: by not signing bills the payment of which devolved on her: by being gentler to her, and not bringing sorrow into her days. Your brother Francis made great amends to her for what she had suffered, by his sweetness and goodness to her through the brief years of his flower-like life. You should have taken him as your model. You were wrong even in fancying that it would have been an absolute delight and joy to your mother if you had managed through me to get your father put into prison. I feel sure you were wrong. And if you want to know what a woman really feels when her husband and the father of her children is in prison dress, in a prison cell, write to my wife and ask her. She will tell you. *I* also had my illusions. I thought life was going to be a brilliant comedy, and that you were to be one of the graceful figures in it. I found it to be a revolting and repellent tragedy, and that the sinister occasion of the great catastrophe, sinister in its concentration of aim and intensity of narrowed will power, was yourself, stripped of that mask of joy and pleasure by which you, no less than I, had been deceived and led astray.

You can now understand—can you not?—a little of what I am suffering. Some paper, the *Pall Mall Gazette*, I think, describing the dress rehearsal of one of my plays, spoke of you as following me about like my shadow: the memory of our friendship is the shadow that walks with me here: that seems never to leave me: that wakes me up at night to tell me the same story over and over till its wearisome iteration makes all sleep abandon me till dawn: at dawn it begins again: it follows me into the prison yard and makes me talk to myself as I tramp round: each detail that accompanied each dreadful moment I am forced to recall: there is nothing that happened in those ill-starred years that I cannot re-create in that chamber of the brain which is set apart for grief or for despair: every strained note of your voice, every twitch and gesture of your nervous hands, every bitter word, every poisonous phrase comes back to me: I remember the street or river down which we passed: the wall or woodland that surrounded us, at what figure on the dial stood the hands of the clock, which way went the wings of the wind, the shape and colour of the moon.

There is, I know, one answer to all that I have said to you, and that is that you loved me: that all through those two and a half years during which the fates were weaving into one scarlet pattern the threads of our divided lives you really loved me. Yes, I know you did. No matter what your conduct to me was, I always felt that at heart you really did love me. Though I saw quite clearly that my position in the world of Art, the interest that my personality had always excited, my money, the luxury in which I lived, the thousand and one things that went to make up a life so charmingly and so wonderfully improbable as mine was, were, each and all of them, elements that fascinated you and made you cling to me: yet besides all this there was something more, some strange attraction for you: you loved me far better than you loved anyone else. But you, like myself, have had a terrible tragedy in your life, though one of an entirely opposite character to mine. Do you want to learn what it was? It was this. In you hate was always stronger than love. Your hatred of your father was of such stature that it entirely outstripped, overthrew, and overshadowed your love of me. There was no struggle between them at all, or but little; of such dimensions was your hatred and of such monstrous growth. You did not realize that there was no room for both passions in the same soul. They cannot live together in that fair carven house. Love is fed by the imagination, by which we become wiser than we know, better than we feel, nobler than we are: by which we can see life as a whole: by which and by which alone we can understand others in their real as in their ideal relation. Only what is fine, and finely conceived, can feed love. But anything will feed hate. There was not a glass of champagne that you drank, not a rich dish that you ate of in all those years, that did not feed your hate and make it fat. So to gratify it you gambled with my life, as you gambled with my money, carelessly, recklessly, indifferent to the consequence. If you lost, the loss would not, you fancied, be yours. If you won, yours, you knew, would be the exultation and the advantages of victory.

Hate blinds people. You were not aware of that. Love can read the writing on the remotest star; but hate so blinded you that you could see no further than the narrow, walled-in and already lust-withered garden of your common desires. Your terrible lack of imagination, the one really fatal defect of your character, was entirely the result of the hate that lived in you. Subtly, silently, and in secret, hate gnawed at your nature, as the lichen bites at the root of some sallow plant, till you grew to see nothing but the most meagre interests and the most petty aims. That faculty in you which love would have fostered, hate poisoned and paralysed. When your father first began to attack me it was as your private friend, and in a private letter to you. As soon as I had read the letter with its obscene threats and coarse violences I saw at once that there was a terrible danger looming on the horizon of my troubled days: I told you I would not be the cat's-paw between you both in your ancient hatred of each other: that I in London was naturally much bigger game for him than a Secretary for Foreign Affairs at Homberg; that it would be unfair to me to place me even for a moment in such a position: and that I had something better to do with my life than to have scenes with a man, drunken, déclassé, and half-witted as he was. You would not be made to see this. Hate blinded you. You insisted that the quarrel had really nothing to do with me that you would not allow your father to dictate to you in your private friendships: that it would be most unfair of me to interfere. You had already, before you saw me on the subject, sent your father a foolish and vulgar telegram as your answer.

That, of course, committed you to a foolish and vulgar course of action to follow. The fatal errors of life are not due to man's being unreasonable. An unreasonable moment may be one's finest moment. They are due to man's being logical. There is a wide difference. That telegram conditioned the whole of your subsequent relations with your father, and consequently the whole of my life. And the grotesque thing about it is that it was a telegram of which the commonest street boy would have been ashamed. From pert telegrams to priggish lawyers' letters was a natural progress, and the result of your lawyers' letters to your father was, of course, to urge him on still further. You left him no option but to go on. You forced it on him as a point of honour, or of dishonour rather, that your appeal should have the more effect. So the next time he attacks me no longer in a private letter and as your private friend, but in public and as a public man. I have to expel him from my house. He goes from restaurant to restaurant looking for me, in order to insult me before the whole world, and in such a manner that if I retaliated I would be ruined, and if I did not retaliate I would be ruined also. *Then* surely was the time when *you* should have come forward and said that you would not expose me to such hideous attacks, such infamous persecution, on your account, but would, readily and at once, resign any claim you had to my friendship. You feel that now, I suppose. But it never even occurred to you then. Hate blinded you. All you could think of (besides, of course, writing to him insulting letters and telegrams) was to buy a ridiculous pistol that goes off in the Berkeley under circumstances that create a worse scandal than ever came to *your* ears. Indeed the idea of your being the object of a terrible quarrel between your father and a man of my position seemed to delight you. It, I suppose, very naturally, pleased your vanity and flattered your self-importance. That your father might have had your body which did not interest me, and left me your soul which did not interest him, would have been to you a distressing solution of the question. You scented the chance of a public scandal and flew to it. The prospect of a battle in which you would be safe delighted you. I never remember you in higher spirits than you were for the rest of that season. Your only disappointment seemed to be that nothing actually happened, and that no further meeting or fracas had taken place between us. You consoled yourself by sending him telegrams of such a character that at last the wretched man wrote to you and said that he had given orders to his servants that no telegrams were to be brought to him under any pretence whatsoever. That did not daunt you. You saw the immense opportunities afforded by the open postcard, and availed yourself of them to the full. You hounded him on in the chase still more. I do not suppose he would ever really have given it up. Family instincts were really strong in him. His hatred of you was just as persistent as your hatred of him, and I was the stalking-horse for both of you, and a mode of attack as well as a mode of shelter. His very passion for notoriety was not merely individual but racial. Still, if his interest had flagged for a moment your letters and postcards would soon have quickened it to its ancient flame. They did so. And he naturally went on further still. Having assailed me as a private gentleman and in private, as a public man and in public, he ultimately determines to make his final and great attack on me as an artist, and in the place where my art is being represented. He secures by fraud a seat for the first night of one of my plays, and contrives a plot to interrupt the performance, to make a foul speech about me to the audience, to insult my actors, to throw offensive or indecent missiles at me when I am called before the curtain at the close, utterly in some hideous way to ruin me through my work. By the merest chance, in the brief and accidental sincerity of a more than usually intoxicated mood, he boasts of his intention before others. Information is given to the police, and he is kept out of the theatre. You had your chance then. Then was your opportunity. Don't you realize now that you should have seen it, and come forward and said that you would not have my art, at any rate, ruined for your sake? You knew what my art was to me, the great primal note by which I had revealed, first myself to myself, and then myself to the world; the great passion of my life; the love to which all other loves were as marsh water to red wine; or the glowworm of the marsh to the magic mirror of the moon. Don't you understand now that your lack of imagination was the only really fatal defect of your character? What you had to do was quite simple, and quite clear before you, but hate blinded you, and you could see nothing. I could not apologize to your father for his having insulted me and persecuted me in the most loathsome manner for nearly nine months. I could not get rid of you out of my life. I had tried it again and again. I had gone so far as actually leaving England and going abroad in the hope of escaping from you. It had all been of no use. You were the only person who could have done anything.

The key of the situation rested entirely with yourself. It was the one great opportunity you had of making some slight return to me for all the love and affection and kindness and generosity and care I had shown you. Had you appreciated me even at a tenth of my value as an artist you would have done so. But hate blinded you. The faculty "by which and by which alone we can understand others in their real, as in their ideal relations" was dead in you. You thought simply of how to get your father into prison. To see him "in the dock," as you used to say: that was your one idea. The phrase became one of the many *scies*[11] of your daily conversation. One heard it at every meal. Well, you had your desire gratified. Hate granted you every single thing you wished for. It was an indulgent master to you. It is so, indeed, to all who serve it. For two days you sat on a high seat with the Sheriffs, and feasted your eyes with the spectacle of your father standing in the dock of the Central Criminal Court. And on the third day I took his place. What had occurred? In your hideous game of hate together, you had both thrown dice for my soul and you happened to have lost. That was all.

You see that I have to write your life to you and you have to realize it. We have known each other now for more than

four years. Half of the time we have been together: the other
half I have had to spend in prison as the result of our friendship. Where you will receive this letter, if indeed it ever
reaches you, I don't know. Rome, Naples, Paris, Venice, some
beautiful city on sea or river, I have no doubt, holds you. You
are surrounded, if not with all the useless luxury you had with
me, at any rate with everything that is pleasurable to eye, ear
and taste. Life is quite lovely to you. And yet, if you are wise,
and wish to find life much lovelier still, and in a different
manner, you will let the reading of this terrible letter—for
such I know it is—prove to you as important a crisis and
turning-point of your life as the writing of it is to me. Your
pale face used to flush easily with wine or pleasure. If, as you
read what is here written, it from time to time becomes
scorched as though by a furnace blast, with shame, it will be
all the better for you. The supreme vice is shallowness. Whatever is realized is right.

I have now got as far as the house of detention, have I
not? After a night passed in the police cells I am sent there in
the van. You were most attentive and kind. Almost every afternoon, if not actually every afternoon, till you go abroad you
took the trouble to drive up to Holloway[12] to see me. You also
wrote very sweet and nice letters. But that it was not your father but you who had put me into prison, that from beginning to end you were the responsible person, that it was
through you, for you, and by you that I was there, never for
one instant dawned upon you. Even the spectacle of me behind the bars of a wooden cage could not quicken that dead
unimaginative nature. You had the sympathy and the sentimentality of the spectator of a rather pathetic play. That you
were the true author of the hideous tragedy did not occur to
you. I saw that you realized nothing of what you had done. I
did not desire to be the one to tell you what your own heart
should have told you, what it indeed would have told you if
you had not let hate harden it and make it insensate. Everything must come to one out of one's own nature. There is no
use telling a person a thing that he does not feel and can't un-

derstand. If I write to you now as I do it is because your own silence and conduct during my long imprisonment have made it necessary. Besides, as things had turned out the blow had fallen upon me alone. That was a source of pleasure to me. I was content for many reasons to suffer, though there was always to my eyes, as I watched you, something not a little contemptible in your complete and wilful blindness. I remember you producing with absolute pride a letter you had published in one of the halfpenny newspapers about me. It was a very prudent, temperate, indeed commonplace production. You appealed to the "English sense of fair play," or something very dreary of that kind, on behalf of a "man who was down." It was the sort of letter you might have written had a painful charge been brought against some respectable person with whom personally you had been quite unacquainted. But you thought it a wonderful letter. You looked on it as a proof of almost quixotic chivalry. I am aware that you wrote other letters to other newspapers that they did not publish. But then they were simply to say that you hated your father. Nobody cared if you did or not. Hate, you had yet to learn, is, intellectually considered, the eternal negation. Considered from the point of view of the emotions it is a form of atrophy, and kills everything but itself. To write to the papers to say that one hates someone is as if one were to write to the papers to say that one had some secret and shameful malady: the fact that the man you hated was your own father, and that the feeling was thoroughly reciprocated, did not make your hate noble or fine in any way. If it showed anything it was simply that it was an hereditary disease.

I remember again, when an execution was put into my house, and my books and furniture were seized and advertised to be sold, and bankruptcy was impending, I naturally wrote to tell you about it. I did not mention that it was to pay for some gifts of mine to you that the bailiffs had entered the house where you had so often dined. I thought, rightly or wrongly, that such news might pain you a little. I merely told you the bare facts. I thought it proper that you should know them. You wrote back from Boulogne in a strain of almost lyrical exultation. You said that you knew your father was "hard up for money" and had been obliged to raise £1,500 for the expenses of the trial and that my going bankrupt was really a "splendid score" off him as he would not then be able to get any of his costs out of me! Do you realize now what hate blinding a person is? Do you recognize now that when I described it as an atrophy destructive of everything but itself, I was scientifically describing a real psychological fact? That all my charming things were to be sold: my Burne-Jones drawings: my Whistler drawings: my Monticelli, my Simeon Solomons: my china: my library with its collection of presentation volumes from almost every poet of my time, from Hugo to Whitman, from Swinburne to Mallarmé, from Morris to Verlaine: with its beautifully bound editions of my father's and mother's works, its wonderful array of college and school prizes: its *éditions de luxe*, and the like: was absolutely nothing to you. You said it was a great bore: that was all. What you really saw in it was the possibility that your father might ultimately lose a few hundred pounds, and that paltry consideration filled you with ecstatic joy. As for the costs of the trial, you may be interested to know that your father openly said in the Orleans Club that if it had cost £20,000 he would have considered the money thoroughly well spent he had extracted such enjoyment, and delight, and triumph out of it all. The fact that he was able not merely to put me into prison for two years but to take me out for an afternoon and make me a public bankrupt was an extra refinement of pleasure that he had not expected. It was the crowning point of my humiliation and of his complete and perfect victory. Had your father had no claim for his costs on me, you, I know perfectly well, would, as far as words go, at any rate have been most sympathetic about the entire loss of my library, a loss irreparable to a man of letters, the one of all my material losses the most distressing to me. You might even, remembering the sums of money I had lavishly spent on you and how you had lived on me for years, have taken the trouble to buy in some of my books for me. The best all went for less than £150: about as much as I would spend on you in an ordinary week. But the mean, small pleasure of thinking that your father was going to be a few pence out of pocket made you forget all about trying to make me a little return, so slight, so easy, so inexpensive, so obvious, and so enormously welcome to me, had you brought it about. Am I right in saying that hate blinds people? Do you see it now? If you don't, try to see it.

How clearly I saw it then, as now, I need not tell you. But I said to myself: "At all costs, I must keep love in my heart. If I go into prison without love what will become of my soul?" The letters I wrote to you at that time from Holloway were my effort to keep love as the dominant note of my own nature. I could if I had chosen have torn you to pieces with bitter reproaches. I could have rent you with maledictions. I could have held up a mirror to you, and shown you such an image of yourself that you would not have recognized it as your own till you found it mimicking back your gestures of horror, and then you would have known whose shape it was, and hated it and yourself for ever. More than that indeed. The sins of another were being placed to my account. Had I so chosen, I could on either trial have saved myself at his expense, not from shame indeed, but from imprisonment. Had I cared to show that the Crown witnesses—the three most important—had been carefully coached by your father and his solicitors, not in reticences merely, but in assertions, in the absolute transference deliberate, plotted and rehearsed, of the actions and doings of someone else on to me, I could have had each one of them dismissed from the box by the judge, more summarily than even wretched perjured Atkins was. I could have walked out of Court with my tongue in my cheek, and my hands in my pockets, a free man. The strongest pressure was put upon me to do so. I was earnestly advised, begged, entreated to do so by people whose sole interest was my welfare, and the welfare of my house. But I refused. I did not choose to do so. I have never regretted my decision for a single moment, even in the most bitter periods of my imprisonment. Such a course of action would have been beneath me. Sins of the flesh are nothing. They are maladies for physicians to cure, if they should be cured. Sins of the soul alone are shameful. To have secured my acquittal by such means would have been a lifelong torture to me. But do you really think that you were worthy of the love I was showing you then, or that for a single moment I thought you were? Do you really think that at any period in our friendship you were worthy of the love I showed you, or that for a single moment I thought you were? I knew you were not. But love does not traffic in a market place, nor use a huckster's scales. Its joy, like the joy of the intellect, is to feel alive. The aim of love is to love: no more, and no less. You were my enemy: such an enemy as no man ever had. I had given you my life: and to gratify the lowest and most contemptible of all human passions, Hatred and Vanity and Greed, you had thrown it away. In less than three years you had entirely ruined me from every point of view. For my own sake there was nothing for me to do but to love you. I knew that if I allowed myself to hate you that in the dry desert of existence over which I had to travel, and am travelling still, every rock would lose its shadow, every palm tree be withered, every well of water prove poisoned at its source. Are you beginning now to understand a little? Is your imagination awakening from the long lethargy in which it has lain? You know already what hate is. Is it beginning to dawn on you what love is and what is the nature of love? It is not too late for you to learn, though to teach it to you I may have had to go to a convict's cell.

After my terrible sentence, when the prison dress was on me, and the prison house closed, I sat amidst the ruins of my wonderful life, crushed by anguish, bewildered with terror, dazed through pain. But I would not hate you. Every day I said to myself: "I must keep love in my heart to-day, else how shall I live through the day?" I reminded myself that you meant no evil, to me at any rate: I set myself to think that you had but drawn a bow at a venture, and that the arrow had pierced a king between the joints of his harness. To have weighed you against the smallest of my sorrows, the meanest of my losses, would have been, I felt, unfair. I determined I would regard you as one suffering too. I forced myself to believe that at last the scales had fallen from your long-blinded eyes. I used to fancy and with pain what your horror must have been when you contemplated your terrible handiwork. There were times, even in those dark days, the darkest of all my life, when I actually longed to console you, so sure was I that at last you had realized what you had done.

It did not occur to me then that you could have the supreme vice, shallowness. Indeed it was a real grief to me when I had to let you know that. I was obliged to reserve for my family business my first opportunity of receiving a letter: but my brother-in-law had written to me to say that if I would only write once to my wife she would, for my own sake and for our children's sake, take no action for divorce. I felt my duty was to do so. Setting aside other reasons, I could not bear the idea of being separated from Cyril, that beautiful, loving, lovable child of mine, my friend of all friends, my companion beyond all companions, one single hair of whose little golden head should have been dearer and more valuable to me than, I will not say you from top to toe, but the entire chrysolite of the whole world: was so indeed to me always, though I failed to understand it till too late.

Two weeks after your application, I get news of you. Robert Sherard, that bravest and most chivalrous of all brilliant beings, comes to see me, and among other things tells me that in that ridiculous *Mercure de France*, with its absurd affectation of being the true centre of literary corruption, you are about to publish an article on me with specimens of my letters. He asks me if it really was by my wish. I was greatly taken aback, and much annoyed, and gave orders that the thing was to be stopped at once. You had left my letters lying about for blackmailing companions to steal, for hotel servants to pilfer, for housemaids to sell. That was simply your careless want of appreciation of what I had written to you. But that you should seriously propose to publish selections from the balance was almost incredible to me. And which of my letters were they? I could get no information. That was my first news of you. It displeased me.

The second piece of news followed shortly afterwards. Your father's solicitors had appeared in prison, and served me with a bankruptcy notice for a paltry £700, the amount of their taxed costs. I was adjudged a public insolvent and ordered to be produced in Court. I felt most strongly, and feel still, and will revert to the subject again, that these costs should have been paid by your family. You had taken personally on yourself the responsibility of stating that your family would do so. It was that which had made the solicitor take up the case in the way he did. You were absolutely responsible. Even irrespective of your engagement on your family's behalf you should have felt that as you had brought the whole ruin on me, the least that could have been done was to spare me the additional ignominy of bankruptcy for an absolutely contemptible sum of money, less than half of what I spent on you in three brief summer months at Goring. Of that, however, no more here. I did, through the solicitor's clerk, I fully admit, receive a message from you on the subject, or at any rate in connexion with the occasion. The day he came to receive my depositions and statements, he leant across the table—the prison warder being present—and, having consulted a piece of paper which he pulled from his pocket, said to me in a low voice: "Prince Fleur de Lys wishes to be remembered to you." I stared at him. He repeated the message again. I did not know what he meant. "The gentleman is abroad at present," he added mysteriously. It all flashed across me, and I remember that, for the first and last time in my entire prison life, I laughed. In that laugh was all the scorn of all the world. Prince Fleur de Lys! I saw—and subsequent events showed me that I rightly saw—that nothing that had happened had made you realize a single thing. You were in your own eyes still the graceful prince of a trivial comedy, not the sombre figure of a tragic show. All that had occurred was as but a feather for the cap that gilds a narrow head, a flower to pink the doublet that hides the heart that hate, and hate alone, can warm, that love, and love alone, finds cold. Prince Fleur de Lys! You were, no doubt, quite right to communicate with me under an assumed name. I myself, at that time, had no name at all. In the great prison where I was then incarcerated, I was merely the figure and letter of a little cell in a long gallery, one of a thousand lifeless numbers, as of a thousand lifeless lives. But surely there were many real names in real history which would have suited you much better, and by which I would have had no difficulty at all in recognizing you at once? I did not look for you behind the spangles of a tinsel vizard suitable only for an amusing masquerade. Ah! had your soul been, as for its own perfection even it should have been, wounded with sorrow, bowed with remorse, and humble with grief, such was not the disguise it would have chosen beneath whose shadow to seek entrance to the House of Pain! The great things of life are what they seem to be, and for that reason, strange as it may sound to you, are often difficult to interpret. But the little things of life are symbols. We receive our bitter lessons most easily through them. Your seemingly casual choice of a feigned name was, and will remain, symbolic. It reveals you.

Six weeks later a third piece of news arrives. I am called out of the hospital ward, where I was lying wretchedly ill, to receive a special message from you through the Governor of the Prison. He reads me out a letter you had addressed to him in which you stated that you proposed to publish an article "on the case of Mr. Oscar Wilde" in the *Mercure de France* (a "magazine," you added for some extraordinary reason, "corresponding to the English *Fortnightly Review*") and were anxious to obtain my permission to publish extracts and selections from . . . what letters? The letters I had written you from Holloway Prison: the letters that should have been to you things sacred and secret beyond anything in the whole world! These actually were the letters you proposed to publish for the jaded *décadent* to wonder at, for the greedy *feuilletoniste*[13] chronicle, for the little lions of the *Quartier Latin* to gape and mouth at. Had there been nothing in your own heart to cry out against so vulgar a sacrilege you might at least have remembered the sonnet he wrote who saw with such sorrow and scorn the letters of John Keats sold by public auction in London and have understood at last the real meaning of my lines

>   . . . I think they love not Art
>   Who break the crystal of a poet's heart
>   That small and sickly eyes may glare and gloat.[14]

For what was your article to show? That I had been too fond of you? The Paris *gamin* was quite aware of the fact. They all read the newspapers, and most of them write for them. That I was a man of genius? The French understood that, and the peculiar quality of my genius, much better than you did, or could have been expected to do. That along with genius goes often a curious perversity of passion and desire? Admirable: but the subject belongs to Lombroso[15] rather than to you. Besides, the pathological phenomenon in question is found also amongst those who have not genius. That in your war of hate with your father I was at once shield and weapon to each of you? Nay more, that in that hideous hunt for my life, that took place when the war was over, he never could have reached me had not your nets been already about my feet? Quite true: but I am told that Henri Bauer had already done it extremely well. Besides, to corroborate his view, had such been your intention, you did not require to publish my letters: at any rate those written from Holloway Prison.

Will you say, in answer to my questions, that in one of my Holloway letters I had myself asked you to try, as far as you were able, to set me a little right with some small portion of the world? Certainly, I did so. Remember how and why I am here at this very moment. Do you think I am here on account of my relations with the witnesses on my trial? My relations, real or supposed, with people of that kind were matters of no interest either to the Government or to Society. They knew nothing of them and cared less. I am here for having tried to put your father into prison. My attempt failed, of course. My own Counsel threw up their briefs. Your father completely turned the tables on me, and had me in prison, has me there still. That is why there is contempt felt for me. That is why people despise me. That is why I have to serve out every day, every hour, every minute of my dreadful imprisonment. That is why my petitions have been refused.

You were the only person who, and without in any way exposing yourself to scorn or danger or blame, could have given another colour to the whole affair, have put the matter in a different light, have shown to a certain degree how things really stood. I would not, of course, have expected, nor indeed wished you to have stated how and for what purpose you had sought my assistance in your trouble at Oxford: or how, and for what purpose, if you had a purpose at all, you had practically never left my side for nearly three years. My incessant attempts to break off a friendship that was so ruinous to me as an artist, as a man of position, as a member of Society even, need not have been chronicled with the accuracy with which they have been set down here. Nor would I have desired you to have described the scenes you used to make with such almost monotonous recurrence: nor to have reprinted your wonderful series of telegrams to me with their strange mixture of romance and finance: nor to have quoted from letters the more revolting or heartless passages as I have been forced to do. Still, I thought it would have been good, as well for you as for me, if you had made some protest against your father's version of our friendship, one no less grotesque than venomous and as absurd in its inference to you as it was dishonouring in its reference to me. That version has now actually passed into serious history: it is quoted, believed, and chronicled: the preacher has taken it for his text, and the moralist for his barren theme: and I who appealed to all the ages have had to accept my verdict from one who is an ape and a buffoon. I have said, and with some bitterness, I admit,

in this letter that such was the irony of things that your father
would live to be the hero of a Sunday school tract: that you
would rank with the infant Samuel: and that my place would
be between Gilles de Retz and the Marquis de Sade. I dare
say it is best so. I have no desire to complain. One of the
many lessons that one learns in prison is, that things are what
they are and will be what they will be. Nor have I any doubt
that the leper of medievalism and the author of *Justine*[16] will
prove better company than *Sandford and Merton*.[17]

But at the time I wrote to you I felt that for both our sakes
it would be a good thing, a proper thing, a right thing, not to
accept that account which your father had put forward
through his Counsel for the edification of a Philistine world,
and that is why I asked you to think out and write something
that would be nearer the truth. It would at least have been
better for you than scribbling to the French papers about the
domestic life of your parents. What did the French care
whether or not your parents had led a happy domestic life?
One cannot conceive a subject more entirely uninteresting to
them. What did interest them was how an artist of my distinction, one who by the school and movement of which he
was the incarnation had exercised a marked influence on the
direction of French thought, could, having led such a life,
have brought such an action. Had you proposed for your article to publish the letters, endless I fear in number, in which
I had spoken to you of the ruin you were bringing on my life,
of the madness of moods of rage that you were allowing to
master you to your own hurt as well as to mine, and of my desire, nay, my determination to end a friendship so fatal to me
in every way, I could have understood it, though I would not
have allowed such letters to be published: when your father's
Counsel desiring to catch me in a contradiction suddenly
produced in Court a letter of mine, written to you in March
1893, in which I stated that, rather than endure a repetition
of the hideous scenes you seemed to take such a terrible
pleasure in making, I would readily consent to be "blackmailed by every renter in London," it was a very real grief to

me that that side of my friendship with you should inadvertently be revealed to the common gaze: but that you should have been so slow to see, so lacking in all sensitiveness, and so dull in apprehension of what is rare, delicate and beautiful, as to propose yourself to publish the letters in which and through which I was trying to keep alive the very spirit and soul of love, that it might dwell in my body through the long years of that body's humiliation,—this was, and still is to me a source of the very deepest pain, the most poignant disappointment. Why you did so, I fear I know but too well. If hate blinded your eyes, vanity sewed your eyelids together with threads of iron. The "faculty by which, and by which alone, one can understand others in their real as in their ideal relations" your narrow egotism had blunted, and long disuse had made of no avail. The imagination was as much in prison as I was. Vanity had barred up the windows, and the name of the warder was hate.

All this took place in the early part of November of the year before last. A great river of life flows between me and a date so distant. Hardly, if at all, can you see across so wide a waste. But to me it seems to have occurred, I will not say yesterday, but to-day. Suffering is one very long moment. We cannot divide it by seasons. We can only record its moods, and chronicle their return. With us time itself does not progress. It revolves. It seems to circle round one centre of pain. The paralysing immobility of a life every circumstance of which is regulated after an unchangeable pattern, so that we eat and drink and lie down and pray, or kneel at least for prayer, according to the inflexible laws of an iron formula: this immobile quality, that makes each dreadful day in the very minutest detail like its brother, seems to communicate itself to those external forces, the very essence of whose existence is ceaseless change. Of seed-time or harvest, of the reapers bending over the corn, or the grape gatherers threading through the vines, of the grass in the orchard made white with broken blossoms or strewn with fallen fruit: of these we know nothing, and can know nothing.

For us there is only one season, the season of sorrow. The very sun and moon seem taken from us. Outside, the day may be blue and gold, but the light that creeps down through the thickly-muffled glass of the small iron-barred window beneath which one sits is grey and niggard. It is always twilight in one's cell, as it is always twilight in one's heart. And in the sphere of thought, no less than in the sphere of time, motion is no more. The thing that you personally have long ago forgotten, or can easily forget, is happening to me now, and will happen to me again to-morrow. Remember this, and you will be able to understand a little of why I am writing, and in this manner writing. . . .

A week later, I am transferred here. Three more months go over and my mother dies. No one knew better than you how deeply I loved and honoured her. Her death was terrible to me; but I, once a lord of language, have no words in which to express my anguish and my shame. Never even in the most perfect days of my development as an artist could I have found words fit to bear so august a burden; or to move with sufficient stateliness of music through the purple pageant of my incommunicable woe. She and my father had bequeathed me a name they had made noble and honoured, not merely in literature, art, archaeology, and science, but in the public history of my own country, in its evolution as a nation. I had disgraced that name eternally. I had made it a low byword among low people. I had dragged it through the very mire. I had given it to brutes that they might make it brutal, and to fools that they might turn it into a synonym for folly. What I suffered then, and still suffer, is not for pen to write or paper to record. My wife, always kind and gentle to me, rather than that I should hear the news from indifferent lips, travelled, ill as she was, all the way from Genoa to England to break to me herself the tidings of so irreparable, so irredeemable, a loss. Messages of sympathy reached me from all who had still affection for me. Even people who had not known me personally, hearing that a new sorrow had broken into my life, wrote to ask that some expression of their condolence should be conveyed to me. . . .

Three months go over. The calendar of my daily conduct and labour that hangs on the outside of my cell door, with my name and sentence written upon it, tells me that it is May.

My friends come to see me again. I enquire, as I always do, after you. I am told that you are in your villa at Naples, and are bringing out a volume of poems. At the close of the interview it is mentioned casually that you are dedicating them to me. The tidings seemed to give me a sort of nausea of life. I said nothing, but silently went back to my cell with contempt and scorn in my heart. How could you dream of dedicating a volume of poems to me without first asking my permission? Dream, do I say? How could you dare do such a thing? Will you give as your answer that in the days of my greatness and fame I had consented to receive the dedication of your early work? Certainly I did so: just as I would have accepted the homage of any other young men beginning the difficult and beautiful art of literature. All homage is delightful to an artist and doubly sweet when youth brings it. Laurel and bay leaf wither when aged hands pluck them. Only youth has a right to crown an artist. That is the real privilege of being young if youth only knew it. But the days of abasement and infamy are different from those of greatness and fame. You had yet to learn that.

Prosperity, pleasure and success, may be rough of grain and common in fibre, but sorrow is the most sensitive of all created things. There is nothing that stirs in the whole world of thought to which sorrow does not vibrate in terrible and exquisite pulsation. The thin beaten-out leaf of tremulous gold that chronicles the direction of forces the eye cannot see is in comparison coarse. It is a wound that bleeds when any hand but that of love touches it, and even then must bleed again, though not in pain.

You could write to the Governor of Wandsworth Prison to ask my permission to publish my letters in the *Mercure de*

France, "corresponding to our English *Fortnightly Review*."
Why not have written to the Governor of the Prison at Reading to ask my permission to dedicate your poems to me, whatever fantastic description you may have chosen to give them? Was it because in the one case the magazine in question had been prohibited by me from publishing letters, the legal copyright of which, as you are, of course, perfectly well aware, was and is vested entirely in me, and in the other you thought that you could enjoy the wilfulness of your own way without my knowing anything about it till it was too late to interfere? The mere fact that I was a man disgraced, ruined and in prison should have made you, if you desired to write my name on the fore-page of your work, beg it of me as a favour, an honour, a privilege: that is the way in which one should approach those who are in distress and sit in shame.

Where there is sorrow there is holy ground. Some day people will realize what that means. They will know nothing of life till they do. Robbie and natures like his can realize it. When I was brought down from my prison to the Court of Bankruptcy, between two policemen, Robbie waited in the long dreary corridor that, before the whole crowd, whom an action so sweet and simple hushed into silence, he might gravely raise his hat to me, as, handcuffed and with bowed head, I passed him by. Men have gone to heaven for smaller things than that. It was in this spirit, and with this mode of love, that the saints knelt down to wash the feet of the poor, or stooped to kiss the leper on the cheek. I have never said one single word to him about what he did. I do not know to the present moment whether he is aware that I was even conscious of his action. It is not a thing for which one can render formal thanks in formal words. I store it in the treasure-house of my heart. I keep it there as a secret debt that I am glad to think I can never possibly repay. It is embalmed and kept sweet by the myrrh and cassia of many tears. When wisdom has been profitless to me, philosophy barren, and the proverbs and phrases of those who have sought to give me consolation as dust and ashes in my mouth, the memory of that little, lovely, silent act of love has un-sealed for me all the wells of pity: made the desert blossom like a rose, and brought me out of the bitterness of lonely exile into harmony with the wounded, broken, and great heart of the world. When people are able to understand, not merely how beautiful Robbie's action was, but why it meant so much to me, and always will mean so much, then, perhaps, they will realize how and in what spirit they should approach me. . . .

The first volume of Poems that in the very springtide of his manhood a young man sends forth to the world should be like a blossom or flower of spring, like the white thorn in the meadow at Magdalen or the cowslips in the Cumnor fields. It should not be burdened by the weight of a terrible and re-volting tragedy; a terrible revolting scandal. If I had allowed my name to serve as herald to such a book, it would have been a grave artistic error; it would have brought a wrong at-mosphere round the whole work, and in modern art atmos-phere counts for so much. Modern life is complex and relative; those are its two distinguishing notes; to render the first we require atmosphere with its subtlety of *nuances*, of suggestion, of strange perspectives; as for the second we re-quire background. That is why sculpture has ceased to be a representative art and why music is a representative art and why literature is, and has been and always will remain the supreme representative art.

I have spoken to you at length on this point in order that you should grasp its full bearings, and understand why I wrote at once to Robbie in terms of such scorn and contempt of you, and absolutely prohibited the dedication, and desired that the words I had written to you should be copied out carefully and sent to you. I felt that at last the time had come when you should be made to see, to recognize, to realize a lit-tle what you had done. Blindness may be carried so far that it becomes grotesque, and unimaginative nature, if something be not done to rouse it, will become petrified into absolute insensibility, so that while the body may eat and drink, and have its pleasures, the soul whose house it is, may, like the soul of Branca d'Oria[18] in Dante, be dead absolutely. My letter seems to have arrived not a moment too soon. It fell on you, as far as I can judge, like a thunderbolt. You described yourself, in your answer to Robbie, as being "deprived of all power of thought and expression." Indeed apparently you can think of nothing better than to write to your mother to complain. Of course, she with that blindness to your real good that has been her ill-starred fortune and yours, gives you every comfort she can think of, and lulls you back, I suppose, into your former unhappy, unworthy condition; while as far as I am concerned, she lets my friends know that she is "very much annoyed" at the severity of my remarks about you. Indeed it is not merely to my friends that she conveys her sentiments of annoyance, but also to those—a very much larger number, I need hardly remind you—who are not my friends; and I am informed now, and through channels very kindly disposed to you and yours, that in consequence of this a great deal of the sympathy that, by reason of my distinguished genius and terrible sufferings, had been gradually but surely growing up for me, has been entirely taken away. People say, "Ah! he first tried to get the kind father put into prison and failed: now he turns around and blames the innocent son for his failure. How right we were to despise him! How worthy of contempt he is!" It seems to me that when my name is mentioned in your mother's presence, if she has no word of sorrow or regret for her share—no slight one—in the ruin of my house, it would be more seemly if she remained silent. And as for you—don't you think now that, instead of writing to her to complain, it would have been better for you, in every way, to have written to me directly, and to have had the courage to say to me whatever you had or fancied you had to say? It is nearly a year ago now since I wrote that letter. You cannot have remained during that entire time "deprived of all power of thought and expression." Why did you not write to me? You saw by my letter how deeply wounded, how outraged I was by your whole conduct. More than that: you saw your entire friendship with me set before you at last in its true light, and by a mode not to be mistaken. Often in old days I had told you that you were ruining my life. You had always laughed. When Edwin Levy at the very beginning of our friendship seeing your manner of putting me forward to bear the brunt and annoyance and expense even of that unfortunate Oxford mishap of yours, if we must so term it, in reference to which his advice and help had been sought, warned me for the space of a whole hour against knowing you, you laughed as at Bracknell I described to you my long and impressive interview with him. When I told you how even that unfortunate young man who ultimately stood beside me in the dock had warned me more than once that you would prove far more fatal in bringing me to utter destruction than any even of the common lads whom I was foolish enough to know, you laughed, though not with such sense of amusement. When my more prudent or less well disposed friends either warned me or left me, on account of my friendship with you, you laughed with scorn. You laughed immoderately when, on the occasion of your father writing his first abusive letter to you about me, I told you that I knew I would be the mere cat's-paw of your dreadful quarrel and come to some evil between you. But every single thing happened as I had said it would happen, as far as the result goes. You had no excuse for not seeing how all things had come to pass. Why did you not write to me? Was it cowardice? Was it callousness? What was it? The fact that I was outraged with you and had expressed my sense of the outrage was all the more reason for writing. If you thought my letter just, you should have written. If you thought it in the smallest point unjust, you should have written. I waited for a letter. I felt sure that at last you would see that, if old affection, much protested love, the thousand acts of ill-requited kindness I had showered on you, the thousand unpaid debts of gratitude you owed me:— that if all these were nothing to you, mere duty itself, most barren of all bonds between man and man, should have made you write. You cannot say that you seriously thought I was obliged to receive none but business communications from members of my family. You knew perfectly that every twelve weeks Robbie writes to me a little budget of literary news. Nothing can be more charming than his letters, in their wit, their clever concentrated criticism, their light touch: they are real letters, they are like a person talking to one; they have the quality of a French *causerie intime*:[19] and in his delicate mode of deference to me, appealing at one time to my judgement, at another to my sense of humour, at another to my instinct for beauty or to my culture, and reminding me in a hundred subtle ways that once I was to many an arbiter of style in art; the supreme arbiter to some; he shows how he has the tact of love as well as the tact of literature. His letters have been the messengers between me and that beautiful unreal world of art where once I was King, and would have remained King indeed, had I not let myself be lured into the imperfect world of coarse uncompleted passion, of appetite without distinction, desire without limit, and formless greed. Yet when all is said surely you might have been able to understand or conceive, at any rate, that on the ordinary grounds of mere psychological curiosity it would have been more interesting to me to hear from you than to learn that Alfred Austin was trying to bring out a volume of poems; that George Street was writing dramatic criticism for the *Daily Chronicle*; or that by one who cannot speak a panegyric without stammering, Mrs. Meynell had been pronounced to be the new Sibyl of style.

Ah! had you been in prison—I will not say through any fault of mine, for that would be a thought too terrible for me to bear—but through fault of your own, error of your own, faith in some unworthy friends, slip in sensual mire, trust misapplied, or love ill bestowed, or none, or all of these—do you think that I would have allowed you to eat your heart away in darkness and solitude without trying in some way, however slight, to help you to bear the bitter burden of your disgrace? Do you think that I would not have let you know that, if you suffered, I was suffering too: that if you wept there were tears in my eyes also: and that if you lay in the house of bondage and were despised of men, I out of my griefs had built a house in which to dwell until your coming, a treasury in which all that man had denied to you would be laid up for your healing, one hundredfold in increase? If bitter necessity, or prudence, to me more bitter still, had prevented my being near you, and robbed me of the joy of your presence, though seen through iron bars and in a shape of shame, I would have written to you in season and out of season in the hope that some mere phrase, some single word, some broken echo even, of love might reach you. If you had refused to receive my letters, I would have written none the less, so that you should have known that at any rate there were always letters awaiting for you. Many have done so to me. Every three months people write to me, or propose to write to me. Their letters and communications are kept. They will be handed to me when I go out of prison. I know they are there. I know the names of the people who have written them. I know that they are full of sympathy, and affection, and kindness. That is sufficient for me. I need know no more. Your silence has been horrible. Nor has it been a silence of weeks and months merely, but of years; of years even as they have to count them who, like yourself, live swiftly in happiness and can hardly catch the gilt feet of the days as they dance by, and are out of breath in a chase after pleasure. It is a silence without excuse; a silence without palliation. I knew you had feet of clay.[20] Who knew better? When I wrote in my aphorisms, that it was simply the feet of clay that made the gold of the image precious, it was of you I was thinking. But it is no gold image with clay feet that you had made for yourself. Out of the very dust of the common highway that the hooves of the horned things pash into mire you have moulded your perfect semblance for me to look at, so that, whatever my secret desire might have been, it would be impossible for me now to have for you any feeling other than that of contempt and scorn. And, on setting aside all other reasons, your indifference, your worldly wisdom, your callousness, your prudence, whatever you may choose to call it, has been made doubly bitter to me by the peculiar circumstances that either accompanied or followed my fall.

Other miserable men when they are thrown into prison, if they are robbed of the beauty of the world, are at least safe in some measure from the world's most deadly slings, most awful arrows. They can hide in the darkness of their cells and of their very disgrace make a mode of sanctuary. The world having had its will goes its way, and they are left to suffer undisturbed. With me it has been different. Sorrow after sorrow has come beating at the prison doors in search of me; they have opened the gates wide and let them in. Hardly if at all have my friends been suffered to see me. But my enemies have had full access to me always; twice in my public appearances in the Bankruptcy Court; twice again in my public transferences from one prison to another have I been shown under conditions of unspeakable humiliation to the gaze and mockery of men. The messenger of Death had brought me his tidings and gone his way; and in entire solitude and isolated from all that could give me comfort or suggest relief I have had to bear the intolerable burden of misery and remorse, which the memory of my mother placed upon me and places on me still. Hardly has that wound been dulled, not healed, by time, when violent and bitter and harsh letters come to me from my wife's solicitors. I am at once tainted and threatened with poverty. That I can bear. I can school myself to worse than that; but my two children are taken from me by legal procedure. That is, and always will remain to me a source of infinite distress, or infinite pain, of grief without end or limit. That the law should decide and take upon itself to decide that I am one unfit to be with my own children is something quite horrible to me. The disgrace of prison is as nothing compared with it. I envy the other men who tread the yard along with me. I am sure that their children wait for them, look for their coming, will be sweet to them.

The poor are wiser, more charitable, more kind, more sensitive than we are. In their eyes prison is a tragedy in a man's life, a misfortune, a casualty, something that calls for sympathy in others. They speak of one who is in prison as of one who is "in trouble" simply. It is the phrase they always use, and the expression has the perfect wisdom of love in it. With people of our own rank it is different. With us, prison makes a man a pariah. I, and such as I am, have hardly any right to air and sun. Our presence taints the pleasures of others. We are unwelcome when we reappear. To revisit the glimpses of the moon is not for us. Our very children are taken away. Those lovely links with humanity are broken. We are doomed to be solitary, while our sons still live. We are denied the one thing that might heal us and keep us, that might bring balm to the bruised heart, and peace to the soul in pain.

And to all this has been added the hard small fact that by your actions and by your silence, by what you have done and by what you have left undone, you have made every day of my long imprisonment still more difficult for me to live through. The very bread and water of prison fare you have by your conduct changed. You have rendered the one bitter and the other brackish to me. The sorrow you should have shared you have doubled, the pain you should have sought to lighten you have quickened to anguish. I have no doubt you did not mean to do so. I know that you did not mean to do so. It was simply that "one really fatal defect in your character, your entire lack of imagination."

And the end of it all is that I have got to forgive you. I must do so. I don't write this letter to put bitterness into your heart, but to pluck it out of mine. For my own sake I must forgive you. One cannot always keep an adder in one's breast to feed on one, nor rise up every night to sow thorns in the garden of one's soul. It will not be difficult at all for me to do so, if you help me a little. Whatever you did to me in the old days I always readily forgave. It did you no good then. Only one whose life is without stain of any kind can forgive sins. But now when I sit in humiliation and disgrace it is different. My forgiveness should mean a great deal to you now. Some day you will realize it. Whether you do so early or late, soon or not at all, my way is clear before me. I cannot allow you to go through life bearing in your heart the burden of having ruined a man like me. The thought might make you callously indifferent, or morbidly sad. I must take the burden from you and put it on my own shoulders.

I must say to myself that I ruined myself, and that nobody great or small can be ruined except by his own hand. I am quite ready to say so. I am trying to say so, though they may not think it at the present moment. This pitiless indictment I bring without pity against myself. Terrible as was what the world did to me, what I did to myself was far more terrible still.

I was a man who stood in symbolic relations to the art and culture of my age. I had realized this for myself at the very dawn of my manhood, and had forced my age to realize it afterwards. Few men hold such a position in their own lifetime, and have it so acknowledged. It is usually discerned, if discerned at all, by the historian, or the critic, long after both the man and his age have passed away. With me it was different. I felt it myself, and made others feel it. Byron was a symbolic figure, but his relations were to the passion of his age and its weariness of passion. Mine were to something more noble, more permanent, of more vital issue, of larger scope.

The gods had given me almost everything. I had genius, a distinguished name, high social position, brilliancy, intellectual daring; I made art a philosophy and philosophy an art; I altered the minds of men and the colours of things; there was nothing I said or did that did not make people wonder. I took the drama, the most objective form known to art, and made it as personal a mode of expression as the lyric or sonnet; at the same time I widened its range and enriched its characterization. Drama, novel, poem in prose, poem in rhyme, subtle or fantastic dialogue, whatever I touched, I made beautiful in a new mode of beauty: to truth itself I gave what is false no less than what is true as its rightful province, and showed that the false and the true are merely forms of intellectual existence. I treated art as the supreme reality and life as a mere mode of fiction. I awoke the imagination of my century so that it created myth and legend around me. I summed up all systems in a phrase and all existence in an epigram. Along with these things I had things that were different. But I let myself be lured into long spells of senseless and sensual ease. I amused myself with being a *flâneur*, a dandy, a man of fashion. I surrounded myself with the smaller natures and the meaner minds. I became the spendthrift of my own genius, and to waste an eternal youth gave me a curious joy. Tired of being on the heights, I deliberately went to the depths in the search for new sensation. What the paradox was to me in the sphere of thought, perversity became to me in the sphere of passion. Desire, at the end, was a malady, or a madness, or both. I grew careless of the lives of others. I took pleasure where it pleased me, and passed on. I forgot that every little action of the common day makes or unmakes character, and that therefore what one has done in the secret chamber one has some day to cry aloud on the house-tops. I ceased to be lord over myself. I was no longer the captain of my soul, and did not know it. I allowed pleasure to dominate me. I ended in horrible disgrace. There is only one thing for me now, absolute humility.

I have lain in prison for nearly two years. Out of my nature has come wild despair; an abandonment to grief that was piteous even to look at; terrible and impotent rage; bitterness and scorn; anguish that wept aloud; misery that could find no voice; sorrow that was dumb. I have passed through every possible mood of suffering. Better than Wordsworth himself I know what Wordsworth meant when he said—

> Suffering is permanent, obscure, and dark,
> And has the nature of infinity.[21]

But while there were times when I rejoiced in the idea that my sufferings were to be endless, I could not bear them to be without meaning. Now I find hidden somewhere away in my nature something that tells me that nothing in the whole world is meaningless, and suffering least of all. That something hidden away in my nature, like a treasure in a field, is humility.

It is the thing left in me, and the best: the ultimate discovery at which I have arrived, the starting-point for a fresh development. It has come to me right out of myself, so I know that it has come at the proper time. It could not have come before, nor later. Had anyone told me of it, I would have rejected it. Had it been brought to me, I would have refused it. As I found it, I want to keep it. I must do so. It is the one thing that has in it the elements of life, of a new life, a *Vita Nuova* for me. Of all things it is the strangest; one cannot give it away and another may not give it to one. One cannot acquire it except by surrendering everything that one has. It is only when one has lost all things, that one knows that one possesses it.

Now I have realized that it is in me, I see quite clearly what I ought to do; in fact, must do. And when I use such a phrase as that, I need not say that I am not alluding to any external sanction or command. I admit none. I am far more of an individualist than I ever was. Nothing seems to me of the smallest value except what one gets out of oneself. My nature is seeking a fresh mode of self-realization. That is all I am concerned with. And the first thing that I have got to do is to free myself from any possible bitterness of feeling against the world.

I am completely penniless, and absolutely homeless. Yet there are worse things in the world than that. I am quite candid when I say that rather than go out from this prison with bitterness in my heart against the world, I would gladly and readily beg my bread from door to door. If I got nothing from the house of the rich I would get something at the house of the poor. Those who have much are often greedy; those who have little always share. I would not a bit mind sleeping in the cool grass in summer, and when winter came on sheltering myself by the warm close-thatched rick, or under the penthouse of a great barn, provided I had love in my heart. The external things of life seem to me now of no importance at all. You can see to what intensity of individualism I have arrived—or am arriving rather, for the journey is long, and "where I walk there are thorns."

Of course I know that to ask alms on the highway is not to be my lot, and that if ever I lie in the cool grass at night-time it will be to write sonnets to the moon. When I go out of prison, Robbie will be waiting for me on the other side of the big iron-studded gate, and he is the symbol, not merely of his own affection, but of the affection of many others besides. I believe I am to have enough to live on for about eighteen months at any rate, so that if I may not write beautiful books, I may at least read beautiful books; and what joy can be greater? After that, I hope to be able to re-create my creative faculty.

But were things different: had I not a friend left in the world; were there not a single house open to me in pity; had I to accept the wallet and ragged cloak of sheer penury: as long as I am free from all resentment, hardness, and scorn, I would be able to face the life with much more calm and confidence than I would were my body in purple and fine linen, and the soul within me sick with hate.

And I really shall have no difficulty. When you really want love you will find it waiting for you.

I need not say that my task does not end there. It would be comparatively easy if it did. There is much more before me. I have hills far steeper to climb, valleys much darker to pass through. And I have to get it all out of myself. Neither religion, morality, nor reason can help me at all.

Morality does not help me. I am a born antinomian.[22] I am one of those who are made for exceptions, not for laws. But while I see that there is nothing wrong in what one does, I see that there is something wrong in what one becomes. It is well to have learned that.

Religion does not help me. The faith that others give to what is unseen, I give to what one can touch, and look at. My gods dwell in temples made with hands; and within the circle of actual experience is my creed made perfect and complete: too complete, it may be, for like many or all of those who have placed their heaven in this earth, I have found in it not merely the beauty of heaven, but the horror of hell also. When I think about religion at all, I feel as if I would like to found an order for those who *cannot* believe: the Confraternity of the Faithless one might call it, where on an altar, on which no taper burned, a priest, in whose heart peace had no dwelling, might celebrate with unblessed bread and a chalice empty of wine. Everything to be true must become a religion. And agnosticism should have its ritual no less than faith. It has sown its martyrs, it should reap its saints, and praise God daily for having hidden Himself from man. But whether it be faith or agnosticism, it must be nothing external to me. Its symbols must be of my own creating. Only that is spiritual which makes its own form. If I may not find its secret within myself, I shall never find it: if I have not got it already, it will never come to me.

Reason does not help me. It tells me that the laws under which I am convicted are wrong and unjust laws, and the system under which I have suffered a wrong and unjust system. But, somehow, I have got to make both of these things just and right to me. And exactly as in Art one is only concerned with what a particular thing is at a particular moment to oneself, so it is also in the ethical evolution of one's character. I have got to make everything that has happened to me good for me. The plank bed, the loathsome food, the hard ropes shredded into oakum till one's fingertips grow dull with pain, the menial offices with which each day begins and finishes, the harsh orders that routine seems to necessitate, the dreadful dress that makes sorrow grotesque to look at, the silence, the solitude, the shame—each and all of these things I had to transform into a spiritual experience. There is not a single degradation of the body which I must not try and make into a spiritualizing of the soul.

I want to get to the point when I shall be able to say quite simply, and without affectation, that the two great turning-points in my life were when my father sent me to Oxford, and when Society sent me to prison. I will not say that prison is the best thing that could have happened to me; for that phrase would savour of too great bitterness towards myself. I would sooner say, or hear it said of me, that I was so typical a child of my age, that in my perversity, and for that perversity's sake, I turned the good things of my life to evil, and the evil things of my life to good.

What is said, however, by myself or by others, matters little. The important thing, the thing that lies before me, the thing that I have to do, if the brief remainder of my days is not to be maimed, marred, and incomplete, is to absorb into my nature all that has been done to me, to make it part of me, to accept it without complaint, fear, or reluctance. The supreme vice is shallowness. Whatever is realized is right.

When first I was put into prison some people advised me to try and forget who I was. It was ruinous advice. It is only by realizing what I am that I have found comfort of any kind. Now I am advised by others to try on my release to forget that I have ever been in a prison at all. I know that would be equally fatal. It would mean that I would always be haunted by an intolerable sense of disgrace, and that those things that are meant for me as much as for anybody else—the beauty of the sun and moon, the pageant of the seasons, the music of daybreak and the silence of great nights, the rain falling through the leaves, or the dew creeping over the grass and making it silver—would all be tainted for me, and lose their healing power and their power of communicating joy. To regret one's own experiences is to arrest one's own development. To deny one's own experiences is to put a lie into the lips of one's own life. It is no less than a denial of the soul.

For just as the body absorbs things of all kinds, things common and unclean no less than those that the priest or a vision has cleansed, and converts them into swiftness or strength, into the play of beautiful muscles and the moulding of fair flesh, into the curves and colours of the hair, the lids, the eye; so the soul in its turn has its nutritive functions also, and can transform into noble moods of thought and passions of high import what in itself is base, cruel, and degrading; nay, more, may find in these its most august modes of assertion and can often reveal itself most perfectly through what was intended to desecrate or destroy.

The fact of my having been the common prisoner of a common gaol I must frankly accept, and, curious as it may seem, one of the things I shall have to teach myself is not to be ashamed of it. I must accept it as a punishment, and if one is ashamed of having been punished, one might just as well never have been punished at all. Of course there are many things of which I was convicted that I had not done, but then there are many things of which I was convicted that I had done, and a still greater number of things in my life for which I was never indicted at all. And as the gods are strange, and punish us for what is good and humane in us as much as for what is evil and perverse, I must accept the fact that one is punished for the good as well as for the evil that one does. I have no doubt that it is quite right one should be. It helps one, or should help one, to realize both, and not to be too conceited about either. And if I then am not ashamed of my punishment, as I hope not to be, I shall be able to think, and walk, and live with freedom.

Many men on their release carry their prison about with them into the air, and hide it as a secret disgrace in their hearts, and at length, like poor poisoned things, creep into some hole and die. It is wretched that they should have to do so, and it is wrong, terribly wrong, of Society that it should force them to do so. Society takes upon itself the right to inflict appalling punishment on the individual, but it also has the supreme vice of shallowness, and fails to realize what it has done. When the man's punishment is over, it leaves him to himself; that is to say, it abandons him at the very moment when its highest duty towards him begins. It is really ashamed of its own actions, and shuns those whom it has punished, as people shun a creditor whose debt they cannot

pay, or one on whom they have inflicted an irreparable, an irredeemable wrong. I can claim on my side that if I realize
what I have suffered, Society should realize what it has inflicted on me; and that there should be no bitterness or hate
on either side.

Of course I know that from one point of view things will
be made different for me than for others; must indeed, by
the very nature of the case, be made so. The poor thieves and
outcasts who are imprisoned here with me are in many re-
spects more fortunate than I am. The little way in grey city or
green field that saw their sin is small; to find those who know
nothing of what they have done they need go no further than
a bird might fly between the twilight at dawn and dawn itself:
but for me the world is shrivelled to a handsbreadth, and
everywhere I turn my name is written on the rocks in lead.
For I have come, not from obscurity into the momentary notoriety of crime, but from a sort of eternity of fame to a sort
of eternity of infamy, and sometimes seem to myself to have
shown, if indeed it required showing, that between the famous and the infamous there is but one step, if as much as
one.

Still, in the very fact that people will recognize me wherever I go, and know all about my life, as far as its follies go, I
can discern something good for me. It will force on me the
necessity of again asserting myself as an artist, and as soon as
I possibly can. If I can produce only one beautiful work of art
I shall be able to rob malice of its venom, and cowardice of its
sneer, and to pluck out the tongue of scorn by the roots.

And if life be, as it surely is, a problem to me, I am no less
a problem to life. People must adopt some attitude towards
me, and so pass judgement both on themselves and me. I
need not say I am not talking of particular individuals. The
only people I would care to be with now are artists and people who have suffered: those who know what beauty is, and
those who know what sorrow is: nobody else interests me.
Nor am I making any demands on life. In all that I have said
I am simply concerned with my own mental attitude towards

life as a whole; and I feel that not to be ashamed of having been punished is one of the first points I must attain to, for the sake of my own perfection, and because I am so imperfect.

Then I must learn how to be happy. Once I knew it, or thought I knew it, by instinct. It was always springtime once in my heart. My temperament was akin to joy. I filled my life to the very brim with pleasure, as one might fill a cup to the very brim with wine. Now I am approaching life from a completely new standpoint, and even to conceive happiness is often extremely difficult for me. I remember during my first term at Oxford reading in Pater's *Renaissance*—that book which has had such a strange influence over my life—how Dante places low in the Inferno those who wilfully live in sadness; and going to the college library and turning to the passage in the *Divine Comedy* where beneath the dreary marsh lie those who were "sullen in the sweet air," saying for ever and ever through their sighs—

*Tristi fummo
Nell' aere dolce, che dal sol s'allegra.*[23]

I knew the Church condemned *accidia,* but the whole idea seemed to me quite fantastic, just the sort of sin, I fancied, a priest who knew nothing about real life would invent. Nor could I understand how Dante, who says that "sorrow remarries us to God," could have been so harsh to those who were enamoured of melancholy, if any such there really were. I had no idea that someday this would become to me one of the greatest temptations of my life.

While I was in Wandsworth Prison I longed to die. It was my one desire. When after two months in the infirmary I was tranferred here, and found myself growing gradually better in physical health, I was filled with rage. I determined to commit suicide on the very day on which I left prison. After a time that evil mood passed away, and I made up my mind to live, but to wear gloom as a king wears purple: never to smile again: to turn whatever house I entered into a house of mourning: to make my friends walk slowly in sadness with me: to teach them that melancholy is the true secret of life: to maim them with an alien sorrow: to mar them with my own pain. Now I feel quite differently. I see it would be both ungrateful and unkind of me to pull so long a face that when my friends came to see me they would have to make their faces still longer in order to show their sympathy; or, if I desired to entertain them, to invite them to sit down silently to bitter herbs and funeral baked meats. I must learn how to be cheerful and happy.

The last two occasions on which I was allowed to see my friends here, I tried to be as cheerful as possible, and to show my cheerfulness, in order to make them some slight return for their trouble in coming all the way from town to see me. It is only a slight return, I know, but it is the one, I feel certain, that pleases them most. I saw Robbie for an hour on Saturday week, and I tried to give the fullest possible expression of the delight I really felt at our meeting. And that, in the views and ideas I am here shaping for myself, I am quite right is shown to me by the fact that now for the first time since my imprisonment I have a real desire for life.

There is before me so much to do that I would regard it as a terrible tragedy if I died before I was allowed to complete at any rate a little of it. I see new developments in art and life, each one of which is a fresh mode of perfection. I long to live so that I can explore what is no less than a new world to me. Do you want to know what this new world is? I think you can guess what it is. It is the world in which I have been living. Sorrow, then, and all that it teaches one, is my new world.

I used to live entirely for pleasure. I shunned suffering and sorrow of every kind. I hated both. I resolved to ignore them as far as possible: to treat them, that is to say, as modes of imperfection. They were not part of my scheme of life. They had no place in my philosophy. My mother, who knew life as a whole, used often to quote to me Goethe's lines— written by Carlyle in a book he had given her years ago, and translated by him, I fancy, also:

Who never ate his bread in sorrow,
Who never spent the midnight hours
Weeping and waiting for the morrow,—
He knows you not, ye heavenly powers.[24]

They were the lines which that noble Queen of Prussia, whom Napoleon treated with such coarse brutality, used to quote in her humiliation and exile; they were the lines my mother often quoted in the troubles of her later life. I absolutely declined to accept or admit the enormous truth hidden in them. I could not understand it. I remember quite well how I used to tell her that I did not want to eat my bread in sorrow, or to pass any night weeping and watching for a more bitter dawn.

I had no idea that it was one of the special things that the Fates had in store for me: that for a whole year of my life, indeed, I was to do little else. But so has my portion been meted out to me; and during the last few months I have, after terrible difficulties and struggles, been able to comprehend some of the lessons hidden in the heart of pain. Clergymen and people who use phrases without wisdom sometimes talk of suffering as a mystery. It is really a revelation. One discerns things one never discerned before. One approaches the whole of history from a different standpoint. What one had felt dimly, through instinct, about art, is intellectually and emotionally realized with perfect clearness of vision and absolute intensity of apprehension.

I now see that sorrow, being the supreme emotion of which man is capable, is at once the type and test of all great art. What the artist is always looking for is the mode of existence in which soul and body are one and indivisible: in which the outward is expressive of the inward: in which form reveals. Of such modes of existence there are not a few: youth and the arts preoccupied with youth may serve as a model for us at one moment, at another we may like to think that, in its subtlety and sensitiveness of impression, its suggestion of a spirit dwelling in external things and making its raiment of earth and air, of mist and city alike, and in its morbid sympathy of its moods, and tones, and colours, modern landscape art is realizing for us pictorially what was realized in such plastic perfection by the Greeks. Music, in which all subject is absorbed in expression and cannot be separated from it, is a complex example, and a flower or a child a simple example, of what I mean; but sorrow is the ultimate type both in life and art.

Behind joy and laughter there may be a temperament, coarse, hard and callous. But behind sorrow there is always sorrow. Pain, unlike pleasure, wears no mask. Truth in art is not any correspondence between the essential idea and the accidental existence; it is not the resemblance of shape to shadow, or of the form mirrored in the crystal to the form itself; it is no echo coming from a hollow hill, any more than it is a silver well of water in the valley that shows the moon to the moon and Narcissus to Narcissus. Truth in art is the unity of a thing with itself: the outward rendered expressive of the inward: the soul made incarnate: the body instinct with spirit. For this reason there is no truth comparable to sorrow. There are times when sorrow seems to me to be the only truth. Other things may be illusions of the eye or the appetite, made to blind the one and cloy the other, but out of sorrow have the worlds been built, and at the birth of a child or a star there is pain.

More than this, there is about sorrow an intense, an extraordinary reality. I have said of myself that I was one who stood in symbolic relations to the art and culture of my age. There is not a single wretched man in this wretched place along with me who does not stand in symbolic relation to the very secret of life. For the secret of life is suffering. It is what is hidden behind everything. When we begin to live, what is sweet is so sweet to us, and what is bitter so bitter, that we inevitably direct all our desires towards pleasures, and seek not merely for a "month or twain to feed on honeycomb," but for all our years to taste no other food, ignorant all the while that we may really be starving the soul.

I remember talking once on this subject to one of the most beautiful personalities I have ever known: a woman, whose sympathy and noble kindness to me, both before and since the tragedy of my imprisonment, have been beyond power and description; one who has really assisted me, though she does not know it, to bear the burden of my troubles more than anyone else in the whole world has, and all through the mere fact of her existence, through her being what she is—partly an ideal and partly an influence: a suggestion of what one might become as well as a real help towards becoming it; a soul that renders the common air sweet, and makes what is spiritual seem as simple and natural as sunlight or the sea: one for whom beauty and sorrow walk hand in hand, and have the same message. On the occasion of which I am thinking I recall distinctly how I said to her that there was enough suffering in one narrow London lane to show that God did not love man, and that wherever there was any sorrow, though but that of a child in some little garden weeping over a fault that it had or had not committed, the whole face of creation was completely marred. I was entirely wrong. She told me so, but I could not believe her. I was not in the sphere in which such belief was to be attained to. Now it seems to me that love of some kind is the only possible explanation of the extraordinary amount of suffering that there is in the world. I cannot conceive of any other explanation. I am convinced that there is no other, and that if the world has indeed, as I have said, been built of sorrow, it has been built by the hands of love, because in no other way could the soul of man, for whom the world was made, reach the full stature of its perfection. Pleasure for the beautiful body, but pain for the beautiful soul.

When I say that I am convinced of these things I speak with too much pride. Far off, like a perfect pearl, one can see the City of God. It is so wonderful that it seems as if a child could reach it in a summer's day. And so a child could. But with me and such as me it is different. One can realize a thing in a single moment, but one loses it in the long hours that follow with leaden feet. It is so difficult to keep "heights that the soul is competent to gain." We think in eternity, but we move slowly through time; and how slowly time goes with us who lie in prison I need not tell again, nor of the weariness and despair that creep back into one's cell, and into the cell of one's heart, with such strange insistence that one has, as it were, to garnish and sweep one's house for their coming, as for an unwelcome guest, or a bitter master, or a slave whose slave it is one's chance or choice to be.

And, though at present my friends may find it a hard thing to believe, it is true none the less, that for them living in freedom and idleness and comfort it is more easy to learn the lessons of humility than it is for me, who begin the day by going down on my knees and washing the floor of my cell. For prison life with its endless privations and restrictions makes one rebellious. The most terrible thing about it is not that it breaks one's heart—hearts are made to be broken—but that it turns one's heart to stone. One sometimes feels that it is only with a front of brass and a lip of scorn that one can get through the day at all. And he who is in a state of rebellion cannot receive grace, to use the phrase of which the Church is so fond—so rightly fond, I dare say—for in life as in art the mood of rebellion closes up the channels of the soul, and shuts out the airs of heaven. Yet I must learn these lessons here, if I am to learn them anywhere, and must be filled with joy if my feet are on the right road and my face set towards "the gate which is called beautiful," though I may fall many times in the mire and often in the mist go astray.

This New Life, as through my love of Dante I like sometimes to call it, is of course no new life at all, but simply the continuance, by means of development and evolution, of my former life. I remember when I was at Oxford saying to one of my friends as we were strolling round Magdalen's narrow bird-haunted walks one morning in the year before I took my degree, that I wanted to eat of the fruit of all the trees in the garden of the world, and that I was going out into the world with that passion in my soul. And so, indeed, I went out, and so I lived. My only mistake was that I confined myself so exclusively to the trees of what seemed to me the sun-lit side of the garden, and shunned the other side for its shadow and its gloom. Failure, disgrace, poverty, sorrow, despair, suffering, tears even, the broken words that come from lips in pain, remorse that makes one walk on thorns, conscience that condemns, self-abasement that punishes, the misery that puts ashes on its head, the anguish that chooses sackcloth for its raiment and into its own drink puts gall:—all these were things of which I was afraid. And as I had determined to know nothing of them, I was forced to taste each of them in turn, to feed on them, to have for a season, indeed, no other food at all.

I don't regret for a single moment having lived for pleasure. I did it to the full, as one should do everything that one does. There was no pleasure I did not experience. I threw the pearl of my soul into a cup of wine. I went down the primrose path to the sound of flutes. I lived on honeycomb. But to have continued the same life would have been wrong because it would have been limiting. I had to pass on. The other half of the garden had its secrets for me also. Of course all this is foreshadowed and prefigured in my books. Some of it is in *The Happy Prince*, some of it in *The Young King*, notably in the passage where the bishop says to the kneeling boy, "Is not He who made misery wiser than thou art?" a phrase which when I wrote it seemed to me little more than a phrase; a great deal of it is hidden away in the note of doom that like a purple thread runs through the texture of *Dorian Gray*; in *The Critic as Artist* it is set forth in many colours; in *The Soul of Man* it is written down, and in letters too easy to read; it is one of the refrains whose recurring *motifs* make *Salomé* so like a piece of music and bind it together as a ballad; in the prose poem of the man who from the bronze image of the "Pleasure that liveth for a moment" has to make the image of the "Sorrow that abideth for ever" it is incarnate. It could not have been otherwise. At every single moment of

one's life one is what one is going to be no less than what one
has been. Art is a symbol, because man is a symbol.

It is, if I can fully attain to it, the ultimate realization of the
artistic life. For the artistic life is simple self-development.
Humility in the artist is his frank acceptance of all experiences, just as love in the artist is simply the sense of beauty
that reveals to the world its body and its soul. In *Marius the
Epicurean* Pater seeks to reconcile the artistic life with the
life of religion, in the deep, sweet, and austere sense of the
word. But Marius is little more than a spectator: an ideal
spectator indeed, and one to whom it is given "to contem-
plate the spectacle of life with appropriate emotions," which
Wordsworth defines as the poet's true aim; yet a spectator
merely, and perhaps a little too much occupied with the
comeliness of the benches of the sanctuary to notice that it is
the sanctuary of sorrow that he is gazing at.

I see a far more intimate and immediate connexion between the true life of Christ and the true life of the artist; and
I take a keen pleasure in the reflexion that long before sorrow
had made my days her own and bound me to her wheel I had
written in *The Soul of Man* that he who would lead a Christ-
like life must be entirely and absolutely himself, and had
taken as my types not merely the shepherd on the hillside
and the prisoner in his cell, but also the painter to whom the
world is a pageant and the poet for whom the world is a song.
I remember saying once to André Gide, as we sat together in
some Paris café, that while metaphysics had but little real interest for me, and morality absolutely none, there was nothing that either Plato or Christ had said that could not be
transferred immediately into the sphere of Art and there find
its complete fulfilment.

Nor is it merely that we can discern in Christ that close
union of personality with perfection which forms the real distinction between the classical and romantic movement in life,
but the very basis of his nature was the same as that of the nature of the artist—an intense and flame-like imagination. He

realized in the entire sphere of human relations that imaginative sympathy which in the sphere of Art is the sole secret of creation. He understood the leprosy of the leper, the darkness of the blind, the fierce misery of those who live for pleasure, the strange poverty of the rich. You once wrote to me in trouble, "When you are not on your pedestal you are not interesting." How remote were you from what Matthew Arnold calls "the Secret of Jesus." Either would have taught you that whatever happens to another happens to oneself, and if you want an inscription to read at dawn and at nighttime, and for pleasure or for pain, write up on the walls of your house in letters for the sun to gild and the moon to silver, "Whatever happens to oneself happens to another."

Christ's place indeed is with the poets. His whole conception of humanity sprang right out of the imagination and can only be realized by it. What God was to the pantheist, man was to him. He was the first to conceive the divided races as a unity. Before his time there had been gods and men, and, feeling through the mysticism of sympathy that in himself each had been made incarnate, he calls himself the Son of the one or the Son of the other, according to his mood. More than anyone else in history he wakes in us that temper of wonder to which romance always appeals. There is still something to me almost incredible in the idea of a young Galilean peasant imagining that he could bear on his own shoulders the burden of the entire world: all that had already been done and suffered, and all that was yet to be done and suffered: the sins of Nero, of Caesar Borgia, of Alexander VI, and of him who was Emperor of Rome and Priest of the Sun: the sufferings of those whose names are legion and whose dwelling is among the tombs: oppressed nationalities, factory children, thieves, people in prison, outcasts, those who are dumb under oppression and whose silence is heard only of God; and not merely imagining this but actually achieving it, so that at the present moment all who come in contact with his personality, even though they may neither bow to his altar nor kneel before his priest, in some way find that the ugliness of their skin is taken away and the beauty of their sorrow revealed to them.

I had said of Christ that he ranks with the poets. That is true. Shelley and Sophocles are of his company. But his entire life also is the most wonderful of poems. For "pity and terror" there is nothing in the entire cycle of Greek tragedy to touch it. The absolute purity of the protagonist raises the entire scheme to a height of romantic art from which the sufferings of Thebes and Pelops' line are by their very horror excluded, and shows how wrong Aristotle was when he said in his treatise on the drama that it would be impossible to bear the spectacle of one blameless in pain. Nor in Aeschylus nor Dante, those stern masters of tenderness, in Shakespeare, the most purely human of all the great artists, in the whole of Celtic myth and legend, where the loveliness of the world is shown through a mist of tears, and the life of a man is no more than the life of a flower, is there anything that, for sheer simplicity of pathos wedded and made one with sublimity of tragic effect, can be said to equal or even approach the last act of Christ's passion. The little supper with his companions, one of whom has already sold him for a price; the anguish in the quiet moon-lit garden; the false friend coming close to him so as to betray him with a kiss; the friend who still believed in him, and on whom as on a rock he had hoped to build a house of refuge for Man, denying him as the bird cried to the dawn; his own utter loneliness, his submission, his acceptance of everything; and along with it all such scenes as the high priest of orthodoxy rending his raiment in wrath, and the magistrate of civil justice calling for water in the vain hope of cleansing himself of that stain of innocent blood that makes him the scarlet figure of history; the coronation ceremony of sorrow, one of the most wonderful things in the whole of recorded time; the crucifixion of the Innocent One before the eyes of his mother and of the disciple whom he loved; the soldiers gambling and throwing dice for his clothes; the terrible death by which he gave the world its most eternal symbol; and his final burial in the tomb of the rich man, his body swathed in

Egyptian linen with costly spices and perfumes as though he
had been a king's son. When one contemplates all this from
the point of view of art alone one cannot but be grateful that
the supreme office of the Church should be the playing of the
tragedy without the shedding of blood: the mystical presentation, by means of dialogue and costume and gesture even, of
the Passion of her Lord; and it is always a source of pleasure
and awe to me to remember that the ultimate survival of the
Greek chorus, lost elsewhere to art, is to be found in the servi-
tor answering the priest at Mass.

Yet the whole life of Christ—so entirely may sorrow and
beauty be made one in their meaning and manifestation—is
really an idyll though it ends with the veil of the temple
being rent, and the darkness coming over the face of the
earth, and the stone rolled to the door of the sepulchre. One
always thinks of him as a young bridegroom with his companions, as indeed he somewhere describes himself; as a
shepherd straying through a valley with his sheep in search
of green meadow or cool stream; as a singer trying to build
out of the music the walls of the City of God; or as a lover for
whose love the whole world was too small. His miracles
seem to me to be as exquisite as the coming of spring, and
quite as natural. I see no difficulty at all in believing that
such was the charm of his personality that his mere presence
could bring peace to souls in anguish, and that those who
touched his garments or his hands forgot their pain; or that
as he passed by on the highway of life people who had seen
nothing of life's mystery saw it clearly, and others who had
been deaf to every voice but that of pleasure heard for the
first time the voice of love and found it as "musical as
Apollo's lute"; or that evil passions fled at his approach, and
men whose dull unimaginative lives had been but a mode of
death rose as it were from the grave when he called them; or
that when he taught on the hillside the multitude forgot
their hunger and thirst and the cares of this world, and that
to his friends who listened to him as he sat at meat the
coarse food seemed delicate, and the water had the taste of

good wine, and the whole house became full of the odour and sweetness of nard.

Renan in his *Vie de Jésus*—the gracious fifth gospel, the gospel according to St. Thomas, one might call it—says somewhere that Christ's great achievement was that he made himself as much loved after his death as he had been during his lifetime. And certainly, if his place is among the poets, he is the leader of all the lovers. He saw that love was the first secret of the world for which the wise men had been looking, and that it was only through love that one could approach either the heart of the leper or the feet of God.

And above all, Christ is the most supreme of individualists. Humility, like the artistic acceptance of all experiences, is merely a mode of manifestation. It is man's soul that Christ is always looking for. He calls it "God's Kingdom," and finds it in every one. He compares it to little things, to a tiny seed, to a handful of leaven, to a pearl. That is because one realizes one's soul only by getting rid of all alien passions, all acquired culture, and all external possessions, be they good or evil.

I bore up against everything with some stubbornness of will and much rebellion of nature, till I had absolutely nothing left in the world but one thing. I had lost my name, my position, my happiness, my freedom, my wealth. I was a prisoner and a pauper. But I still had my children left. Suddenly they were taken away from me by the law. It was a blow so appalling that I did not know what to do, so I flung myself on my knees, and bowed my head, and wept, and said, "The body of a child is as the body of the Lord: I am not worthy of either." That moment seemed to save me. I saw then that the only thing for me was to accept everything. Since then—curious as it will no doubt sound—I have been happier. It was of course my soul in its ultimate essence that I had reached. In many ways I had been its enemy, but I found it waiting for me as a friend. When one comes in contact with the soul it makes one simple as a child, as Christ said one should be.

It is tragic how few people ever "possess their souls" before they die. "Nothing is more rare in any man" says Emerson "than an act of his own." It is quite true. Most people are other people. Their thoughts are someone else's opinions, their lives a mimicry, their passions a quotation. Christ was not merely the supreme individualist, but he was the first individualist in history. People have tried to make him out an ordinary philanthropist, or ranked him as an altruist with the unscientific and sentimental. But he was really neither one nor the other. Pity he has, of course, for the poor, for those who are shut up in prisons, for the lowly, for the wretched; but he has far more pity for the rich, for the hard hedonists, for those who waste their freedom in becoming slaves to things, for those who wear soft raiment and live in kings' houses. Riches and pleasure seemed to him to be really greater tragedies than poverty or sorrow. And as for altruism, who knew better than he that it is vocation not volition that determines us, and that one cannot gather grapes of thorns or figs from thistles?

To live for others as a definite self-conscious aim was not his creed. It was not the basis of his creed. When he says, "Forgive your enemies," it is not for the sake of the enemy, but for one's own sake that he says so, and because love is more beautiful than hate. In his own entreaty to the young man, "Sell all that thou hast and give to the poor," it is not of the state of the poor that he is thinking, but of the soul of the young man, the soul that wealth was marring. In his view of life he is one with the artist who knows that by the inevitable law of self-perfection, the poet must sing, and the sculptor think in bronze, and the painter make the world a mirror for his moods, as surely and as certainly as the hawthorn must blossom in spring, and the corn turn to gold at harvest-time, and the moon in her ordered wanderings change from shield to sickle, and from sickle to shield.

But while Christ did not say to men, "Live for others," he pointed out that there was no difference at all between the lives of others and one's own life. By this means he gave to man an extended, a Titan personality. Since his coming the history of each separate individual is, or can be made, the history of the world. Of course, culture has intensified the personality of man. Art has made us myriad-minded. Those who have the artistic temperament go into exile with Dante and learn how salt is the bread of others, and how steep their stairs; they catch for a moment the serenity and calm of Goethe, and yet know but too well that Baudelaire cried to God—

O Seigneur, donnez-moi la force et le courage
De contempler mon corps et mon coeur sans dégoût.[25]

Out of Shakespeare's sonnets they draw, to their own hurt it may be, the secret of his love and make it their own; they look with new eyes on modern life, because they have listened to one of Chopin's nocturnes, or handled Greek things, or read the story of the passion of some dead man for some dead woman whose hair was like threads of fine gold, and whose mouth was as a pomegranate. But the sympathy of the artistic temperament is necessarily with what has found expression. In words or in colours, in music or in marble, behind the painted masks of an Aeschylean play, or through some Sicilian shepherds' pierced and jointed reeds, the man and his message must have been revealed.

To the artist, expression is the only mode under which he can conceive life at all. To him what is dumb is dead. But to Christ it was not so. With a width and wonder of imagination that fills one almost with awe, he took the entire world of the inarticulate, the voiceless world of pain, as his kingdom, and made of himself its external mouthpiece. Those of whom I have spoken, who are dumb under oppression and "whose silence is heard only of God," he chose as his brothers. He sought to become eyes to the blind, ears to the deaf, and a cry in the lips of those whose tongues had been tied. His desire was to be to the myriads who had found no utterance a very trumpet through which they might call to heaven. And feeling, with the artistic nature of one to whom suffering and sorrow were modes through which he could realize his conception of the beautiful, that an idea is of no value till it becomes incarnate and is made an image, he made of himself the image of the Man of Sorrows, and as such has fascinated and dominated art as no Greek god ever succeeded in doing.

For the Greek gods, in spite of the white and red of their fair fleet limbs, were not really what they appeared to be. The curved brow of Apollo was like the sun's disc over a hill at dawn, and his feet were as the wings of the morning, but he himself had been cruel to Marsyas and had made Niobe childless. In the steel shields of Athena's eyes there had been no pity for Arachne; the pomp and peacocks of Hera were all that was really noble about her; and the Father of the Gods himself had been too fond of the daughters of men. The two most deeply suggestive figures of Greek mythology were, for religion, Demeter, an earth goddess, not one of the Olympians, and for art, Dionysos, the son of a mortal woman to whom the moment of his birth had proved also the moment of her death.

But Life itself from its lowliest and most humble sphere produced one far more marvellous than the mother of Proserpina or the son of Semele. Out of the Carpenter's shop at Nazareth had come a personality infinitely greater than any made by myth and legend, and one, strangely enough, destined to reveal to the world the mystical meaning of wine and the real beauties of the lilies of the field as none, either on Cithaeron or at Enna, had ever done.

The song of Isaiah, "He is despised and rejected of men, a man of sorrows and acquainted with grief: and we hid as it were our faces from him," had seemed to him to prefigure himself, and in him the prophecy was fulfilled. We must not be afraid of such a phrase. Every single work of art is the fulfilment of a prophecy: for every work of art is the conversion of an idea into an image. Every single human being should be the fulfilment of a prophecy: for every human being should be the realization of some ideal, either in the mind of God or in the mind of man. Christ found the type and fixed it, and the dream of a Virgilian poet, either at Jerusalem or at Babylon, became in the long progress of the centuries incarnate in him for whom the world was "waiting." "His visage was marred more than any man's, and his form was more than the sons of men," are among the signs noted by Isaiah as distinguishing the new ideal, and as soon as art understood what was meant it opened like a flower at the presence of one in whom truth in art was set forth as it had never been before. For is not truth in art, as I have said, "that in which the outward is expressive of the inward; in which the soul is made flesh and the body instinct with spirit in which form reveals."

To me one of the things in history the most to be regretted is that the Christ's own renaissance which has produced the Cathedral at Chartres, the Arthurian cycle of legends, the life of St. Francis of Assisi, the art of Giotto, and Dante's *Divine Comedy*, was not allowed to develop on its own lines, but was interrupted and spoiled by the dreary classical Renaissance that gave us Petrarch, and Raphael's frescoes, and Palladian architecture, and formal French tragedy, and St. Paul's Cathedral, and Pope's poetry, and everything that is made from without and by dead rules, and does not spring from within through some spirit informing it. But wherever there is a romantic movement in art there somehow, and under some form, is Christ, or the soul of Christ. He is in *Romeo and Juliet*, in the *Winter's Tale*, in Provençal poetry, in the *Ancient Mariner*, in *La Belle Dame sans merci*, and in Chatterton's *Ballad of Charity*.

We owe to him the most diverse things and people. Hugo's *Les Misérables*, Baudelaire's *Fleurs du Mal*, the note of pity in Russian novels, Verlaine and Verlaine's poems, the stained glass and tapestries and the quattrocento work of Burne-Jones and Morris, belong to him no less than the tower of Giotto, Lancelot and Guinevere, Tannhäuser, the troubled romantic marbles of Michael Angelo, pointed architecture, and the love of children and flowers—for both of which, indeed, in classical art there was but little place, hardly enough for them to grow or play in, but which, from the twelfth century down to our own day, have been continually making their appearances in art, under various modes and at various times, coming fitfully and wilfully, as children, as flowers, are apt to do: spring always seeming to one as if the flowers had been in hiding, and only came out into the sun because they were afraid that grown-up people would grow tired of looking for them and give up the search; and the life of a child being no more than an April day on which there is both rain and sun for the narcissus.

It is the imaginative quality of Christ's own nature that makes him this palpitating centre of romance. The strange figures of poetic drama and ballad are made by the imagination of others, but out of his own imagination entirely did Jesus of Nazareth create himself. The cry of Isaiah had really no more to do with his coming than the song of the nightingale has to do with the rising of the moon—no more, though perhaps no less. He was the denial as well as the affirmation of prophecy. For every expectation that he fulfilled there was another that he destroyed. "In all beauty," says Bacon, "there is some strangeness of proportion," and of those who are born of the spirit—of those, that is to say, who like himself are dynamic forces—Christ says that they are like the wind that "bloweth where it listeth, and no man can tell whence it cometh and whither it goeth." This is why he is so fascinating to artists. He has all the colour elements of life; mystery, strangeness, pathos, suggestion, ecstasy, love. He appeals to the temper of wonder, and creates that mood in which alone he can be understood.

And to me it is a joy to remember that if he is "of imagination all compact," the world itself is of the same substance. I said in *Dorian Gray* that the great sins of the world take place in the brain: but it is in the brain that everything takes place. We know now that we do not see with the eyes or hear with the ears. They are really channels for the transmission, adequate or inadequate, of sense impressions. It is in the brain that the poppy is red, that the apple is odorous, that the skylark sings.

Of late I have been studying with diligence the four prose

poems about Christ. At Christmas I managed to get hold of a
Greek Testament, and every morning, after I had cleaned my
cell and polished my tins, I read a little of the Gospels, a
dozen verses taken by chance anywhere. It is a delightful way
of opening the day. Everyone, even in a turbulent, ill-
disciplined life, should do the same. Endless repetition, in
and out of season, has spoiled for us the freshness, the
naïveté, the simple romantic charm of the Gospels. We hear
them read far too often and far too badly, and all repetition is
anti-spiritual. When one returns to the Greek, it is like going
into a garden of lilies out of some narrow and dark house.

And to me, the pleasure is doubled by the reflexion that it
is extremely probable that we have the actual terms, the *ip-
sissima verba*, used by Christ. It was always supposed that
Christ talked in Aramaic. Even Renan thought so. But now
we know that the Galilean peasants, like the Irish peasants of
our own day, were bilingual, and that Greek was the ordinary
language of intercourse all over Palestine, as indeed all over
the Eastern world. I never liked the idea that we knew of
Christ's own words only through a translation of a translation.
It is a delight to me to think that as far as his conversation was
concerned, Charmides[26] might have listened to him, and
Socrates reasoned with him, and Plato understood him: that
he really said ἐγώ εἰμι ὁ ποιμὴν ὁ καλός,[27] that when he
thought of the lilies of the field and how they neither toil nor
spin, his absolute expression was καταμάθετε τὰ κρίνα τοῦ
ἀγροῦ πῶς αὐξάνει οὐ κοπιᾷ οὐδὲ νήθει,[28] and that his last
word when he cried out "my life has been completed, has
reached its fulfilment, has been perfected," was exactly as St.
John tells us it was: τετέλεσται[29]—no more.

While in reading the Gospels—particularly that of St.
John himself, or whatever early Gnostic took his name and
mantle—I see the continual assertion of the imagination as
the basis of all spiritual and material life, I see also that to
Christ imagination was simply a form of love, and that to him
love was lord in the fullest meaning of the phrase. Some six
weeks ago I was allowed by the doctor to have white bread to

eat instead of the coarse black or brown bread of ordinary
prison fare. It is a great delicacy. It will sound strange that dry
bread could possibly be a delicacy to anyone. To me it is so
much so that at the close of each meal I carefully eat whatever
crumbs may be left on my tin plate, or have fallen on the
rough towel that one uses as a cloth so as not to soil one's
table; and I do so not from hunger—I get now quite sufficient
food—but simply in order that nothing should be
wasted of what is given to me. So one should look on love.

Christ, like all fascinating personalities, had the power of
not merely saying beautiful things himself, but of making
other people say beautiful things to him; and I love the story
St. Mark tells us about the Greek woman, who, when as a
trial of her faith he said to her that he could not give her the
bread of the children of Israel, answered him that the little
dogs—(κυνάρια, "little dogs" it should be rendered)—who
are under the table eat of the crumbs that the children let
fall. Most people live for love and admiration. But it is by love
and admiration that we should live. If any love is shown us we
should recognize that we are quite unworthy of it. Nobody is
worthy to be loved. The fact that God loves man shows us
that in the divine order of ideal things it is written that eternal
love is to be given to what is eternally unworthy. Or if that
phrase seems to be a bitter one to bear, let us say that every
one is worthy of love, except him who thinks that he is. Love is
a sacrament that should be taken kneeling, and *Domine, non
sum dignus*[30] should be on the lips and in the hearts of those
who receive it.

If ever I write again, in the sense of producing artistic
work, there are just two subjects on which and through which
I desire to express myself: one is "Christ as the precursor of
the romantic movement in life": the other is "The artistic life
considered in its relation to conduct." The first is, of course,
intensely fascinating, for I see in Christ not merely the essentials
of the supreme romantic type, but all the accidents,
the wilfulnesses even, of the romantic temperament also. He
was the first person who ever said to people that they should

live "flower-like lives." He fixed the phrase. He took children as the type of what people should try to become. He held them up as examples to their elders, which I myself have always thought the chief use of children, if what is perfect should have a use. Dante describes the soul of a man as coming from the hand of God "weeping and laughing like a little child," and Christ also saw that the soul of each one should be *a guisa di fanciulla che piangendo e ridendo pargoleggia.*[31] He felt that life was changeful, fluid, active, and that to allow it to be stereotyped into any form was death. He saw that people should not be too serious over material, common interests; that to be unpractical was to be a great thing: that one should not bother too much over affairs. The birds didn't, why should man? He is charming when he says, "Take no thought for the morrow; is not the soul more than meat? is not the body more than raiment?" A Greek might have used the latter phrase. It is full of Greek feeling. But only Christ could have said both, and so summed up life perfectly for us.

His morality is all sympathy, just what morality should be. If the only thing that he ever said had been, "Her sins are forgiven her because she loved much," it would have been worth while dying to have said it. His justice is all poetical justice, exactly what justice should be. The beggar goes to heaven because he has been unhappy. I cannot conceive a better reason for his being sent there. The people who work for an hour in the vineyard in the cool of the evening receive just as much reward as those who have toiled there all day long in the hot sun. Why shouldn't they? Probably no one deserved anything. Or perhaps they were a different kind of people. Christ had no patience with the dull lifeless mechanical systems that treat people as if they were things, and so treat everybody alike: for him there were no laws: there were exceptions merely, as if anybody, or anything, for that matter, was like aught else in the world!

That which is the very keynote of romantic art was to him the proper basis of natural life. He saw no other basis. And when they brought him one taken in the very act of sin and showed him her sentence written in the law, and asked him what was to be done, he wrote with his finger on the ground as though he did not hear them, and finally when they pressed him again, looked up and said, "Let him of you who has never sinned be the first to throw the stone at her." It was worth while living to have said that.

Like all poetical natures he loved ignorant people. He knew that in the soul of one who is ignorant there is always room for a great idea. But he could not stand stupid people, especially those who are made stupid by education: people who are full of opinions not one of which they even understand, a peculiarly modern type, summed up by Christ when he describes it as the type of one who has the key of knowledge, cannot use it himself, and does not allow other people to use it, though it may be made to open the gate of God's Kingdom. His chief war was against the Philistines. That is the war every child of light has to wage. Philistinism was the note of the age and community in which he lived. In their heavy inaccessibility to ideas, their dull respectability, their tedious orthodoxy, their worship of vulgar success, their entire preoccupation with the gross materialistic side of life, and their ridiculous estimate of themselves and their importance, the Jews of Jerusalem in Christ's day were the exact counterpart of the British Philistine of our own. Christ mocked at the "whited sepulchre" of respectability, and fixed that phrase for ever. He treated worldly success as a thing absolutely to be despised. He saw nothing in it at all. He looked on wealth as an encumbrance to a man. He would not hear of life being sacrificed to any system of thought or morals. He pointed out that forms and ceremonies were made for man, not man for forms and ceremonies. He took Sabbatarianism as a type of the things that should be set at nought. The cold philanthropies, the ostentatious public charities, the tedious formalisms so dear to the middle-class mind, he exposed with utter and relentless scorn. To us, what is termed orthodoxy is merely a facile unintelligent acquiescence; but to them, and in their hands, it was a terrible and paralysing tyranny. Christ swept it aside. He showed that the spirit alone was of value. He took a keen pleasure in pointing out to them that though they were always reading the law and the prophets, they had not really the smallest idea of what either of them meant. In opposition to their tithing of each separate day into the fixed routine of prescribed duties, as they tithe mint and rue, he preached the enormous importance of living completely for the moment.

Those whom he saved from their sins are saved simply for beautiful moments in their lives. Mary Magdalen, when she sees Christ, breaks the rich vase of alabaster that one of her seven lovers had given her, and spills the odorous spices over his tired dusty feet, and for that one moment's sake sits for ever with Ruth and Beatrice in the tresses of the snow-white rose of Paradise. All that Christ says to us by the way of a little warning is that every moment should be beautiful, that the soul should always be ready for the coming of the bridegroom, always waiting for the voice of the lover, Philistinism being simply that side of man's nature that is not illumined by the imagination. He sees all the lovely influences of life as modes of light: the imagination itself is the world of light. The world is made by it, and yet the world cannot understand it: that is because the imagination is simply a manifestation of love, and it is love and the capacity for it that distinguishes one human being from another.

But it is when he deals with a sinner that Christ is most romantic, in the sense of most real. The world had always loved the saint as being the nearest possible approach to the perfection of God. Christ, through some divine instinct in him, seems to have always loved the sinner as being the nearest possible approach to the perfection of man. His primary desire was not to reform people, any more than his primary desire was to relieve suffering. To turn an interesting thief into a tedious honest man was not his aim. He would have thought little of the Prisoners' Aid Society and other modern movements of the kind. The conversion of a publican into a Pharisee would not have seemed to him a great achievement.

But in a manner not yet understood of the world he regarded sin and suffering as being in themselves beautiful holy things and modes of perfection.

It seems a very dangerous idea. It is—all great ideas are dangerous. That it was Christ's creed admits of no doubt. That it is the true creed I don't doubt myself.

Of course the sinner must repent. But why? Simply because otherwise he would be unable to realize what he had done. The moment of repentance is the moment of initiation. More than that: it is the means by which one alters one's past. The Greeks thought that impossible. They often say in their Gnomic aphorisms, "Even the Gods cannot alter the past." Christ showed that the commonest sinner could do it, that it was the one thing he could do. Christ, had he been asked, would have said—I feel quite certain about it—that the moment the prodigal son fell on his knees and wept, he made his having wasted his substance with harlots, his swineherding and hungering for the husks they ate, beautiful and holy moments in his life. It is difficult for most people to grasp the idea. I dare say one has to go to prison to understand it. If so, it may be worth while going to prison.

There is something so unique about Christ. Of course, just as there are false dawns before the dawn itself, and winter days so full of sudden sunlight that they will cheat the wise crocus into squandering its gold before its time, and make some foolish bird call to its mate to build on barren boughs, so there were Christians before Christ. For that we should be grateful. The unfortunate thing is that there have been none since. I make one exception, St. Francis of Assisi. But then God had given him at his birth the soul of a poet, as he himself when quite young had in mystical marriage taken poverty as his bride: and with the soul of a poet and the body of a beggar he found the way to perfection not difficult. He understood Christ and so he became like him. We do not require the Liber Conformitatum[32] to teach us that the life of St. Francis was the true *Imitatio Christi*, a poem compared to which the book of that name is merely prose.

Indeed, that is the charm about Christ, when all is said: he is just like a work of art. He does not really teach one anything, but by being brought into his presence one becomes something. And everybody is predestined to his presence. Once at least in his life each man walks with Christ to Emmaus.

As regards the other subject, the Relation of the Artistic Life to Conduct, it will no doubt seem strange to you that I should select it. People point to Reading Gaol and say, "That is where the artistic life leads a man." Well, it might lead to worse places. The more mechanical people to whom life is a shrewd speculation depending on a careful calculation of ways and means, always know where they are going, and go there. They start with the ideal desire of being the parish beadle, and in whatever sphere they are placed they succeed in being the parish beadle and no more. A man whose desire to be something separate from himself to be a member of Parliament, or a successful grocer, or a prominent solicitor, or a judge, or something equally tedious, invariably succeeds in being what he wants to be. That is his punishment. Those who want a mask have to wear it.

But with the dynamic forces of life, and those in whom those dynamic forces become incarnate, it is difficult. People whose desire is solely for self-realization never know where they are going. They can't know. In one sense of the word it is of course necessary, as the Greek oracle said, to know oneself: that is the first achievement of knowledge. But to recognize that the soul of a man is unknowable, is the ultimate achievement of wisdom. The final mystery is oneself. When one has weighed the sun in the balance, and measured the steps of the moon, and mapped out the seven heavens star by star, there still remains oneself. Who can calculate the orbit of his own soul? When the son went out to look for his father's assets, he did not know that a man of God was waiting for him with the very chrism of coronation, and that his own soul was already the soul of a king.

I hope to live long enough and to produce work of such a

character that I shall be able at the end of my days to say, "Yes! this is just where the artistic life leads a man!" Two of the most perfect lives I have come across in my own experience are the lives of Verlaine and of Prince Kropotkin: both of them men who have passed years in prison: the first, the one Christian poet since Dante; the other, a man with a soul of that beautiful white Christ which seems coming out of Russia. And for the last seven or eight months, in spite of a succession of great troubles reaching me from the outside world almost without intermission, I have been placed in direct contact with a new spirit working in this prison through man and things, that has helped me beyond any possibility of expression in words: so that while for the first year of my imprisonment I did nothing else, and can remember doing nothing else, but wring my hands in impotent despair, and say, "What an ending, what an appalling ending!" now I try to say to myself, and sometimes when I am not torturing myself do really and sincerely say, "What a beginning, what a wonderful beginning!" It may really be so. It may become so. If it does I shall owe much to this new personality that has altered every man's life in this place.

You may realize it when I say that had I been released last May, as I tried to be, I would have left this place loathing it and every official in it with a bitterness of hatred that would have poisoned my life. I have had a year longer of imprisonment, but humanity has been in the prison along with us all, and now when I go out I shall always remember great kindnesses that I have received here from almost everybody, and on the day of my release I shall give many thanks to many people, and ask to be remembered by them in turn.

The prison style is absolutely and entirely wrong. I would give anything to be able to alter it when I go out. I intend to try. But there is nothing in the world so wrong but that the spirit of humanity, which is the spirit of love, the spirit of the Christ who is not in churches, may make it, if not right, at least possible to be borne without too much bitterness of heart.

I know also that much is waiting for me outside that is very delightful, from what St. Francis of Assisi calls "my brother the wind, and my sister the rain," lovely things both of them, down to the shop-windows and sunsets of great cities. If I made a list of all that still remains to me, I don't know where I should stop: for, indeed, God made the world just as much for me as for anyone else. Perhaps I may go out with something that I had not got before. I need not tell you that to me reformations in morals are as meaningless and vulgar as Reformations in theology. But while to propose to be a better man is a piece of unscientific cant, to have become a deeper man is the privilege of those who have suffered. And such I think I have become.

If after I am free a friend of mine gave a feast, and did not invite me to it, I should not mind a bit. I can be perfectly happy by myself. With freedom, flowers, books, and the moon, who could not be perfectly happy? Besides, feasts are not for me any more. I have given too many to care about them. That side of life is over for me, very fortunately, I dare say. But if after I am free a friend of mine had a sorrow and refused to allow me to share it, I should feel it most bitterly. If he shut the doors of the house of mourning against me, I would come back again and again and beg to be admitted, so that I might share in what I was entitled to share in. If he thought me unworthy, unfit to weep with him, I should feel it as the most poignant humiliation, as the most terrible mode in which disgrace could be inflicted on me. But that could not be. I have a right to share in sorrow, and he who can look at the loveliness of the world and share its sorrow, and realize something of the wonder of both, is in immediate contact with divine things, and has got as near to God's secret as anyone can get.

Perhaps there may come into my art also, no less than into my life, a still deeper note, one of greater unity of passion, and directness of impulse. Not width but intensity is the true aim of modern art. We are no longer in art concerned with the type. It is with the exception that we have to do. I cannot put my sufferings into any form they took, I need hardly say. Art only begins where Imitation ends, but something must come into my work, of fuller memory of words perhaps, of richer cadences, of more curious effects, of simpler architectural order, of some aesthetic quality at any rate.

When Marsyas was "torn from the scabbard of his limbs"—*della vagina della membra sue*,[33] to use one of Dante's most terrible Tacitean phrases—he had no more song, the Greek said. Apollo had been victor. The lyre had vanquished the reed. But perhaps the Greeks were mistaken. I hear in much modern art the cry of Marsyas. It is bitter in Baudelaire, sweet and plaintive in Lamartine, mystic in Verlaine. It is in the deferred resolutions of Chopin's music. It is in the discontent that haunts Burne-Jones's women. Even Matthew Arnold, whose song of Callicles tells "of the triumph of the sweet persuasive lyre," and the "famous final victory," in such a clear note of lyrical beauty, has not a little of it; in the troubled undertone of doubt and distress that haunts his verses, neither Goethe nor Wordsworth could help him, though he followed each in turn, and when he seeks to mourn for *Thyrsis* or to sing of the *Scholar Gipsy*, it is the reed that he has to take for the rendering of his strain. But whether or not the Phrygian Faun was silent, I cannot be. Expression is as necessary to me as leaf and blossoms are to the black branches of the trees that show themselves above the prison walls and are so restless in the wind. Between my art and the world there is now a wide gulf, but between art and myself there is none. I hope at least that there is none.

To each of us different fates are meted out. My lot has been one of public infamy, of long imprisonment, of misery, of ruin, of disgrace, but I am not worthy of it—not yet, at any rate. I remember that I used to say that I thought I could bear a real tragedy if it came to me with purple pall and a mask of noble sorrow, but that the dreadful thing about modernity was that it put tragedy into the raiment of comedy, so that the great realities seemed commonplace or grotesque or lacking in style. It is quite true about modernity. It has probably always been true about actual life. It is said that all martyrdoms seemed mean to the looker-on. The nineteenth century is no exception to the rule.

Everything about my tragedy has been hideous, mean, repellent, lacking in style; our very dress makes us grotesque. We are the zanies of sorrow. We are clowns whose hearts are broken. We are specially designed to appeal to the sense of humour. On 13th November 1895, I was brought down here from London. From two o'clock till half-past two on that day I had to stand on the centre platform of Clapham Junction in convict dress, and handcuffed, for the world to look at. I had been taken out of the hospital ward without a moment's notice being given to me. Of all possible objects I was the most grotesque. When people saw me they laughed. Each train as it came up swelled the audience. Nothing could exceed their amusement. That was, of course, before they knew who I was. As soon as they had been informed they laughed still more. For half an hour I stood there in the grey November rain surrounded by a jeering mob.

For a year after that was done to me I wept every day at the same hour and for the same space of time. That is not such a tragic thing as possibly it sounds to you. To those who are in prison tears are part of every day's experience. A day in prison on which one does not weep is a day on which one's heart is hard, not a day on which one's heart is happy.

Well, now I am really beginning to feel more regret for the people who laughed than for myself. Of course when they saw me I was not on my pedestal, I was in the pillory. But it is a very unimaginative nature that only cares for people on their pedestals. A pedestal may be a very unreal thing. A pillory is a terrific reality. They should have known also how to interpret sorrow better. I have said that behind sorrow there is always sorrow. It were wiser still to say that behind sorrow there is always a soul. And to mock at a soul in pain is a dreadful thing. In the strangely simple economy of the world people only get what they give, and to those who have not enough imagination to penetrate the mere outward shell of things, and feel pity, what pity can be given save that of scorn?

I write this account of the mode of my being transferred here simply that it should be realized how hard it has been for me to get anything out of my punishment but bitterness and despair. I have, however, to do it, and now and then I have moments of submission and acceptance. All the spring may be hidden in the single bud, and the low ground nest of the lark may hold the joy that is to herald the feet of many rose-red dawns. So perhaps whatever beauty of life still remains to me is contained in some moment of surrender, abasement, and humiliation. I can, at any rate, merely proceed on the lines of my own development, and, accepting all that has happened to me, make myself worthy of it.

People used to say of me that I was too individualistic. I must be far more of an individualist than ever I was. I must get far more out of myself than ever I got, and ask for less of the world than ever I asked. Indeed, my ruin came not from too great individualism of life, but from too little. The one disgraceful, unpardonable, and to all time contemptible action of my life was to allow myself to appeal to Society for help and protection. To have made such an appeal would have been from the individualist point of view bad enough, but what excuse can there ever be put forward for having made it? Of course once I had put into motion the forces of Society, Society turned on me and said "Have you been living all this time in defiance of my laws, and do you now appeal to those laws for protection? You shall have those laws exercised to the full. You shall abide by what you have appealed to." The result is I am in gaol. Certainly no man ever fell so ignobly, and by such ignoble instruments, as I did. I say in *Dorian Gray* somewhere that "A man cannot be too careful in the choice of his enemies." I little thought that it was by a pariah I was to be made a pariah myself.

The Philistine element in life is not the failure to understand art. Charming people, such as fishermen, shepherds, ploughboys, peasants and the like, know nothing about art, and are the very salt of the earth. He is the Philistine who upholds and aids the heavy, cumbrous, blind, mechanical forces of Society, and who does not recognize dynamic force when he meets it either in a man or a movement.

People thought it dreadful of me to have entertained at dinner the evil doings of life, and to have found pleasure in their company. But then, from the point of view through which I, as an artist in life, approach them they were delightfully suggestive and stimulating. It was like feasting with panthers; the danger was half the excitement. I used to feel as a snake-charmer must feel when he lures the cobra to stir from the painted cloth or reed basket that holds it and makes it spread its hood at his bidding and sway to and fro in the air as a plant sways restfully in a stream. They were to me the brightest of gilded snakes, their poison was part of their perfection. I did not know that when they were to strike at me it was to be at another's piping and at another's pay. I don't feel at all ashamed at having known them, they were intensely interesting; what I do feel ashamed of is the horrible Philistine atmosphere into which I was brought. My business as an artist was with Ariel, I set myself to wrestle with Caliban. Instead of making beautiful coloured musical things such as *Salomé* and the *Florentine Tragedy* and *La Sainte Courtisane*, I forced myself to send long lawyer's letters and was constrained to appeal to the very things against which I had always protested. Clibborn and Atkins were wonderful in their infamous war against life. To entertain them was an astounding adventure; Dumas *père*, Cellini, Goya, Edgar Allan Poe, or Baudelaire would have done just the same. What is loathsome to me is the memory of interminable visits paid by me to the solicitor Humphreys, when in the ghastly glare of a bleak room I would sit with a serious face telling serious lies to a bald man till I really groaned and yawned with ennui. There is where I found myself, right in the centre of Philistia, away from everything that was beautiful or brilliant or wonderful or daring. I had come forward as the champion of respectability in conduct, of puritanism in life, and of morality in art. *Voilà où mènent les mauvais chemins.*[34]

And the curious doing to me is that you should have tried to imitate your father in his chief characteristics. I cannot understand why he was to you an exemplar, where he should have been a warning, except that whenever there is hatred between two people there is bond or brotherhood of some kind. I suppose that, by some strange law of the antipathy of similars, you loathed each other, not because in so many points you were so different but because in some you were so like. In June 1893, when you left Oxford, without a degree and with debts, petty in themselves, but considerable to a man of your father's income, your father wrote you a very vulgar, violent and abusive letter. The letter you sent him in reply was in every way worse, and of course far less excusable, and consequently you were extremely proud of it. I remember quite well your saying to me with your most conceited air that you could beat your father "at his own trade." Quite true. But what a trade! What a competition! You used to laugh and sneer at your father for retiring from your cousin's house where he was living in order to write filthy letters to him from a neighbouring hotel. You used to do just the same to me. You constantly lunched with me at some public restaurant, sulked or made a scene during luncheon, and then retired to White's Club and wrote me a letter of the very foulest character. The only difference between you and your father was that after you had dispatched your letter to me by special messenger, you would arrive yourself at my rooms some hours later not to apologize, but to know if I had ordered dinner at the Savoy, and if not, why not. Sometimes you would actually arrive before the offensive letter had been read. I remember on one occasion you had asked me to invite to luncheon at the Café Royal two of your friends, one of whom I had never seen in my life. I did so, and at your special request ordered beforehand a specially luxurious luncheon to be prepared. The chef, I remember, was sent for, and particular instructions given about the wines. Instead of coming to luncheon you sent me at the Café an abusive letter timed so as to reach me after we had been waiting half an hour for you. I read the first line, and saw what it was, and putting the letter in my pocket explained to your friends that you were suddenly taken ill, and that the rest of the letter referred to your symptoms. In point of fact I did not read the letter till I was dressing for dinner at Tite Street that evening. As I was in the middle of its mire, wondering with infinite sadness how you could write letters that were really like the froth and foam on the lips of an epileptic, my servant came in to tell me that you were in the hall and very anxious to see me for five minutes. I at once sent down and asked you to come up. You arrived, looking, I admit, very frightened and pale, to beg my advice and assistance, as you had been told that a man from Lumley, the solicitor, had been enquiring for you at Cadogan Place, and you were afraid that your Oxford trouble or some new danger was threatening you. I consoled you, and told you, what proved to be the case, that it was merely a tradesman's bill probably, and let you stay to dinner and pass your evening with me. You never mentioned a single word about your hideous letter, nor did I. I treated it simply as an unhappy symptom of an unhappy temperament. The subject was never alluded to. To write to me a loathsome letter at 2:30 and fly to me for help and sympathy at 7:15 the same afternoon, was a perfectly ordinary occurrence in your life. You went quite beyond your father in such habits, as you did in others. When his revolting letters to you were read in open Court he naturally felt ashamed and pretended to weep. Had your letters to him been read by his own Counsel still more horror and repugnance would have been felt by everyone. Nor was it merely in style that you beat him at "his own trade," but in the mode of attack you distanced him completely. You availed yourself of the public telegram, and the open postcard. I think you might have left such modes of annoyance to people like Alfred Wood[35] whose sole source of income it is. Don't you?

What was a profession to him and his class was a pleasure to you, and a very evil one. Nor have you ever given up your horrible habit of writing offensive letters, after all that has happened to me through them and for them. You still regard it as one of your accomplishments, and you exercise it on my friends, or those who have been kind to me in prison like Robert Sherard and others. That is disgraceful of you. When Robert Sherard heard from me that I did not wish you to publish any article on me in the *Mercure de France*, with or without letters, you should have been grateful to him for having ascertained my wishes on the point, and for having saved you from inflicting, without intending it, more pain on me than you had already done. You must remember that a patronizing and Philistine letter about "fair play" for a "man who is down" is all right for an English newspaper. It carries on the old traditions of English journalism in regard to its attitude towards artists. But in France such a tone would have exposed me to ridicule and you to contempt. I could not have allowed any article till I had known its aim, temper, mode of approach and the like. In art, good intentions are not of the smallest value. All bad art is the result of good intentions.

Nor is Robert Sherard the only one of my friends to whom you have addressed acrimonious and bitter letters because they sought that my wishes and my feelings should be consulted in matters concerning myself, the publication of articles on me, the dedication of your verses, the surrender of my letters and presents, and such like. You have annoyed or sought to annoy others also.

Does it ever occur to you what an awful position I would have been in if for the last two years, during my appalling sentence, I had been dependent on you as a friend? Do you ever think of that? Do you ever feel any gratitude to those who by kindness without stint, devotion without limit, cheerfulness and joy in giving have lightened my black burden for me, have visited me again and again, have written to me beautiful and sympathetic letters, have managed my affairs for me, arranged my future life, and stood by me in the teeth of obloquy, taunt and open sneer, or insult even? I owe everything to them. The very books in my cell are paid for by Robbie out of his pocket-money; from the same source are to come clothes for me when I am released. I am not ashamed of taking a thing that is given in love and affection; I am proud of it. Yes, I think of my friends, such as More Adey, Robbie, Robert Sherard, Frank Harris, Arthur Clifton, and what they have been to me, in giving me help, affection, and sympathy. I think of every single person who has been kind to me in my prison life down to the warder who gives me a "Good-morning" and a "Good-night" (not one of his prescribed duties) down to the common policemen who, in their homely, rough way strove to comfort me on my journeys to and from the Bankruptcy Court under conditions of terrible mental distress—down to the poor thief who recognizing me as we tramped round the yard at Wandsworth, whispered to me in the hoarse prison voice men get from long and compulsory silence: "I am sorry for you; it is harder for the likes of you than it is for the likes of us." I suppose that has never dawned on you. And yet—if you had any imagination in you—you would know that there is not one, not one of them all, I say, the very mire from whose shoes you should not be proud to kneel down and clean.

Have you not imagination enough to see what a fearful tragedy it was for me to have come across your family? What a tragedy it would have been for anyone at all, who had a great position, and great name, anything of importance to lose? There is hardly one of the elders of your family—with the exception of Percy, who is a really good fellow—who did not in some way contribute to my ruin.

I have spoken of your mother to you with some bitterness, and I strongly advise you to let her see this letter, for your own sake chiefly. If it is painful for her to read such an indictment against one of her sons, let her remember that my mother, who intellectually ranks with Elizabeth Barrett Browning, and historically with Madame Roland, died broken-hearted because the son of whose genius and art she had been proud, and whom she had regarded always as a worthy continuer of a distinguished name, had been condemned to the treadmill for two years. You will ask me in what way your mother contributed to my destruction. I will tell you. Just as you strove to shift on me all your immoral responsibilities, so your mother strove to shift on me all her moral responsibilities with regard to you. Instead of speaking directly to you about your life, as a mother should, she always wrote privately to me with earnest, frightened entreaties not to let you know that she was writing to me. You see the position in which I was placed between you and your mother. It was one as false, as absurd, and as tragic as the one in which I was placed between you and your father. In August 1892 and on the 8th day of November of the same year I had two long interviews with your mother about you. On both occasions I asked her why she did not speak directly to you herself. On both occasions she gave me the same answer: "I am afraid to: he gets so angry when he is spoken to." The first time I knew you so slightly that I did not understand what she meant. The second time I knew you so well that I understood perfectly. (During the interval you had had an attack of jaundice and been ordered by the doctor to go for a week to Bournemouth, and had induced me to accompany you as you hated being alone.) But the first duty of a mother is not to be afraid of speaking seriously to her son. Had your mother spoken seriously to you about the trouble she saw you were in in July 1892, and made you confide in her, it would have been much better and much happier ultimately for both of you. All the underhand and secret communications with me were wrong. What was the use of your mother sending me endless little notes, marked "Private" on the envelope, begging me not to ask you so often to dinner, and not to give you any money, each note ending with an earnest postscript: "On no account let Alfred know that I have written to you"? What good could come of such a correspondence? Did you ever wait to be asked to dinner? Never. You took all your meals as a matter of course with me. If I remonstrated you always had one observation: "If I don't dine with you, where am I to dine? You don't suppose that I am going to dine at home." It was unanswerable. And if I absolutely refused to let you dine with me, you always threatened that you would do something foolish, and always did it. What possible result could there be from letters such as your mother used to send me, except that which did occur, a foolish and fatal shifting of the moral responsibility on to my shoulders? Of the various details in which your mother's weakness and lack of courage proved so ruinous to herself, to you and to me, I don't want to speak any more; but surely, when she heard of your father coming down to my house to make a loathsome scene and create a public scandal, she might then have seen that a serious crisis was impending, and taken some steps to try to avoid it? But all she could think of doing was to send down plausible George Wyndham with his pliant tongue to propose to me—what? That I should gradually "drop you." As if it had been possible for me to "gradually" drop you! I had tried to end our friendship in every possible way, going so far as actually to leave England and give a false address abroad in the hopes of breaking at one blow a bond that had become irksome, hateful and ruinous to me. Do you think that I *could* have "gradually" dropped you? Do you think that would have satisfied your father? You knew it would not. What your father wanted, indeed, was not the cessation of our friendship, but a public scandal. That is what he was striving for. His name had not been in the papers for years. He saw the opportunity of appearing before the British public in an entirely new character, that of an affectionate father. His sense of humour was roused. Had I severed my friendship with you it would have been a terrible disappointment to him, and the small notoriety of a second divorce suit, however revolting its detail and origin, would have proved but little consolation to him. For what he was aiming at was popularity, and to pose as the champion of purity, as it is termed, is in the present condition of the British public the surest mode of becoming for once a heroic figure. Of this public I have said in one of my plays, that if it is Caliban for one half of the year, it is Tartuffe for the other: and your father, in whom both characters may be said to have become incarnate, was in this way marked out as the proper representative of Puritanism in its aggressive and most characteristic form. No "gradual" dropping of you would have been of avail, even had it been practicable. Don't you feel now that the only thing for your mother to have done was to have asked me to come to see her, and had you and your brother present, and said definitely that the friendship must absolutely cease? She would have found in me her warmest seconder, and with Drumlanrig and myself in the room she need not have been afraid of speaking to you. She did not do so. She was afraid of her responsibilities, and tried to shift them on to me. One letter she did certainly write to me. It was a brief one to ask me not to send the lawyer's letter to your father warning him to desist. She was quite right. It was ridiculous my consulting lawyers and seeking their protection. But she nullified any effect her letter might have produced by her usual postscript: "On no account let Alfred know that I have written to you." You were entranced at the idea of my sending lawyers' letters to your father, as well as yourself. It was your suggestion. I could not tell you that your mother was strongly against the idea, for she had bound me with the most solemn promises never to tell you about her letters to me, and I foolishly kept my promise to her. Don't you see that it was wrong of her not to speak directly to you? That all the backstairs interviews with me, and the area-gate correspondence were wrong? Nobody can shift his responsibilities on to anyone else. They always return ultimately to the proper owner. Your one idea of life, your one philosophy, if you are to be credited with a philosophy, was that whatever you did was to be paid for by someone else: I don't mean merely in the financial sense—that was simply the practical application of your philosophy to everyday life—but in the broadest, fullest sense of transferred responsibility. You made that your creed. It was very successful as far as it went. You forced me into taking action because you knew that your father would not attack your life or yourself in any way and that I would defend both to the utmost, and take on my own shoulders whatever would be thrust on me. You were quite right. Your father and I, each from different motives, of course, did exactly as you counted on our doing. But somehow, in spite of everything, you have not really escaped. The "infant Samuel theory," as for brevity's sake one may term it, is all very well as far as the general world knows. It may be a good deal scorned in London, and a little sneered at in Oxford, but that is merely because there are a few people who know you in each place, and because in each place you left traces of your passage. Outside of a small set in those two cities, the world looks on you as the good man who was very nearly tempted into wrongdoing by the wicked and immoral artist, but was rescued just in time by his kind and loving father. It sounds all right. And yet, you know you have not escaped. I am not referring to a silly question asked by a silly juryman which was, of course, treated with contempt by the Crown and Judge. No one cared about that. I am referring perhaps principally to yourself. In your own eyes, and some day, you will have to think of your conduct; you are not, cannot be, quite satisfied at the way in which things have turned out. Secretly you must think of yourself with a good deal of shame. A brazen face is a capital thing to show to the world, but now and then when you are alone, and have no audience, you have, I suppose, to take the mask off for breathing purposes. Else, indeed, you would be stifled.

And in the same manner your mother must at times regret that she tried to shift her grave responsibilities on to someone else, who already had enough of a burden to carry. She occupied the position of both parents to you. Did she really fulfil the duties of either? If I bore with your bad temper and your rudeness and your scenes, she might have borne with them too. When last I saw my wife—fourteen months ago now—I told her that she would have to be to Cyril a father as well as a mother. I told her everything about your mother's code of dealing with you in every detail as I have set it down in this letter, only, of course, far more fully. I told her the reasons of the endless notes with "Private" on the envelope that used to come to Tite Street from your mother, so constantly that my wife used to laugh and say we must be collaborating in a society novel or something of the kind. I implored her not to be to Cyril what your mother was to you. I told her that she should bring him up so that if he shed innocent blood he would come and tell her, that she might cleanse his hands for him first, and then teach him how by penance or expiation to cleanse his soul afterwards. I told her that if she was frightened of facing the responsibility of the life of another, though her own child, she should get a guardian to help her. That she has, I am glad to say, done. She has chosen Adrian Hope, a man of high birth and culture and fine character, her own cousin, whom you met once at Tite Street, and with him Cyril and Vyvyan have a good chance of a beautiful future. Your mother, if she was afraid of talking seriously to you, should have chosen someone among her own relatives to whom you might have listened. But she should not have been afraid. She should have had it out with you and faced it. At any rate, look at the result. Is she satisfied and pleased?

I know she puts the blame on me. I hear of it, not from people who know you, but from people who do not know you, and do not desire to know you. I hear of it often. She talks of the influence of an elder over a younger man, for instance. It is one of her favourite attitudes towards the question, as it is always a successful appeal to popular prejudice and ignorance. I need not ask you what influence I had over you. You know I had none. It was one of your frequent boasts that I had none, and the only one, indeed, that was well founded. What was there, as a mere matter of fact, in you that I could influence? Your brain? It was undeveloped. Your imagination? It was dead. Your heart? It was not yet born. Of all the people who have ever crossed my life, you were the one, and the only one, I was unable in any way to influence in any direction. When I lay ill and helpless in fever caught from tending on you I had not sufficient influence over you to induce you to get me even a cup of milk to drink, or to see that I had the ordinary necessities of a sickroom, or to take the trouble to drive a couple of hundred yards to a bookseller to get me a book at my own expense. When I was actually engaged in writing, and penning comedies that were to beat Congreve for brilliancy, and Dumas *fils* for philosophy, and I suppose everybody else for every other quality, I had not sufficient influence with you to get you to leave me undisturbed as an artist should be left. Wherever my writing room was, it was to you an ordinary lounge, a place to smoke and drink hock and seltzer in, and chatter about absurdities. The "influence of an elder over a younger man" is an excellent theory till it comes to my ears. Then it becomes grotesque. When it comes to your ears, I suppose you smile—to yourself you are certainly entitled to do so. I hear also much of what she says about money. She states, and with perfect justice, that she was ceaseless in her entreaties to me not to supply you with money. I admit it. Her letters were endless, and the postscript "Pray do not let Alfred know that I have written to you" appears in them all. But it was no pleasure to me to have to pay for every single thing for you from your morning shave to your midnight hansom. It was a horrible bore. I used to complain to you again and again about it. I used to tell you—you remember, don't you?—how I loathed your regarding me as a "useful" person, because the artist, like art itself, is of his very essence quite useless. You used to get very angry when I said it to you. The truth always made you angry. Truth, indeed, is a thing which is most painful to listen to and most painful to utter. But it did not make you alter your views or your mode of life. Every day I had to pay for every single thing you did all day long. Only a person of absurd good nature or of indescribable folly would have done so. I unfortunately was a complete combination of both. When I used to suggest that your mother should supply you with the money you wanted, you always had a very pretty and graceful answer. You said that the income allowed her by your father— some £1,500 a year, I believe—was quite inadequate to the wants of a lady of her position, and that you would not go to her for more money than you were already getting. You were quite right about her income being one absolutely unsuitable to a lady of her position and tastes, but you should not have made that an excuse for living in luxury on me: it should on the contrary have been a suggestion to you for economy in your own life. The fact is that you were, and are I suppose still, a typical sentimentalist. For a sentimentalist is simply one who desires to have the luxury of an emotion without paying for it. To propose to spare your mother's pocket was beautiful. To do so at my expense was ugly.

I think that if you look back to your attitude towards your mother's income, and your attitude towards my income, you will not feel proud of yourself, and perhaps you may some day, if you don't show your mother this letter, explain to her that your living on me was a matter in which my wishes were not consulted for a moment. It was simply a peculiar and, to me personally, most distressing form that your devotion to me took. To make yourself dependent on me for the smallest as well as for the largest sums, lent you in your own eyes all the charm of childhood, and in the insisting on my paying for every one of your pleasures you thought that you had found the secret of eternal youth. I confess that it pains me when I hear of your mother's remarks about me, and I am sure that on reflexion you will agree with me that if she has no word of regret or sorrow for the ruin your race has brought on me it would be better if she remained silent. Of course, there is no reason she should see any portion of this letter that refers to any mental development I have been going through, or to any point of departure I hope to attain to. It would not be interesting to her. But the parts concerned purely with your life I should show her if I were you.

If I were you, in fact, I would not care about being loved on false pretences. There is no reason why a man should show his life to the world. The world does not understand things. But with people whose affection one desires to have it is different.

A great friend of mine—a friend of ten years' standing—came to see me some time ago, and told me that he did not believe a single word of what was said against me, and wished me to know that he considered me quite innocent, and the victim of a hideous plot. I burst into tears at what he said, and told him that while there was much amongst the definite charges that was quite untrue and transferred to me by revolting malice, still that my life had been full of perverse pleasures, and that unless he accepted that as a fact about me and realized it to the full I could not possibly be friends with him any more, or ever be in his company. It was a terrible shock to him, but we are friends, and I have not got his friendship on false pretences. I have said to you to speak the truth is a painful thing. To be forced to tell lies is much worse.

I remember that as I was sitting in the dock on the occasion of my last trial listening to Lockwood's appalling denunciation of me—like a thing out of Tacitus, like a passage in Dante, like one of Savonarola's indictments of the Popes of Rome—and being sickened with horror at what I heard, suddenly it occurred to me, *How splendid it would be, if I was saying all this about myself.* I saw then at once that what is said of a man is nothing. The point is, who says it. A man's very highest moment is, I have no doubt at all, when he kneels in the dust, and beats his breast, and tells all the sins of his life. So with you. You would be much happier if you let your mother know a little at any rate of your life from yourself. I told her a good deal about it in December 1893, but of course I was forced into reticences and generalities. It did not seem to give her any more courage in her relations with you. On the contrary, she avoided looking at the truth more persistently than ever. If you told her yourself it would be different. My words may perhaps be often too bitter to you, but the facts you cannot deny. Things were as I have said they were, and if you have read this letter carefully as you should have done you have met yourself face to face.

I have now written, and at great length, to you in order

that you should realize what you were to me before my imprisonment, during those three years' fatal friendship; what you have been to me during my imprisonment, already within two moons of its completion almost; and what I hope to be to myself and to others when my imprisonment is over. I cannot reconstruct my letter or rewrite it. You must take it as it stands, blotted in many places with tears, in some with the signs of passion or pain, and make it out as best you can, blots, corrections, and all. As for the corrections and errata, I have made them in order that my words should be an absolute expression of my thoughts, and err neither through surplusage nor through being inadequate. Language requires to be tuned, like a violin: and just as too many or too few vibrations in the voice of the singer or the trembling of the string will make the note false, so too much or too little in words will spoil the message. As it stands, at any rate, my letter has its definite meaning behind every phrase. There is in it nothing of rhetoric. Whenever there is erasion or substitution, however slight, however elaborate, it is because I am seeking to render my real impression, to find for my mood its exact equivalent. Whatever is first in feeling comes away last in form.

I will admit that it is a severe letter. I have not spared you. Indeed you may say that, after admitting that to weigh you against the smallest of my sorrows, the meanest of my losses would be really unfair to you, I have actually done so, and made scruple by scruple the most careful assay of your nature. That is true. But you must remember that you put yourself in the scales.

You must remember that, if when matched with one mere moment of my imprisonment the balance in which you lie kicks the beam. Vanity made you choose the balance, and Vanity made you cling to it. *There* was the one great psychological error of our friendship, its entire want of proportion. You forced your way into a life too large for you, one whose orbit transcended your power of vision no less than your power of cyclic motion, one whose thoughts, passions and actions were of intense import, of wide interest, and fraught, too heavily indeed, with wonderful or awful consequences. Your little life of little whims and moods was admirable in its own little sphere. It was admirable at Oxford, where the worst that could happen to you was a reprimand from the Dean or a lecture from the President, and where the highest excitement was Magdalen becoming head of the river, and the lighting of a bonfire in the Quad as a celebration of the august event. It should have continued in its own sphere after you left Oxford. In yourself you were all right. You were a very complete specimen of a very modern type. It was simply in reference to me that you were wrong. Your reckless extravagance was a crime. Youth, is always extravagant. It was your forcing me to pay for your extravagances that was disgraceful. Your desire to have a friend with whom you could pass your time from morning to night was charming. It was almost idyllic. But the friend you fastened on should not have been a man of letters, an artist, one to whom your continual presence was utterly destructive of all beautiful work as it was actually paralysing to the creative faculty. There was no harm in your seriously considering that the most perfect way of passing an evening was to have a champagne dinner at the Savoy, a box at a music hall to follow, and a champagne supper at Willis's as a *bonne bouche* for the end. Heaps of delightful young men in London are of the same opinion. It is not even an eccentricity. It is a qualification for becoming a member of White's. But you had no right to require of me that I should become the purveyor of such pleasures for you. It showed your lack of any real appreciation of my genius. Your quarrel with your father, again, whatever one may think about its character, should obviously have remained a question entirely between the two of you. It should have been carried on in a back yard. Such quarrels I believe usually are. Your mistake was in insisting on its being played as a tragicomedy on a high stage in history, with the whole world as an audience, and myself as the prize for the victor in the contemptible contest. The fact that your father loathed you, and that you loathed your father, was not a matter of any interest to the English public. Such feelings are very common in English domestic life, and should be confined to the place they characterize: the home. Away from the home circle they are quite out of place. To translate them is an offence. Family life is not to be treated as a red flag to be flaunted in the streets, or a horn to be blown hoarsely on the housetop. You took domesticity out of its proper sphere, just as you took yourself out of your proper sphere. And those who quit their proper sphere change their surroundings merely, not their natures. They do not acquire the thoughts or passions appropriate to the sphere they enter. It is not in their power to do so.

Emotional forces, as I say somewhere in *Intentions*, are as limited in extent and duration as the forces of physical energy. The little cup that is made to hold so much can hold so much and no more, though all the purple vats of Burgundy be filled with wine to the brim, and the treaders stand knee-deep in the gathered grapes of the stony vineyards of Spain. There is no error more common than that of thinking that those who are the causes or occasions of great tragedies share in the feelings suitable to the tragic mood: no error more fatal than expecting it of them. The martyr in his "shirt of flame" may be looking on the face of God, but to him who is piling the faggots or loosening the logs for the blast the whole scene is no more than the slaying of an ox is to the butcher, or the felling of a tree to the charcoal burner in the forest, or the fall of a flower to one who is mowing down the grass with a scythe. Great passions are for the great of soul, and great events can be seen only by those who are on a level with them. We think we can have our emotions for nothing. We cannot. Even the finest and the most self-sacrificing emotions have to be paid for. Strangely enough, that is what makes them fine. The intellectual and emotional life of ordinary people is a very contemptible affair. Just as they borrow their ideas from a sort of circulating library of thought—the *Zeitgeist* of an age that has no soul and send them back soiled at the end of each week—so they always try to get their emotions on credit, or refuse to pay the bill when it comes in. We must pass out of that conception of life; as soon as we have to pay for an emotion we shall know its quality and be the better for such knowledge. Remember that the sentimentalist is always a cynic at heart. Indeed sentimentality is merely the bank holiday of cynicism. And delightful as cynicism is from its intellectual side, now that it has left the tub for the club, it never can be more than the perfect philosophy for a man who has no soul. It has its social value; and to an artist all modes of expression are interesting, but in itself it is a poor affair, for to the true cynic nothing is ever revealed.

I know of nothing in all drama more incomparable from the point of view of art, nothing more suggestive in its subtlety of observation, than Shakespeare's drawing of Rosencrantz and Guildenstern. They are Hamlet's college friends. They have been his companions. They bring with them memories of pleasant days together. At the moment when they come across him in the play he is staggering under the weight of a burden intolerable to one of his temperament. The dead have come armed out of the grave to impose on him a mission at once too great and too mean for him. He is a dreamer, and he is called upon to act. He has the nature of the poet, and he is asked to grapple with the common complexity of cause and effect, with life in its practical realization, of which he knows nothing, not with life in its ideal essence, of which he knows so much. He has no conception of what to do, and his folly is to feign folly. Brutus used madness as a cloak to conceal the sword of his purpose, the dagger of his will, but the Hamlet madness is a mere mask for the hiding of weakness. In the making of fancies and jests he sees a chance of delay. He keeps playing with action as an artist plays with a theory. He makes himself the spy of his proper actions, and listening to his own words knows them to be but "words, words, words." Instead of trying to be the hero of his own history, he seeks to be the spectator of his own tragedy. He disbelieves in everything, including himself, and yet his doubt helps him not, as it comes not from scepticism but from a divided will.

Of all this Guildenstern and Rosencrantz realize nothing. They bow and smirk and smile, and what the one says the other echoes with sickliest intonation. When, at last, by means of the play within the play, and the puppets in their dalliance, Hamlet "catches the conscience" of the King, and drives the wretched man in terror from his throne, Guildenstern and Rosencrantz see no more in his conduct than a rather painful breach of Court etiquette. That is as far as they can attain to in "the contemplation of the spectacle of life with appropriate emotions." They are close to his very secret and know nothing of it. Nor would there be any use in telling them. They are the little cups that can hold so much and no more. Towards the close it is suggested that, caught in a cunning springe set for another, they have met, or may meet, with a violent and sudden death. But a tragic ending of this kind, though touched by Hamlet's humour with something of the surprise and justice of comedy, is really not for such as they. They never die. Horatio, who in order to "report Hamlet and his cause aright to the unsatisfied,"

> Absents him from felicity a while,
> And in this harsh world draws his breath in pain,

dies, though not before an audience, and leaves no brother. But Guildenstern and Rosencrantz are as immortal as Angelo and Tartuffe, and should rank with them. They are what modern life has contributed to the antique ideal of friendship. He who writes a new *De Amicitia* must find a niche for them, and praise them in Tusculan prose. They are types fixed for all time. To censure them would show "a lack of appreciation." They are merely out of their sphere: that is all. In sublimity of soul there is no contagion. High thoughts and high emotions are by their very existence isolated. What Ophelia herself could not understand was not to be realized by "Guildenstern and gentle Rosencrantz," by "Rosencrantz and the gentle Guildenstern." Of course, I do not propose to compare you. There is a wide difference between you. What with them was chance, with you was choice. Deliberately and by me uninvited you thrust yourself into my sphere, usurped there a place for which you had neither right nor qualifications, and having by curious persistence and by the rendering of your very presence a part of each separate day, succeeded in absorbing my entire life and could do no better with that life than break it in pieces. Strange as it may sound to you it was but natural that you should do so. If one gives to a child a toy too wonderful for its little mind, or too beautiful for its but half awakened eyes, it breaks the toy if it is willful; if it is listless it lets it fall and goes its way to its own companions. So it was with you. Having got hold of my life, you did not know what to do with it. You couldn't have known. It was too wonderful a thing to be in your grasp. You should have let it slip from your hands and gone back to your own companions at their play. But unfortunately you were willful; and so you broke it. That, when everything is said, is perhaps the ultimate secret of all that has happened. For secrets are always smaller than their manifestations. By the displacement of an atom a world may be shaken. And that I may not spare myself any more than you I will add this: that dangerous to me as my meeting with you was, it was rendered fatal to me by the particular moment in which we met. For you were at that time of life when all that one does is no more than the sowing of the seed, and I was at that time of life when all that one does is no less than the reaping of the harvest.

There are some few things more about which I must write to you. The first is about my bankruptcy. I heard some days ago, with great disappointment I admit, that it is too late now for your family to pay your father off, that it would be illegal, and that I must remain in my present painful position for some considerable time to come. It is bitter to me because I am assured on legal authority that I cannot even publish a book without the permission of the Receiver, to whom all the accounts must be submitted. I cannot enter into a contract with the manager of a theatre, or produce a play without the receipts passing to your father and my few other creditors. I think that even you will admit now that the scheme of "scoring off" your father by allowing him to make me a bankrupt has not really been the brilliant all-round success you imagined it was going to turn out to be.

It has been so to me at any rate, and my feelings of pain and humiliation at my pauperism should have been consulted rather than your own sense of humour, however caustic or unexpected. In point of actual fact, in permitting my bankruptcy, as in urging me on to the original trial, you really were playing right into your father's hands, and doing just what he wanted.

Alone, and unassisted, he would from the very outset have been powerless. In you—though you did not mean to hold such a horrible office—he has always found his chief ally.

I am told by More Adey in his letter that last summer you really did express on more than one occasion your desire to repay me "a little of what I spent" on you. As I said to him in my answer, unfortunately I spent on you my art, my life, my name, my place in history, and if your family had all the marvellous things in the world at their command, or what the world holds as marvellous, genius, beauty, wealth, high position and the like, and laid them all at my feet, it would not repay me for one tithe of the smallest things that have been taken from me, or one tear of the least tears that I have shed. However, of course, everything one does has to be paid for. Even to the bankrupt it is so.

You seem to be under the impression that bankruptcy is a convenient means by which a man can avoid paying his debts, a "score off his creditors" in fact. It is quite the other way.

It is the method by which a man's creditors "score off" him, if we are to continue your favourite phrase, and by which the law, by the confiscation of all his property, forces him to pay every one of his debts, and if he fails to do so leaves him as penniless as the commonest mendicant who stands in an archway or creeps down a road, holding out his hand for the alms for which, in England, at any rate, he is afraid to ask. The law has taken from me not merely all that I have, my books, furniture, pictures, my copyright in my published works, my copyright in my plays, everything in fact from *The Happy Prince* and *Lady Windermere's Fan* down to the stair carpets and door-scraper of my house, but also all that I am ever going to have. My interest in my marriage settlement, for instance, was sold.

Fortunately, I was able to buy it in through my friends. Otherwise, in case my wife died, my two children during my lifetime would be as penniless as myself. My interest in our Irish estate, entailed on me by my own father, will, I suppose, have to go next.

I feel very bitterly about it being sold, but I must submit.

Your father's seven hundred pence—or pounds is it?—stand in the way, and must be refunded. Even when I am stripped of all I have, and am ever to have, and am granted a discharge as a hopeless insolvent, I have still got to pay my debts. The Savoy dinners—the clear turtle soup; the luscious ortolans wrapped in their crinkled Sicilian vine-leaves, the heavy amber-coloured, indeed almost amber-scented champagne—Dagonet, 1880, I think was your favourite wine—all have still to be paid for. The suppers at Willis's, the special *cuvées* of Perrier-Jouet reserved always for us, the wonderful *pâtés* procured directly from Strasburg, the marvellous *fine-champagne* served always at the bottom of great bell-shaped glasses that its bouquet might be the better savoured by the true epicures of what was really exquisite in life—these cannot be left unpaid, as bad debts of a dishonest client. Even the dainty sleeve-links—four heart-shaped moonstones of silver mist girdled by alternate ruby and diamond for their setting—that I designed and had made at Henry Lewis's as a special little present to you, to celebrate the success of my second comedy—these even—though I believe you sold them for a song a few months afterwards—have to be paid for. I cannot leave the jeweller out of pocket for the presents I gave you, no matter what you did with them. So, even if I get my discharge, you see I have still my debts to pay.

And what is true of a bankrupt is true of everyone else in life. For every single thing that is done someone has to pay. Even you yourself—with all your desire for absolute freedom from all duties, your insistence on having everything supplied to you by others, your attempts to reject any claim on your affection, or regard, or gratitude—even you will have some day to reflect seriously on what you have done, and try, however unavailingly, to make some attempt at atonement. The fact that you will not be able really to do so will be part of your punishment. You can't wash your hands of all responsibility, and propose, with a shrug or a smile, to pass on to a new friend and a freshly spread feast. You can't treat all that you have brought upon me as a sentimental reminiscence to be served up occasionally with the cigarettes and liqueurs, a picturesque background to a modern life of pleasure like an old tapestry hung in a common inn. It may for the moment have the charm of a new sauce or a fresh vintage, but the scraps of a banquet grow stale, and the dregs of a bottle are bitter. Either to-day, or to-morrow, or some day you have to realize it. Otherwise you may die without having done so, and then what a mean, starved, unimaginative life you would have had. In my letter to More I have suggested one point of view from which you had better approach the subject as soon as possible. He will tell you what it is. To understand it you will have to cultivate your imagination. Remember that imagination is the quality that enables one to see things and people in their real as in their ideal relations. If you cannot realize it by yourself, talk to others on the subject. I have had to look at my past face to face. Look at your past face to face. Sit down quietly and consider it. The supreme vice is shallowness. Whatever is realized is right. Talk to your brother about it. Indeed, the proper person to talk to is Percy. Let him read this letter, and know all the circumstances of our friendship. When things are clearly put before him, no judgement is better.

Had we told him the truth what a lot would have been saved
to me of suffering and disgrace! You remember that I proposed to do so the night you arrived in London from Algiers.
You absolutely refused. So when he came in after dinner we
had to play the comedy of your father being an insane man
subject to absurd and unaccountable delusions. It was a capital comedy while it lasted, none the less so because Percy
took it all quite seriously. Unfortunately it ended in a very revolting manner. The subject on which I write now is one of its
results, and if it be a trouble to you, pray do not forget that it
is the deepest of my humiliations, and one I must go through.
I have no option. You have none either.

   The second thing about which I have to speak to you is
with regard to the conditions, circumstances, and place of
our meeting when my term of imprisonment is over. From
extracts from your letter to Robbie written in the early summer of last year, I understand that you have sealed up in two
packages my letters and my presents to you—such at least as
remain of either—and are anxious to hand them personally to
me. It is, of course, necessary that they should be given up.
You did not understand why I wrote beautiful letters to you,
any more than you understood why I gave you beautiful presents. You failed to see that the former were not meant to be
published any more than the latter were meant to be
pawned. Besides, they belong to a side of life that is long
over, to a friendship that somehow you were unable to appreciate at its proper value. You must look back with wonder
now to the days when you had my entire life in your hands. I
too look back to them with wonder and with other, with far
different, emotions.

   Of course to one so modern as I am, *enfant de mon siècle*,
merely to look at the world will be always lovely. I tremble
with pleasure when I think that on the very day of my leaving
prison both the laburnum and the lilac will be blooming in
the gardens, and that I shall see the wind stir into restless
beauty the swaying gold of the one, and make the other toss
the pale purple of its plumes so that all the air shall be Arabia

for me. Linnaeus fell on his knees and wept for joy when he saw for the first time the long heath of some English upland made yellow with the tawny aromatic blossoms of the common furze; and I know that for me, to whom flowers are part of desire, there are tears waiting in the petals of some rose. It has always been so with me from my boyhood. There is not a single colour hidden away in the chalice of a flower, or the curve of a shell, to which, by some subtle sympathy with the very soul of things, my nature does not answer. Like Gautier, I have always been one of those *pour qui le monde visible existe.*[36]

Still, I am conscious now that behind all this beauty, satisfying though it may be, there is some spirit hidden of which the painted forms and shapes are but modes of manifestation, and it is with this spirit that I desire to become in harmony. I have grown tired of the articulate utterances of men and things. The Mystical in Art, the Mystical in Life, the Mystical in Nature—this is what I am looking for. It is absolutely necessary for me to find it somewhere.

I have a strange longing for the great simple primeval things, such as the sea, to me no less of a mother than the Earth. It seems to me that we all look at Nature too much, and live with her too little. I discern great sanity in the Greek attitude. They never chattered about sunsets, or discussed whether the shadows on the grass were really mauve or not. But they saw that the sea was for the swimmer, and the sand for the feet of the runner. They loved the trees for the shadow that they cast, and the forest for its silence at noon. The vineyard-dresser wreathed his hair with ivy that he might keep off the rays of the sun as he stooped over the young shoots, and for the artist and the athlete, the two types that Greece gave us, they plaited with garlands the leaves of the bitter laurel and of the wild parsley, which else had been of no service to men.

We call ours a utilitarian age, and we do not know the uses of any single thing. We have forgotten that water can cleanse, and fire purify, and that the Earth is mother to us all. As a consequence our art is of the moon and plays with shadows, while Greek art is of the sun and deals directly with things. I feel sure that in elemental forces there is purification, and I want to go back to them and live in their presence.

All trials are trials for one's life, just as all sentences are sentences of death; and three times have I been tried. The first time I left the box to be arrested, the second time to be led back to the house of detention, the third time to pass into a prison for two years. Society, as we have constituted it, will have no place for me, has none to offer; but Nature, whose sweet rains fall on unjust and just alike, will have clefts in the rocks where I may hide, and secret valleys in whose silence I may weep undisturbed. She will hang the night with stars so that I may walk abroad in the darkness without stumbling, and send the wind over my footprints so that none may track me to my hurt: she will cleanse me in great waters, and with bitter herbs make me whole.

I am to be released, if all goes well with me, towards the end of May, and hope to go at once to some little seaside village abroad with Robbie and More.

The sea, as Euripides says in one of his plays about Iphigenia, washes away the stains and wounds of the world.

At the end of a month, when the June roses are in all their wanton opulence, I will, if I feel able, arrange through Robbie to meet you in some quiet foreign town like Bruges, where grey houses and green canals and cool still ways had a charm for me years ago. For the moment you will have to change your name. The little title of which you were so vain—and indeed it made your name sound like the name of a flower!—you will have to surrender, if you wish to see me; just as my name once so musical in the mouth of Fame will have to be abandoned by me in turn. How narrow and mean, and inadequate to its burdens is this century of ours: it can give to success its palace of porphyry, but for sorrow and shame it does not keep even a wattled house in which they may dwell: all it can do for me is to bid me alter my name into some other name, where even medievalism would have given me the cowl of a monk or the face of the leper behind which I might be at peace.

I hope that our meeting will be what a meeting between you and me should be, after everything that has occurred. In old days there was always a wide chasm between us, the chasm of achieved art and acquired culture; there is a still wider chasm between us now, the chasm of sorrow: but to humility there is nothing that is impossible, and to love all things are easy.

As regards your letter to me in answer to this, it may be long or as short as you choose. Address the envelope to "The Governor, H.M. Prison, Reading." Inside, in another, and an open envelope, place your own letter to me: if your paper is very thin do not write on both sides, as it makes it hard for others to read. I have written to you with perfect freedom. You can write to me with the same. What I must know from you is why you have never made any attempt to write to me since the August of the year before last, more especially after, in the May of last year, eleven months ago now, you knew and admitted to others that you knew how you made me suffer, and how I realized it.

I waited month after month to hear from you. Even if I had not been waiting but had shut the doors against you, you should have remembered that no one can possibly shut the doors against love for ever. The unjust judge in the Gospels rises up at length to give a just decision because justice comes knocking daily at his door; and at night time the friend in whose heart there is no real friendship yields at length to his friend "because of his importunity." There is no prison in any world into which love cannot force an entrance. If you did not understand that, you did not understand anything about love at all. Then, let me know all about your article on me for the *Mercure de France*. I know something of it. You had better quote from it. It is set up in type. Also, let me know the exact terms of your dedication of your poems. If it is in prose, quote the prose; if in verse, quote the verse. I have no doubt that there will be beauty in it. Write to me with full frankness, about yourself: about your life: your friends: your occupations: your books. Tell me about your volume and its reception. Whatever you have to say for yourself, say it without fear. Don't write what you don't mean: that is all. If anything in your letter is false or counterfeit I shall detect it by the ring at once.

It is not for nothing, or to no purpose, that in my lifelong cult of literature I have made myself

Miser of sound and syllable, no less
Than Midas of his coinage.[37]

Remember also that I have yet to know you. Perhaps we have yet to know each other. For yourself, I have but this last thing to say. Do not be afraid of the past. If people tell you that it is irrevocable, do not believe them. The past, the present and the future are but one moment in the sight of God, in whose sight we should try to live. Time and space, succession and extension, are merely accidental conditions of thought. The imagination can transcend them, and more in a free sphere of ideal existences. Things, also, are in their essence what we choose to make them. A thing is, according to the mode in which one looks at it. "Where others," says Blake "see but the dawn coming over the hill, I see the sons of God shouting for joy." What seemed to the world and to myself my future I lost irretrievably when I let myself be taunted into taking the action against your father: I had, I dare say, lost it in reality long before that. What lies before me is my past. I have got to make myself look on that with different eyes, to make the world look on it with different eyes, to make God look on it with different eyes. This I cannot do by ignoring it, or slighting it, or praising it, or denying it. It is only to be done fully by accepting it as an inevitable part of the evolution of my life and character: by bowing my head to everything that I have suffered. How far I am away from the true temper of soul, this letter in its changing uncertain moods, its scorn and bitterness, its aspirations and its failures to realize those aspirations, shows you quite clearly. But do not forget in what a terrible school I am sitting at my task. And incomplete, imperfect, as I am, yet from me you may have still much to gain. You came to me to learn the pleasure of life and the pleasure of art. Perhaps I am chosen to teach you something much more wonderful—the meaning of sorrow and its beauty.

Your affectionate friend,

OSCAR WILDE

THE BALLAD OF READING GAOL

IN MEMORIAM
C. T. W.
Sometime Trooper of the Royal Horse Guards
obiit H.M. Prison, Reading, Berkshire
July 7, 1896

1

He did not wear his scarlet coat,
　For blood and wine are red,
And blood and wine were on his hands
　When they found him with the dead,
The poor dead woman whom he loved,
　And murdered in her bed.

He walked amongst the Trial Men
　In a suit of shabby grey;
A cricket cap was on his head,
　And his step seemed light and gay;
But I never saw a man who looked
　So wistfully at the day.

I never saw a man who looked
　With such a wistful eye
Upon that little tent of blue
　Which prisoners call the sky,
And at every drifting cloud that went
　With sails of silver by.

I walked, with other souls in pain,
    Within another ring,
And was wondering if the man had done
    A great or little thing,
When a voice behind me whispered low,
    "That fellow's got to swing."

Dear Christ! the very prison walls
    Suddenly seemed to reel,
And the sky above my head became
    Like a casque of scorching steel;
And, though I was a soul in pain,
    My pain I could not feel.

I only knew what hunted thought
    Quickened his step, and why
He looked upon the garish day
    With such a wistful eye;
The man had killed the thing he loved,
    And so he had to die.

———

Yet each man kills the thing he loves,
    By each let this be heard,
Some do it with a bitter look,
    Some with a flattering word.
The coward does it with a kiss,
    The brave man with a sword!

Some kill their love when they are young,
    And some when they are old;
Some strangle with the hands of Lust,
    Some with the hands of Gold:
The kindest use a knife, because
    The dead so soon grow cold.

Some love too little, some too long,
    Some sell, and others buy;

Some do the deed with many tears,
    And some without a sigh;
For each man kills the thing he loves,
        Yet each man does not die.

He does not die a death of shame
    On a day of dark disgrace,
Nor have a noose about his neck,
    Nor a cloth upon his face,
Nor drop feet foremost through the floor
    Into an empty space.

He does not sit with silent men
    Who watch him night and day;
Who watch him when he tries to weep,
    And when he tries to pray;
Who watch him lest himself should rob
    The prison of its prey.

He does not wake at dawn to see
    Dread figures throng his room,
The shivering Chaplain robed in white,
    The Sheriff stern with gloom,
And the Governor all in shiny black,
    With the yellow face of Doom.

He does not rise in piteous haste
    To put on convict-clothes,
While some coarse-mouthed Doctor gloats, and notes
    Each new and nerve-twitched pose,
Fingering a watch whose little ticks
    Are like horrible hammer-blows.

He does not feel that sickening thirst
    That sands one's throat, before
The hangman with his gardener's gloves
    Comes through the padded door,

And binds one with three leathern thongs,
    That the throat may thirst no more.

He does not bend his head to hear
    The Burial Office read,
Nor, while the anguish of his soul
    Tells him he is not dead,
Cross his own coffin, as he moves
    Into the hideous shed.

He does not stare upon the air
    Through a little roof of glass:
He does not pray with lips of clay
    For his agony to pass;
Nor feel upon his shuddering cheek
    The kiss of Caiaphas.

2

Six weeks the guardsman walked the yard,
    In the suit of shabby grey:
His cricket cap was on his head,
    And his step seemed light and gay,
But I never saw a man who looked
    So wistfully at the day.

I never saw a man who looked
    With such a wistful eye
Upon that little tent of blue
    Which prisoners call the sky,
And at every wandering cloud that trailed
    Its ravelled fleeces by.

He did not wring his hands, as do
    Those witless men who dare
To try to rear the changeling Hope
    In the cave of black Despair:

He only looked upon the sun,
    And drank the morning air.

He did not wring his hands nor weep,
    Nor did he peek or pine,
But he drank the air as though it held
    Some healthful anodyne:
With open mouth he drank the sun
    As though it had been wine!

And I and all the souls in pain,
    Who tramped the other ring,
Forgot if we ourselves had done
    A great or little thing,
And watched with gaze of dull amaze
    The man who had to swing.

For strange it was to see him pass
    With a step so light and gay,
And strange it was to see him look
    So wistfully at the day,
And strange it was to think that he
    Had such a debt to pay.

———

For oak and elm have pleasant leaves
    That in the spring-time shoot:
But grim to see is the gallows-tree,
    With its adder-bitten root,
And, green or dry, a man must die
    Before it bears its fruit!

The loftiest place is that seat of grace
    For which all worldlings try:
But who would stand in hempen band
    Upon a scaffold high,
And through a murderer's collar take
    His last look at the sky?

It is sweet to dance to violins
    When Love and Life are fair:
To dance to flutes, to dance to lutes
    Is delicate and rare:
But it is not sweet with nimble feet
    To dance upon the air!

So with curious eyes and sick surmise
    We watched him day by day,
And wondered if each one of us
    Would end the self-same way,
For none can tell to what red Hell
    His sightless soul may stray.

At last the dead man walked no more
    Amongst the Trial Men,
And I knew that he was standing up
    In the black dock's dreadful pen,
And that never would I see his face
    For weal or woe again.

Like two doomed ships that pass in storm
    We had crossed each other's way:
But we made no sign, we said no word,
    We had no word to say;
For we did not meet in the holy night,
    But in the shameful day.

A prison wall was round us both,
    Two outcast men we were:
The world had thrust us from its heart
    And God from out His care:
And the iron gin that waits for Sin
    Had caught us in its snare.

3

In Debtors' Yard the stones are hard,
    And the dripping wall is high,
So it was there he took the air
    Beneath the leaden sky,
And by each side a Warder walked,
    For fear the man might die.

Or else he sat with those who watched
    His anguish night and day;
Who watched him when he rose to weep,
    And when he crouched to pray;
Who watched him lest himself should rob
    Their scaffold of its prey.

The Governor was strong upon
    The Regulations Act:
The Doctor said that Death was but
    A scientific fact:
And twice a day the Chaplain called,
    And left a little tract.

And twice a day he smoked his pipe,
    And drank his quart of beer:
His soul was resolute, and held
    No hiding-place for fear;
He often said that he was glad
    The hangman's day was near.

But why he said so strange a thing
    No Warder dared to ask:
For he to whom a watcher's doom
    Is given as his task,
Must set a lock upon his lips
    And make his face a mask.

Or else he might be moved, and try
    To comfort or console:
And what should Human Pity do
    Pent up in Murderers' Hole?
What word of grace in such a place
    Could help a brother's soul?

With slouch and swing around the ring
    We trod the Fool's Parade!
We did not care: we knew we were
    The Devil's Own Brigade:
And shaven head and feet of lead
    Make a merry masquerade.

We tore the tarry rope to shreds
    With blunt and bleeding nails;
We rubbed the doors, and scrubbed the floors,
    And cleaned the shining rails:
And, rank by rank, we soaped the plank,
    And clattered with the pails.

We sewed the sacks, we broke the stones,
    We turned the dusty drill:
We banged the tins, and bawled the hymns,
    And sweated on the mill:
But in the heart of every man
    Terror was lying still.

So still it lay that every day
    Crawled like a weed-logged wave:
And we forgot the bitter lot
    That waits for fool and knave.
Till once, as we tramped in from work,
    We passed an open grave.

With yawning mouth the yellow hole
    Gaped for a living thing;

The very mud cried out for blood
    To the thirsty asphalte ring;
And we knew that ere one dawn grew fair
    Some prisoner had to swing.

Right in we went, with soul intent
    On Death and Dread and Doom:
The hangman, with his little bag,
    Went shuffling through the gloom:
And I trembled as I groped my way
    Into my numbered tomb.

———

That night the empty corridors
    Were full of forms of Fear,
And up and down the iron town
    Stole feet we could not hear,
And through the bars that hide the stars
    White faces seemed to peer.

He lay as one who lies and dreams
    In a pleasant meadow-land,
The watchers watched him as he slept,
    And could not understand
How one could sleep so sweet a sleep
    With a hangman close at hand.

But there is no sleep when men must weep
    Who never yet have wept:
So we—the fool, the fraud, the knave—
    That endless vigil kept,
And through each brain on hands of pain
    Another's terror crept.

Alas! it is a fearful thing
    To feel another's guilt!
For, right within, the Sword of Sin

Pierced to its poisoned hilt,
And as molten lead were the tears we shed
    For the blood we had not spilt.

The Warders with their shoes of felt
    Crept by each padlocked door,
And peeped and saw, with eyes of awe,
    Grey figures on the floor,
And wondered why men knelt to pray
    Who never prayed before.

All through the night we knelt and prayed,
    Mad mourners of a corpse!
The troubled plumes of midnight shook
    The plumes upon a hearse:
And bitter wine upon a sponge
    Was the savour of Remorse.

———

The grey cock crew, the red cock crew,
    But never came the day:
And crooked shapes of Terror crouched,
    In the corners where we lay:
And each evil sprite that walks by night
    Before us seemed to play.

They glided past, they glided fast,
    Like travellers through a mist:
They mocked the moon in a rigadoon
    Of delicate turn and twist,
And with formal pace and loathsome grace
    The phantoms kept their tryst.

With mop and mow, we saw them go,
    Slim shadows hand in hand:
About, about, in ghostly rout
    They trod a saraband:

And the damned grotesques made arabesques,
    Like the wind upon the sand!

With the pirouettes of marionettes,
    They tripped on pointed tread:
But with flutes of Fear they filled the ear,
    As their grisly masque they led,
And loud they sang, and long they sang,
    For they sang to wake the dead.

"Oho!" they cried, "The world is wide,
    But fettered limbs go lame!
And once, or twice, to throw the dice
    Is a gentlemanly game,
But he does not win who plays with Sin
    In the secret House of Shame."

No things of air these antics were,
    That frolicked with such glee:
To men whose lives were held in gyves,
    And whose feet might not go free,
Ah! wounds of Christ! they were living things,
    Most terrible to see.

Around, around, they waltzed and wound;
    Some wheeled in smirking pairs;
With the mincing step of a demirep
    Some sidled up the stairs;
And with subtle sneer, and fawning leer,
    Each helped us at our prayers.

The morning wind began to moan,
    But still the night went on:
Through its giant loom the web of gloom
    Crept till each thread was spun:
And, as we prayed, we grew afraid
    Of the Justice of the Sun.

The moaning wind went wandering round
    The weeping prison-wall:
Till like a wheel of turning steel
    We felt the minutes crawl:
O moaning wind! what had we done
    To have such a seneschal?

At last I saw the shadowed bars,
    Like a lattice wrought in lead,
Move right across the whitewashed wall
    That faced my three-plank bed,
And I knew that somewhere in the world
    God's dreadful dawn was red.

At six. o'clock we cleaned our cells,
    At seven all was still,
But the sough and swing of a mighty wing
    The prison seemed to fill,
For the Lord of Death with icy breath
    Had entered in to kill.

He did not pass in purple pomp,
    Nor ride a moon-white steed.
Three yards of cord and a sliding board
    Are all the gallows' need:
So with rope of shame the Herald came
    To do the secret deed.

We were as men who through a fen
    Of filthy darkness grope:
We did not dare to breathe a prayer,
    Or to give our anguish scope:
Something was dead in each of us,
    And what was dead was Hope.

For Man's grim Justice goes its way,
    And will not swerve aside:

It slays the weak, it slays the strong,
    It has a deadly stride:
With iron heel it slays the strong,
    The monstrous parricide!

We waited for the stroke of eight:
    Each tongue was thick with thirst:
For the stroke of eight is the stroke of Fate
    That makes a man accursed,
And Fate will use a running noose
    For the best man and the worst.

We had no other thing to do,
    Save to wait for the sign to come:
So, like things of stone in a valley lone,
    Quiet we sat and dumb:
But each man's heart beat thick, and quick,
    Like a madman on a drum!

With sudden shock the prison-clock
    Smote on the shivering air,
And from all the gaol rose up a wail
    Of impotent despair,
Like the sound that frightened marshes hear
    From some leper in his lair.

And as one sees most fearful things
    In the crystal of a dream,
We saw the greasy hempen rope
    Hooked to the blackened beam,
And heard the prayer the hangman's snare
    Strangled into a scream.

And all the woe that moved him so
    That he gave that bitter cry,
And the wild regrets, and the bloody sweats,
    None knew so well as I:

For he who lives more lives than one
    More deaths than one must die.

4

There is no chapel on the day
    On which they hang a man:
The Chaplain's heart is far too sick,
    Or his face is far too wan,
Or there is that written in his eyes
    Which none should look upon.

So they kept us close till nigh on noon,
    And then they rang the bell,
And the Warders with their jingling keys
    Opened each listening cell,
And down the iron stair we tramped,
    Each from his separate Hell.

Out into God's sweet air we went,
    But not in wonted way,
For this man's face was white with fear,
    And that man's face was grey,
And I never saw sad men who looked
    So wistfully at the day.

I never saw sad men who looked
    With such a wistful eye
Upon that little tent of blue
    We prisoners called the sky,
And at every happy cloud that passed
    In such strange freedom by.

But there were those amongst us all
    Who walked with downcast head,
And knew that, had each got his due,
    They should have died instead:

He had but killed a thing that lived,
   Whilst they had killed the dead.

For he who sins a second time
   Wakes a dead soul to pain,
And draws it from its spotted shroud,
   And makes it bleed again,
And makes it bleed great gouts of blood,
   And makes it bleed in vain!

———

Like ape or clown, in monstrous garb
   With crooked arrows starred,
Silently we went round and round
   The slippery asphalte yard;
Silently we went round and round,
   And no man spoke a word.

Silently we went round and round,
   And through each hollow mind
The Memory of dreadful things
   Rushed like a dreadful wind,
And Horror stalked before each man,
   And Terror crept behind.

———

The Warders strutted up and down,
   And watched their herd of brutes,
Their uniforms were spick and span,
   And they wore their Sunday suits,
But we knew the work they had been at,
   By the quicklime on their boots.

For where a grave had opened wide,
   There was no grave at all:
Only a stretch of mud and sand
   By the hideous prison-wall,

And a little heap of burning lime,
    That the man should have his pall.

For he has a pall, this wretched man,
    Such as few men can claim:
Deep down below a prison-yard,
    Naked for greater shame,
He lies, with fetters on each foot,
    Wrapt in a sheet of flame!

And all the while the burning lime
    Eats flesh and bone away,
It eats the brittle bone by night,
    And the soft flesh by day,
It eats the flesh and bone by turns,
    But it eats the heart alway.

——

For three long years they will not sow
    Or root or seedling there:
For three long years the unblessed spot
    Will sterile be and bare,
And look upon the wondering sky
    With unreproachful stare.

They think a murderer's heart would taint
    Each simple seed they sow.
It is not true! God's kindly earth
    Is kindlier than men know,
And the red rose would blow more red,
    The white rose whiter blow.

Out of his mouth a red, red rose!
    Out of his heart a white!
For who can say by what strange way,
    Christ brings His will to light,
Since the barren staff the pilgrim bore
    Bloomed in the great Pope's sight?

But neither milk-white rose nor red
    May bloom in prison-air;
The shard, the pebble, and the flint,
    Are what they give us there:
For flowers have been known to heal
    A common man's despair.

So never will wine-red rose or white,
    Petal by petal, fall
On that stretch of mud and sand that lies
    By the hideous prison-wall,
To tell the men who tramp the yard
    That God's Son died for all.

————

Yet though the hideous prison-wall
    Still hems him round and round,
And a spirit may not walk by night
    That is with fetters bound,
And a spirit may but weep that lies
    In such unholy ground,

He is at peace—this wretched man—
    At peace, or will be soon:
There is no thing to make him mad,
    Nor does Terror walk at noon,
For the lampless Earth in which he lies
    Has neither Sun nor Moon.

They hanged him as a beast is hanged:
    They did not even toll
A requiem that might have brought
    Rest to his startled soul,
But hurriedly they took him out,
    And hid him in a hole.

The Warders stripped him of his clothes,
    And gave him to the flies:

They mocked the swollen purple throat.
    And the stark and staring eyes:
And with laughter loud they heaped the shroud
    In which the convict lies.

The Chaplain would not kneel to pray
    By his dishonoured grave:
Nor mark it with that blessed Cross
    That Christ for sinners gave,
Because the man was one of those
    Whom Christ came down to save.

Yet all is well; he has but passed
    To Life's appointed bourne;
And alien tears will fill for him
    Pity's long-broken urn,
For his mourners will be outcast men,
    And outcasts always mourn.

5

I know not whether Laws be right,
    Or whether Laws be wrong;
All that we know who lie in gaol
    Is that the wall is strong;
And that each day is like a year,
    A year whose days are long.

But this I know, that every Law
    That men have made for Man,
Since first Man took his brother's life,
    And the sad world began,
But straws the wheat and saves the chaff
    With a most evil fan.

This too I know and wise it were
    If each could know the same—

That every prison that men build
   Is built with bricks of shame,
And bound with bars lest Christ should see
   How men their brothers maim.

With bars they blur the gracious moon,
   And blind the goodly sun:
And they do well to hide their Hell,
   For in it things are done
That Son of God nor son of Man
   Ever should look upon!

———

The vilest deeds like poison weeds,
   Bloom well in prison-air;
It is only what is good in Man
   That wastes and withers there:
Pale Anguish keeps the heavy gate,
   And the Warder is Despair.

For they starve the little frightened child
   Till it weeps both night and day:
And they scourge the weak, and flog the fool,
   And gibe the old and grey,
And some grow mad, and all grow bad,
   And none a word may say.

Each narrow cell in which we dwell
   Is a foul and dark latrine,
And the fetid breath of living Death
   Chokes up each grated screen,
And all, but Lust, is turned to dust
   In Humanity's machine.

The brackish water that we drink
   Creeps with a loathsome slime,
And the bitter bread they weigh in scales

Is full of chalk and lime,
And Sleep will not lie down, but walks
    Wild-eyed, and cries to Time.

———

But though lean Hunger and green Thirst
    Like asp with adder fight,
We have little care of prison fare,
    For what chills and kills outright
Is that every stone one lifts by day
    Becomes one's heart by night.

With midnight always in one's heart,
    And twilight in one's cell,
We turn the crank, or tear the rope,
    Each in his separate Hell,
And the silence is more awful far
    Than the sound of a brazen bell.

And never a human voice comes near
    To speak a gentle word:
And the eye that watches through the door
    Is pitiless and hard:
And by all forgot, we rot and rot,
    With soul and body marred.

And thus we rust Life's iron chain
    Degraded and alone:
And some men curse, and some men weep,
    And some men make no moan:
But God's eternal Laws are kind
    And break the heart of stone.

———

And every human heart that breaks,
    In prison-cell or yard,
Is as that broken box that gave

Its treasure to the Lord.
And filled the unclean leper's house
    With the scent of costliest nard.

Ah! happy they whose hearts can break
    And peace of pardon win!
How else may man make straight his plan
    And cleanse his soul from Sin?
How else but through a broken heart
    May Lord Christ enter in?

————

And he of the swollen purple throat,
    And the stark and staring eyes,
Waits for the holy hands that took
    The Thief to Paradise;
And a broken and a contrite heart
    The Lord will not despise.

The man in red who reads the Law
    Gave him three weeks of life,
Three little weeks in which to heal
    His soul of his soul's strife,
And cleanse from every blot of blood
    The hand that held the knife.

And with tears of blood he cleansed the hand,
    The hand that held the steel:
For only blood can wipe out blood,
    And only tears can heal:
And the crimson stain that was of Cain
    Became Christ's snow-white seal.

6

In Reading gaol by Reading town
    There is a pit of shame,

And in it lies a wretched man
    Eaten by teeth of flame,
In a burning winding-sheet he lies,
    And his grave has got no name.

And there, till Christ call forth the dead,
    In silence let him lie:
No need to waste the foolish tear,
    Or heave the windy sigh:
The man had killed the thing he loved,
    And so he had to die.

And all men kill the thing they love,
    By all let this be heard,
Some do it with a bitter look,
    Some with a flattering word,
The coward does it with a kiss,
    The brave man with a sword!

NOTES

THE PICTURE OF DORIAN GRAY

Chapter I

1. **laburnum:** Tree or shrub with yellow flowers.
2. **tussore silk:** An Asian yellow or brown silk.
3. **bourdon:** A low, deep sound from an organ.
4. **The Grosvenor:** An art gallery important to aesthetics; Wilde often reviewed its art shows.
5. **The Academy:** The Royal Academy, an art gallery that was traditional and part of the establishment.
6. **Adonis:** An extremely good-looking man from Greek mythology with whom the goddess of love fell in love.
7. **Narcissus:** Beautiful young man in Greek legend so entranced by his own reflection in the water that he starved to death. The flower that grew where he died is the narcissus; the term "narcissism," self-love to the exclusion of connection with others, comes from the story.
8. **crush:** Slang for a party.
9. **Stars and Garters:** Symbols of knighthood.
10. **précis:** An abstract or summary.

11. *salon:* A regular gathering of artists and intellectuals.
12. **Antinous:** The Roman emperor Hadrian's beautiful lover. Hadrian had him deified after his death, and had hundreds of statues in his likeness erected throughout the empire.
13. **East End:** A working-class section of London.

Chapter II

1. **Schumann:** A Romantic composer (1810–56).
2. **Orleans:** A club for gentlemen on King's Street.
3. **Curzon Street:** Street in a fashionable part of London.
4. *moue:* A pout or grimace.
5. **Eton:** A prestigious preparatory school populated by the children of wealthy and noble people.
6. **viol:** A popular violinlike Renaissance and baroque instrument, whose popularity died out in the 1700s.
7. **lute:** A harplike old-fashioned instrument popular in medieval times, up to the 1700s.
8. **Tyrian convolvulus:** A multipetaled purple flower.
9. **Hermes:** Messenger of the Greek gods; also a trickster.
10. **Faun:** Mythological creature who was half man, half goat.
11. **deal:** A cheap kind of wood, usually fir or pine.
12. **Georgian:** An aesthetic style derived from classicism (1714–90).
13. **White's:** A club for gentlemen.
14. **hansom:** A closed two-wheeled horse-drawn carriage.

Chapter III

1. **Isabella . . . Prim:** Queen Isabella II of Spain (reign 1843–68), who was overthrown in the Spanish Revolution. Juan Prim, a general, led the forces which overthrew her.
2. **collieries:** Coal mine.
3. **Tory:** The British conservative party.

4. **buttonhole:** A flower for a buttonhole.
5. **English Blue book:** Official report of Parliament and the Privy Council.
6. **arcade:** A lane with shops.
7. **Burlington Street:** A street full of shops, mostly ladies' apparel stores.
8. **Buonaroti:** Michelangelo Buonarroti (1475–1564), the famous Italian Renaissance painter, sculptor, and poet. He was accused of immorality in his art.
9. **Whitechapel:** Rough section of London. Jack the Ripper murdered prostitutes there.
10. **Silenus:** A mythological Greek satyr who was tutor to Dionysus, god of wine, and son of the messenger god Hermes. He was often depicted drunk. The bacchante mentioned are female worshippers of Bacchus who celebrate his arrival in the spring with wild drinking and dancing.
11. **Athenaeum:** A club for people who patronized or participated in the fine arts, literature, or science.

Chapter IV

1. **Clodion:** Eighteenth-century French sculptor.
2. *Les Cent Nouvelles:* A collection of bawdy medieval French tales.
3. **Margaret of Valois:** Queen of France and Navarre (1553–1615), known for her well-written memoirs and her lascivious lifestyle.
4. **Clovis Eve:** A famous and accomplished bookbinder specializing in remarkable gilded decorations.
5. *Manon Lescaut:* Abbé de Prévost's classic novel about tragic romance, sometimes thought of as a cautionary tale about the dangers of passion.
6. **Louis Quatorze:** A very luxurious style of furniture dating from or modeled on the furniture of the court of French king Louis XIV.
7. *Lohengrin:* The most popular of Wagner's operas in 1880s London; it was inspired by tales of the Holy Grail.

8. **frangipanni:** A fragrant flower.
9. **Park:** London's central and very popular Hyde Park; called by Charles Dickens the "lounge of London."
10. **Piccadilly:** A beautiful main road, which leads to some of the fashionable districts.
11. *Les grandpères ont toujours tort:* Grandfathers are always wrong.
12. **Romeo, Mercutio, Juliet:** Characters in Shakespeare's tragedy *Romeo and Juliet.*
13. **hautbois:** A kind of oboe used between the seventeenth and early nineteenth centuries.
14. **Rosalind:** A woman who disguises herself as a man in Shakespeare's *As You Like It*; one of several gender-bending characters mentioned.
15. **Imogen:** Another Shakespearean character (from the play *Cymbeline*), who dresses as a boy.
16. **Arden:** The forest of Arden is the setting for *As You Like It.*
17. **Giordano Bruno:** A priest and philosopher (1548–1600) who shocked Europe by disagreeing with Aristotle and supporting Copernicus. He was eventually burned at the stake.

Chapter V

1. **bismuth:** An ingredient in makeup; still used as an ingredient in modern cosmetics.
2. *tableau:* A group of carefully posed people, arranged for dramatic effect.
3. **smart:** Fashionable.
4. **orris-root:** A plant that smells like violets.
5. **Achilles Statue:** A bronze statue erected in 1822 to honor the Duke of Wellington and shocked London with its nudity.
6. **Marble Arch:** A gate in Hyde Park.
7. **omnibus:** A method of public transportation, often crowded, for those not wealthy.

Chapter VI

1. **whitewashing:** To gloss over, cover up.
2. **Messalina:** The wife of the Roman emperor Claudius, Messalina (A.D. 22–48) has come to be emblematic of manipulative and licentious women.
3. **Orlando:** Romantic partner to Rosalind in *As You Like It*.
4. **Tanagra figurine:** Terra-cotta figures from the the the ancient Greek city Tanagra.
5. **Verona:** *The Two Gentlemen of Verona* was a Shakespearean play.
6. *fine-champagne:* A kind of brandy or cognac.
7. **brougham:** A closed four-wheel carriage.

Chapter VII

1. **Miranda, Caliban:** Characters from Shakespeare's *Tempest*. Miranda is a lovely and passive heroine and Caliban, a monster.
2. **Cordelia:** King Lear's loving daughter.
3. **Covent Garden:** Fresh fruit, flowers, and vegetables were sold here early in the morning.
4. **Doge:** The leader of the Venice republic. The republic fell in 1797.
5. **Renaissance:** After the so-called Dark Ages, the Renaissance was a "rebirth"—re (again) naissance (birth)—of arts, philosophy, and science spanning the early fourteenth to late sixteenth centuries.

Chapter VIII

1. **Sèvres:** A very beautiful translucent French china.
2. **Louis-Quinze:** A reference to the decorative and luxurious style of the arts during King Louis XV's reign in France.
3. **prussic acid:** Cyanide.
4. **Patti:** Adelina Patti, an enormously popular opera singer.

5. **gold-latten:** Gold-plated.
6. **poppies, violets, asphodel:** In Victorian times, flowers were highly symbolic and could be used to speak "the language of flowers." Violets meant faithfulness, poppies stood for sleep, and asphodels were connected to the underworld.
7. **sixth act:** Most plays have three or five acts.
8. **Desdemona, Ophelia:** Both these Shakespearean characters were killed, directly or indirectly, by their beloveds.
9. **Jacobean:** The literary period during which Shakespeare wrote some of his greatest tragedies.
10. **Webster, Ford, Cyril Tourneur:** Three Jacobean playwrights.
11. **daughter of Brabantio:** Desdemona in *Othello*.

Chapter IX

1. **Gautier:** Théophile Gautier, the French decadent who put forward the idea, so important to the aesthetes, of art for art's sake.
2. **Paris:** The beautiful youth who ran away with Helen of Troy and began the Trojan War.
3. **Adrian's barge:** Adrian is another form of Hadrian, the Roman emperor whose lover Antinous drowned in the Nile.

Chapter X

1. **Michelangelo, Montaigne, Winckelmann, Shakespeare:** Great male artists and writers who were known to have had male lovers.
2. **Fonthill:** A major auction was held at the Fonthill Abbey in 1822.
3. **Italian *cassone*:** An ornate wooden chest.
4. **nacre:** Pearly interior of shell.
5. **yellow book:** J. K. Huysman's decadent 1884 novel *À*

Rebours (*Against the Grain*) was very influential among members of the Aesthetic Movement. It was commonly referred to as "the yellow book."

6. *Symbolistes:* A group of primarily French poets important to the decadent and aesthetic movements. Mallarmé, Rimbaud, and Baudelaire are included among this group.

Chapter XI

1. Chapter XI bridges the first and second halves of the novel by showing how Dorian fills the interim eighteen years, and demonstrates Dorian's growing dissolution. Many of the references are to homosexuality; religion, especially Catholicism; and philosophy, including aestheticism. Rich descriptions of Dorian's collections of jewels and tapestries offer evidence of Dorian's commitment to beautiful things. The overall effect of the overwhelming allusions is of a testament to Dorain's full commitment to a decadent life.

2. **antinomianism:** The rejection of obedience as a legal obligation.

3. **macaroni:** A travelled young Englishman who affected foreign ways.

Chapter XII

1. **Gladstone bag:** A large leather suitcase, or light portmanteau.

2. **ulster:** A long, loose overcoat of rough cloth frequently closed with a waist belt. First introduced in Belfast, Ireland.

3. **marqueterie:** Ornamental inlays.

4. *Anglomanie:* Anglophilism, or love of the English and things English.

5. **hock-and-seltzer:** Drink made with a sweet wine and seltzer.

6. **Mentone:** Menton, a French Riviera resort.

Chapter XIII

1. **satyr:** A hedonistic mythological creature who is part man, part goat; Roman counterpart to the Greek faun.
2. **"Each of us has . . . him":** Adapted from Milton's *Paradise Lost*, bk. 1, st. 255.
3. **"Though your sins . . . snow":** See Isaiah 1:118.
4. **bull's-eye:** A lantern.
5. **the Blue book:** A society directory.

Chapter XIV

1. **Gautier's *Emaux et Camées*:** Translated as *Enamels and Cameos and other Poems*, it was a very influential collection; the poem quoted in French is from it.
2. **Charpentier's:** There were six editions published; Charpentier was one of the publishers.
3. **Jacquemart:** Jules-Ferdinand Jacquemart (1837–80), a famous etcher.
4. **Lacenaire:** A notorious French killer.
5. *du supplice encore mal lavée:* Still dirty from torture.
6. *doigts de faune:* Fingers of a faun.
7. **Lido:** A small island near Venice.
8. **Campanile:** Bell tower.
9. **Tintoretto:** Jacopo Tintoretto (1519–94), a prolific Venetian painter.
10. **Smyrna:** A city in Turkey, now called Izmir.
11. **Hadjis:** Muslims who have journeyed to Mecca.
12. *monstre charmant:* Charming monster.
13. **Louvre:** The most famous museum in Paris, and one of the most famous in the world.
14. **good class:** In English universities, people graduate with first-, second-, or third-class degrees.
15. **Tripos:** Exams at Cambridge.
16. **Rubinstein:** Anton Rubinstein (1830–94), a Russian pianist and composer whose talent rivaled Liszt's.
17. **Astrakhan:** The fur or skin of a particular Russian-bred

lamb; a lustrous cloth of wool or cotton or a blend of both with a curled and looped pile cut to imitate astrakhan fur.

18. **ague:** An illness marked by fevers and chills; like malaria.

Chapter XV

1. **Queen Elizabeth:** Powerful English queen (1533–1603), who saw the rise of the British Empire. She was sometimes called the "Virgin Queen" because she never married, most likely for political reasons. She often referred to herself as a man.
2. **ormolu:** Copper and zinc alloy, usually used on furniture.
3. *chaudfroid:* Literally, "hot cold." Cooked meats served in a chilled aspic, a jelly made from meat stock and gelatin.
4. *décolletée:* A low neckline exposing the tops of the breasts.
5. *édition de luxe:* A luxurious edition.
6. **Marguerite de Navarre:** Margaret of Valois.
7. *trop de zèle:* Overenthusiastic.
8. *trop d'audace:* Overly audacious, too bold.
9. *fin de siècle:* Literally, "end of the century," but also refers to the attitudes in the 1890s, particularly one of a jaded, cynical world-weariness.
10. *fin du globe:* End of the world.
11. **Debrett:** A directory of the nobility.
12. *doctrinaire:* Someone who sticks to his opinion arbitrarily or arrogantly.
13. **Union Jack:** The United Kingdom flag.
14. **Algerian pastilles:** A kind of incense.
15. **green paste:** Opium.

Chapter XVI

1. **Malays:** People from Malaysia.
2. **half-caste:** An offensive word to describe a person of mixed racial origins.
3. **Daly's:** A theater.

Chapter XVII

1. **realism in literature:** Realistic literature focuses on portraying events and people as realistically as possible, uncolored by ideals; anathema to aesthetics.
2. **Tartuffe:** A religious hypocrite, the main character of Molière's play of the same name.
3. **survival of the pushing:** A play on the Darwinian phrase "survival of the fittest."
4. **Trojans:** The Trojans fought the Greeks in the war recorded in Homer's *Iliad*. The war was started by a political battle over the beautiful Helen of Troy.
5. **Parthian:** The Parthians, who fought the Roman Empire, would shoot at enemies as they retreated.

Chapter XVIII

1. **Artemis:** The Greek virgin goddess of the hunt.
2. **strawberry leaves:** The symbol of ducal rank; here, they refer to the Duchess.
3. **button, mask:** Protective gear in fencing; here, the fencing is verbal rather than physical.

Chapter XIX

1. **Perdita, Florizel:** Characters from Shakespeare's *A Winter's Tale*. Perdita was abandoned by her parents because of her mother's supposed infidelity, though by the end her name is cleared. Florizel is a prince and her faithful husband.
2. **vinaigrette box:** Container for aromatic or smelling salts.
3. **Chopin:** Frédéric Chopin (1810–49), a Romantic composer Wilde was fond of.
4. **Waterbury:** A cheap watch.
5. **Velásquez:** Diego Rodríguez de Silva y Velásquez (1599–1660), famous baroque Spanish painter.

6. **"Like the painting . . . heart":** From *Hamlet*, act 4, scene 7.
7. **"what does it profit . . . soul":** Mark 8:36.
8. **Majorca:** A Spanish resort town, where Chopin wrote some of his best music.
9. **Apollo:** Among other things, Apollo was the god of music.
10. **Marsyas:** A satyr who challenged Apollo to a musical contest; Marsyas lost and was flayed alive.
11. **Browning:** Poet Robert Browning (1812–89), who returned to those themes often in his work.
12. *lilas blanc:* White lilac.

DE PROFUNDIS

1. **Bosie:** Lord Alfred Douglas (1870–1945), Wilde's lover. Bosie's father brought the charges of gross indecency against Wilde, resulting in his jail stay.
2. **Robbie:** Robert Ross (1869–1918). He claimed to have initiated Wilde into homosexuality. He stood by Wilde through the trial and afterward and became his literary executor.
3. *moyen de vivre:* Way of life.
4. **Gilles de Retz:** Gilles de Laval, seigneur de Retz (1404–40). A companion of Joan of Arc, he later confessed to kidnapping, abusing, and killing children.
5. **Marquis de Sade:** Donatien Alphonse François, comte de Sade (1740–1814), notoriously the author of elegantly written stories of eroticized pain, featuring graphic descriptions of inventive sexual games. The term "sadism" comes from his name.
6. **Aeschylus:** Ancient Greek tragedian; the lines are from *Agamemnon*.
7. **your tutor:** Campbell Dodgson (1867–1948) was Bosie's tutor at Oxford.
8. *candidissima anima:* Very candid soul.
9. *lacrimae rerum:* Tearful or sad event or state.

10. **Hylas . . . Hyacinth, Jonquil . . . Narcisse:** Mytholog- ical figures known for their youthful, seductive beauty.

11. *scies:* An old saying or saw.

12. **Holloway:** The prison where Wilde awaited trial.

13. *feuilletoniste:* A person who writes fanciful stories purely for amusement.

14. **"I think they . . . gloat":** From Wilde's poem "On the Sale by Auction of Keats's Love Letters."

15. **Lombroso:** Cesare Lombroso (1835–1909), Italian phy- sician and criminologist, who was among the first to study the criminal as well as the crime.

16. **Justine:** Book by the marquis de Sade featuring female heroine.

17. **Sandford and Merton:** Thomas Day's landmark chil- dren's book from 1783.

18. **Branca d'Oria:** A reference to Dante's *Inferno*. Oria was such a terrible sinner the devils took his soul to hell be- fore his body had died and left a devil in its place.

19. *causerie intime:* Intimate conversation.

20. **"feet of clay":** From *Dorian Gray*, chapter 15, p. 193.

21. **"Suffering is permanent . . . infinity":** From Wordsworth's play *The Borderers*.

22. **antinomian:** Person who rejects moral law.

23. *"Tristi fummo . . . s'allegra":* From the *Inferno*, canto 7. Essentially, the line recalls that we were sad once in the sweet air of the sun; Nostalgic, in the underworld, for the wasted days of living.

24. **"Who never ate . . . powers":** From book 2, chapter 13 of *Wilhelm Meister's Apprenticeship* by Johann Wolfgang von Goethe.

25. **"O Seigneur . . . dégoût":** From the poem "Un Voyage à Cythère" in French poet Charles Baudelaire's *Les Fleurs du Mal* (1857). Roughly, "Oh God, give me the courage and strength to think about my heart and body without disgust."

26. **Charmides:** The central figure in a Platonic dialogue about moderation, and the subject of Wilde's intemperate

poem "Charmides," which described necrophilia and other scandalous acts.

27. **"I am the good Shepherd":** John 10:11 and 10:14.
28. **"Consider the lilies of the field, how they grow; they toil not, neither do they spin":** Matthew 6:28.
29. **"It is finished":** John 19:30.
30. *Domine, non sum dignus:* Lord, I am not worthy.
31. *"a guisa . . . pargoleggia":* From Dante's *Purgatorio*, canto 16, lines 86–87.
32. **Liber Conformitatum:** By Bartolomaeus of Pisa; compares the lives of Christ and St. Francis.
33. *"della . . . sue":* From Dante's *Paradiso*, canto 1, line 20.
34. *Voilà . . . chemins:* Now there is where bad ways lead.
35. **Afred Wood:** A blackmailer who gave evidence at Wilde's trial.
36. *pour qui . . . existe:* For whom the visible world exists.
37. **"Miser of sound . . . coinage":** From "Sonnet on the Sonnet" by John Keats.

INTERPRETIVE NOTES

THE PICTURE OF DORIAN GRAY

The Plot

The Picture of Dorian Gray tells the story of a young man who retains his youthful beauty, while his portrait is ravaged by his dissolute life. It calls into question the separation of art and morality, and explores the dangers of a decadent life lived only for beauty and art.

As the novel opens, an innocent Dorian sits in a studio "filled with the rich odours of roses," posing for the painter Basil Hallward. Hallward introduces Dorian to the witty aesthete Lord Henry, who praises his youth and beauty, flattering him to such an extreme that Dorian wishes the portrait would grow old, and let him remain untouched by time or life.

As the friendship between Henry and Dorian grows, Henry plies the youth with ideas about "the search for beauty being the real secret of life" and scoffs when Dorian announces he has fallen in love with a poor but talented actress, Sibyl Vane. The affair doesn't last. Sibyl can no longer act once she has felt real love, and without her art, Dorian no longer loves her and casts her aside. Returning home, he looks at his portrait and realizes it has changed: the expression on its face is now colored by cruelty.

By morning Dorian decides to make amends with Sibyl, but it is too late: she has committed suicide. Under the guidance of Lord Henry, Dorian comes to view her death as an artistic parallel to her stage roles, rather than as a human, real tragedy. That night, he goes to the opera. His descent into living only for his senses has truly begun.

Influenced by a "little yellow book" (a reference to Joris Karl Huysmans's *À Rebours*), a gift from Lord Henry, Dorian spends the next eighteen years studying beautiful objects—perfumes, jewels, flowers, tapestries—and seeks fulfillment of the senses through them, through drugs, and through a series of love affairs with both men and women. He becomes thoroughly dissolute, but his portrait, not his face, bears the marks of his unbridled sensuality.

The night before his thirty-eighth birthday, Basil Hallward stops by to warn Dorian of the gossip being spread about him in society, and Dorian shows him the portrait. Basil is shocked, and in his horror, calls out to God and asks Dorian to pray. Dorian murders him, and submerges whatever twinges of remorse he has with opium. It is in an opium den that James Vane, Sibyl's brother, discovers him by chance. Intending to kill him, James yields to Dorian's request to be viewed under light. James determines Dorian is "too young" to be Sibyl's jilter. Still, it's not until James is killed accidentally that Dorian breathes freely.

Dorian is determined to reform his life, but his debauchery has gone too far. He ends up killing himself.

The Characters

Dorian Gray. Initially, a beautiful, vain, callow young man, Dorian goes on to become a famously dissolute sensualist, seemingly untouched by time.

Lord Henry Wotton. Wealthy, witty, and depraved, Lord Henry is a confirmed sensualist and aesthete. By playing on Dorian's vanity, Lord Henry seduces him into the sensual life. Wilde places many of his famous epigrams in Henry's mouth.

Basil Hallward. An artist and friend to Dorian and Lord Henry. He worships beautiful things, including Dorian. Basil's portrait of Dorian reveals Basil's feelings about the young man. Dorian murders Basil shortly after he talks about God and repentance.

Sibyl Vane. A beautiful, lowborn actress who falls in love with Dorian. Her first name means "a female prophet." When Sibyl falls in love with Dorian she loses her ability to act: having felt genuine passion, she can no longer pretend onstage. She later commits suicide.

James Vane. Sibyl's brother is a gruff, inarticulate sailor, passionately devoted to his sister and her happiness. When Dorian wrongs her, he vows to avenge her death.

Mrs. Vane. Sibyl's mother, and a self-centered, histrionic faded beauty. In her most emotional moments she still thinks about how the "scene" looks.

Alan Campbell. A music lover, scientist, and ambivalent member of Dorian's circle of friends. Alan was an intimate friend of Dorian's for some time before cutting him off and giving up music to devote himself to science. Dorian later blackmails him into helping him dispose of Basil's body.

Themes and Symbols

The Pursuit of Beauty and Beautiful Objects

The characters in *Dorian Gray* are all driven by their devotion to beauty, a devotion that often passes into obsession, and a disregard for truth and consequences. Lord Henry, whose praise first flatters Dorian's vanity, later won't believe anything bad about Dorian because he is still beautiful. Basil's passionate devotion to Dorian's beauty produces the supernatural portrait that later becomes so monstrous. The aesthetes are not the only ones susceptible to beauty: though he commits many atrocious acts, Dorian is never formally ostracized from society.

Dorian's youthful beauty is sometimes referred to as though it were one more object to possess, like a beautiful painting, a jewel, or a flower. It is Dorian's intense desire to hold on to his prized beauty that prompts his fateful wish. "Youth! Youth! There is absolutely nothing in the world but youth!" Lord Henry cries to Dorian. Dorian clearly believes him, but that does not stop him from collecting many other beautiful things—and people. Chapter XI, which relates how Dorian spent the eighteen years that take place between the first and second halves of the book, lists some of Dorian's possessions—the rich tapestries, furnishings, and ornaments with which he is surrounded—and details his evolved and complete dedication to beautiful things.

Implicit in all this pursuit and collection is the question of what, exactly, constitutes beauty, and whether or not it can, in fact, be possessed. Many of the objects associated with beauty, including youth itself, are fragile and ephemeral. In fact, they are beautiful in proportion to the brevity of their existence. Dorian's beauty, on the other hand, becomes stranger and more monstrous the longer he holds on to it.

Classical Beauty and Homosexuality

There are numerous references in *Dorian Gray* to classical figures known for their beauty and implicitly or explicitly tied to homosexuality: in particular, Adonis, Narcissus, and Antinous. All three of these figures are icons of young male beauty. The first two are figures from mythology. Adonis was a young man so beautiful that the goddess of love herself fell in love with him, but he rejected her advances and was gored to death by a male boar. Narcissus was a stunningly beautiful young man who cruelly rejected the female nymph who loved him (Echo, who wasted away into nothing but a repeated sound) and fell in love with his own image instead. He sat staring at his own beautiful reflection in a pool of water until he starved to death. Antinous was, as far as we can tell from ancient history, a beautiful young man deeply loved by the Roman Emperor Hadrian. After he drowned under mysterious circumstances in AD 130, Hadrian raised a city dedicated to him on the ruins near the river where he drowned and ordered sculptures of his image to be placed throughout the empire.

While the classical world provided Wilde with access to a culture where homosexuality was an everyday fact of life, clearly these particular references also suggest the brevity and dangers of beautiful youth. Wilde's use of these references also seems to imply a certain unique beauty in homosexuality itself, as the love of two men, at least as described in *Dorian Gray*, can be seen as a purely aesthetic experience. It is the enjoyment of physical beauty that drives the relationships between the male lovers in the novel. Heterosexual love, on the other hand, is driven by biological imperatives and societal expectations, and so it is not just about beauty.

Doubling

Dorian is a man split into two: himself and his portrait, each a reflection of the other. The painting has become his "other self," so separate that Dorian comes to hate the portrait, and so connected that when he acts out his hatred by slashing the image he inflicts the damage on himself. Hallward also experiences a kind of doubling with the painting. After all, he created it, he put himself in it, and he too experiences its changes. When he goes with Dorian to see the ravaged portrait, he says that it is "his own picture"—a turn of phrase that can be read as a statement of authorship (he painted the portrait) or recognition (it is a picture of himself).

Self-Development and the Dangers of Influence

"The aim of life is self-development," Lord Henry avers. His statement echoes the advice of the ancient Greek philosophers who stressed self-knowledge and careful reflection as the keys to a meaningful life. However, none of the characters seem truly committed to reflection or development. In the same moment that Lord Henry urges Dorian to develop himself, he decides "to dominate" Dorian. He fills Dorian with new ideas, gives him "the little yellow book," and urges Dorian toward hedonism. Dorian's quest to live life as though it were a work of art fails miserably precisely because it is not a quest of pure self-development. Dorian sets off on his path toward dissolution in response to the goading influence of Lord Henry. His adventures, therefore, are not a sign of brave risk-taking and defiance, but merely the result of his initial weakness, and doomed to fail.

Basil Hallward also suffers from a weakness of character. He sublimates his emotions into his art—particularly, of course, into Dorian's portrait. Lord Henry seems to live his life as a voyeur, feeding off the actions of others. He remains stagnant, unable to change or grow. In some ways, then, the tragedy of *Dorian Gray*'s characters is their inability to "know themselves."

DE PROFUNDIS and THE BALLAD OF READING GAOL

Wilde wrote *De Profundis* while in jail following his obscenity trial. He was at the lowest point of his life: he had lost his lover, Lord Alfred Douglas, his wife and children had left him and changed their last name, and his mother had died. The voice and feeling of the work are entirely different from anything he had ever before penned. Gone are the bravado and flashy wit. In their place, readers find Wilde's immense intelligence and emotional anguish turned inward on himself. He writes with humility and honesty of his past pride and selfishness, and he resolves to purify himself of all hatred and malice and truly know and accept himself for who he is. Wilde manages to see his new humility as part of a natural progression in his artistic life, "for the artistic life," he writes, "is simply self-development." It seems as if a glittering mask has been stripped away, and we see Wilde truly for the first time.

In some sense, *De Profundis* fits the literary genre of the conversion narrative, in which a writer traces his or her spritual awakening. The classical example is St. Augustine's *Confessions* (written between 397 and 401), but a more recent popular example of a conversion narrative is *The Autobiography of Malcolm X*. Whereas conversion narratives usually involve acceptance of Christianity or Christian principles, Wilde's conversion is more of an acceptance of sorrow and love as both necessary and beautiful. *De Profundis* also fits into the genre of prison literature, in which authors write about incarceration or while incarcerated themselves. Writers of prison literature focus on the psychological, physical, and sociological effects of imprisonment (often their own imprisonment). Prominent writers of prison literature have included: Alexander Solzhenitsyn (author of *One Day in the Life of Ivan Denisovich*), Fyodor Dostoevsky (author of *Memoirs from the House of the Dead*), and Jean Genet (author of *Our Lady of the Flowers*).

In *De Profundis*, Wilde writes: "I must say to myself that I ruined myself, and that nobody great or small can be ruined except by his own hand." *The Ballad of Reading Gaol* picks up this idea and gives it an anguished, human embodiment. The speaker in the poem sees a prisoner, a man who had "killed the thing he loved," in the jail yard, looking wistfully at the sky, thinking of his lost love and freedom. But, says the speaker in the poem, "each man kills the thing he loves." In Wilde's case, his goal, his life, had centered around the pursuit of beauty and pleasure for their own sake. In the end, however, he was friendless, reviled, and poor. He, with his own actions, had exterminated all that was beautiful in his life. The poem takes up again the idea Wilde puts forth in *De*

Profundis—that sorrow is necessary for the full appreciation of the beauty of life, and even for redemption. He writes: "Ah! happy they whose hearts can break/And peace of pardon win!/How else may man make straight his plan/And cleanse his soul from Sin? / How else but through a broken heart/May Lord Christ enter in?" Wilde's almost heavy-handed use of Christian symbols—blood, the color white, the crucifix—drives home the point that the "prisoner" of the poem is not, as society sees him, a foul and damned beast, but a soul purified by sorrow and welcomed by Christ.

The ballad form in poetry dates back to the troubadours of the Middle Ages, who entertained at royal courts with their songs of romance, adventure, and sorrow. A ballad is, on the basic level, just a story told in song, usually in four-line stanzas with a refrain or repeated section. The classic Irish ballads "Barbara Allen" and "Wearing of the Green" are good examples. The ballad form remains popular in music even in modern times, especially with writers of protest songs or folk songs. Woody Guthrie's "Ballad of Harriet Tubman" and Bob Dylan's "The Lonesome Death of Hattie Carroll," for example, protest racism in the United States. The simple structure and lyrical power of the ballad give it a blunt, powerful force. Wilde made use of that force in his protest of the treatment of prisoners in Reading Gaol.

CRITICAL EXCERPTS

Biographies and Biographical Studies

Ellman, Richard. *Oscar Wilde*. New York: Alfred A. Knopf, 1988.

Weighing in at nearly 700 pages, this definitive biography won the Pulitzer Prize in 1989 and was the result of more than twenty years of research. More exhaustive than the important but largely anecdotal 1946 biography by Hesketh Pearson, and aided by the critically important 1962 publication of Wilde's letters (edited by Sir Rupert Hart-Davis), it connects Wilde's life to his work.

> What he did [in *Dorian Gray*] . . . was to write the tragedy of aestheticism. It was also the premonitory of his own tragedy, for Dorian, like Wilde, has experimented with two forms of sexuality, love of women and love of men. . . . The life of mere sensation is uncovered as anarchic and self-destructive. Dorian Gray is a test case. He fails. Life cannot be lived on such terms.

Early Reviews and Interpretations

"A Study in Puppydom." *St. James Gazette*. June 24, 1890.

This review is of the *Lippincott's* version of *Dorian Gray* and is indicative of the general reaction of many readers.

> Not being curious in ordure, and not wishing to offend the nostrils of decent persons, we do not propose to analyse "The Picture of Dorian Gray": that would be to advertise the developments of an esoteric prurience. . . . The puzzle is that a young man of decent parts, who enjoyed (when he was at Oxford) the opportunity of associating with gentlemen, should put his name (such as it is) to so stupid and vulgar a piece of work.

Wilde, Oscar. "To the Editor of the *St. James Gazette*." *St. James Gazette*. June 26, 1890.

The above review led to a correspondence between Wilde and the editors of the *Gazette*, published in that paper's pages. Wilde has the best lines: "To say that a book such as mine should be 'chucked into the fire' is silly. That is what one does with newspapers." In this letter, Wilde gives an oft-cited exposition of his novel.

> All excess, as well as all renunciation, brings its own punishment. The painter, Basil Hallward, worshipping physical beauty far too much, as most painters do, dies by the hand of one in whose soul he has created a monstrous and absurd vanity. Dorian Gray, having led a life of mere sensation and pleasure, tries to kill conscience, and at that moment kills himself. Lord Henry Wotton seeks to be merely the spectator of life. He finds that those who reject the battle are more deeply wounded than those who take part in it. Yes; there is a terrible moral in *Dorian Gray*—a moral which the prurient will not be able to find in it, but which will be revealed to all whose minds are healthy. Is this an artistic error? I fear it is. It is the only error in the book.

Pater, Walter. "A Novel by Mr. Oscar Wilde." From *The Bookman* (October 1891).

Walter Pater, whose own writing profoundly influenced Wilde, wrote one of the few truly positive reviews of *Dorian Gray*.

> . . . his story is also a vivid, though carefully considered, exposure of the corruption of a soul, with a very plain moral, pushed home, to the effect that vice and crime make people coarse and ugly. General readers, nevertheless, will probably care less for this moral, less for the fine, varied, largely appreciative culture of the writer, in evidence from page to page, than for the story itself, with its adroitly managed supernatural incidents, its almost equally wonderful applications of natural science; impossible, surely, in fact, but plausible enough in fiction.

Ransome, Arthur. *Oscar Wilde: A Critical Study*. London: M. Seeker, 1912.

In this early study, Ransome revealed that *De Profundis* had been written to Bosie. He was one of the first critics to focus on Wilde's work instead of his life. The comments below are on *Dorian Gray*.

> It is unbalanced; and that is a fault. It is a mosaic hurriedly made by a man who reached out in all directions and took and used in his work whatever scrap of jasper, or porphyry or broken flint was put into his hand; and that is not a virtue. But in it there is an individual essence, a private perfume, a colour whose secret has been lost. There are moods whose consciousness that essence, perfume, colour, is needed to intensity. . . .

Modern Critical Interpretations, 1940s–1960s

Nethercot, Arthur H. "Oscar Wilde and the Devil's Advocate." *PMLA* 59.3 (1944).

This essay is typical of the opining on Wilde's moral state that dominated Wilde scholarship during the first part of the century. Nethercot examines "the full extent and method of self-portrait" in Dorian Gray. In the original text, when he mentions Wotton's views on marriage, he goes on to quote a passage about the "absolutely necessary" life of deception from *Dorian Gray*.

> In his creation of Lord Henry Wotton . . . Wilde produced an even closer replica of himself. Wotton too is a dandy, with a contempt for the drab conventional costumes of the nineteenth century. . . . When Lord Henry speaks of marriage, he is clearly airing his author's views, which had matured very shortly after his ecstatic union with the loyal and devoted Constance. . . . At heart Wilde was a moral man. At any rate, judged by his writings he was a moral man, though judged by his life he was not.

Roditi, Edouard. *Oscar Wilde*. Norfolk, CT: New Directions, 1947.

In the late 1940s, Wilde scholars began focusing more on Wilde's work than his life. This study was one of the most important in that transition. In his remarks on *Dorian Gray*, Roditi argues that Wilde borrowed from Charles Maturin's *Melmoth the Wanderer* (1820), as described below.

> There, amidst "a great deal of decayed and useless lumber" such as that which later furnished the locked and abandoned school-room where Dorian Gray concealed his compromising portrait, young Melmoth's eyes were "in a moment, and as if by magic, riveted on a portrait." . . . This portrait represents an evil ancestor, a third Melmoth who, by a pact with the devil, has been permitted to live one hundred and fifty years without showing any signs of aging, much as Dorian Gray was mysteriously permitted to retain the appearance of his youth in spite of his crimes and debauchery.

Ellmann, Richard, ed. *Oscar Wilde: A Collection of Critical Essays*. Englewood Cliffs, NJ: Spectrum, 1969.

Though this collection wasn't published until 1969, it largely reflects the early twentieth-century tendency toward biographical criticism. Authors include W. B. Yeats, W. H. Auden, George Bernard Shaw, Jorge Luis Borges, André Gide, and Thomas Mann. The excerpt below is from Yeats's "My First Meeting with Oscar Wilde."

My first meeting with Oscar Wilde was an astonishment. I never before heard a man talking with perfect sentences, as if he had written them all overnight with labour and yet all spontaneous. . . . Wilde asked me to tell his little boy a fairy story, and I had but got as far as "Once upon a time there was a giant" when the little boy screamed and ran out of the room. Wilde looked grave and I was plunged into the shame of clumsiness that afflicts the young.

1970s to 1980s

Knott, Charles E. and Donald J. Lawler. "The Context of Invention: Suggested Origins of 'Dorian Gray.' " *Modern Philology* 73.4, 1976.

Wilde has been accused of being lazy because he borrows heavily from other authors, including himself. In this article, the authors propose that much of *Dorian Gray* originates from two earlier short stories of Wilde's.

During this particular phase of his career, Wilde frequently resorted to stock expressions which are found with sometimes tiresome frequency through the two stories and the novel. . . . Those easy repetitions in *Dorian Gray* are indications that Wilde did, in fact, reuse materials which came readily to mind because they had been so recently employed in writing "The Portrait of Mr. W. H." and "The Fisherman and His Soul." That such borrowing may indicate an indolence of the imagination or even a lack of artistic integrity is not the point. Such cases of self-appropriation emphasize the fact that Wilde was resynthesizing his material at many levels when he began writing *Dorian Gray* and he continued to do so in the course of his revisions.

Cohen, Philip K. *The Moral Vision of Oscar Wilde*. Rutherford, NJ: Fairleigh Dickinson University Press, 1976.

In these comments on *Dorian Gray*, Cohen asserts a connection between *The Picture of Dorian Gray* and *De Profundis*.

> Just as he acknowledges that one must enter life in order to be fully human, so he vaguely suggests that great art must somehow encompass reality. But he did not know how this could be achieved positively at the time of *Dorian Gray*, when, though he knew that separations between art and life are morally wrong, he could discover no benefit from their union. Only in *De Profundis*, after he recognized the value of suffering itself, could he celebrate a unified vision in which the artist's life becomes the supreme work of art precisely because it encompasses and expresses reality.

Oates, Joyce Carol. "Wilde's Parable of the Fall." *Contraries*. New York: Oxford University Press, 1981.

Oates, a celebrated writer of fiction, argues that it "might be possible for readers to underestimate" *Dorian Gray*. She explores the complexities of the novel, and rather than resolving, highlights them as one of the book's strengths.

> The ceremonially correct punishment of Dorian Gray seems to complete the novel; but it merely ends the novel. The preoccupation with the questionable morality of the artist's interference with life—Basil Hallward's appropriation of Dorian's image, for instance, for his uncanny portrait—is never satisfactorily resolved, and even the final

appearance of the aging and somewhat attenuated Lord Henry hints at another level of human concern which Wilde has no space to investigate. What the strangely moved reader is likely to carry away from *Dorian* is precisely this sense of something riddling and incomplete. One feels about it as one feels about the most profoundly haunting works of art—that it has not been fully understood.

Paglia, Camille. "Wilde and the English Epicene." *Raritan* (Winter 1985).

Paglia, well known (and in some cases notorious) for her writings on feminism and gender studies, here tackles feminization and masculinity in the dialogue of *The Picture of Dorian Gray*.

Dorian Gray says to Lord Henry Wotton, "You cut life to pieces with your epigrams." It is no coincidence that terms describing a witty exchange—thrust, parry, riposte, repartee—are drawn from swordplay. The close interrelations of language and martial contention in Western culture are demonstrated by fencing parlance which speaks of a "conversation" or "phrase" of action. In other words, a fencing match is imagined as a sequence of competitive speech. It is plain how a woman of the salon who commands this sharp, challenging rhetoric is masculinized into an Androgyne of Manners. The male Androgyne of Manners achieves his hermaphroditism by combining aggressive language with a feminine manner, graceful and languid, archly flirtatious and provocative. The persona which Wilde projects in his epicene witticisms is a conflation of masculine intimidation and attack with feminine seduction and allure.

1990s and Beyond

Glick, Elisa. "The Dialectics of Dandyism." *Cultural Critique* 48.1 (2001).

Glick examines the homosexual identities of the three main characters in *Dorian Gray* in light of the theory that homosexual identity is marked by secrecy and disclosure and is therefore paradoxical.

> Declaring that his love for Dorian must remain secret, Basil here exemplifies the love that dare not speak its name. But we must remember that the "secret" of the portrait exceeds Basil's unspeakable desire for Dorian, since the portrait eventually becomes the emblem of (and medium for) Dorian's double identity. Although the portrait functions as a sign for the homosexual as eternally beautiful youth, Wilde does not define gay identity solely through this image. Finally, queerness in the text inheres not in the image of Dorian Gray, but in the networks of secrecy that constitute this image . . . it is the site for a circulation of secrecy in which all three characters—Basil, Dorian, and Lord Henry—are implicated.

Joyce, Simon. "Sexual Politics and the Aesthetics of Crime: Oscar Wilde in the Nineties." *ELH* 69.2 (2002).

Here, Joyce argues that Dorian's habit of slumming in lower-class neighborhoods and committing crimes correlate to Wilde's ideas on poverty and crime, and in effect are a criticism of society.

> But there's a more serious point here, which he expresses in "The Soul of Man under Socialism" as well as in the essay on Wainewright: that, given the harshness of working-class life, and especially the constant search for the means of subsistence rather than pleasure, Wilde felt that the poor criminal was entirely exonerated. But for someone like Dorian to commit murder is ultimately to

borrow a form of justification which is unwarranted in his case, and which cannot be secured by simply renaming murder as an art form: since he has the wealth, leisure, and cultural training which are necessary for finding enjoyment in the aesthetic, an aristocrat really has no business committing crimes which can be supported only as a response to material need and suffering. . . .

QUESTIONS FOR DISCUSSION

One of the tenets of aestheticism, the philosophy Oscar Wilde helped to create, was that art should not teach lessons. What do you think about this idea? Is it enough for art to be beautiful? Can beautiful art ever be bad or dangerous? Think about a recent work of art—visual, literary, or musical. Does that work teach a lesson? Is it a better work of art because it does/does not teach a lesson? What exactly does it mean for art to "teach a lesson"?

Dorian's obsession with his own beauty and his delight in being able to escape aging were profound, but in the end they ruined him. How does our society value youth and beauty? Can you think of any modern parallels to Dorian's story?

Dorian's life was changed by a book. Do you think books still have the power to change people? Can ideas be dangerous? Why or why not? If so, what sorts of ideas?

How does reading *De Profundis* change your understanding of *The Picture of Dorian Gray*? Is it important or helpful to know about an author's life while reading one of his or her books?

In *De Profundis*, Wilde sees his sorrow and disgrace as part of a progression in his artistic devotion to beauty. He argues that his anguish gave him the ability to see the beauty of life more clearly. Do you believe this is true? Is sorrow necessary for a deep appreciation of beauty?

One of the techniques this book uses is doubling—the picture is Dorian's double, and James Vane seems to be another double, embodying Dorian's conscience or better self. Why do you think Oscar Wilde used doubling to tell his story? What effect did it have on you while reading the story? Can you think of any other books or movies with doubles in them?

Do you believe, as Wilde writes in *The Ballad of Reading Gaol*, that "each man kills the thing he loves"? What, exactly, do you think he meant?

SUGGESTIONS FOR THE INTERESTED READER

If you enjoyed *The Picture of Dorian Gray*, you might also be interested in the following:

Writers from Christopher Marlowe to Thomas Mann have been seduced by the legend of Faust, the man who sells his soul to Mephistopheles to get the power and knowledge he wants from life. *The Picture of Dorian Gray* is another version of this story. The most famous version is Johann Wolfgang von Goethe's play *Faust*, which took him sixty years to write. Numerous translations are available. The musical *Damn Yankees* is a modern version of the story, in which a man sells his soul to become a baseball star.

Wilde, 1997 (VHS, DVD). This biographical film, based on Wilde scholar Richard Ellman's biography, faithfully re-creates much of Wilde's life. The movie boasts an excellent cast, including Stephen Fry, Jude Law, and Jennifer Ehle.

The Strange Case of Dr. Jekyll and Mr. Hyde by Robert Louis Stevenson. Another novel from the Victorian age, this is the famous story of a man who tries to split off his evil self from his good self with disastrous results.

The Importance of Being Earnest, 1952 (VHS, DVD). Wilde's most famous play and certainly one of his wittiest is translated into an excellent film by Anthony Asquith.

American Psycho by Bret Easton Ellis. This book, like *Dorian Gray*, was very controversial when it came out because the young, well-educated, handsome protagonist murders indiscriminately and without emotion. Many have argued that the novel is a critique of the society that produces him.

BESTSELLING ENRICHED CLASSICS

JANE EYRE
Charlotte Brontë
0-671-01479-X
$5.99

WUTHERING HEIGHTS
Emily Brontë
0-7434-8764-8
$4.95

THE GOOD EARTH
Pearl S. Buck
0-671-51012-6
$6.99

THE AWAKENING AND SELECTED STORIES
Kate Chopin
0-7434-8767-2
$4.95

HEART OF DARKNESS AND THE SECRET SHARER
Joseph Conrad
0-7434-8765-6
. $4.95

GREAT EXPECTATIONS
Charles Dickens
0-7434-8761-3
$4.95

A TALE OF TWO CITIES
Charles Dickens
0-7434-8760-5
$4.95

THE COUNT OF MONTE CRISTO
Alexandre Dumas
0-7434-8755-9
$6.50

10210 (1 of 2)

FROM
POCKET BOOKS

Not sure what to read next?

Visit Pocket Books online at
www.SimonSays.com

Reading suggestions for
you and your reading group
New release news
Author appearances
Online chats with your favorite writers
Special offers
And much, much more!